SONG OF MAGDALA

THE UNTOLD STORY OF MARY MAGDALENE,
CONFIDANT OF JESUS OF NAZARETH

SONG

OF

MAGDALA

Marilyn Mueller Onoda

Edited by Jennifer P. Tanabe
Cover and interior design by Jonathan Gullery

Palestine map © https://visualunit.me. Approval pending.

ISBN: 978-0-578-34486-7

Printed in the United States of America

To my Parents, Husband and Children

PALESTINE IN THE TIME OF JESUS

Damascus ●

SYRIA

● Sidon
● Zarephath

▲ Mt. Hermon

● Caesarea Philippi

● Tyre

PHOENICIA

TRACHONITIS

● Seleucia

Ptolemais ●

Korazin
Capernaum
Gennesaret ● ● Bethsaida
Magdala ●

Naveh ●

Cana ●
Sepphoris ●
Nazareth ●

Tiberias ● ● Gergesa

Sea of
Galilee

▲ Mt.
Tabor

● Dium
● Abilene
● Gadara

MEDITERRANEAN SEA

GALILEE ● Nain

● Caesarea

Scythopolis ●

DECAPOLIS

● Pella

SAMARIA

● Samaria
Shechem ● ● Sychar
▲ Mt. Gerizim

● Gerasa

● Antipatris

● Arimathea

Joppa ●

● Lydda

● Ephraim

● Gedora

PEREA

● Jamnia

Emmaus ●

Jericho ●

● Philadelphia

● Azotus

Jerusalem ✪

▲ Mt. Olives

Bethany ● ●— Qumran

Bethlehem ●

JUDEA

Ashkelon ●

● Machaerus

Gaza ●

● Hebron

En Gedi ●

Dead
Sea

IDUMEA

Masada ●

● Raphia

Beersheba ●

● Elusa

Zoar ● NABATEA

● Mampsis

Jordan River

N
↑

Contents

Preface

Song of Magdala is a fictionalized account of Mary Magdalene's life and how she became the person she was and close confidant of Jesus of Nazareth. When I first got the inspiration to write about Mary Magdalene, back in 1996, I began researching all that I could find written about her in a library. The few times she is mentioned in the New Testament, and in other various religious papers, the paradigm was the same. Mostly she is portrayed as a prostitute and she applied fragrant oil to Jesus' feet, wiping it away with her hair.

I realized that there was very little known about her that was different than what is written in the Bible. I also discovered that she is second only to Mother Mary as the most painted woman in the history of art. I reasoned that if she had inspired so many paintings, and she walked beside Jesus Christ, there could be a deeper story to her life. This spurred me on further. With a hypothesis that came from inspiration and with more research, and a desire to look deeper into the ancient words of the New Testament gospels, I continued to search for a more comprehensive feeling and understanding of her story.

I found the Apocryphal Gospel of Mary and Gospel of Thomas which, curiously enough, gave descriptions and images, though incomplete, of her relationships with the apostles and with Jesus himself. It was not much to go on, but my imagination and inspiration took off. I began to realize different concepts about her character and relationship to Jesus that I could almost tangibly imagine and perceive. My imagination took flight and within days I could see a whole story just longing to be told.

Many of the words spoken by Jesus were taken from the New Testament gospels, and from a more recent book published in 2007 called *Christ Returns*. Older sources of his words were the Gospel of Mary and Gospel of Thomas.

The following are the sources that I used to write her story.

- New Testament: Revised Standard Version
- *Exposition of the Divine Principle*, Rev. Sun Myung Moon
- *Christ Returns: Reveals Startling Truth*, author anonymous
- Apocryphal Gospels of Mary and Thomas
- *Israel's Royal House, The Davidic Dynasty*, A Genealogy, by David Hughes © 2012

I also chose not to use the English word for God but to use the Aramaic and Hebrew words that Jesus and his contemporaries would have used. Although Jesus usually used Abba or Elah from his mother tongue, Aramaic, he also used different Hebrew terms for God out of respect for the people he was speaking to, the orthodoxy and citizens of Judea. The following are the Aramaic and Hebrew words used for God.

- Aramaic: Elah - absolute God
  Abba - Father
- Hebrew/Judean: Elohim, Elohim hayyim - the living God,
  Adonai - my Lord, reverence for God
  Ha Shem - the name referring to God
  El Shaddai - Almighty
  Ha Elohim - the God

Names of the Apostles:

- Simon Peter and Andrew, brothers from Bethsaida
- James and John, sons of Salome of Zebedee, first cousin of Mother Mary

- Jude Thaddeus (Lebbaeus) and James Alpheus, sons of Mary of Clopas, the sister of Salome and first cousin of Mother Mary
- Matthew/Levi
- Thomas
- Bartholomew/Nathaniel
- Phillip
- Simon the Zealot
- Judas (only Judean disciple)

I never imagined I would write a manuscript. But it all began that one day back in 1996, sitting in front of my new personal computer, I began typing out the story without much foresight beyond that which comprised most of the first chapter.

Finally, I would like to acknowledge my husband, Takao Thomas Onoda, for his support and patience during the many years and time I spent researching, preparing and writing this manuscript.

And also I commend with great praise and gratitude Jennifer Tanabe, my editor and Jonathan Gullery at jonathangullery.design my publisher. These professionals were one in heart with my vision and story. Their sincerity and dedication, professionalism and expertise were exceptional as they applied their skills which brought my dream and manuscript to fruition.

Marilyn Mueller Onoda
November 2021

PART I

Chapter 1

Mary's Early Years

12 CE
Magdala, Galilee

I believe that I shall see the goodness of the Lord in the land of the living.
Wait for the Lord; be strong and let your heart take courage.
Wait for the Lord!
(Psalm 27:13-14)

The ancient land of Palestine was in the 16th year of the reign of Herod Antipas, Tetrarch of Galilee, the fifth son of Herod the Great. He was a mere puppet in his land, though, as the whole world was under the occupation of the great Roman army and the Emperor, Caesar Augustus. In order to maintain his position, Herod ruled with an iron hand and with hundreds of Roman soldiers at his disposal. In this way, he maintained peace with all the different factions of peoples living in the land of Palestine.

From time to time, the Zealots, religious men of the ancient Hebrew faith, caused rebellious outbreaks in an attempt to regain autonomous rule over the holy land of their forefathers. The deadly hand of the Roman soldiers deployed by Herod put an end to their lofty ventures almost as quickly as they began.

However, most ordinary Hebrew Palestinians were consumed with the problems of their daily lives, leaving little time to worry about the larger picture and the political make-up of their homeland. For most, just to give their taxes and tithes and to provide for their families was all they could do.

Disease and poverty, always looming amongst them like hidden sand snakes, gave their lives a fearful uncertainty.

In this simple life, their belief in Elohim and observance of their faith traditions provided them with an invisible shield of assurance. This unseen protection came to them through their strictly guided lives, regimented by ancient religious tenets. Every action and aspect of their lives was dictated for them.

If there were questions, and there were so many, they would ask their holy men, called rabbis, who would search their scriptures for answers. Most of the people believed these revered men had an answer for everything. Their rigid lifestyle, regulated by the rules of their auspicious religion, was enough to distract them from ever thinking about the secular rulers.

For centuries, the Palestinian Hebrews had been an unusual and unchanging people, keeping much to themselves. In this land nestled on the eastern shore of the Great Sea, they were a people who believed in only one Elohim hayyim. Their scriptures predicted a mighty leader who would redeem the Holy Temple and deliver them from sinful, oppressive rulers. Their Elohim promised them this one hope.

***

In a small Galilean fishing village called Magdala, on the western shore of the Sea of Galilee, a young mother, Ruth, and her daughter, Mary, made their way along a well-worn, narrow path toward the market at the center of their village. The high holy days of Passover were only a few days away and they were preparing to celebrate with many traditional foods. They always made this a special occasion.

There were rules concerning choice and preparation of foods served on these auspicious days. It was not a strain for them as they were a moderately well-to-do Jewish family. Mary's father had provided well for his family before he died. Their home, a modest adobe single family house with a shaded back porch, was a bit larger than most of the other dwellings, but the style of their home was almost identical to all the other residences. However, other families, especially those with large households, had to save all year for this event which commemorated their liberation from Egypt by Moses over a thousand years before.

Normally, mothers began educating their young daughters conscientiously from the age of five or six to run a household and care for the family. Then, by twelve or thirteen years of age, fathers betrothed them to worthy young men from good families. Shopping was an essential skill. Daughters were trained to choose the freshest traditional foods, barter for the best prices, and help carry the groceries back home. The girl who excelled was considered an excellent bridal candidate.

Mother Ruth struggled throughout the years, weighing the social norms and the health of her daughter. However, now that this was Mary's tenth year, Ruth could no longer delay her daughter's education, even though her health problem was not resolved. The child's constant pleading to accompany her to the market was also a factor. Thus, putting caution aside, mother and daughter set off along the path into the village.

Mary's maiden journey into the outside world began on a warm sunny morning. Ruth noticed how much younger her daughter looked than others of her age, especially with her small, gaunt frame and frail complexion. But her only daughter's excitement and joy temporarily abated Ruth's concern and she relaxed, feeling confident that it was the correct decision.

She's grown and matured this year. Perhaps she will surprise everyone and overcome this horrible illness. Only Elah knows! Nonetheless, sighing with resignation, Ruth thought, *She's a fighter. I know that without a doubt.*

Mary smiled up at her mother as if reading her thoughts, and proclaimed with assurance, "Mother! I finally have your approval to go to the market. I'm so happy! I know I can do this!" Then she added as she looked up at her mother and then back to herself, taking notice of their similar clothing, "Mother, we look alike, don't we?"

Mother and daughter were dressed identically, with the traditional white skull caps, meant to keep their hair in place and away from their face, covered with a modest homespun beige headscarf falling to the waist. Each wore an ecru colored long sleeve, flax woven dress, with a sleeveless variegated brown and beige wool robe over it and tied above the waist with a matching belt.

Their modest outfits reached right down to their ankles. Small for her age, the daughter could barely stand up under the weight of the layered clothing.

Mary proudly took notice of her outdoor clothes and sandals. Worn so seldom each piece was practically new. She felt her white cap tilt askew under her headscarf and felt errant brown curls sticking out from under her cap and scarf. She tried to adjust her head cap, but it only caused more hair to become loose. Nevertheless, this did not dampen her excitement.

The atmosphere was fresh and there was a cooling breeze as they strolled together along the winding, well-worn, cinnamon colored dirt path leading from their home to the market. Mary relished the new vistas and sounds. *I'm finally allowed to leave home and accompany mother to the market,* she reflected joyfully.

She noticed the swaying yellow stalks of tall grass with billowing white puffy tops and the meandering stream running alongside their path. Black birds with red neck feathers, and other yellow ones flying past, caught her eye as they tweeted in and out of the vegetation.

Ruth made use of this maiden journey to teach her daughter: "Those stalks are wheat, my dear, and on the tops are the seeds that we collect and grind for flour. The white flowers with yellow centers are chamomile. I make your tea after drying and crushing them." Pointing to the middle of the field, she explained, "The birds have nests hidden in the fields where they raise their young."

Suddenly, in the midst of the lesson, there came a loud commotion interrupting her and causing her to halt abruptly. Standing perfectly still they listened, trying to figure out where all the noise came from.

Over the hills ahead, loud shouting and heavy footsteps were coming their way. Mary and her mother stretched their necks and stood on their toes trying to see over the hill ahead of them.

Ruth whispered and pointed, "The sound is getting louder and coming from over there. Step back, daughter." Feeling uncertain, she gently pushed Mary behind her to shield her. Mary grabbed her mother's skirt, but peeked curiously around it.

Topping the hill, a man came into view and then a moment later a crowd of men scrambled a distance behind him. As they ran closer toward them, Mary saw three men chasing after the man in front, up and down the hills, along the curving narrow path. Continuing toward them, they shouted while waving their hands, "Get him, he's a thief. He stole from us!"

The fleeing man came toward them. As he drew closer, Mary observed his red and perspiring face and frayed, dirty clothing. Then he ran past to their left side, ignoring both mother and daughter, down the hill and under a large, flat protruding rock where he hid himself. Mother and daughter turned with their backs to the thief and innocuously faced the pursuers.

The angry elders hollered breathlessly toward them, "Have you seen the thief!"

Without a word, Ruth turned to her right indicating a fork in their path and reflexively pointed to it. The men hastily followed her signal and took the path down the hill and away from the hiding man.

Naively Mary looked up in wonderment at her mother, trying to understand the incident. She did recognize the huffing and puffing, as she was accustomed to breathlessness and gasping for breath. After they all disappeared, the innocent child asked her mother, "What is going on?"

Ruth took Mary's hand and said kindly, "Let us go and speak to the man under the rock." Together, they turned off the path and headed toward him. He was completely hidden under the rock.

Mother and daughter squatted down to take a look at him. Curled up and lying on his side in a hollowed-out space, he was trembling and winded. Mary felt his distress, seeing that he was perspiring and uncomfortable.

"The men are gone," Ruth gently informed the fearful, unfortunate man.

Coming out from under the rock, he quickly spoke in his defense, "My family is starving. Without steady work, they still come to my door to collect taxes that I am unable to pay. Even the rabbis give no consolation. They constantly ask for tithes. How am I to feed my family? And for Passover, how can I buy the special food, attend Passover in Jerusalem, and meet all the religious demands!"

Clutching a bulging, brown cloth bag, the desperate man breathlessly continued explaining his frustrations, "I know it is against Elah's law to steal, but this is all I have for my wife and children."

Ruth reached into her drawstring purse and compassionately handed him a handful of shekels. "There you go. We live in a terrible time, especially for families. Please use this to buy food for your family!" With a slight bow, she added, "Elah be with you."

Ruth held her daughter's hand as they walked away and back to the path toward the center of the village. Mary felt proud of her mother for helping the man. She hoped that he and his family would have a good dinner with the money.

A few moments later they arrived at the marketplace, where mother and daughter paused at the entrance. They stood on an embankment which gave them a birds-eye view of the hustle and bustle of shoppers. Mary's eyes sparkled at the new sights and sounds, feeling thrilled and excited at the unimaginable sight before her.

Comforted by her mother's warm hand, she gazed in awe at the activity of the village square in front of her and considered her introductory excursion, *This is the furthest I've ever traveled from home.* Still, she silently admitted, *My chest feels heavy and …my legs hurt. But I'm not going to think about my discomfort!* Bravely she commanded herself, *Be thankful. It will be a good day!*

Interrupting Mary's thoughts, Ruth waved her hand introducing the surroundings, "This is the marketplace, Magdala's main hub where all the villagers gather for the necessities of daily living. You are finally here, my dear! Let's begin your first shopping lessons together. How are you feeling?"

Mary noticed her mother's concerned expression and examination of her countenance for any sign of exhaustion. Then she nodded with a broad smile, exclaiming, "I am very happy, Mother. I am ready!" However, to herself she determined, *I refuse to let my aches and pains ruin our day.*

They surveyed the shops and crowds. Mary quickly forgot her discomfort and delighted in all that her eyes perceived.

However, not long after that thrilling moment, as they descended into the fray of the crowded village market, the fragile child immediately noted the changing atmosphere and began to cough, thinking, *This is unlike the fresh and light air of the hills.* She noticed the many scurrying shoppers, wagons, beast of burden, goats and dogs stirring up the fine powder from the clay covered pathway. And the heat wasn't helping.

Encouraging her, Mother continued the training, "Mary, notice the quilt-like awnings over some of the storefronts. These create shade where buyers can escape from the burning rays of the sun. We will definitely stand under them so that you don't get too hot!"

Mary listened, trying her best to be attentive, though at the same time she became helplessly distracted by all the exciting and lively commotion. The hubbub of merchants chanting their wares, children chasing dogs and goats, and buyers shouting their prices at the shoppers and shoppers at buyers. Momentarily captivated, Mary thought, *...so much excitement!*

Hand in hand they descended into the dense atmosphere. There was no escape from the mix of human and animal stench. The lack of a breeze and the hot rays of the sun made the stale air even thicker. Mother and child walked briskly through the crowd.

Anyone who took notice of the child could recognize from her slight body and pallid complexion that she was not healthy and that she was struggling. However, everyone was busy concentrating on their buying and selling.

Though fascinated and thrilled, the heat and fetid aromas overwhelmed Mary as she struggled to stay close to her mother. Try as she might, she could not ignore her situation. Within minutes, it became excruciating to breathe. Instinctively, she buried her face in the material of her mother's rough robe. Nonetheless, her nose and throat burned and the cloth hardly helped.

As she constantly tried to clear her dry throat, between determination and tears she reminded herself, *I finally got Mother's approval. I must show her that I can endure!*

No longer could she ignore the pain in her chest and she grimly accepted her frailty, *Now I understand... mother never allowed me to go to the market because she knew I...* Now that she was face to face with her illness, she understood.

But in between episodes it was difficult to accept how sick she really was. She remembered overhearing whispered conversations, "Your daughter's life will be a short one." Even her beloved rabbi whispered his concern. On days like this one, she stayed shuttered away in her home out of the heat and dust.

To make it worse, Mary had been unable to attend the high holy day celebrations in Jerusalem like most devout Jewish families. Because of her severe illness her mother and grandmother had requested and received a special dispensation from their rabbi to remain at home during all the holy days.

Tearful memories of her insisting and pleading arguments over the past years came to her, "Mother, I am old enough now, please let me go with you to the market! I will be careful, and I will not make a problem for you. Don't worry about me! Passover is very important, and it is time I helped you shop. You cannot keep me stuck in the house forever!" Until Mother finally relented.

The joyful words of her mother just days ago echoed in her ears, "Alright, you are old enough now, but because of your health we will only make a short trip to the market, there and back, as quickly as we can. Do you understand?" Mary remembered her mother's loving but stern mien.

Being tugged along, she did feel strength surging through her mother's hand, and initially it helped reassure her. As long as she kept up with her mother's pace Mary felt confident.

However, finally the atmosphere overwhelmed her and, as her self-confidence waned, she quickly tired from her wheezing and difficulty catching her breath. As they walked into the first shop, she could not ignore the harsh sound of wheezing coming from her throat and her struggling breath. Neither could Ruth.

One woman turned around and looked at them, "Ruth, it seems that your daughter is struggling. Poor child! Let's get her some water."

Ashamed but trying to overcome, Mary looked up regretfully at her mother, not knowing what to do. Though she knew she had to get out of there, nonetheless she wanted to will herself forward.

Distracted and in haste to finish quickly, Ruth's sweet voice said, "Let's get the dates, figs, and cashews here in this shop and then we will go home. Can you make it that long, Mary? I'll come back tomorrow and finish the shopping."

Mary heard her mother's voice but, with what little effort she could feebly muster, only a scratchy painful sound emerged, "Ma---Ma." It was the last thing she remembered.

Mary awoke to find that she was lying on her pallet at home. Groggily, she tried to remember why she was dizzy with an aching head. When she tried to sit up, she could not lift her head. She sniffed the usual sweet medicinal incense, a common treatment for her ailment, and that gave her a clue as to why she was lying down. Now her breathing was easy and normal.

Slowly, she remembered the market. *Oh! What happened,* she wondered, staring at the ceiling. She did not remember going to bed. She just remembered the market and the pain in her chest.

There was some light coming through the slats of her shuttered window. The house was quiet. It seemed like no one was home. *Maybe mother is still out shopping,* she thought.

Suddenly the outside door opened, letting in the bright sunlight, and her grandmother came into their comfortable home. The sound of Grandmother's skirts coming closer lifted Mary's spirits.

If she had been a strong and healthy child, Mary would have bounded out of bed, but she remained still and asked, "Grandmother, how long have I been like this? Why am I here and why am I so tired?"

Mary saw Grandmother's joyful expression upon seeing her awake, "Praise Elah, you almost look like your normal self! You are a bit pale but definitely better than when Mama brought you home."

Mary was heartened at the sound of Grandmother's voice. Sitting down carefully on Mary's bed and caressing her granddaughter's cool hand, Grandmother kindly related the incident to her granddaughter.

"The whole marketplace witnessed you collapse," she told Mary, with tears in her eyes. "You become so ill in the market, and you could not breathe. Mama said that you fell and hit your head. You even had a shaking spell. After your body stopped shaking, a kind man carried you home. Mama will be so happy to see that you are better. It has taken you two days to wake up. Praise Elah that He has not taken you from us. We were so worried about you. Ruth never left your bed, but just before you awoke, she went to the temple to pray for you and to tell Rabbi Ben Levi that you were very ill."

"Grandmother, am I going to be alright? I'm so sorry to cause Mother and you so much trouble. Now I'm sorry I insisted on going to the market."

Mary was quiet for the rest of the afternoon. She did not feel like doing anything, even when Grandmother asked her to help prepare the special holiday bread.

Grandmother brought her broth and bread and her favorite hummus peas and Mary realized that she was hungry. She felt comforted to hear her grandmother's soft, familiar voice.

"You must be very hungry. This soup and peas will make you strong again. Eat as much as you can. Elah is always taking care of us, Mary. Elah has special plans for you," the wise woman predicted. "No matter what happens, He is always with us."

Mary's grandmother was a devoutly religious woman. She did not speak often, but when she did, the word "Elah" was mentioned at least once in every conversation. She prayed constantly for the Messiah to come. She, like most of the populace of Galilee, echoed the same sentiment, "We are Elah's chosen people and He promised to send us a savior!"

Grandmother expressed this mantra passionately, and many times a day, "The signs are all about and the time is ripe. We must watch and keep ready, for the time of our liberation is near. Our king is coming!"

Mary watched her grandmother making her customary gesticulation with both hands lifted and waving above her head. At times it seemed like the woman was speaking directly to Elah, reminding Him of His promise.

The elderly woman continued, "We are being ruled by these barbarian Romans. They have no idea of the one true Elah. Soon the Messiah will come and lead us in our faith. Our nation will become Elah's Holy Nation and we won't have to worry about influence from outsiders anymore."

Mary was accustomed to her grandmother's repetitive chanting and today she felt unusually comforted by her words. She ate eagerly, and felt strength coming back into her frail body. She was used to being sick and overcoming.

She had hoped that the market visit would demonstrate that she could be responsible like other girls her age, but now she admitted that she was wrong. Sadly, it was clear to her that she had to remain at home. Thankfully, though, she did have one positive capability. She whispered a prayer, "Thank you, Elah, for giving me my studies."

Life for the young girl was boring until that special day her rabbi brought her a religious scroll. Rabbi Ben Levi had given authorization for her to study. Their kind and considerate rabbi was unorthodox in allowing and promoting the education of a girl. This special man was a long-time acquaintance of her grandmother and grandfather since their marriage. He had eulogized and prayed at her father's funeral.

After years of watching Mary mature, Rabbi Levi had recognized that she was a bright child. But sadly, after being called many times to anoint her during her serious bouts of illness, he had assumed that she probably would not make it to maturity. Consequently, he took it on himself to disregard social norms and felt that studying would help bring her closer to Elah and distract her from loneliness.

Radically, in secret and for this reason alone, he taught her how to speak and read Hebrew, the religious language of the ancient Word, as the colloquial language in Galilee was Aramaic. Every week he introduced her to a different scroll of scriptures. As she was the only girl he had ever taught, she surprised him with her quick and eager ability to learn. He loved her challenging spirit and he himself felt exhilarated.

Mary enjoyed studying and put many hours a day into it. She especially appreciated the chance to read Elah's beautiful words. Nevertheless, on this day, even though she was a hopeful child, she began to realize the seriousness of her illness.

Sighing to herself as she sat on her bed finishing her bread and broth, Mary whispered, "Now I understand why mother is so careful with me." And with tears in her eyes, she continued, "Oh Elah, help me get well so I can go outside and walk in the fields and climb the hills and return to the market!"

That evening after dinner Mary climbed the steps to the flat rooftop of their home. The cool outdoor air was clean and light. There she could breathe comfortably and effortlessly. As darkness descended, she sat hugging her legs and looking into the sky. The moon was shining brightly, bathing the other adobe roofs in its silvery light. Usually, the stars seemed to understand her plight but tonight she did not care. In better times she imagined that the twinkling heavenly bodies were forming shapes, sending her special messages and consoling her. Tonight, though, she was too distracted to feel anything.

Abstractedly, Mary heard her mother and grandmother downstairs cleaning and hastily preparing for the Passover dinner. Depressed and with a headache, she felt too feeble to help them as she normally did. She also knew that they had lost time taking care of her, which made her feel guilty and even worse.

Therefore, she escaped to the roof, glumly thinking with more deep sighs, *Passover is only a few days away. I love this holiday and always want to participate in the baking.* Pausing, she stood up and walked weakly over to the edge of the roof. *I love the excitement and anticipation but right now, I am truly useless.*

Mary recalled earlier how her mother's face had lit up when she returned from her visit to the synagogue and Grandmother dramatically exclaimed with joy, "Ruth, your daughter Mary has recovered!"

"Praise Elah! My prayers are answered," Mama cried and rushed to embrace her precious child.

Then, at the dinner table, her mother explained her plan, though the words echoed hopelessly in Mary's consciousness. It was a repeat of the same plan after the many episodes she had before. "After Passover I am going to look for another rabbi to help you, Mary. Surely there are other remedies and herbs to strengthen and heal you… and more prayers. Look at you my dear, Elah helped you this time! Prayer works! Thank you, Elohim!"

Mother was obviously overjoyed to find me awake and nearly back to my old self. But why am I not happy that she is happy? Mary groaned and realized the answer, *I am ashamed for constantly making her worry. Oh, Elah! I am so sorry for the grief I give my poor mother!*

All the while, Mary ate quietly during dinner, listening cynically to the two women's conversation. *When will they finally realize there is no hope? I am tired of their ideas. It is a false wish! How many pretenders will she look for to find that they are all liars.*

Today was the first time Mother admitted to Grandmother, with frustration, "The last rabbi didn't help her at all." And then she seemed unable to catch herself from uttering, "She even seems to be getting worse."

Yet Grandmother repeated her reassurance and hope to Mary, "Elah has special plans for you, Mary. You must never give up. There are unseen spirits trying to take your precious life, for reasons only Elah knows. You must determine never to give up and continue your studies."

Mary caught Grandmother's words and internally thought of her secret, *I agree, Grandmother, what you say does have a semblance of truth. Not often, but there have been times when I felt something invade my dreams. I never told you or Mother about them because I didn't want to frighten you or seem strange. Sometimes a vividly frightful dream comes, after which my chest becomes tight and feels exactly like one of my breathing episodes. In one particular recurring dream, I feel a kind of force hold me down while rain drips into my eyes. I am helpless and paralyzed and tongue-tied. Although I try to call for help, no one hears my pleas, and all the while I am wheezing and coughing until at last I am able to wake, feeling normal but tired.* Mary quickly wiped away her tears so that her mother and grandmother would not notice her internal struggle.

During her lonely days, reading and studying Hebrew and religious scriptures gave her inspiration. She learned that many past heroes had to endure struggles and grave challenges, but they were able to survive. Therefore, she felt hope and inferred that she might survive as they did.

As she grew older, her idealism became realism. The scriptures clearly spelled out the roles and duties of women. Childbearing and homemaking were to be their central roles. There were no scriptures she could recall speaking of women scholars. Thus, she became inhibited and self-conscious.

Though she was proud of her ability and thrived on her studies, nevertheless, Mary knew how peculiar she was. She became sensitive and secretive, embarrassed for anyone to know her proficiency. After all, she realized how useless and unattractive she would be to a possible husband. However, through it all, Mary's grandmother praised her work and reminded her that Elah had plans for her.

Sitting on the roof, she found comfort and no judgment from her consolers, the stars. She whispered her secrets and dreams to them. And in a strange sort of way, she was satisfied with the return of their sparkling light as acknowledgement of their pride and encouragement toward her.

Years passed and miraculously she reached her sixteenth year. This birthday marked a special time in most girls' lives. At this age, the entire village community welcomed them as adults and joyfully prepared for their marriage. Mary's cousins told her of their engagements and their plans for the future. Though happy for them, she anguished about her own pitiful life, because she could only recline on her pallet and listen.

She had already outlived anyone ever known to have such an affliction. She made no plans for the future and had no hope for marriage. She knew there were no parents willing to marry their son to such a feeble woman, especially one not strong enough to bear children.

Despite all this, though, she never felt totally hopeless. Somewhere deep inside her heart she felt the love of Elah, and that He had given her this life of illness for a reason. At least that idea came to her from her grandmother, who had died a year before. She had managed to convince Mary of the value of her suffering.

One day Mary had a fleeting thought about her grandmother. She realized that Grandmother's dream of the Messiah coming during her lifetime had not come true. *Grandmother lived her whole life believing absolutely that she would see the Messiah. How sad that she never did!*

Chapter 2

The Marketplace News

For whoever would save his life will lose it,
and whoever loses his life for my sake will find it.
(Matt. 16:25)

Listening to her mother's daily reports of the news she had gathered in the marketplace was the most exciting part of Mary's lonesome days. The bits of gossip, personal stories, and sometimes up-to-date news of what was happening in the greater Galilee area opened Mary's awareness of the world outside her cloistered life in this, her seventeenth year.

The most exciting report of all concerned expectations regarding the imminent arrival of the Messiah, Elah's prophesied Anointed One. Ruth described what one of her friends had told her: "Tzipporah dreamed that she was sitting right at the feet of the Messiah, asking him questions with all her family members watching."

She continued, "I tell you, my precious daughter, there are many reports from outstanding seers saying that 'the fruit is ripe on the vine.' There are even exhilarating sermons spoken by rabbis and priests every Sabbath."

Lifting her hands above her head, Ruth expressed her delight, mimicking their exhortations by deepening her voice and enacting their words, "Prepare your home and life, for the signs are all about, predicting the imminent arrival of our Redeemer!"

She began another tale about a young preacher from the Essene sect, "They say he is the son of a high priest in Bethlehem, a town in the hill country of Judea. Instead of following his esteemed priestly father into the orthodoxy this young man, who is called John, chose to follow the Essenes, an eccentric group of religious Hebrews."

Mary realized she was more receptive today than other days and, as she relaxed, she let herself become mesmerized by her mother's lilting voice and her melodramatic antics.

Altogether she magically uplifts me. I can actually visualize the market and momentarily lose the feeling of the hermit that I am. Unlike other days, she is actually coaxing me to live through her eyes. Today, curiously I feel excited instead of annoyed, she reflected.

Unusually receptive, Mary felt like laughing, an emotion she seldom experienced. Her disinterest and gloominess dissipated, she spoke kindheartedly, "Mother, today I see that you're filled with the spirit and really enjoying this. You're trying so hard to tell your tale that your cheeks have flushed. You seem to be demonstrating all of this to me like I am a child, but you know I am not?"

Ruth slumped, a bit deflated and surprised at her daughter's comment, "I am trying to give you some delight and inspire you, my daughter."

Mary smiled respectfully and responded, "Yes Mama, I see that you have gleaned much to tell me. I'm really grateful to hear all the news today. It surely gives me a lot to think about. Please tell me more. Your enthusiasm is contagious, and I feel truly inspired. You're certainly more emotional than usual, though. It's good to see that you are so inspired and full of delight! Please continue."

Ruth paused to catch her breath, drinking a few sips of her lukewarm tea. She admitted, "Yes, I am quite excited." Smiling sheepishly, she repositioned herself and felt her burning cheeks with the back of her hand. "I am so thrilled about what I heard today. I couldn't wait to come home and share it with you."

Ruth continued, though with a bit more restraint, "I am not finished, there are even more interesting things to tell you about."

Mary's curiosity grew as her mother's expression filled with wonder and she thought, *What more can there be?*

Ruth was already speaking again. Mary asked, "Mama, can you please repeat that?"

Ruth took a deep breath and repeated what she had just said, realizing that she was still overly excited. "The Essenes are known for their outlandish practices as they seriously believe Elijah is soon to return and announce the arrival of the Messiah. Elijah will present our Redeemer to the nation.

"These holy men practice celibacy. That means they never take a woman to marry. They lead a very strict and austere life of fasting and prayer in a very arid and uncomfortable region of our country."

Ruth searched her daughter's face for the same excitement and awe she felt. After all, she was trying so hard to inspire her lonely daughter. She was overjoyed to see that Mary was still listening with interest.

"I know that today I am much more excited than usual, Mary. But I was filled with the spirit today as was my friend, Tzipporah. There is more!" Ruth looked at Mary to make sure she was still interested, and with a smile Mary nodded for her to continue.

"The itinerant preacher, John, the one I spoke about already, many think he is preparing for Elijah to return. He has no possessions and for sustenance he eats only food given to him, or he finds plants or roots, or he doesn't eat at all. Oddly, he wears a rough and primitive animal hide for clothing. He proclaims that his only purpose is to prepare for the imminent arrival of the Redeemer, the Messiah!"

Again, Ruth was flushed and out of breath. But, as if she could not stop, she continued, "Oh, and another unusual thing, he declares to everyone who listens to him, shouting with strong conviction, 'You must all repent for your day of reckoning is at hand!' They say that he is very unconventional in his speeches. Uncivilized and desperate he is. Screaming with desperation like a madman out to the crowds."

Nodding her head Ruth continued, "Yes, he is charismatic and intriguing, and they say he looks crazy as he desperately screams, 'The Messiah is coming! Repent and make yourselves ready!'" She kept going on and on, sometimes acting out what she imagined him to be like.

Mary again became distracted as her attention was caught up by the curious word, *'repentance.' Why do we have to repent? I thought we are Elah's chosen people. Our sins are overlooked by Elah, aren't they?*

Her mind began to buzz with many questions, trying to remember her grandmother's point of view. *Did Grandmother ever speak of the need for repentance?* Disquieted by the surprising notion of repentance, she desired her grandmother's wise advice. However, recounting her own knowledge of scriptures, Mary did recall that the old prophets were known for their fiery sermons, and some were certainly about repentance.

Maybe this preacher is irrational or maybe he is a modern-day prophet, she could not decide. Finally, she decided to dispel that uncomfortable idea for the present.

Breaking from her bewilderment, Mary realized she was staring right into her mother's eyes but she was not sure what her mother had said. Sheepishly she smiled back.

Ruth paused, recognizing that her daughter was not paying attention. She cleared her throat and admitted awkwardly, "Oh dear, I was a bit out of control. Let me go and prepare something to eat."

Wishing to ponder the morning's excitement further, Mary climbed the stairs to the roof. The unanswered question lingered and left her with an uncomfortable element of curiosity. Pensively, she made a plan, *Tomorrow I will do a special study on a few of the scriptures in Isaiah and the other prophets and see what they had to say about repentance.*

Mary's plan to study would have to wait. The following morning when she woke, she inhaled a waft of the sweetly pungent familiar herb, Felty Germander. Its strong medicinal odor filled the dim room, telling her that she was not dreaming.

She managed to lift her head. The steaming concoction wafted in the air and she saw her mother lying asleep next to her, immediately remembering her sleepless night from another breathing attack.

With little strength to do more than raise her throbbing head, she remained flat on her pallet. She wanted to go back to sleep but her mind spun out a depressing insight. *It seems that the older I get, my struggle to stay alive gets more intense and desperate.*

Remorsefully she recalled thinking in the midst of the gasping and wheezing during the night, *Perhaps, these are my last moments on this earth and I won't live to see my eighteenth year.*

But here I am, still alive and at this moment feeling relief, though my head and chest ache. There is no doubt that my wheezing and struggles are getting worse. Mother stayed up all through the night and tried hard to keep me alive and as comfortable as possible. Her worries fill me with sadness and helplessness. I'm sorry that my whole life has caused her so much worry.

Weakened and tired of the fight, her spirit helplessly gave in to her reality. She began to accept and believe in the inevitable. In the midst of the pain, she no longer cared about the thought of dying. Exhaustion overtook her. After days of suffering and without energy or the will power to live, she fell into a deep sleep.

There was no way for Mary to know that this year, although not without great effort, would be not the end but rather the beginning of her legendary life. Her bitter path of suffering would lead directly to the heart of the Anointed One, the Messiah.

This last attack, as she lingered at death's door, would change Mary's attitude toward life. She realized, *Another episode like this one, and I will no longer have enough strength to gasp for air.* Now she understood and decided that she had to live each day to its fullest. With a renewed sense of the value of her short life, she determined to find a way to go beyond her limitations.

Weeks had passed since the attack, and as she was feeling stronger Mary dared to face her greatest fear, the fear of dying. She determined to try something new. She began to search her soul audaciously for ideas on how she could face her destiny. She put aside her fear of the dust and heat and determined, *No longer will I cling to past restrictions.*

Thus, she entertained different possibilities and considered her situation rationally. *This season is cooler. I know I have to avoid the dust and stale air of the marketplace. Where can I go?*

One windy evening on her roof, no longer feeling the effects of her ailment, Mary inhaled the fresh but fishy aroma of the balmy sea breeze coming from the east. *The Sea of Galilee is over there. Maybe I can go to the shore where the air is fresh.* Then she remembered that Grandmother once told her that it was not too far away.

Mary seriously entertained the possibility, *This is a brazen idea. I could lose my life. Am I ready? Yes, it is time to live, if only for a brief time.*

Enthused by her inspiration, and with youthful undaunted spontaneity, she hastily descended the stairs to announce her plan to her mother. Without setting up her inspiration in a way her mother could receive it, Mary blurted out her bold idea, "Mother, I want to go to the shore."

The release of her preposterous suggestion brought Mary face to face with the reality of her shocking words. She swallowed hard as she observed her mother's aghast and speechless expression. Mary's countenance reddened, realizing how unfair she was being to her mother.

Clearing her throat, she dared to continue, though attempting to sound normal and trying to comfort her shaken mother, "The air is fresh there, and the sea breezes are comfortable, and it might help my condition and give me strength. Last Sabbath, I heard you speaking with Uncle about his upcoming journey to the sea. You know, his seasonal trip to procure fish. He asked if you needed any goods from the newly built city of Tiberius."

Ruth tried to interrupt, but Mary quickly continued, speaking breathlessly, "Do you think he would let me go with him on his wagon? It's only a day's journey to the fishing port. I'd like to go."

Mary noticed Mother's appalled expression. Then immediately it softened and with a positive nod of acceptance she surprised Mary by answering, "It sounds like a good idea! I will ask Uncle tomorrow."

During the following week, mother and daughter worked together preparing for Mary's fledgling journey. Even though Mary rested often so as to not exacerbate her condition, she remained determined to go. Mother fed her frail daughter hearty food and herbs to aid and strengthen her for the three-day journey.

As planned, Ruth had proposed the idea to her brother. She was not surprised when he immediately agreed to take Mary. He was an independent soul who in the past had even chided Ruth for not allowing Mary to venture out of the house. Of course, he knew why, but as Mary matured, he felt it necessary for her to have experiences beyond their walls.

Mary intuited her mother's silent angst, but was impressed that she did not speak one word of discouragement. They both supported each other for the challenging trek ahead.

Ruth did all the packing and heavy lifting. She prepared meals for the journey, special herbs that seemed to fortify her daughter, and a bedroll. She washed Mary's practically new clothing, an outer shift and robe, and even sewed her a new scarf.

Finally, she brought all the supplies to the front of the house, where she and Mary waited for the wagon. Ruth was thrilled at Mary's bright appearance and expression of anticipation for the first time in her daughter's life.

Sitting together, Mary nervously made small talk, trying to ease her mother's concern. Even though she herself was anxious, she knew that her mother was concealing her own uneasiness. "This morning, I breathed the sea air on the roof. I know it will be exciting seeing such a large body of water. Mother, I promise I will not be a burden to Uncle." She chattered and embraced her mother, trying to give her mother and herself reassurance.

They heard wagon wheels before her uncle's wagon came into sight. Mary stood up boldly, kissed her mother's cheek, and waited while the wagons drove up.

Uncle Simeon, a short and stocky, jovial man, sat on the top board of his wagon, pulled by an ox. There were two other wagons following behind him. He jumped off and picked up Mary's bundle that held the specially prepared food and herbs. Then he turned to his sister, "Ruth, don't you worry! We will be just fine. Before you know it, we will be back, and Mary will have much to tell you."

Confidently, in his manly way, Uncle commanded her, "Come on, Niece, let's get going." Mary boarded the wagon, and sat next to her uncle. Even though her eyes were moist and there was a lump in her throat, she smiled and waved bravely to her mother as they rounded the bend in the road.

The road was dusty as their little caravan made its way out of the village. Breezes helped to clear the air while Mary used her scarf to cover her mouth and nose. She remembered the tears in Mother's eyes, but Mary was confident that she had made the right decision. She would return with many stories and more reasons to get well.

This was an exciting moment for the frail young maiden of seventeen who had never ventured further than that one time visit to the marketplace. It was unusual, also, because an unmarried woman rarely left home without a female guardian, especially on an overnight trip. However, Uncle Simeon, her late father's brother, was like a father to Mary and so it was allowed. Bravely, she thought that she had nothing to lose. Her goal, after all, was to strengthen her body and embrace the life that she could not even imagine.

The sun beamed right into Mary's eyes as the bouncing ox carts squeaked loudly as they rolled along the rugged path toward the lake. Magdala, situated in the western hills of Galilee, was a slow day's journey east to the water's edge.

From the shore they would turn southward to their destination, a well-known fishing port where the water was fresh and the fish were abundant. It was a central deep-water port and market for the region. All the fish were brought by fishing boats daily to be processed and cured for preservation before being transported back to Magdala and other towns and villages in the area.

The new cosmopolitan city of Tiberius was about a day's journey further south. It was the region's international market for dry goods, food stuffs, meats, textiles, hides and delicacies from all over the Mediterranean. Mary's uncle made the trip once or twice a season and brought back items that only the city was known to have, to be sold in Magdala's market.

Uncle Simeon seemed to be the leader of the group. When he began to sing the other traders followed, echoing the same song, an old Hebrew folk song. Uncle sang one phrase and the others answered in a chorus.

Mary immediately felt excited and relaxed with a smile from ear to ear. She observed the noisy screeching seagulls circling each wagon greedily, looking for savory scraps of food. She noticed that the birds' squealing was almost in rhythm with the men's voices. The boisterous and manly words of the song were invigorating, making Mary laugh quietly while hiding her face under her scarf. Life became tangible and delicious.

Mary watched the sun, beginning on the horizon in the east, rising high in the sky, all the while jerking about and trying to keep her balance as she sat on the top board of the wagon. She felt every jolt and bounce. The new experience was surprisingly arduous. However, the sights and sounds distracted her from her physical pain.

When the bright sun was directly overhead in the clear blue sky, her uncle turned around to the other wagon drivers behind them and announced in a loud voice, "We'll stop just over the next hill to have lunch and rest."

Mary looked at her uncle's well-worn face and shyly spoke for the first time, "Uncle, you must have made this trip many times."

Uncle Simeon looked at his niece and grinned. Mary noticed that a few teeth were missing. "Yes, my father took me and your father on my first trip when I was only six years old. I was like you, very excited to see all the new sights. He taught me from that time how to keep the family business going. So, since then I go four times and sometimes as many as six times each year.

"Niece, we are very fortunate. We are able to feed and clothe our whole family. There are so many in our land who are not so fortunate. Do you know that our family has been doing this for many generations? Your father also participated until his illness; Yahweh bless his soul."

As they reached the top of the next hill, Mary got her first glimpse of the lake in the distance. She could hardly believe the breathtaking vista and pointed with excitement, "Is that the Sea of Galilee ahead?" In her wildest imagination she could not have envisioned its vastness and beauty.

Her uncle nodded as he focused on navigating the rocks and pathway. "We will stop here," he motioned with his hand above his head to the others.

Although Mary felt bruised and tired, her spirit soared with happiness like the birds. She felt like the winged seagulls that followed them and like a newborn baby as she began experiencing the outside world for the first time.

She was grateful that her uncle had allowed her to travel with him. Even though she admitted feeling a gnawing pain in her back, which reminded her of her weakness, she reasoned, *I haven't forgotten my limitations and that there is a chance that my wheezing could return. I don't regret taking this trip. I'm so grateful to Uncle for his support as well!*

The ox pulled the wagon under one of the only trees in the area. The welcome shade gave much-needed relief from the afternoon heat. As she looked up into the aged branches of the ancient tree, Mary appreciated its comfort. Meditatively she whispered, "You must have given many travelers comfort."

Mary hopped gingerly out of the wagon with undeniable discomfort, but as she walked around and stretched, she forgot her aches and pains. Fascinated by the vista of browns, greens and the occasional yellow and lavender flowered landscape beside the wind-swept rocks, she gazed downward into the bluish grey waters of the inland sea on the other side of the hills.

There were only a few trees and shrubs dispersed scantily across the hilly area where they had stopped. The different tones of brown and splashes of other earthen colors appeared to the reclusive girl to form a beautiful mosaic. Taking a deep breath, her nostrils caught the aroma of the sea. *Elah!* she exclaimed inwardly. *I love your creation! It fills my senses with joy. My being is stimulated simultaneously with sight, sound, taste, touch, and smell!*

The travelers ate their lunch of bread and figs. Though the taste was familiar, eaten in this environment to Mary it seemed as if it were a new delicacy. Even the watered-wine that she drank from her waterskin revived her tired body so deliciously.

Mary was not sure how much of her emotional experience was obvious to the men in her caravan. Reticently, she continued sharing her excitement alone with Elah. She avoided talking with the men who gathered together taking their meal. She was beginning to feel free but not that free. In fact, in her whole life, she had never spoken to any man other than her uncle and her rabbi.

Life in Galilee was based on age-old Hebrew traditions; very little had changed in centuries. Men and women had their own division of labor and there was little social interaction between the sexes. Mary was traveling with her uncle, who was like a father to her as her own father had died when she was a baby. Uncle Simeon had a dear and caring heart toward her, but still it was not a usual occurrence. Other than making sure she was comfortable, he and the other men kept to their customary distance and duties and ignored her.

They took some time to rest. Mary lay down on her quilt next to a large rock under the shade tree. Before she knew it, she fell into a peaceful sleep. As she drifted off, she had an unforgettable dream.

Standing and looking into the distance, she saw a figure, very tiny, on the horizon. It was coming toward her and getting larger. After a while the figure became recognizable as that of a man dressed in gold and shining in the sun. As he came closer, she saw his beautiful fine clothing, bedecked with fine jewelry. On his head he wore a golden turban-like head covering, and she realized he was dressed in wedding clothes.

There was a bright light shining around him. He turned his head, looking to his left. Then Mary saw another figure nearing. It appeared to be a woman dressed in beautiful red and golden wedding clothes, with a golden veil over her head and face. The man's face was clear but because of the fine material she could not see the woman's face. The scene filled Mary with excitement and wonder. In joy she fell to her knees.

"Niece … Niece," she heard her uncle calling her, and she opened her eyes to find herself lying under the shade tree. Her dream was so clear and beautiful that she did not want to wake up. However, her uncle was calling her to come back to the wagon to resume their journey. Rubbing the sleep from her eyes, she stood and returned to the wagon.

She kept the scarf over her face, shielding herself from the sun, sitting on a wooden box in the bed of the rickety wagon as her uncle thought she might be more comfortable there. She held on to the sides of the wagon as it swayed back and forth, as they made their way along the sandy and rocky path to the fishing port.

Mesmerized by the gently rocking wagon bed, she thought about her curious dream. *What an interesting dream! I wonder who the man and woman were?* Mary had never had such a fascinating dream. *They must be from a royal family.* She had a while to ponder the dream for there was nothing else to do but just hold on to the swaying wagon.

The sun, which had been baking Mary for the last few hours, was settling toward the horizon as the wagons neared the port. The smell of the water, now stronger in her nostrils, and numerous seagulls swooping around the caravan, continued giving Mary unforgettable joy. There was also a breeze that helped to cool her.

As their path neared the port, they also came closer to the edge of the water. "The water! It's a deep bluish green!" Mary exclaimed. Her heart leaped. The sparkling water gleamed with silvery patches caught by the rays of the sun. It looked more like a mirror than water. Its color was a welcome change from the brown countryside.

She stared at the other side of the lake, far in the distance. There were many boats dispersed far and wide: some stationery in the center of the lake; others sitting still near the shore; while others were sailing toward the little fishing port with their bounty. *That must be where we are going?* Mary guessed.

Bravely standing to look forward in the direction they were going, she saw a gathering of about a dozen wagons along the shore. *Those wagons are from other communities?* she speculated.

Mary's uncle pulled his wagon into the same area, followed by the others in their party. As he pulled the reins of the ox to stop, feeling like a child Mary jumped from the back of the wagon to the sandy ground, which gave way under her feet. She could hardly wait to touch the water. Her sandals and feet were covered with sand. Even though she was stiff from the long ride, she could hold back no longer. Half walking and half running she headed for the water's edge.

In her haste, Mary did not notice that her scarf slipped off and strands of her hair were now waving in the breeze. She inhaled the fresh, balmy air. The sight was more than she had ever imagined. "Oh, Elah, thank you for giving me this glimpse of heaven!" she whispered.

Standing on the water's edge, and ignoring the people around her, like a child she shook off her sandals and jumped into the shallow water, kicking it up with her feet. The breeze caught the water and sprayed it back onto her uncovered face and hair. She gathered her skirt and crouched down, dipping her hands into the lake's life-giving water. She splashed its coolness over her hands and onto her face. The clean, crystal-clear water ran down her face, following the creases of her smile into her welcoming mouth. *How refreshing!* she thought.

Still not noticing that her scarf was missing, for she was lost in the world of innocence, she forgot herself and became immersed in playfulness. Keeping the hem of her skirt out of the water, she again squatted and looked closer into the water and at the plants along the shore.

Moments later, she heard the voice of a man standing behind her. Suddenly her mind sprang back to reality. She reached for her scarf, which was not there, and jumped to her feet in embarrassed surprise.

The man was talking for a few seconds before Mary began to comprehend his meaning. His deep voice sounded almost foreign because of its rough Aramaic dialect. She could not look up, for shame. She was not used to speaking to a man, especially without a scarf covering her face and shoulders.

The peculiar sounding man was holding her scarf and asked, "Is this yours?"

"Oh! Yes, thank you," she said timidly as she reached and grabbed it from him, promptly covering her head and then reaching for the end to modestly cover her face.

As she looked up at him, she could see only a silhouette of his face with the sun behind him. She smiled shyly and awkwardly began to walk back toward her uncle's wagon, clinging to her wrap.

As she glanced over her shoulder, she was surprised to see that he was still watching her. It was then that she saw his broad and bearded face. Still embarrassed to be caught without her wrap, she blushed deeply, especially surprised when she saw that he continued to observe her as she walked away.

Chapter 3

The Burning Ember

Never let the fire in your heart go out!
When you hope, be joyful, when you suffer be patient,
when you pray be faithful.
(Romans 12: 11-12)

Dusk was setting in. At least twelve wagons, including Uncle Simeon's three, were preparing for the end of the day. The moonlit sky was filled with puffy drifting clouds being spread quickly about the heavens by the mild easterly breeze coming off the water. The clouds made it difficult to view more than a few stars. The breeze pushed the heat of the day away, making a comfortable temperature at the campsite.

Men were setting up for the night, moving the oxen away from the campfires. Some were moving their empty wagons, in a last-minute attempt to be situated before total darkness.

There were male voices, talking, laughing, and singing as all were preparing the campfires for warmth and cooking. Mary noticed a dozen or so fires each with several men gathered around, walking to and from their wagons. She observed a few women and children as well.

Aromas of cooking abounded, some acrid while others were delightful. Smoke intermingled with the savory roasted meats and vegetables seasoned with dill, coriander, and a familiar whiff of lentil stew that caused her stomach to grumble and reminded her of home.

Her uncle and his company had already built a fire and set their pallets around it. They hardly noticed Mary as she entered the camp. She had been so caught up in the mesmerizing scenes that she had not noticed her pangs of hunger.

Her uncle was beginning to roast a fish over the fire and called her to sit next to him. *How delightful is its aroma!* she thought. She opened her bundle from home and shared the bread, figs, and nuts her mother had packed for her. Then she sat down quietly by the fire, patiently waiting for the fish to cook.

Her attention turned back toward the spellbinding water and again her senses were alive like she had never known before. The pleasing outdoor cooking aromas were bathing her skinny malnourished physique and she felt her stomach longing for the tasty food. The crispy fish tasted wonderful with all the other contributions of food. It was a memorable supper.

Staring at the dancing flames and red-hot coals, she noticed the human voices all around intermingled with the distant lapping of the water on the shore. The simplicity of being outdoors and at the seashore seemed to heal her from within. On the other hand, she thought of home and surely felt a pang of loneliness for her mother. Trying to ignore the conflicting feelings, she chided herself with a reminder that this was her chance to make a new beginning.

Darkness enveloped the travelers. The only lights came from the fires burning at the center of the camps, the few tiny stars, and the crescent moon appearing off and on over their heads. It was hard to imagine the lake, if not for the occasional reflection of moonlight on the water.

As their fire smoldered to red coals, Mary rose and thanked her uncle graciously. She formally wished him a 'Good Night,' and proceeded to prepare for sleep. She laid her pallet on the opposite side of the wagon, away from the men and farthest from the warming fire. It was chilly but with her wraps and blanket she was quite comfortable. Sleep came quickly.

The next morning when she opened her eyes, she beheld a blue sky. She had no idea what time it was, but smoke from the fireplace filled the air around her. *The men put out the campfire!* Mary thought. She jumped up quickly, covering her nose and mouth with her scarf as the smoke brought on her wheezing and coughing.

Her uncle heard her coughing and ran to help her. Together they walked toward the water's edge. He gave her a waterskin and she drank, which seemed to relieve her cough, but her wheezing continued.

"Uncle let me walk away from the camp. I think everything will clear up with this breeze off the water." Though she felt a wave of dizziness Mary continued on alone along the water's edge and slowly her breathing began to improve.

The sight of the azure water caught her off guard. Its deep blue and glass like stillness filled her with wonder. Never could she imagine such a scene of beauty. The morning breeze blew into her face and seemed to chase the smoke away. This relieved her sick feeling. After her breathing eased, she returned to carry her things to the wagon.

She noticed her uncle walking away from their camp toward the fishing boats and ran to catch up to him. She wanted to go with him and watch the boats unload their catch.

Uncle Simeon smiled broadly and proudly at her and spoke encouragingly, "You found a way to help yourself. Elah bless you!"

Then he began to tell her his schedule, "Now I begin my day. I will bring fish back to our village after the fresh fish is roasted, smoked, and cured. That will take a day. The building over there with a gutter and a smoker is the preparation facility.

"Niece, I will be busy for the morning and then I will make a trip into Tiberius. You are welcome to come with me right after taking a quick meal about noontime."

"Yes, I would love to come with you. I will meet you near the wagon. Thank you."

As her uncle took the pathway toward the docks, her eye caught an unexpected sight. There was a strange person standing waist deep in the water some twenty span away along the curving shoreline. Intrigued, she turned and joined the few people who also seemed as curious as she was, wondering, *What is this bizarre bearded man doing? It's a bit chilly to be waist deep in the water this early in the morning.*

Close up, she gawked at the scraggy, ill-kempt man with a dark brown full beard and long stringy hair, wearing what looked like a rough brown sack draped over his shoulder. The sun was rising above the horizon behind him in the cloudless sky.

Mary thought, with concern for him, *The rays of the sun will warm the chilly morning air which will be good for him, standing there in the cold water.* Captivated by the strange man, she listened to him calling out to the crowd standing on the dry sand and staring at him.

"Hear my message. Repent and be baptized!"

There is that word again, repent! Mary whispered to herself. *I didn't remember to look for it in my studies. I wonder what view scripture takes of repenting. I wonder why I feel uncomfortable about it. It's something I must ask Rabbi Levi about when I get home.*

The man continued speaking loudly and beckoning to his audience, "Come into the water and be baptized."

He speaks with such passion and conviction, Mary said to herself.

Though she was shocked when he bellowed out, "You are of your father the devil and you must repent and prepare yourselves to receive the Messiah!"

What is he talking about? she thought. *I am a Hebrew waiting for the Messiah. I am one of Elah's chosen people, so why does he say that I am the child of the devil? Is he a foreigner? Is he a Hebrew? Who can this man be?* Mary was perplexed but admittedly curious.

As she listened, she became interested in the other people standing around. There were fishermen and a few women and children. Some stayed to listen, while others left shaking their heads.

The strange man continued pleading for his audience to come into the water and be baptized. No one responded.

It is certainly too cold, she thought sympathetically. She was curious though and wondered, *What is baptism?* She admitted to herself that it was kind of exciting, so she stayed to see if anyone would go in to be baptized.

Feeling uninhibited, Mary curiously glanced around at the few remaining observers. Suddenly she spotted the young man who had recovered her scarf the day before. Before she could cover her face to remain anonymous, she realized that he must have felt her attention as he looked straight into her eyes. He recognized her immediately, smiled, and walked amiably over to her.

Respectfully he offered a greeting. "Good morning. I am James," he introduced himself. "I hope you slept well."

His casual familiarity stunned her. She nodded woodenly, unable to lift her face to him. She noticed her cheeks were hot, as she stood speechless. The shock of his attention was so great that the unexpected emotion brought tears to her eyes. Dumbfounded, she thought, *This is the first time a man paid any attention to me.*

She was an oddity and a social outcast. Most girls were already married and had children by their seventeenth year. Finally, she managed to stammer, "My name is Mary."

James, unaware of her state of mind, questioned her further, "Are you with the caravan from Magdala?"

"Yes, I am," she flushed and answered with a nod. She noticed that James was not much older than she was. His skin was rough and brown, baked by the sun, and his beard grew unevenly around his mouth and throat. His friendly, brown eyes seemed to pierce her soul. Unsure of herself, she could not look him directly in the eye. She found herself looking at the ground and listening to his rustic sounding voice. Surprisingly, she even liked the sound of his accent.

"Have you been listening to this preacher very long?" he inquired.

"No, I've only been here a short time." Mary surprised herself when she quickly added a question to prolong his wonderful attention, "Have you?"

"Yes, well, not too long today, but his words are interesting to me and I have seen him here a few other times. He speaks with strength and conviction of his faith in Elah."

James went on to give more information because she seemed interested. "I overheard someone say that he is the son of a high priest and his name is John. And a fisherman I know who was just here told me that he is a wandering preacher who encourages people to be baptized and that he is from an Essene sect. His main message is our need to repent and how we come from the devil...."

As James continued talking, Mary noticed that she enjoyed listening to the sound of his coarse but rhythmic voice. However, his forward manner went against her customs and upbringing which forbade women to converse with men, especially strangers. Nevertheless, she could not pull herself away. Also, she was interested in his information about this unusual evangelist. As though compensating for her burning conscience, she tightened her scarf and kept her eyes lowered.

James continued, "They say he has no worldly possessions and that those who come to listen to him give him the only food that he eats. He does not speak like usual religious men..."

Oh Yes! Suddenly Mary remembered the news her mother brought her from the marketplace. *This must be the same man,* she surmised.

"...What do you think?" James asked her opinion. He caught her off guard, shocking her with the question and again bringing tears to her eyes.

She responded after clearing her throat, "Ah, yes, he is very curious to me as well." Then she added the obvious, "But he is unable to get anyone to join him in the water."

James answered sincerely, "Yes, that's right. As for me, I am curious, but not enough to go into the water. Anyway, I would like to listen to him a bit longer, but I have to go back to my brother who is readying our fishing boat. Will you be staying here longer?"

The personal question caused Mary's face to blush, warming her heart, and sending a tingling sensation throughout her whole body. Feeling a cough coming she quickly swallowed and held it back. "No, I will be returning to my village in the morning." Reality filled her with remorse as she realized her unfortunate condition and that she would never see him again.

Oh well, she thought. *He's probably married or promised to someone, anyway.*

From a distance they heard someone calling, "James!" The voice was coming from a fishing boat that was already beginning to leave the water's edge. James bowed politely and bid her farewell with a blessing for a safe journey home. As Mary bowed her head in response, he ran toward the boat. He was already halfway to the boat when Mary lifted her head and caught sight of his agile body, running along the shore.

The ache in Mary's heart consumed her. Never had she felt such a sensation. Pitifully she wondered, *Is this the feeling men and women have toward each other?*

Until this moment, due to her fragile condition, she never imagined such an experience. But after this albeit natural realization, she knew that she could never forget it. Although brief, it ignited a spark in her heart, a sensation of fire throughout her whole consciousness and her whole being. It consumed her, catching her completely by surprise.

What do I do with this feeling now? she thought hopelessly, knowing that she would never see him again. Yet, what was she to do with the burning sensation deep within her chest? She made her way slowly and pensively back to her campsite.

Mary forgot about the preacher as she returned to her uncle's wagon. She was overwhelmed by the newly discovered and unintended fire within her heart. *What a wonderful feeling that men and women have toward each other. I am grateful to experience it even if only for a moment.*

When she reached her uncle's wagon, he was already preparing to leave for Tiberius. The two of them were going to the markets there during the time the fish were being cured and preserved. Tiberius was a short journey farther south, along the shore. Uncle Simeon prepared to buy additional products, textiles, dry goods and such for the vendors in the Magdala market, as well as items for his family.

The women were expecting linens for sewing into tunics, robes, scarves, and veils. The men were looking forward to tools of their trades, and the children were dreaming of the delicious foreign sweets that could only be obtained there, one of the most modern and cosmopolitan towns in Galilee. Egyptian, Phoenician, and other foreign delicacies were procured there.

To Mary, a country girl, all the sights and sounds were new. Had she seen them yesterday she would have been thrilled. Today, however, there was no comparison between the town's sights and the attention of the young man, James. Everywhere she looked she saw his face.

Uncle Simeon dropped Mary off to explore the town and market while he went to procure his goods. As Mary walked around, she vaguely remembered the marketplace of Magdala from many years before.

Tiberius was much bigger than Magdala and aesthetically more sophisticated with marble columns and stone paved streets. There was trading of every kind of commodities from around the world, textiles from the coastal city of Tyre, adornments from Phoenicia, and food from all over the known world such as she had never seen before. The goods were displayed on table after table, row after row, and there were many plazas where people congregated. Animals to be sold for riding, carrying, and pulling were everywhere.

It truly was fascinating. But, just as the air in Magdala's marketplace was filled with the strong odors of livestock, the air here was also heavy and dusty. Mary quickly covered her face and sat down in one of the outer plazas waiting for her uncle's return.

Nonetheless, her breathing became labored and her throat tightened. Instinctively she stood up and walked closer toward the exit. She chose a large stone-paved street that led away from the market. As she walked, she noticed there were Roman soldiers standing guard. She also noticed that the buildings were bigger and more elaborate than any she had ever seen. Just ahead was the largest building yet. It was made of smooth, white stone with ornate curves on the top of the pillars. The doors were very large.

She thought to herself, *This must be the temple*. As she neared its steps, she saw priests dressed in familiar white robes coming out. They spoke in Hebrew to each other, unaware that she could understand their discourse. They were loudly debating verses in Isaiah. She really wanted to take time to listen, but it was unacceptable for a woman to show an intellectual interest.

Forlorn and discouraged, she moved away from the dusty market. As her breathing continued to cause her pain, she thought, *Alas! The wheezing*.

Since beginning her trip, it was her plan to ignore the reality of her life. Though she tried to escape and dispel her limitations, she realized it was only a wishful illusion. She only wanted to forget and pretended to be a young woman of good health. *What folly!* she chided herself.

Thus, with no choice but to face her nagging weak body, she slowly turned around. With shoulders slumped she decided to head back to their meeting place. *How did I ever think I could escape from the reality of my life?* Cynically, she rebuked herself.

Heavy with her reality, she thought, *I hope Uncle is back by now and that I will not get worse before... I get home.* She struggled but she knew she could not give up and thus she prayed, *Elah, please smile on me and give me strength. If we get back soon enough, I will sleep early to be ready for the trip back home.*

Mary could not deny the heaviness and sadness that she felt. She wanted to run away from her body. Inwardly she was crying out to Elah.

They planned to arrive home before the beginning of the Sabbath because they were not able to work on that day according to their religious code. Time was of the essence so they needed to work diligently with purpose and with no time to waste.

As she reached her uncle, he was loading the last of the supplies. It was a big load and the wagon was filled. Climbing up to the top board with her uncle took all her strength, and she climbed clumsily. She knew that her feeling of despondency was not only her tired physical body, but it was her tired and discouraged spirit.

"You're having another attack, aren't you?" Mary's uncle asked with sympathy and kindness.

"Yes, Uncle, but I will be all right as soon as we get away from the dust of the city. I will be better back by the sea and the countryside where the air is lighter," she reassured him, silently wanting to believe it was so.

She could only hope and pray that it was true. She prayed that she would be able to make it all the way home before a full attack came. *This was my original plan to embrace life and this is what I did. Dear Elah, please be kind to me and allow me to get home without becoming a burden to my uncle.*

Her prayer was answered when she made it through the night and all the way home. She continued to breathe heavily and cough, but she endured all the way.

As they rode along, her back ached and she felt the bruises from the first day. However, the excitement she had felt on her way to the seashore was gone. Without that, she felt her failing body more. Depression set in. The momentary meeting with the young man was a fading memory and she had nothing else, save her mother and her books, to look forward to.

Late in the afternoon of the third day, their caravan neared the outskirts of her village. So much had happened to Mary in three days. It was as if she had lived a lifetime, and she felt it in her weak body. Home was a welcome sight.

Ruth and other relatives gathered as they drove into view. Mary managed to climb down from the wagon and sank into her mother's waiting arms. Her mother heard the wheezing and immediately took her inside. She gave Mary much-needed broth and bread, and then Mary went to her pallet and quickly fell asleep. Her last thought was that she was not the same girl who had lain on that pallet only three days before.

Chapter 4

Love That Would Not Go Away

Hope deferred makes the heart sick,
but a desire fulfilled is a tree of life.
(Prov. 13:12)

Six years had passed since Mary's awakening journey to the Sea of Galilee and her happenstance meeting with James, the fisherman. Gone was her innocence and simplistic understanding of life. In its place she felt an empty hole in her heart and frustration that there was no solution.

Lying helpless on her bed day after day, she realized that she was a prisoner of her incurable physical malady. *I thought I only needed to escape the fear of death and live life to its fullness! But in my search, I found a greater vexation. Now I realize that as a woman it is only natural to desire the companionship of a man. Elah made me like that. I wonder how much more I do not know.*

The brief emotional taste of attention from the stranger would not go away and Mary wanted so much to spill out the whole experience to her mother, her only companion. She wanted to share every emotion and thrill of being noticed, and the emergent realization of attraction between the two of them.

However, she struggled with the shame of boldly speaking to the stranger without her uncle as chaperone, not just once but several times. Also, that she craved his attention. At the same time, though, she knew that she could not hide her abrupt change of character from her mother. From the first day home Mary noticed in her mother's hurt expression the disappointment and pain at the loss of their close relationship, and being unable to know why. But Mary did not know how to explain.

From the first whole day back from the trip, Mary longed to tell her mother of the young man's attention and her attraction to him. Of course, she wanted to tell her everything. But in the light of the next day, Mary realized that the experience was only a one-sided imagination, which also added to her shame.

Several times she prepared herself with a deep breath to explain everything, but she could not muster the words. And, her practical mind candidly taunted her for holding on to the shallow and imaginary affair in the first place. Thus, day after day, Mary mutely buried the experience deep in her heart without sharing, hoping that it would eventually disappear. On the contrary and to her surprise it multiplied and consumed her. It was her first thought every day, and her last one before sleeping.

Like a festering wound, over time she became increasingly angry and resentful. Any attempt that her mother made to get her to talk only drove them further apart. This separation hurt them both deeply. They became strangers.

As the years passed, Mary continued reading religious texts brought to her by her rabbi. In this way she distracted herself and suppressed the distant and nagging memory. However, she reluctantly accepted that she would never experience the love meant for men and women. Nevertheless, its absence drove her closer and closer to insanity.

Her wheezing attacks continued frequently. Thus, she endured her reclusive and lonely life. The only time she dared to venture outdoors was in the cool evening air on the rooftop of her home.

Over the years, friends of her mother and relatives visited, trying to uplift her and thereby help their friend Ruth. However, they found that regardless of their attempts to uplift her spirit, Mary was not a pleasant person to be around. Unhappy and resentful, she did not try to be agreeable, expressing angry outbursts even to her once beloved rabbi. In this way and in her hopeless manner she deliberately drove everyone away.

Over the next seven years, she and her mother traveled to many villages and towns seeking a healer. Though Mary rebelled and rued the attempts, Ruth forced her to visit healers and holy men. Nevertheless, no one was able to release her from her infirm body. Thus, finally, she refused to go on any more treks.

When Mary was not suffering from her tortuous condition, she continued reading any religious texts she could get her hands on. The study helped distract her as she whiled away the hours and days. Forcefully resigning herself in her cynicism to never experience love, she learned to push the old memory away from her consciousness. But that which once was sweet now had become a monster.

Ruth, however, never gave up and continued searching. This only enraged Mary. In her despondent state, she shrieked at her mother, "Just let me die! Why, can't you let me die?" She sputtered and wheezed. Her mental and physical pain was unbearable. "Just let me die," she repeated.

It seemed to her that Elah was truly punishing her from every angle of thought and desire. Because at the same time, the inexorable question of repentance, this unresolved query, remained a puzzlement to her. Muttering to herself in great consternation, she asked, "How could that preacher whom I met so long ago speak about repentance for Hebrews?" For hours she sat and thought about this theological question. Her mind was unable to come up with any answer, which made her even more confused and more frustrated.

The memories haunted her like an addiction that she could not resist. The warm feeling of infatuation, though she knew was imagined, was all she lived for. There were times when she tried to forget, but she only sank deeper into morbid depression. There was nowhere to turn. Even sleep waited with its nightmares to further pound her spirit, driving her toward madness.

Thus, she lost the will to live and even developed an unhealthy, welcoming desire for death. She lost her appetite so that her mother had to force her to eat. She was already quite thin but became even more emaciated. She no longer wanted to care for herself, even to brush her hair or to bathe. She was frail, disheveled, and melancholic, and lay on her pallet in her dark room from morning to night.

Through it all, that tiny spark kept glowing deep within her heart. She tried to push it deeper and deeper away from her consciousness. It was like an animal that burrowed deep inside. It would not be extinguished, it would not disappear, and it would not leave her alone.

Ten years passed, with Mary living in the depths of depression. Miraculously, she survived to her twenty-seventh year, despite her efforts to give up.

One afternoon she heard her mother enter their house. She was not sure what time of day it was or even whether it was day or night. "Mother," she called.

After a few moments, Ruth entered the room where she found Mary, as usual, lying on her pallet in the dark. As she opened the door, light streamed in, slicing through the darkness of despair. The bright light caught the invalid by surprise, causing her to wince from the brilliance. "Where have you been?" Mary demanded feebly.

Ruth replied softly and casually, so as to not arouse her pitiful daughter's usual resentment. She had something to ask her daughter but waited for the right moment. "I came from the well, abuzz with the usual gossip and news."

When there was no response from her daughter, charily, not wanting to provoke her daughter's angry tantrums, she asked, "Would you like me to tell you something unusual that I heard?"

Mary was not interested but she was also too weak to resist. Without answering, she lay there quietly, cynically knowing she was going to hear it anyway.

"There is a report of an itinerant rabbi who is visiting Magdala. He is joined by a group of followers, mostly fishermen from the Sea of Galilee. The rumors are that he has healed some very sick people; he even healed lepers."

Purposely nonchalant, Ruth avoided looking directly at her daughter. She slowly went around the room picking up and cleaning the room while relating the news, keeping herself restrained to prevent a negative response.

"Fishermen!" The word burst from Mary's lips, stunning her as she feebly looked up at her mother. The unusual response seemed to stop time, catching both by surprise as they held their breath. Both of their eyes were suddenly wide open.

Ruth saw an unusual spark of life emanating from her daughter. It had been many years since she had seen such kind of a reaction. She noted her heart pounding, feeling out of breath like she had run home. Holding back the desire to embrace her pitiful daughter, she swallowed and waited for her daughter's next response.

Instantly, memories of long ago streamed quickly through Mary's mind as she remembered the preacher standing in the waters of the lake. She felt her skin immediately burn and blushed, from deathly pale to crimson. It was too late for her to squelch the emotion. Hope sprang in her heart, startling the cynical invalid.

Everything happened so quickly that she could not conceal her elation from her mother. Trying not to appear totally besotted, impulsively she asked a bizarre question, "Do you know what kind of clothes he wears?" As soon as she blurted it out, Mary realized how pathetic she sounded. It caused a cascade of emotions and tears to spill out. The sudden release actually relieved an ache in her heart and this time she did not try to conceal it.

How long had it been since Mary spoke with such spontaneity and spirit! Shocked, Ruth turned to examine her daughter. She noticed Mary's manner and flushed face. "What just happened?" she asked, not sure what had caused Mary's reaction.

Mary managed to regain her usual coolness as her mind tried to take command of her heart. Internally she bounced back to rigid rationalization as had been her habit all those long years. Furtively she thought, *How ridiculous of me to entertain those old feelings! Besides, I'm an invalid and I have already given up.* Her skepticism continued, *There is no reason to get hopeful over any such news of another rabbi-healer. They're all the same.*

Her mind was about to win its habitual game, again, but then Ruth stepped in. Although surprised at her daughter's response, she realized that here was an opportunity to help Mary. She wanted to nurse the sudden emotion, the tiny ember she felt in her daughter's lonely heart, to allow it to grow.

She had not seen this kind of hopeful reaction since her daughter left for the coast. Something had aroused her daughter, something about the news she brought today. But it did not matter to her what, only that her curiosity had started to reemerge.

Wisely choosing her words, Ruth agreed, "Yes, I know he is just another one of those good for nothing rabbis." Glancing sideways at Mary to see her reaction, she continued. "I imagine you don't want to go and see another rabbi. They are all alike. They promise things and…."

Ruth could not finish before Mary burst out with emotion, "Alright mother! I would like to see that rabbi!"

Her resignation to die suddenly disappeared. Mary tried to compose herself so that she would not cause a horrid breathing attack. Nonetheless, she began to struggle helplessly and motioned for assistance to stand up. With newly found enthusiasm, something her mother had not seen for years, she admitted, "Please take me to the Rabbi!"

There was curiosity in Ruth's face, but she dared not ask for a reason. She quietly granted Mary's request with pleasure, "All right, I would like to go with you. This is a good day to take a walk."

With that, Ruth prepared water for a bath and helped Mary rise from her cot. As her mother poured the water over her, Mary felt a renewal, cleansing her of hopelessness. She dressed in her robe which she had not worn for years. She could not remember the last time she put it on. Finally, Ruth combed and braided her long hair and gave her a cap and traditional scarf.

After the years of despair and then this sudden change, Mary realized her selfishness and dismissive attitude to her mother. Now she felt gratitude toward her mother for never giving up on her. Taking her mother's hand, she pressed it to her cheek, "Mother, I am ashamed of my callous attitude toward you and others all these years. I know you saw a difference in me right away after returning from my trip with Uncle. Please forgive me."

Tears welled up in Ruth's eyes as she replied, "I am so sorry that you had to endure this difficult life. You have fought long and hard. Remember, though, what Grandmother always told you, that Elah has plans for you."

They smiled together at the mention of Grandmother. The feeling of relief was cathartic for both women. As Mary looked at her mother, it felt good to see joy in her mother's expression after all the misery she had caused.

The unusual activity brought on Mary's wheezing. However, she ignored her labored breathing while she slipped on her sandals and tied her tunic and then opened the door of their home and her heart. It was extraordinary to find that love and hope still existed there.

The sunlight was so bright that it brought tears to Mary's eyes. The tears precipitated a flood of emotion, and she began crying uncontrollably. How much she wanted to be normal! How much she wanted to find love! But she also cried because she knew that her appearance was pitiful and feeble.

Ruth, hearing Mary's weary and tearful weeping, turned to dry her tears. The teardrops were contagious and now both mother and daughter were crying. They shed tears long held back all those years. Mary's were about the undeniable hope and love that were still in her heart, and Ruth's were from the years of weariness and longing to help her daughter.

Mary no longer wanted to push her mother away, rather she relished her mother's arms of support and allowed her mother to comfort her as she wanted to console her mother. After embracing for a few minutes, their grief came to an end. A comforting release from the loneliness and despair came over each woman.

Mary smiled at her mother and took her arm. Taking a rattling deep breath, she said, "I'm ready. Let's go."

Chapter 5

Rebirth

I revealed myself to those who did not ask for me;
I was found by those who did not seek me.
To a nation that did not call on my name,
I said, 'Here am I, here am I.'
(Isaiah 65:1)

A s the two women walked arm and arm, Mary noticed the weakness of her frail body. It had been years since she had walked any distance. Her legs shook and, being so fragile, she leaned on her mother. Initially she felt faint, but once she moved forward, she regained strength and with a renewed sense of humility she allowed her mother to lead.

Ruth explained, "It was early this morning when I heard the news, so I am not sure where the visitors will be. Though it's not too late so they must still be here." Remaining positive, she suggested, "Let's try the eastern outskirts of the village near the cliffs and trees. When there are village meetings, that is where people usually gather."

Together, they strolled carefully and slowly in that direction, each with hopeful expectations of what they would find. Ruth prayed that this would be the rabbi whom she had sought to heal her daughter, while Mary had an uncanny feeling that there was somehow a link to her experience with the young man whom she had met those many years ago.

As the two neared the edge of the village, they saw a gathering of people, which encouraged and reassured them. Ruth broke their silence, "The rabbi must be here!"

Mary, grateful for Ruth's supportive arm, listened as Ruth asked a few of the villagers standing around if the rabbi was there. A man who seemed to know her pointed, "Those fellows up there are part of the rabbi's entourage and are preparing for him."

Just then one of the strangers made an announcement, motioning toward the hills above, "Our master is praying on the cliffs and will come down soon to speak to you. Please take a seat."

It was hard for Mary to tell the difference between the villagers and the visitors. First because she hardly knew anyone from her village, and second because they wore the same simple Galilean attire of linen tunics cinched by a belt around the waist and a mantle resting upon their shoulders and flowing down to their knees. Around their heads they wore rolled linen material tied in the back or around their forehead. The men greeted the curious villagers affably, answering questions and introducing themselves.

Even though they had walked only a short distance, Mary tired quickly and needed to lean heavily on Ruth as they inched their way through the crowd. Suddenly and unexpectedly her gaze caught sight of the back of a man's head that looked strangely familiar. Her heart began to race. *Could that be him?* Mary blinked her eyes a few times in disbelief and stuttered, *How can he be here?*

Instantaneously, her heart was confident it was him, but realistically it was hard to believe. Moments went by as she considered the possibility. *Could it really be him? What is he doing here, so far from the sea and his boat and with this rabbi?*

Regretting her appearance and wretched state of health, she resisted the desire to continue moving forward and even to run to him. As she considered her sad state, her rationalization as usual overcame her heart. *I am an appalling invalid*, she reminded herself.

Out of a feeling of self-preservation, she wrenched away from Ruth's arm, wanting to turn and run. *I cannot face him to find that he is repulsed by me or does not recognize me!* This intense emotional struggle affected her physically, causing her to gasp breathlessly as she fell to her knees. *He certainly will not remember me!* That thought depressed her further.

Ruth, stunned by her daughter's collapse and, unaware of her internal struggle, exclaimed in confusion, "What's the matter?"

"I … I want to go home," Mary stammered, choking back a sob with each painful and strained breath.

Her struggle, audible and growing louder, became apparent to the crowd. Her pasty complexion became even more sallow as moisture dripped from her face. Instead of remaining anonymous, she was becoming the center of attention.

I am going to faint! she realized as she tried to speak, but her voice was inaudible. Weakly and in anguish, she thought, *Let me leave. Dear Elah, I don't want to collapse in front of everyone, especially in front of James. Please let me disappear!*

Just then, as if he heard his name whispered, James turned around. However, in reality it was only the sound of her wheezing that had caused him and the whole crowd to turn and look at her.

Oh no! I cannot escape. I cannot bear this embarrassment. Though she tried to remain upright she collapsed into her mother's arms. Breaking her fall, Ruth gently laid her down on the ground, protecting her daughter's head in her lap. Immediately her friends and the visitors, James included, rushed to her side.

Ruth spoke desperately through her sobs to the young man, "Please, could you help us? My daughter is ill. We thought that the rabbi might help her. We heard that he has healed others. Can the rabbi help her?" she asked humbly through her tears.

Mary could not open her eyes. She had no energy to speak or hide. All those nearby heard her gasps, as she felt her body stiffen and shake.

Nearing unconsciousness, though still aware of the clamoring crowd, suddenly there was silence. Then she felt a warm hand upon her forehead and immediately her labored breathing stopped. Breathing easily, she wondered, *Am I alive or dead?* Opening her eyes, she was stunned to see a man kneeling beside her with his hand upon her head.

Is this the rabbi? she wondered. He does not look like other rabbis with their curls and formal attire. Although strangely he looks familiar. Curious, she tried to remember where she had seen him.

She immediately noticed his warm and gentle expression as he prayed over her, and felt energy flowing from his hand, filling her with strength and peace and causing her to breath easily. Feeling a surge of strength fill her body, Mary blushed and sat up. Her eyes remained fixed on the rabbi. It was as if the two of them were the only people in the world.

Mary asked herself, *Is this a dream? Am I dead?* It was hard to understand why she felt unusually relaxed and comfortable. Looking at her arms and legs and feeling her face and then the earth beside her, she spoke, "I'm alive?"

Ruth wept beside her, which caused a cascade of tears from Mary's own eyes. Those gathered around were standing in shock and amazement at what they had witnessed.

Ruth's cousin, who knew of Mary's years of torment, knelt down and reached out to touch Mary, affirming for herself that it was all really happening. Then Mary took Ruth's hand into hers, whispering, "I am alive and breathing, dear Mother!"

Finally, Ruth, smiling through her tears, stood and bowed to the rabbi healer. She exclaimed in praise, "You have healed my daughter! At last, we found you. Praise Elah!"

And the crowd shouted together with her a second time, "Praise Elah and His benevolence!"

Continuing to marvel, Mary sat up and watched the rabbi stand up. Without a single word of explanation, he left her side. Surprising everyone, and especially Mary, at his humility and simplistic nature, he showed no surprise or awe.

By contrast, the crowd of onlookers began to praise Elah and dance at the miracle they beheld. Many started bringing their infirm to the rabbi. After a few cases were healed, the attendants announced that Rabboni Jesus would visit with every family after his sermon. They asked everyone to take a seat.

Mary could not take her eyes off the rabbi as he went to the front of the crowd. She continued to marvel, *It all happened so quickly. Did he really heal me? I want to thank him!*

The man began to speak. "I would like to speak to you of Elah our Creator. I often refer to Him as 'Abba' because we are all His children, young and old, Hebrew and Pagan, good and bad, believer and heathen, rich and poor.

"Abba is everywhere. He cannot be constrained to one place, like an altar. I know because I experienced Him, 'That which created everything,' our Abba.

"Let me tell you about my experience in the desert, where I experienced that everything began from His love and thus everything was made lovingly with a purpose. He gave every entity an ability to multiply itself, to protect and feed itself and its offspring, to seek comfort, and even in many cases to teach and raise its young."

While he spoke, he motioned above and around, continuing, "He is invisible in the air around you. He is even within you.

"In this way, you are already living in His Kingdom. He is my Abba, your Abba. He is not up in the sky or way over there on the other side of the mountain or on an altar. He is right here."

After witnessing the rabbi's kindness and concern for Mary and others in the crowd, the villagers erupted with enthusiasm and shouted! "Why haven't we known this before?"

The great healer laughed and motioned to the clamoring witnesses to sit down, encouraging them to hear his "Good News."

Mary was full of excitement, *I am well! Who is this magnificent man? He speaks of Elah as if he met Him!*

Mary whispered to Ruth, who also was mesmerized by the rabbi, "What is his name and where is he from?"

Ruth answered that she had heard that the man is a Galilean from Nazareth and his name is Rabbi Jesus.

Mary's whole body felt light and tingled with excitement. She realized how oddly uninhibited she felt. She wanted to run and prostrate herself before him, however she composed herself and remained seated. She repented for her shameful attitude and begged Elah's pardon and thanked Him for her healing.

Then she felt the need to repent to her mother and whispered. "Mother

I caused you and others much strife and heartache." She admitted to herself, *My heart was so dark for so long as I denied my faith and hated Elah.* Inwardly she cried, *I am so sorry!*

With great emotion, she suddenly remembered the young preacher standing in the waters calling to everyone to repent! *He was right! He was so very right! I understand! Oh! Thank you, Elah, Creator of my fathers,* she silently screamed in prayer. She felt a surge of power come from within her, with the desire to run and shout with joy. Trembling, heat seemed to explode from within her. And after a few moments, another wonderful feeling came over her, a feeling of total peace.

Finally, confidently and with complete assurance, Mary stood up and walked with strength that she did not remember, to the front of the crowd of listeners and sat on the ground in front of the rabbi.

She could not take her eyes off him. Every aspect of him enthralled her. She observed his wavy dark brown hair tied with a cloth band in a knot on the top of his head. She noticed his Galilean dialect, so comfortable and familiar. There was no hint of the Hebrew dialect as was common with most educated rabbis. His eyes were like pools of black ink, warm and embracing. His skin was tanned by the sun.

Again, his words caught her attention, "The Kingdom of Elah, the Creator of all things is at hand. I come to your village not to those who think they are righteous but to those who are humble and know that they need to repent. I come to tell you Good News of the coming Kingdom and much more.

"If any one of you is healthy, do you need a physician?"

The engaged multitude shouted, "No!"

"Of course not," he answered. "Only those of you who are sick need a physician. No one puts an unshrunk cloth on an old garment. What will happen?"

The crowd roared with laughter as if Rabbi Jesus had told them a joke. He continued laughing with his countrymen, "Of course, everyone knows that the patch will pull away making the tear worse. Likewise, you can't put new wine into an old wineskin because the skin bursts and the wine and skin will be destroyed."

Mary, fascinated by everything he said, thought, *His voice and concepts are as refreshing as water rippling over rocks in a stream. It is all pleasant to my heart and sensibilities! His words are what I have thirsted for all my life. I want to continue to taste this water of truth.*

She admitted her struggles, *It is true that over the last few years, it was harder for me to find any scripture that impressed me. Certainly, the scrolls became dry and lifeless and even confusing.*

These fresh concepts came clear to her heart and mind. She felt like she had found an oasis and that she did not want to stop drinking. She vowed that from this moment on that she would never leave this man, *He is my wellspring of life.*

After the Rabbi spoke for a long while, he asked if anyone had questions. A few men raised their hands and asked simple questions. One asked if he had learned all that he spoke from the teachers in the synagogue.

Smiling, Jesus answered, "My words come on the foundation of the scriptures, but I have a new message from Abba, Elah. It is time that Elah wants to enlighten his children."

There was not a negative response in the whole audience. Rabbi Jesus left the front of the crowd as some of the people began to leave. Others brought their infirm to him, and he prayed for Elah's blessing over them.

Daylight was fading. Mary remained seated and continued to watch him. At last, after he had prayed over the last of the sick, he moved to the side and humbly and modestly sat down and began to pray.

Tears came to Mary's eyes. Within a few seconds she wept uncontrollably, "I am sorry for doubting you, Elah. Thank you for allowing me to experience his life-giving words. Thank you for healing my soul and body."

Resolving what she knew she must do, with determination she dried her tears and rose from her place on the ground. When she stood up, she saw that Jesus had gathered all the men who were with him and was speaking with them. It seemed that they were preparing to leave.

Reality struck her, *He's leaving!* Her thoughts began to race, *Will I ever see him again? Where are they going for the night?*

As if the rabbi picked up on her thoughts, he turned toward her and stepped forward to the remaining villagers, calling out to them, "To any of you who feels called, I invite you to come follow me."

Struck with wonder at the past moments she heard her inner voice speak, *This is the Messiah, the Anointed One!* At that moment Mary remembered her grandmother. *This is the Messiah!* She heard it again!

Again, she began to cry. Spontaneously she called out in a loud voice and bowed her face the hard dry earth, "You are my savior, and you are the one whom we are awaiting! Let me go with you, wherever you go!" She whispered desperately, "Please, don't leave me here alone. I want to help you! How can I help you?"

Several of the Nazarene's followers rushed to her side, James among them. They saw that she was no longer ill and that she had had a similar, profound experience to what they themselves had experienced. They wanted to comfort her, but at the same time wondered if she would become sick again.

However, turning to James whom she felt close to, she implored him, "May I go with Rabbi Jesus and assist him?"

As she spoke, she no longer thought self-consciously. She no longer pined for James. She realized that the longing for James had kept her alive all those years. And, though it nearly drove her insane, that it was for this very moment. Instantly, she was released from the past. In its place she became aware of him as a brother that she never had. Instantaneously, she was a new person.

James told Mary that he remembered her at the fishing port and was so happy to see her again. Sharing this moment seemed to tie them together as a family.

"James, I want to stay with Rabbi Jesus and attend him as Elah's Chosen One. I believe he is the Anointed One! Is this possible? I am no longer sick, and I won't be a burden!"

James felt Mary's desperation and heard her plea. He understood her fervor, "I will go ask my master." Still, he thought it was impossible because of their rugged lifestyle, *It is probably too austere for this fragile woman.*

Mary desperately watched James as he walked toward the remarkable rabbi and prayed that there might be some way that she could go with him. "Do not leave me behind!" she whispered. She wanted to leave the past behind her and believed that she would not get sick again.

***

"Rabboni, the young woman whom you healed wants to stay with us and help you."

Simon, a more mature follower of Jesus, overheard James' request, and immediately tried to advise Jesus, "Rabboni, I would not permit my own daughter to travel with a group of single men."

Simon was a traditional elder concerned with traditional mores. He tried to exert his opinion over his master, hoping to avert a scandal. He continued, "After all, we are traveling and sleeping in close proximity. Only mature women are acceptable."

However, much to Simon's chagrin, Jesus ignored his advice.

***

Mary ran to Ruth who remained sitting on the ground, still overcome with emotion from the miraculous healing. Certainly, the faithful woman had believed unceasingly that Elah would heal her daughter; but the reality overwhelmed her. As Mary approached her, she gazed at her daughter in amazement.

"Mother, I am well, look at me. I am well! I can breathe without effort!" Mary took a deep breath of air without effort and spun around, "Look, I can breathe!"

Ruth noticed her daughter's face, more colorful than it had ever been. It was so pink and bright. Gone were her sunken eyes and cheeks. Her face was truly beautiful to behold.

Ruth stood up and her eyes sparkled with tears of happiness as she embraced her daughter. Their joy was profound. Several relatives and friends gathered around. In delight, they broke into a jubilant Galilean fishing song. Her uncle and a few other men began to dance. Uncle Simeon lifted Mary upon his shoulders and continued to dance with her. To these simple people, this moment was exhilarating and cause for celebration.

Her uncle was going to carry her all the way home, but Mary called out, "Uncle, put me down!" He did as she wished, and she began to speak. But what she said next was more bizarre than anything he could have imagined.

"I want to stay with Rabbi Jesus and attend him in his work. I cannot return home now. I am a new person and I want to learn more from him and his lessons of life. If I can, I want to help him!"

Her fellow villagers stared at her incredulously. They could not believe her proposal. Firstly, she was well but probably only for a while, and secondly, because of their strict laws. Unmarried and unaccompanied, she could not travel with the preacher and his band of followers. Single women did not do that. It would be immoral. Besides, in this moment she was cured of the breathing illness, but for how long. Who would take care of her? They believed that she needed shelter and nurturing to stay healthy.

Mary saw that her mother was in a state of shock. This afternoon's inexplicable occurrence had overwhelmed her. She realized that her request was not practical and very confusing to her mother.

Uncle Simeon and everyone looked to Ruth for an answer. She sighed and spoke, "I feel like I am living a wonderful dream. My prayers have been answered! I hear your request, dear daughter. But I do not know how to answer you."

Mary took her mother's dear hand in hers and pressed it against her cheek, "Mother, I am well! Elah, through this rabbi, healed me and I am whole person. I have no other desire but to serve him."

She admitted, "I know what I ask sounds preposterous, but I must follow my heart." Mary reminded her mother, "Remember, you and Grandmother always encouraged me by telling me that Elah had a purpose for me. I believe, today, Elah showed me my purpose."

Looking into Ruth's eyes, she spoke slowly and softly to help her understand, "I want to learn from him and follow him as he instructs me. He has given purpose to my life. Mother, I believe that he is the one that Grandmother spoke of and waited her whole life for. Through me, Grandmother can see her dream fulfilled. He is the one that Israel is waiting for, the one that all the prophets foretold.

"How can I do anything else when I am the fruit of all my ancestors' yearnings? I can see now that all my suffering was for this moment. This is what my life is meant for. Elah must have watched my suffering and I think even He prayed that I would not give up before I met Rabbi Jesus."

Ruth realized the truth in her speech, spoken with no breathlessness.

Mary continued to explain her decision, "How can I turn my back and go home as if nothing happened?"

Ruth understood. She felt the zeal in her daughter's voice and heart, and she was convinced that Mary was right. This was a situation without precedent. In response to the otherwise unbelievable question, surprisingly she answered, "Go as Elah is leading you. You have my blessing."

While Ruth was speaking, James came over to Mary and respectfully proclaimed, "Sister, Rabboni welcomes you and anyone else who would like to follow him."

James spoke kindly with her mother and uncle, "We will take care of your daughter. Do not worry. Your blessing will be great! Rabboni Jesus asks that you all join us tonight for a great celebration of Mary's new life."

This was her new beginning. From that day forward, Mary never regretted her decision to leave her home. The next few years cast her into eternal memory. She became known as Mary Magdalene, one of the most famous women in all of human history.

PART II

Chapter 6

The Source of Life

Arise, shine; for your light has come,
and the glory of the Lord has risen upon you.
(Isaiah 60:1)

That evening at their campsite, Jesus and his followers, whom he called "Friends," and the village people came together to celebrate Mary's new life. Many of the humble folk, genuinely inspired, brought food for the festivities as an offering to Rabbi Jesus in gratitude and appreciation. From what they had witnessed, they believed and felt that he was a man of Elah. Jesus and his Friends were astounded by the outpouring of love and support from the village of Magdala.

Earlier in the afternoon, at the conclusion of the meeting in which Mary was healed, she had gone home with her mother and uncle. Together, they had prepared for her journey and her new life.

While Mary packed her clothes and prepared a woolen covered quilt bedroll, Ruth and Uncle Simeon astonished her with all that they had prepared for her and the rabbi in such a short time. Ruth led her outside to an ox-drawn wagon full of bags of foodstuff, fresh and imperishable food, including loaves of bread, dried fish, pomegranates, olives, figs, cheese, and cashew nuts; and vats of wine. It was enough for a hundred people.

Mary embraced her uncle and mother together, and with her scarf wiped Ruth's tears away. It was a bittersweet moment.

Ruth spoke for both herself and her brother as she smiled through wet, sparkling eyes. Clearing her throat, she joyfully praised Mary, "My daughter, you have filled my life with joy and happiness. Elah has always been beside us on this journey. He will not stop showing you the way. You must know that my prayers are always with you. Now, at last, we have found the one to heal you."

Full of emotion, Mary answered, "Mother, I am happy to see your joyful expression. We can see that Elah heard your prayers. Something once unimaginable has now come to pass. I am a new person, and I will make you proud of me. Thank you for all the encouragement you gave me. Your love and sacrifice, with Elah's help, kept me alive, an almost impossible task."

Ruth nodded and took Mary's hands in hers. Squeezing them, she motioned to her brother and he placed a leather bag of shekels in his niece's hands. Overwhelmed, Mary wept again. "Mother, Uncle, how generous you are, I have nothing to match your generosity. With your permission, I will certainly give this gift to Rabbi Jesus."

"Brother," Ruth said, brimming with pride and joy, "let's board the wagon and take our most precious offerings to this man of Elah and his followers."

Mary recollected the first time she rode in the wagon to the Sea of Galilee. Now, once again, she sat upon its rickety top board, recalling that time of her innocence, the joy and excitement she had experienced. Now she understood that, though it had set her on a painful path, in fact it was the beginning of her long journey from death to life.

***

As the evening star appeared in the sky, they pulled up to the gathering place, astonishing the group of about forty Friends and villagers whose faces filled with joy. It was difficult to tell the difference between the villagers and the newcomers.

One man came forward out of the crowd and thanked everyone for the outpouring of offerings brought by the residents. "Good evening, I am Simon. May I formally introduce Rabbi Jesus from Nazareth." He indicated and bowed respectfully to Jesus, who was standing humbly at the edge of the crowd. "As you already heard from his sermon this afternoon, he is a man of Elah. He is chosen for this time and your support is greatly appreciated. We are traveling throughout Galilee and hopefully will then take his message to Judea and to the Holy Temple in Jerusalem."

Simon acknowledged the foods and gifts, including the wagon that Mary's uncle offered. "I would like to repeat Rabbi Jesus' final message. Anyone is welcome to join us in our mission. The time is ripe for the accomplishment of Elah's will and the Anointed One is near at hand. Rabbi Jesus prepares everyone to hear and appreciate the word of Elah. Please join me in a prayer of gratitude for your blessing." The prayer was short but left many with hope and moist eyes. Most of the humble people truly believed that it was an auspicious time.

Rabbi Jesus asked their permission to sing a joyful psalm of King David, encouraging everyone to join together in singing and clapping their hands.

Adonai, Adonai,
How excellent is Your name in all of the earth!
Oh Lord, how excellent is Your name.
When I consider Your heavens,
the work of Your fingers, the moon and
the stars which You have set in place,
What is man, that You are mindful of him,
And the son of man that You care for him?
(Psalm 8:1-3-4)

After the song, Simon, the elder, called out, "Let us get to know each other and celebrate and eat!"

Dusk set in but the campfire burned brightly. Villagers and Friends mingled, sharing a supper of smoked fish, dates, figs, nuts, bread, and wine, with food left over.

Mary had noticed two women preparing the feast and realized happily that she would not be the only woman. This gave her confidence and a comforting sense of comradery. Later, one of the women played a lyre while a young man accompanied her with his rhythmic drumming.

When all were satisfied, Rabbi Jesus thanked everyone for the delicious food and suggested, "Perhaps we are witnessing an example of the Kingdom of Elah, where everyone's needs are met."

Gaiety ensued with singing and storytelling of the most outlandish fish tales. Jesus sat with them and shared their happiness. Together with Jesus they laughed at the tales and sang loudly and exuberantly. The joy was contagious. Mary thought that even the stars above seemed to join in their glee.

She noticed how the warm air embraced her, as she breathed freely and easily. She did not want the night to end as this was the first time in her life that she had attended a celebration. And even though it was getting late, she was not tired.

It was hard for Mary to take her eyes off the man who had given her new life, and she thought, *His face is strong and handsome.* Immediately, she felt her countenance blush for thinking such a private thought. *It seems we are about the same age but maybe he's older... like an older brother.* She continued to muse to herself, *I wonder who his wife is and how many children he has?* It was customary for rabbis to have large families.

What is it about him that seems familiar to me? Searching her memory, she tried hard to remember where she had seen him. *Maybe one of the few times I went to temple? Maybe at the seashore? He looks like the fishermen as his shoulders are broad and his skin is suntanned.*

Suddenly she remembered and whispered to herself, intrigued, *Oh! It is him, the bridegroom in the dream I had on my way to the shore. But he isn't wearing the golden robes of a bridegroom. What could the dream mean? I will have to reflect on it,* she thought in curious wonderment. During her years of solitude, she had often daydreamed about that dream and others. But this one was beautiful and vivid. It had brought her joy and hope during the darkest days of her life.

Jolted out of her thoughts, Mary heard her name called, "Mary, how do you feel?" Rabbi Jesus was staring at her curiously, with a smile.

Her face burned with embarrassment at being called out in front of the crowd of people, and also that Rabbi Jesus, himself, had asked her. However, with a freshly mature attitude of confidence she answered, "I feel alive and content."

Continuing to engage her, he asked inquisitively, "Could you sing us a song?" To the musician he directed, "Martha, accompany her with your lyre."

Surprised at his request, Mary blushed. She had never sung before, but now, since she could breathe so easily, she was willing to try. She chose the song that she had heard her uncle sing on their way to the shore. As she opened her mouth, she surprised herself. Remembering the lyrics and melody, a pleasant, feminine voice emerged. To her, as everything did tonight, it felt good and natural.

Everyone was moved by her voice stood and applauded when she finished. Ruth was especially thrilled and naturally wanted to hear more. She stood proudly and with a bow asked respectfully of Jesus, "Rabbi, could my daughter sing another?

"Of course," he agreed.

Wishing that this night would never end, Mary sang a familiar hymn, often sung in religious ceremonies:

Sh'ma Yisrael
Adonai Eloheu
Adonai, Adonai Echad
(Hear O Israel, the Lord is our Adonai.
The Lord is one!)

Baruch Shem
K'vod Malchuto
L'olam, L'olam Vaed
(Blessed be His name,
Whose glorious Kingdom
is forever and ever.
He is my defense
I shall not be moved.)

There was great applause and then Elder Simon stood, respectfully bowed to Jesus, and invited him to sing, "Before we close, would you like to hear a song from Rabboni, himself?"

There was a loud sound of disappointment from the entertained crowd, but everyone understood the time was coming to an end, so they shouted gleefully, "Yes!"

Jesus stood and began to sing an old Hebrew hymn which was given to Moses by Elah.

> *May the Lord bless and keep you.*
> *May His grace and His face shine upon you.*
> *May the Lord lift up His countenance upon you.*
> *And give you peace and give you peace.*
> *And give you peace.*
> *This is the way you shall be blessed from day to day.*
> *He'll be your rest.*
> (Numbers 6:24-26)

Everyone applauded, shouting for more. Then Jesus raised his arms, indicating that all should stand and invited the lyrist and drummer to play their instruments for the popular circle dance. Joining hands to his right and left, they began dancing around the campfire. Keeping time with the rapping of the drumbeat, they circled to the left and then to the right and then to the center in jubilation, all the while continuing the song that Jesus sang. The flames in the fire leaped into the air and the sparks flew.

Finally, as the celebration drew to a close, Jesus folded his hands and offered his heartfelt, spontaneous prayer in Aramaic, their mother tongue. It was unusual to use their colloquial language, as rabbis usually prayed and recited scriptural verses in Hebrew.

Humbly he beseeched Elah, always with an unusual familiarity as his Abba. It was as if he was speaking directly to his own earthly father. His use of the tender term of endearment moved their hearts and made many shed tears.

Then Jesus sincerely expressed his gratitude once again for the outpouring of gifts and support from all the people of Magdala, "Abba, who is leading us," motioning to all his followers, "will never forget your receptive and benevolent actions this day."

He raised his hands in blessing, and everyone bowed their heads, "Abba, bless the people of this fertile ground. Let Your light shine upon them and give them abundance and Your love. Amen."

The time had come to say goodbye. Mary embraced her mother, who cried truly out of joy and happiness for her daughter. Then her uncle, as head of their family, bowed, smiling through tears, and blessed her, "May Elah give you joy and happiness and you may not tire in your service to this holy man. Remember you are always welcome in our house. Shalom!"

Ruth also offered her own blessing to her daughter, "Go with Elah."

Finally, with trust in Elah, Ruth and her brother turned and left for home, leaving the wagon, oxen, and bountiful foods.

Martha and Joanna introduced themselves and gathered Mary's belongings and brought her to a sleeping area near the campfire and away from the men. Familiar with the customs of Jesus' entourage, the women helped her set up her bedroll.

Immediately, Mary felt at ease with Martha, who was about her age. She reminded Mary of one of her cousins; short in stature and outgoing with an expressive, warm smile.

Joanna was older, but younger than Mary's mother. She was more formal in her actions and did not speak unless spoken to, but she was kind and practical. She helped Mary position her bed and also helped her feel comfortable.

After the excitement of the evening and sleeping outdoors, Mary could hardly sleep as she reflected upon the unusual evening, *I sang two songs! I'm sleeping outside and the atmosphere is refreshing, and all the while my breathing is easy.* For the first time she thanked Elah as Abba, mimicking Jesus! As her mind continued to whirl from her healing she thought, *I think I must be reborn.*

Finally, she prayed, "Abba Elah, thank you for my healing, my new life, and for Rabbi Jesus. Please continue to bless my family and help me not become a burden to anyone! I…." She drifted off to sleep.

Chapter 7

The Journey Begins

Let your light so shine before men,
that they may see your good works,
and glorify your Father which is in heaven.
(Matt 5:16)

Surprising nearly everyone, including herself, Mary kept pace with Jesus and the small band of attendants. Elder Simon was the only person who kept a wary eye on her. She noticed his sideway glances, but he never interfered or spoke to her. From mid-morning they trekked up and down the western hills of Galilee along the coast near Tiberius. Though her feet blistered and she changed her sandals many times, she had no complaints.

During their long walks, there was time to think about her new life. *Though it's only a few weeks since I joined Rabboni's disciples, I can hardly remember the person I was before. I've changed so much that I'm a totally different person, spiritually and physically. And it's only been a few weeks. Thank you, Elah! I wish Mother could see me enduring long days of walking between villages, and thriving. She would be so amazed!*

As she followed the path with Rabbi Jesus and the disciples on the way to another village, she meditated about the sermon he had given to the inhabitants of Cana the day before. She went over the key points to imprint them upon her heart.

She pictured Rabbi Jesus standing confidently, speaking in front of the villagers, "Many of you are concerned about tomorrow. How will you care for your family? You are burdened by life's ups and downs. Your minds are concerned with physical attachments, but do you know that Abba is waiting for you to ask Him for help? If you do, it will surely be given unto you.

"Listen to your conscience, your inner voice. For example, if you see a friend or a stranger in need, many times your first feeling is to reach out and help them. But have you ever noticed that, after this first thought, you have a second one telling you all the practical reasons you should not give aid? The first thought is your conscience. This conscience is from Abba for you to connect to Him.

"Therefore, let go of your old ideas and habits of protecting your self-interest. These are burdens to you that, over time, build up and weigh you down, eventually causing you to become ill.

"If you seek to give joy to another at your own expense, it may be a burden to you; nonetheless you will feel joy. If you see that your neighbor is ill and unable to care for his family, expend your energy and take time to care for his family until he heals.

"Remember, if you try to keep what you have, guard and covet it, you will eventually lose it. But the more you offer yourself and things to others, the more abundance and satisfaction you will find in your own life."

Breaking her train of thought, she heard her name called. "Mary, it is your turn to ride on the wagon," Martha coaxed her, knowing that Mary would not ask for herself.

Today, Mary felt strong and knowing that Joanna was probably tired, asked, "Can Sister Joanna ride instead? I am enjoying the rhythm of my steps and my thoughts."

"Thank you, but I am fine."

She usually followed Martha and Joanna behind the wagon. They took turns riding on the top board with one of the brothers holding the reins driving the oxen.

Once in a while, memories of her pain and helplessness invaded her consciousness, but she rejected them and refused to give them any attention. With Rabboni leading the way, staring at the back of his head gave her strength and courage. Mary learned quickly, and each of Rabbi Jesus' messages day after day gave her strength.

Jesus's early morning service was her favorite time. She felt bathed in the light of truth and warmth of love when listening to his refreshing words as he referred to Elah as Abba. As she walked, she reviewed this morning's message.

"Abba is not a being sitting on a throne in the sky, but He is our loving father. 'Abba' is living, walking, and experiencing everything with you! Look around, you see trees and rocks and even little animals. Elah's essence, His consciousness, is within everything of this physical world and certainly His essence is within you, His sons and daughters."

She recognized that Jesus sought to cast away their ancient concepts, trying to correct their misinformed understanding of Elah. Also, he loved everyone. He even loved the skeptical members of their group who often questioned his decisions or displayed doubts about him.

Mary loved to watch his facial expressions and mannerisms. When he smiled at her, she felt the whole world smiled, and when he wept, she felt the whole world weep. It was also surprising to her that though he was a strong man, he could be tender and gentle.

Every breath she took, she imagined breathing in air he exhaled, giving her life. She truly loved being in his presence and thanked Elah repeatedly. Inside, she also made a promise to Elah that she would always stay and assist him on his journey and look for ways to lighten his path.

***

Today, their journey took them north to Capernaum. A threatening storm gathered in the distance to their right, in the center of the great Sea of Galilee. The winds blew off the waters, cooling the hot and humid atmosphere. Large bolts of lightning streaked through the immense black clouds above the freshwater lake. Though menacing, it was a beautiful phenomenon as above them the sky was yet clear. It caused them to hasten their pace along the sandy path.

Mary jogged to the side of the wagon where Martha sat on the top board. "Martha, this morning Rabboni announced happily that we were going to Simon's house in Capernaum."

Martha nodded. "Yes, Elder Simon offered his house as the hub of our work in Galilee. It is nice to have a comfortable place to come and go from.

His wife, Perpetua, and his mother-in-law are naturally hospitable. With their servants, they prepare for our lodging and dining. Both love Rabboni Jesus. And Perpetua is happy because it brings her husband home to her."

Martha continued, "You know that Simon is a fisherman. He cannot fish while helping Jesus though, so he pays men to use his boat. This helps him continue to pay his taxes while allowing him to accompany Jesus." She added, "We will be able to bathe and have a roof over our heads. Elah is taking care of His son and us!"

Martha started to tell Mary a short testimony about the first time Elder Simon met Rabboni. Mary enjoyed this especially because of the way she mimicked the different disciples' voices, particularly Simon's.

"One afternoon, after Simon had little result fishing, Rabboni walked up to him on the dock and engaged him in conversation, 'I see from your expression that the day did not go so well.' 'Very astute!' Simon retorted sarcastically, whilst pulling his boat to dock. Later on, ashamed of his response to Rabboni, Simon explained to us that he apologized to Jesus for being rude, saying it was because he was tired."

Both women laughed, imaging the scene in their mind's eye. Martha continued on, mimicking the cantankerous Simon, "You know how strong Simon's character is, right? Well, at that first meeting, he was really annoyed by the stranger, Jesus, bothering him and taking notice of his lack of result.

"Then Rabboni surprised him with a challenge. 'Take me out to the middle of the lake. Over there.' Rabboni Jesus spoke brusquely, pointing. And with complete confidence, Rabboni promised him, 'You will have more than you can hold.'

"Well, Simon was not one to let the dare go. So, he accepted it, forgetting his fatigue. In an aside comment, he said that the last thing he wanted to do was prepare the skiff for another sail after his fishless day. However, he could not deny his gnawing curiosity to do what Jesus asked.

"Not only did Simon overload his boat with fish, but they also noticed other boats near their spot, filled to the brim."

Interrupting their chat as they rounded a bend in the road, they heard

Rabboni call out to Simon, "Did you send John ahead to announce our arrival?"

Elder Simon answered affirmatively, "I also reminded him to have Perpetua prepare for dinner and for our lodging. I believe we will make it before nightfall and before the coming storm."

Jesus signaled his approval and continued on at the head of their procession.

Mary was surprised at how quickly she had adjusted and learned their schedule. It helped that she was eager to serve and fit into their way of life. Joanna and Martha patiently taught her and gave her responsibilities.

From several recent experiences, Mary knew that John, being the youngest man and most agile, was often used as a messenger. He was also the brother of James and they were cousins of Rabboni Jesus.

She also noticed and became familiar with the different characters and idiosyncrasies of the other disciples. Elder Simon was the first person she knew she had to understand, as he was the most skeptical toward her. She was not alone in this.

Martha made comments about him under her breath, "He obviously doesn't like us traveling with the men. He is always concerned with public opinion." Martha's assessment helped Mary realize she wasn't the only thorn in Simon's side.

The most curious thing she learned about Rabboni Jesus was that he was not married. This surprised her because it was certainly unusual in their culture for a mature man, a religious leader, to be unmarried. From her mother she had learned how parents usually arranged their children's marriages at about sixteen years of age. And, that rabbis were the most sought-after marriage partners.

How could this be? He is a healthy and good man. I wonder why his parents did not seek a wife for him. Maybe they did? she thought, questioning.

She knew that Elder Simon was the only married follower. Though it was unusual, Mary felt at ease knowing that being unmarried at her age was no longer exceptional.

As she became acquainted with the different characters of her companions, she found that some were a bit distant and grim and somewhat argumentative. James and his brother John were truly unique in their youthful enthusiasm and being highly energetic. However, more importantly, she observed them all to be exceptional people. Although their itinerant lifestyle was austere and regimented, she perceived their sincere motivation in following Rabboni. Each person's love and manner of meeting him was remarkable, and they were all devoted to him.

They were mostly fishermen and common people. They claimed to be devout Hebrews, but were unsophisticated when it came to religion, unable to read the Torah or speak Hebrew. Theirs was just a practical understanding of the ancient religious language. The only real contact they had with religious men was in trading fish or selling goods.

Along with cooking, Mary also learned to use herbs. Jesus taught them his practical knowledge of useful herbs. He gave them advice about which spices to use with certain foods, and how certain herbs helped strengthen them and keep them healthy. He found most of the herbs while walking along the roads and on the hills along their journey.

At times she became nostalgic, thinking of her loving mother and uncle, and prayed as if sending them a message, *I wish you could see me walking and cooking and keeping pace with everyone. It would make you so happy!*

The sole problem she had experienced so far was becoming accustomed to walking long distances. She had gone through at least four pairs of sandals already, and thankfully calluses had replaced the blisters on her feet. These were minor cares, though, and mostly she prayed that her wheezing would never return.

"Sister Mary," James called, breaking into her thoughts. "Rabboni is asking for you to meet with him at the next rest stop."

Surprised, she nodded, modestly avoiding direct eye contact. *Really, Rabboni wants to speak with me!* she thought.

Since the day of her healing, Mary had not been invited to meet with him personally. In fact, this was also the first time that James had spoken directly to her since she had become part of their group.

As she covered her smile with her scarf, she recollected, *Oh, James, you may never know how you kept me alive. Your memory was like a thorn in my heart, but without it I might not be here this day or even alive. The memory of you was a torment to my soul, though strangely a hope that kept me going all those years of suffering. You don't know how close we really are. You truly are my brother!*

"Mary, are you listening to me?" James asked, when he received no response to his comment.

Quickly and truthfully responded, "Oh, Brother! I am sorry. I was thinking about our meeting at the sea. Do you remember it? Do you remember that preacher speaking in the water?"

He nodded, "Yes, you cannot imagine what happened to me after that. I actually met him a few months later. I gave up fishing and left my parents to assist him in his mission. I traveled all over the land of Judea. Someday, I will tell you all about it."

Looking up ahead, he said, "It looks like we are nearing the rest stop. It seems that you are managing well in your new life. Let me know if you need my help with anything. Elah is pouring out blessings to us all because we are willing to help Rabboni Jesus. Elah be with you, Sister Mary." Customarily, he bowed and excused himself.

As he turned to leave, Mary suddenly and brashly asked, "Brother James, why did Rabboni ask to see me? Do you know what he wants to speak with me about?"

"No, he will see you soon, though. Please come as soon as you have washed up at our next stop. I have to go back." And then as an aside, before he ran back to his place in the line, he added, "Someday, I will share with you why I am so grateful to Rabboni."

Mary eagerly kept step with the person in front of her. Soon they arrived at the last resting spot before Capernaum.

She hurried over to the women who had gathered to one side of their small troop, preparing to replenish everyone's waterskins. Excitedly, Mary announced, "Martha, Joanna, Rabboni asked to speak with me!"

Although they were busy taking care of everyone's needs, Martha looked up and gave her a wink and handed her an allotment of water, hastily instructing her, "Go behind us over there." She indicated behind a bush. "And freshen up. Be sure to wash your hands and feet."

Mary hid herself on the other side of the women, farthest from the men. She was glad for Martha's advice. She relished a refreshing gulp of water and then rinsed her mouth. Since she needed the liquid to prepare to meet Rabboni Jesus, she did not quench her thirst.

After cleaning herself, she recombed her hair and braided its long, dark-brown strands. She made an effort to show how happy and healthy she was. Then she straightened her tunic and donned a fresh scarf and started over to Jesus.

As she entered their gathering, the men were talking about the day's events and their happiness to be nearing Elder Simon's house, where they would have a roof to sleep under and home cooked food. Mary, quietly and unassumingly, walked over to Rabboni Jesus, stopping first to present herself to Elder Simon.

"Yes, woman, what is it that you want?" Elder Simon spoke sternly and gruffly. His manner reminded her of her first meeting with him and his reaction when she requested to join Rabboni's entourage, and also his lack of patience with her and the other women.

Modestly, she pulled her scarf over her mouth. Respectfully and humbly with her eyes gazing at the ground, she reported to him, "Elder Simon, Brother James carried a message to me that Rabboni asked to speak with me." He could not see her brash smile and countenance hidden under her scarf. As a good Hebrew woman, she knew her place.

Satisfied with her request and manner, Simon went to Jesus' side. When he announced her, Rabboni looked up and unceremoniously motioned for her to join him with the others. Sitting on the ground in a circle, a place was made for Mary to sit between Simon and James.

Jesus opened their meeting with a surprise for all. In a respectful tone, he inquired, "Mary, is it true that you, a Galilean woman, speak and read Hebrew?"

What! She gasped wordlessly and felt her cheeks burn with embarrassment. *How does he know that I speak Hebrew?* She wanted to disappear she was so embarrassed. *Why does he reveal this in front of all the men? They will surely think I am disgusting.* Unable to control herself she burst into tears and tried to hide her face with her scarf. Then she nodded modestly, but could not look up at him nor the others.

Jesus spoke warmly, confusing her with his gentleness, "I can see you are embarrassed, but do not be ashamed." Then he continued praising her, and even marveling about her, "How is it possible that you are fluent in the language of our Holy Scriptures?"

Again, Mary's complexion became scarlet and nearly purple. She could not look up at him or anyone else. She wondered why he was calling her out in front of everyone.

His announcement was so unexpected and outlandish that it caused a gasp of astonishment from Simon and others. Jesus looked around, taking notice of his befuddled followers. "Fight this tendency every moment!" he chided the astounded men. "It is incorrect to think that a woman should not be educated. You must rid yourself of that old traditional and narrow-minded thinking. Your understanding is outdated and meaningless to me. I am trying to teach you a new understanding of Abba. All your current thoughts are getting in the way. Simply love people."

Jesus continued with pride, "Yes, a woman, this woman can read and speak Hebrew. You men must not hate her for this breach of custom. You must examine your thinking. There are many fallacies in our culture. This is one of them."

Abruptly Mary realized that Rabboni Jesus was not trying to embarrass her but that he was actually proud of her. She realized that she had been small minded. She also held the same wrongful attitude toward her education.

"Do you want to hide your talent?" Rabboni Jesus challenged her. "On the contrary, your ability encourages me. I see Abba Elah's hand at work here. Indeed, He is helping us on our path. I am grateful that Elah prepared you. Think of it. Who can help me witness to the religious leaders since my Friends know so little of our scriptures and language?" He continued humbly, "I also appreciate your modesty and open heart! Will you help me witness to the religious leaders?" Jesus paused and waited for her to respond.

"I … I," awkwardly, Mary stammered. She was surprised at his broad-minded viewpoint. For the first time in her life, Mary began to appreciate the knowledge she had acquired. As with her illness that within moments was gone, now her self-consciousness was gone within moments.

Suddenly she recognized her value, *Yes! I can be a benefit to others because of Rabboni's appreciation and I will gladly assist him, to the best of my ability.*

Graciously, she responded. "Yes, Rabboni, I will help you." Clearing her throat, she boldly affirmed with a newly found confidence, "Whatever you ask of me I will do my best."

She continued, "I learned these things when I was young. During my illness, I could do very little. My grandmother explained her concern to her rabbi and after thinking it over he suggested I study the holy manuscripts. He was a broad minded and concerned man of Elah."

"After meeting with me, compassionately he felt that education would be good for me. Over the next few years, he coached me weekly in Hebrew and brought many scrolls for me to read and to review with him."

Noticing her rapidly beating her heart and needing to catch her breath, she paused, feeling overwhelmed, and thought, *I can't believe I'm speaking to this group of men.* But because of Jesus' attention and acceptance, she had the confidence to continue.

"You see the truth was that I was not expected to live beyond my youth." Shrugging her shoulders, she added, "I suppose that is why he permitted me to study privately the same as the boys in our village." Mary ended her brief account. Though it did bring back harsh memories, by clearing her throat, she disguised the sound of sadness in her voice.

Sensitive to her recollection, Jesus said, "We are grateful for your extraordinary resilience not to give up. We can see that Abba Elah undoubtedly prepared you for this mission."

Smiling broadly, Jesus looked around at the astonished men, teasing them, "Never mind these scruffy men who realize their own limitations." Then with a twinkle in his eye, he added his new plan, "I am sure they will be pleased to hear my plan. I want you to accompany me visiting the temples and synagogues."

Jesus looked at Simon and asked, "What do you think of this plan?"

Simon humbly acknowledged his plan, "Now we see how valuable she will be for you."

As the meeting came to an end, the men understood and smiled hopefully. Everyone agreed that Mary would bring much needed assistance to Jesus and the mission.

Motioning for all to stand, Rabboni spoke to Simon, "Ask Martha and Joanna to prepare the dinner."

As Mary and the disciples stood waiting, Rabboni Jesus whispered in Hebrew, as if in a prayer, though it was loud enough for only Mary to understand, "Elah has truly prepared you and nurtured you through your long suffering. Now He sends you to His Son. I am pleased and grateful. I pray that you will be able to bear the course ahead."

Mary, again flushed from Rabboni's attention and prayer for her, whispered her own silent prayer, *Abba, please help me, as I am but a humble woman. I will do my best. Thank you, Abba, Elah.*

When Simon signaled that dinner was ready, Jesus instructed all, "Come gather around. Mary, could you please lead us in the blessing prayer to our Abba Elah?"

Mary began to pray in the colloquial language, but Rabboni Jesus interrupted, "Please pray in the words of the scriptures."

Nodding, she obliged. Praying in Hebrew, she expressed her gratitude to Abba Elah. But after Rabboni's secret prayer about her, she trembled as tears flowed from her eyes.

Her sincerity was contagious. Although they could not fully understand the familiar religious language, they could sense her sentiment, and all renewed their gratitude to Abba that day.

The humble dinner was a welcome sight for the weary travelers. Radically, Rabboni Jesus requested that all the women join their circle and share the meal amongst the men. Though it was not easy for Elder Simon, he realized it was not the time to disagree and that perhaps times were changing.

As the men ate, the change of custom did not come easily. They remembered times when Jesus addressed the women as part of their group, but none had ever joined them in a meal. However, several of the young disciples agreed with the wisdom of their Rabboni and determined to overcome their old way of thinking.

While they shared the food, Rabboni asked Mary to formally introduce herself. While Mary explained about her family and her illness, she noticed Jesus making shapes in the dirt with a stick. He nodded but did not speak as she related her anguished suffering and loneliness. Revealing the past seemed to help her finally separate from that life of emptiness and begin anew. When she finished, she again expressed her gratitude to Rabboni for freeing her.

He smiled and assured her that she was released from more than physical illness, "Satan holds all in bondage. This is the bondage I can release you from."

Jesus prophesied, "Mary, your life has great purpose and in time we will see. Again, I express joy at your knowledge about scripture and the language. You will help make my path smoother. You are Abba's gift to us all. He recognizes your open, sincere, and humble heart."

Then Rabboni Jesus stood and directed everyone to resume the journey onward to Capernaum. The wind was strengthening and the clouds darkening. They hastened to reach their destination before the arrival of the storm.

Mary cherished Jesus' personal attention. Satisfied and happy, she determined to do anything she could to help him in his mission.

Chapter 8

Fishing

For I know the plans I have for you,
declares the Lord,
plans to prosper and not harm,
plans to give you hope and a future.
(Jeremiah 29:11)

The fishing village of Capernaum, situated on the northwestern shore of the Sea of Galilee, was a relatively modern port. Roman-built roads made it a central hub for transporting goods and ideas from the northern regions of Galilee to southern Galilee, and vice versa. It was also Elder Simon's home.

As Jesus and his followers emerged from the lesser populated countryside onto the flat seashore, they began to experience the more populated area. Their pace became easier and quicker as they neared their destination along the level stone thoroughfare. They followed it directly into Capernaum, past blocks of adobe houses and finally reaching Simon's home.

As the wind whistled around them, Mary noticed the odor of fish coming off the Sea of Galilee, intermingled with the tainted odors of human living. Not stopping at his home, Simon led them to a bluff that overlooked the harbor to give the newcomers their first sight of his beloved waterfront.

Mary and her fellow travelers looked at the many boats anchored off shore. Wharfs reached out from the land like fingers into the water. With the storm nearing, they watched the frantic fishermen hastily securing their vessels filled with bounty.

Simon proudly pointed out a boat that was rolling back and forth in the stormy waters, "There she is over there! Andrew, she looks secure."

Mary noticed Simon's expression momentarily relax and soften, replacing his habitual strict, authoritarian mien. In its place was a look of pride and pleasure. It was at that moment that she appreciated Simon's sacrifice, leaving his craft and family to attend Jesus.

"Thank you, Abba," Mary whispered. "I realize now what an unusual man he is. He gave up so much. I will try harder to support him!" she prayed sincerely.

Water droplets filled the air. Simon took them back to the well-worn path and followed it quickly to his dwelling.

Mary was fascinated by the different types of adobe and stone houses. The town was much larger that Magdala and the buildings were arranged along straight and narrow roadways. Though there were people coming and going in haste, there was a feeling of an orderly and prosperous society. They passed women carrying urns of water on their heads and children tagging alongside them. Men dressed in practical, lightweight clothing appeared to be laborers or fishermen, talking and laughing in groups.

Elder Simon's home was a one-story family house mere meters from the lake. It was similar to other homes they had passed, made of dark basalt rock and clay plaster. Wooden beams covered with clay panels formed the roof.

Perpetua and her servants received them warmly and welcomed everyone with basins of cool water to cleanse away the grime and tiredness from their feet. Mary knew that everyone standing under the porch was relieved to have a roof over their heads as claps of thunder and flashes of lightning streaked across the sky.

Soon enough, they were led to their quarters to settle all their belongings. Martha put her bag down with a sigh, and sat on her bedroll, obviously tired, "This is a gift from Elah. How are the both of you feeling?"

Joanna, who had ridden on the wagon, mostly out of respect to her being the elder, nevertheless also seemed tired, "I have come to appreciate the comforts of life. Simon's home is certainly a welcome reprieve. Let us be refreshed and thank Elah for this generous household." Her drained smile revealed more than her words.

They both turned to Mary, and Martha commented, "Your youthful and hopeful spirit are exceptional and inspiring to us. We remember you, weeks ago, in your struggle to live. No one could know at that time how healthy and enduring your physical body and spirit would become. You are a testament to us all of Rabboni's healing power, a sign of his closeness to Elah!"

Mary responded, "I am grateful and amazed at Rabboni's power of love as well. He is truly the one my mother and grandmother expected. I thank Elah that I now have the health to help His son." She bowed to her sisters, "Thank you also for your support!"

A servant came to the door of their room and requested the women to follow her. They entered a large open room with one south facing window. In a circle were small low tables where everyone waited for them, and they were invited to sit. The aroma of the dinner made Mary aware of her empty stomach.

Jesus stood beside the tables of food surrounded by the brothers and announced, "Elder Simon's wife, Perpetua, and her family and servants have prepared this array of delicious food. Let us pray!

"Most loving Elah Abba, You are our constant support and the fulfillment of our every need. It is through the kindness of others that we see Your spirit illuminated in our presence. Because of Elder Simon and his household giving so much to us, we have an example of the Kingdom of Heaven. The Kingdom of Heaven is at hand! Bless all here today and reassure them of their value to You and to me. Amen." Jesus motioned to Simon and gave him the floor.

Elder Simon bowed and welcomed everyone, "This is my home but treat it as your own and now eat to your heart's content."

The women sat on the floor around a small table separate from the men. The tantalizing aroma of freshly baked bread and baked fish seasoned with parsley and chives greeted them. Each platter of fish was surrounded with black walnuts, and beside each place setting was a fresh cup of watered wine.

The taste was invigorating. Mary ate heartily and each time she emptied her cup a servant refilled it. She realized that she was even more thirsty than hungry, but not by much.

As she ate, Mary silently observed Perpetua's gracious hosting and directing of the servants to replenish each dish and every cup, and sensed their sincerity. A middle-aged woman, Perpetua seemed happy that her husband was home, and she seemed comfortable with his master, Rabboni Jesus. Mary counted twelve of their group and about seven others who were residents, including servants. The room, quiet at first as everyone devoured the food, became filled with laughter and loud talking among themselves.

Simon's home was arranged into a natural and comfortable meeting place. The large central room was not at all filled and could accommodate at least double the amount of people that were present. The window looked out onto a roof covered patio. Though there were other houses, it was positioned in such a way as to have a clear view of the lake. Mary imagined that this window provided a beautiful scene to look upon every day. Above the dining hall, the wooden beams of the roof were exposed and the whole room gave everyone a welcoming comfortable feeling.

She observed everyone enjoying their dinner. *We are all so hungry and tired from the weeks of traveling. How nice to end a good day this way!*

When everyone had finished, and the tables and remaining food had been carried away, Jesus asked Simon to give direction. "The men will use this room to sleep in and women, you will be guided back to your quarters. Our bathing area will be open for the women tonight and tomorrow morning it is open for the men. Please refresh yourselves. Our servants will wash your clothes tomorrow. Please rest well."

Jesus then called everyone to pray and end the day.

While the men gathered in the front room, a servant guided the women back to their small room where they prepared their rolled mats and sleeping quilts.

Mary and her sisters went to the bathing area. It was delightful to wash away all the dirt and grime. It had been a while since their last bath and the first for Mary away from home. At last, they were ready for sleep. After many days and nights of traveling and living in the open, they really appreciated sleeping under a roof.

Mary listened to the whistling wind, cracks of thunder, and the raindrops hitting the clay roof. Feeling safe inside and wondering what tomorrow would bring, she fell asleep before her next thought.

Again, she dreamed of the handsome bridegroom. This time he was alone; his expression was no longer bright and triumphant, but dark and solemn. It seemed that he could not find his bride. Though Mary slept deeply, the dream woke her in the middle of the night. She lay awake thinking of the lonesome man whom she now recognized was Jesus.

Rabboni cares for all his countrymen and followers and yet he has no woman of his own. How truly unfortunate. Again, she thought of her nagging question, *Why did his parents not fulfill their duty to find him a spouse? Did he want it this way? Did Elah require that way of life from him?* Closing her eyes, she slept until she was called to awake.

The bright, sun-lit morning was fresh and clean. The rain storm was over, and Mary and her sisters joined the household on the veranda. Just as she had imagined, the view overlooked the great lake. Rested and energetic, she stretched and took a deep breath. She noticed the air was clear of the dust and grime of human living and whispered, *It's a beautiful day that Rabboni can walk in the fresh atmosphere.*

Mary heard Jesus asking Elder Simon and Andrew, his brother, to prepare the fishing boats, "We will go fishing today."

Joanna handed Mary a fresh warm roll of bread and a cup of watered wine and commented, "It is so beautiful here, is it not my sister?" Joanna's warm smile indicated to Mary that through their common experience, and over their time together, they were drawing closer together and that they really were sisters. Together they peered out toward the water.

A little while later, after finishing the morning meal, they heard Martha calling from a stairway descending toward the shore, "Mary and Joanna. Are you ready? Rabboni has asked us to go with him on the fishing boat and Elder Simon and Brother Andrew are preparing the boat now. Come quickly."

The house was on an incline above the lake. Using the sandy pathway down to the shore, the women descended to the water's edge. The waves lapped the sides of the boat and washed against the pebbles on the shore. The sun sparkled on the water and warmed their skin.

They were eight men and three women on the boat. Mary noticed that Joanna was feeling just as insecure as she was, but Martha, who had experience sailing, looked steady and trusting. Martha suggested that they stay out of the way of the men preparing to launch the craft, and the sisters took a place toward the back of the boat. Martha gave Mary confidence, and she was grateful for her support. She hoped that she would soon feel as sure of herself as Martha.

Mary was fascinated with everything. She noticed the excitement of the experienced fishermen who were returning to their craft. Jesus sat in the back of the vessel while everyone not preparing the sail had to get out of the way.

They sailed in a southerly direction and the breeze invigorated everyone. *What a joyful day!* Mary thought. *Every day is an adventure following Rabboni. I wish Mother could see me! And my first time on a boat!* As the water splashed and sprayed her face and clothes, she welcomed the coolness as openly as a child. It reminded her of the day so long ago, on her first trip to the sea, when the spray of water hit her face as she kicked at the waves standing at the water's edge. But then she was a child.

In a strange way the memory was ambiguous. On one hand it was a joyful and thrilling experience but on the other hand there remained uncomfortable feelings still. Quickly Mary caught the melancholic thought that was from the past and dismissed it. Purposefully, she focused on this new experience.

The rolling unsteadiness and swaying of the vessel began to lead to apprehension and queasiness in her stomach. But again, she reminded herself that she was near Jesus, and this tamped down her feeling of self-protection.

Cleverly, she thought to focus her eyes on the shoreline. It seemed to help relieve her uncomfortable queasy feeling. As she relaxed, soon enough she began to notice the beauty all around and the boats surrounding them. Not for long though, as unexpectedly she was caught off guard as she and her sisters lost their balance when a gust of wind filled the sail, tossing them to the side of the boat.

Determined to let go of her fear, she persuaded herself that the sudden movements were kind of exciting and thrilling. She boldly leaned over the wooden rim along the inside of the boat. Clutching it tightly, she looked over the side and into the water. She was surprised to see fish swimming up to the boat and then scattering when the boat made sudden jerks as it hit the waves.

A sudden splash of water on her face surprised her. As she wiped the water out of her eye, she looked up and stared into the mischievous face of James. He laughed with glee and Mary joined in his merriment. This also resolved her nervousness and from that point she relaxed.

Speaking to him as a brother and covering her gleeful expression with her scarf, she chided him, "James, you are used to this, but you tease me. Are you trying to help me or scare me?" Defiantly, she declared, "Well, I am not scared, anymore."

Acting like a big brother, he said, "It is good for you sisters to join us. Don't worry because we will protect you and Rabboni will protect us, as always." Then he respectfully bowed and made his way back to his responsibility in the bow.

As a novice she had no idea what to expect, and she continued watching everyone scurrying around. Andrew taught the inexperienced brothers how to prepare the fishing nets, while Simon worked at the helm. Those who were skilled tended the sails and prepared the nets.

The boat gently rolled from side to side as it sailed across the water. It was wonderful. After letting go of her fear, Mary was enjoying the movement of the boat and the splashing of the waves, which actually increased her exhilaration. With Jesus in the bow, Mary was no longer wary. *He is my guide and my master. I will live or die for him!* She determined, pledging her life to him and his mission.

The sisters leaned over the side of the boat together, looking up into the sky and down into the swirling water. It was a good day, and sailing on the water gave them a special bonding experience.

As a respite from their long journey, Mary guessed that Jesus was using this natural and effortless moment to reconnect to Elah and to each of his fellow companions. She took notice that they were now far from the shore. It was about midday, with the sun directly above them, in a cloudless sky.

Suddenly in a loud voice, Jesus commanded dramatically, "Get the nets ready!" Mary thought, *He speaks with the same authority as during his sermons to the congregants.* She noticed that even the experienced fishermen loved it. It was obvious that he enjoyed their craft as much as they did.

As everyone went to their assigned spot next to the nets, John and James began their customary boisterous fishing song, along with the other experienced fishermen. Mary was surprised when even Martha chimed in and Jesus sang wholeheartedly. It was a joyful experience.

"All hands lower the nets," Jesus instructed. Everyone worked in synchronicity, following the rhythm of his words and still singing as they lowered the nets carefully into the water. Mary realized that the process took their complete unity. She also noticed the delight in Simon's expression and on all the other men's faces.

Earlier, it had been natural for Elder Simon to give directions to the seasoned fisherman, but now he respectfully deferred to Master Jesus. Mary perceived how Jesus completely had won Simon's heart and allegiance.

After the nets were in the water, Simon made an announcement, "You all have worked hard, now it is time for the fish to do their work. Take a rest as we wait."

Martha stood and instructed Mary to help distribute their lunch and the watered wineskins. Joanna was not feeling well. Nonetheless, she stood and tried to help. Everyone, thirsty and hungry, appreciated the simple meal of bread and cheese with some cashews and olives, and they drank heartily. This was the time for all to rest.

Finally, when the sun was traveling toward the western sky, Jesus instructed loudly, "Raise the nets."

The men jumped to their prearranged positions and began pulling in the nets full of fish. All hands pulled with all their strength in unity to the rhythm of James' chanting, "Pull…Pull…Pull!"

Mary noted how he united their efforts. The full nets were heavy and it seemed impossible to drag them into the boat, but skillfully they all managed it together. The craft tilted to the side from the weight of the fish in each net, and the women, forewarned, clung to the sides in the back of the boat.

Mary watched with childlike fascination. From over the side of the boat, hundreds of fish poured onto the floor of the vessel, jumping and thrashing about. It was fascinating and memorable. She had never seen so many live fish. Mary reached out and picked up one of the slippery creatures, and with pure exuberance she cried out, "A live fish!" *Oh my Elah! They are so alive, living beings, moving and squirming. Jesus taught us that Elah provides these creatures for human's sustenance, for His dearly loved children!*

By the time they finished filling the tall reed baskets, there were twenty or so baskets full. Mary and Martha shouted with delight, "These will provide us a healthy dinner and fetch a good price in the marketplace to replenish our purse."

Finally, Jesus broke into another hearty fishing song as he gathered everyone together, and then he thanked Elah for His magnificent creation. He offered a prayer, blessing their hard work. Then he instructed Simon, "Set your course northeast for the village of Bethsaida."

Lastly, Rabboni gave instructions for when they landed, "Simon and Matthew, you are responsible to take care of the catch while we bring Elah's new words to the people of this village. Martha, go with them, and carry the purse. Also, buy and prepare enough food for the next week. Be frugal and return any money to Matthew, who will report to me."

Again, John and James led them in another song, singing joyfully and exuberantly at the top of their lungs, while everyone cheered their great bounty. It was a joyful moment for all!

With a bright and hopeful face, Jesus taught his disciples, "Through fishing together you have experienced how your unity with each other brought a great result. Therefore, let us adopt the same accord with each other when witnessing to the people. It will ensure a great result for Abba the Creator."

Sailing to the port of Bethsaida gave most everyone some time to rest. The women found a small corner to talk among themselves. It was a good opportunity to get to know each other better, as at other times they were always busy with chores.

While the men rested, Martha told Mary and Joanna her testimony of meeting Jesus, "One afternoon during the harvest time in Bethany, my brother Lazarus brought home a stranger. Lazarus explained how he found the man, Jesus, sitting by the side of the road outside our compound. Despite his poor appearance, my brother was taken by his unusually bright countenance and felt naturally drawn to speak with him. So, they sat together and talked under a tree.

"Jesus explained to him that he had just left the desert where he had sought solitude and prayer for forty days to understand his life, and in the process, he had met the Being who created him and all things.

"Lazarus, greatly moved with compassion for Jesus, brought him into our home. And during the short time that he stayed with us, we were inspired by the richness of his words and humility of his spirit.

"Jesus humbly recounted his time in the desert with the Creator of all things. He claimed an incredible awareness of the Creator's immense love and mercy for His children, humankind, and that He had asked Jesus to help Him. We were surprised to hear his fascinating and refreshing story and were deeply inspired.

"Jesus told us that he was as surprised about Elah as we were. He explained that all his life he was told that we had to be good so that we would not be punished by Elah, as that was how Elah kept human beings from sinning. Jesus was overjoyed to realize that in fact the great Creator of all things unconditionally loved His children, men and women alike.

"Jesus told us that he was excited to tell his mother and family in Nazareth. Even though we offered him time to rest at our house, nevertheless he took his leave with a promise to return.

"My brother offered him a purse of money which Jesus refused, 'You have already given me so much. I now have the strength to return to Nazareth. Abba has a plan for all of us which I must put together in order to bring this message to our whole nation of Israel.'

"We were greatly inspired by him but saddened when Jesus left. We never forgot him and spoke of him daily, wondering how he was doing.

"Months later we heard about healings in Galilee by a man called Jesus of Nazareth. I asked my brother if he would allow me to go to Capernaum where he was reported to be. I promised my brother to return at harvest time. He agreed and even sent a servant with me to help me get there safely."

Sailing on the calm waters, the three women felt closer from Martha's testimony. Standing up to stretch their legs, they held tight to the rim of the craft. Leaning over the side, they joyfully caught the waves that splashed on their hands. It was exciting and refreshing. Even Joanna felt at ease.

There was more time before reaching port, so Martha asked, "Joanna, I am curious about how you met Rabboni?"

"Thank you, sister Martha, for asking," Joanna responded.

Mary observed Joanna as she began her story and considered what she already knew about this matron, *She's mature and reserved and she's from Sepphoris, and always dresses formally wearing a scarf wound around her head like a turban. Her posture is noble and her speech is soft and cultured and just seems to be out of place living this humble life.* Mary was excited to hear her testimony.

Joanna sat down, cleared her throat, and began, "My husband, Elia of Chuza, is a steward in Herod's household. He is a practical man, but he respects the sincere devotion I have to my faith and religious upbringing.

"One day on my return to Sepphoris from visiting family in Nain, by chance I met Jesus speaking to travelers along the road. From my carriage window, I sleepily watched the people rushing here and there. When my eyes caught sight of Jesus' face, I noticed a sincerity in his expression, so foreign in my surroundings that it moved my heart. Awakening fully, I felt a strong desire to meet him.

"Halting my carriage, I boldly walked up to him and inquired what he was doing and his name. Actually, this was so unlike me. I hardly ever risked my safety, speaking with strangers. However, my fascination was remarkably strong.

"Rabbi Jesus impressed me deeply. When I felt his humility and love for Elah, I immediately wanted to help him, so I gave him all the denarii in my purse. Another thing I don't usually do.

"I am not a mother, but strangely I felt a maternal heart toward him. I felt the need to take him into my heart as my son. When he spoke to me, I was filled with joy.

"Like Martha, he told me of his experience in the desert. He told me that he experienced Abba Elah's love for him and all things of creation. He expressed to me about Elah, 'Not only is Abba Elah the fulfiller of every need and our constant supporter, our protector, He also has a vision for His chosen people.'

"I still remember Rabbi Jesus' eyes brimming with tears of love for Elah. His spirit spurred something deep inside me. And, by the way, I also believe that this is the time of the Messiah's coming and I am expecting his coming.

"Yes! like you Martha, I believe he is truly different from any other religious man I have ever met. Whilst most of them speak of Elah's vengefulness, he clearly explains that love not fear is Elah's motivator.

"Nevertheless, because of my responsibility toward my husband, I continued on my way home. Over the next month, I could not forget Jesus. I decided to fast and pray that Elah would help me decide whether or not to search for him.

"While I waited for an answer, I continued loving and serving my husband. After many dreams of Jesus, I finally told my husband that Elah was directing me to search for him and attend him. I asked him if he would let me go.

"Of course, he did not understand my unusual fascination, but he knew me well enough to know that I would not give up. Finally, with Elah's help, Elia allowed me to go to Jesus, with my promise to return at the new year.

"I searched for Jesus. He had moved on from where I first met him. But, after several days, I found him preaching to fishermen along the shore. From there, I joined with him as one by one he gathered his followers." Joanna paused pondering her experience.

Then Martha added, "Like your healing, Mary! I witnessed him heal others. Do you know that he is not afraid to touch even lepers and heal them?"

Joanna added her appreciation for Jesus' attitude, "Unlike the haughty rabbis, his love for the common folk is astounding. I witnessed that he never passed a pauper or the outstretched hand of the infirm without giving care, or his last coin, or healing them outright. We witnessed many times his tears for the poor and downtrodden. He gives hope and his prayers are always welcoming and compassionate."

Joanna loved him particularly because he addressed her own passionate concern, the hypocrisy of the rabbis, "They fear Rome and they love money. Their attitude corrupts the synagogues," she declared passionately. "Many of our nation's people are starving and unable to care for their own families. Nonetheless, the priests use religious law unrelentingly to force tithing on everyone regardless of their ability to pay."

As she listened, Mary remembered the first time she had witnessed Rabboni give away all the coins in his pocket and also instructed Simon to give out all the shekels from their community purse to the poor. And she had witnessed him sincerely placing his hands upon their heads or shoulders, praying and blessing them with peace and prosperity.

Joanna commented on witnessing to the leadership of upper classes, "Rabbi Jesus began with the simple, openhearted people with good results. However, it will not be so easy for him with the educated and wealthy. They are bound by society and religious precepts, and are led by traditional leadership. Their hearts are rigid and controlled by custom and habit and desire for wealth. Trying to introduce Elah's new message means that he will need to break through the inflexible religious culture to change them."

Martha, surprised by Joanna's perspective, spoke in Jesus' defense, "Jesus knows what the best course will be able to reach the center of the culture, the hearts of the religious leaders. Elah will guide him. Though I have to admit, Joanna, you do have a point. The priests' minds are steeped in the letter of the law and desensitized by comfort and habit." She added hopefully, "Jesus knows that with Elah's help, our unity with him and hard work, we can find prepared people to open doors for him to speak to the leaders of our faith."

How can we break through to the people? Mary asked herself. Wondering she remembered Rabboni's words, *First to receive something new you must empty yourself, refresh all your concepts and knowledge. Become like a new wineskin.* This made sense to her.

As the day came to an end, Simon gave a report of the day's affairs. Then Jesus asked Mary to share a testimony about something that she had learned.

She stood and bowed, "Lord! My sisters and I realized how damaging old ideas and customs are. One cannot learn new concepts unless the heart and mind are cleansed and emptied of old ideas and old commitments. I promise to avoid misunderstandings from preconceived ideas and biases. I want to receive your fresh concepts with an open mind and pure heart."

Jesus listened with his eyes closed and smiled. Opening them he stared back at her and then to Martha and Joanna, "You cannot know how comforting your words are to me. Thank you, sisters."

Chapter 9

Work to Be Done

The harvest is plentiful, but the laborers are few, therefore,
Ask the Lord of the harvest to send out laborers into his harvest.
(Matt. 9:37-38)

Sailing into Bethsaida harbor, Mary stood at the bow with the sea breeze upon her face filling her spirit with joy and excitement. Through their day together, she had experienced much about her companions and conquered her fears on this her maiden voyage.

As they pulled close to the pier, Jesus spoke purposefully, inspiring and refocusing everyone after their early morning fishing adventure, "This evening I will speak with the people and introduce myself to them. I want to bring them Abba's love and truth, and to connect their hearts to me that I may connect them to Abba Elah. Did you feel the power that we created through our unity of spirit? Consequently, we were able to bring in a large catch of fish that will aid us in our work for Abba."

Everyone answered in unison, "Yes!"

Masterfully, Jesus continued, "Just as we spent the morning fishing for the nourishment of our physical body, let us carry the same principle of unity in reaching out to the minds and hearts of the men and women of Bethsaida." He suggested an inspiring plan, "Spread out into the community. It is a busy time to meet many people. Women will be drawing water from the well for their daily use. There are fishermen all around the dock. Many will be walking to and from the market. Our day is ripe for success!" Jesus asked, "Does this sound like a good plan?" Everyone nodded in agreement.

Aware of the struggle that some of his disciples felt, Jesus continued, "Let's build on our past experiences. Go in pairs around the village, tell them your own personal story and why you are so motivated by my sermons. We still have a good amount of time to draw a crowd. Tell them I will speak near the well after the evening meal."

Mary overheard two brothers at the back of their gathering grumbling quietly about feeling tired. However, James' voice, so noticeably enthusiastic, caused everyone to unite and answer agreeably.

Admittedly, Mary also felt reticent, though she was also excited to visit the new and larger community. She had a plan, *I will speak with the women at the well. Surely, they will be interested and curious to meet my healer and evangelist, Jesus the Nazarene.*

Jesus suddenly and good-naturedly added a comment to lighten their spirit, "While you are fishing…" Everyone laughed at Rabboni's choice of the word 'fishing.' His remark quickly uplifted everyone, giving them vitality and a lighter more agreeable confidence. They all recognized how laughter influenced their attitude. It cleared their negative feelings, reminding them why they loved and followed him.

Jesus continued in earnest, "Yes, and while you are fishing for the minds and hearts of our people, I will visit the synagogue and speak with the religious elders." With great expectation and confidence, he continued to encourage them, "There is no time to waste. Everyone in Galilee must be given a chance to hear Elah's words before I leave here and go to Judea. I am desperate, and so is Elah, to bring new life to everyone, the high and the low."

The men and women disciples fanned out in pairs. Joanna chose Mary as her partner. On their way to the community well, Mary recalled her first witnessing experiences, especially how she had overcome her shyness at approaching strangers. That was her biggest struggle. Smiling to herself, she remembered her first time trying to catch someone's attention, *I tried to catch them by surprise, using a bold and straightforward approach. Of course, my bright smile and enthusiasm helped.*

Since some had not yet heard of Rabbi Jesus, she soon learned to use a softer and more deferential manner, more relaxed, which seemed to inspire curiosity about Jesus. She also found out that the main topic to attract their interest was about the expected arrival of the Anointed One. Also, she decided she would give her testimony of being healed by Jesus.

As she and Joanna entered the center of the village, there were dozens of women around the well, talking and drawing water. Alongside them their children played among themselves and men stood on the outskirts, enjoying conversations with occasional boisterous outbursts of laughter. Mary thought, *It was a good idea to come here. We can bring a good result.*

Joanna interrupted Mary's thoughts and suggested her plan, pointing, "Over there are two women drawing water. Would you like to speak with the younger woman, and I will speak with the other one?"

Mary agreed and walked up to the woman as she was lifting her water bucket. Graciously Mary introduced herself. The young woman was startled but not offended by Mary's bold friendliness. To Mary's surprise she was interested to hear what Mary had to say and immediately set her bucket down.

Mary asked, "Have you heard of Rabbi Jesus? He preaches an inspiring message about Elah's love and plan for His children. He is also a healer." Mary continued with a positive attitude before the woman had time to refuse, "There are many people who are interested in meeting him, all over Galilee. In fact, Rabbi Jesus is speaking here later today, after the evening mealtime."

"What is your name?" Mary asked boldly.

"Rebecca," the woman answered. "I will surely come to hear a religious speaker."

The woman's interest gave Mary confidence. The rest of the afternoon she spoke to many, explaining that Jesus healed her only months before. Some were interested but a few were either too busy or too shy to speak with her. Nevertheless, she invited them all to bring their husbands and neighbors to the well.

Another woman overheard Mary speaking about her healing and walked up to her, introducing herself as the wife of a rabbi. Miriam was her name and she asked Mary, "How did this Jesus heal you? You look like you have never been sick!"

Mary answered. "A season ago, he and his friends came to my village of Magdala to hold a meeting like this. I was very ill and had been since birth. My mother was desperate to save my life. She asked Jesus to help me and miraculously, when Jesus laid his hands on my head, I was healed. Because of my renewed spirit and healthy body, I decided to join his ministry to help Rabbi Jesus give life to others."

Mary's testimony and sincerity made Miriam curious. She promised that she would come to meet the healer, and that she would also inform her husband about the meeting, "I think my husband will be interested in what your Jesus will have to say."

News of the interesting conversations and meetings with Jesus' disciples spread throughout the village. That evening after dinner, scores of residents with their children gathered to meet and listen to the healer, Jesus of Nazareth.

Jesus was pleased with the large numbers of common folk who displayed eager enthusiasm to hear his speech. There were many who came early to get a good seat and there was a lot of talk among them about a fellow Galilean from the other side of the lake.

Watching their excitement to meet and listen to Rabboni, Mary was encouraged and thought whimsically, *As we stand around a well because we thirst for water, likewise we are thirsting for truth about Elah.*

It seemed to Mary that with each town and village Jesus visited the interest grew among the common Galileans. Mary compared this evening to the other speeches, *Their response here is more enthusiastic than in the first towns we visited. There is a lot of excitement and so many are curious.* However, Mary did notice a few cynical faces. They were mostly people dressed in religious garments.

In each town, Mary enjoyed observing the many expressions. On every occasion the people showed more and more interest in Rabbi Jesus' message because he spoke in Aramaic. It was becoming the talk of the town. Never had a religious man spoken so clearly to them about Elah. Many savored every word and were refreshed in their understanding of the ways of Elah.

Today, Mary noticed that there were several rabbis in their official garb. One of the rabbis stood next to the woman, Miriam, whom she had met at the well. *That must be her husband,* she guessed. Mary was glad that she could inspire the wife enough that she would bring her husband.

Jesus began his sermon, "Elah is our Abba, our creator. I received much of this awareness of the living Elah while fasting in the desert. Therefore, I am inspired to introduce all that I learned to you. I think you will find it a fresh perspective about Elah.

"Many of us have a rebellious nature while others find themselves just naturally and humbly deferring to and obeying the religious and secular establishment. It is because Elah created each person with a unique character. Have you ever noticed that?

"Let me give you an example by looking at nature. Have you ever noticed the difference between sheep and goats? Sheep listen to and follow the shepherd's voice. They huddle tightly in pens, peacefully eating the grass without damaging it so that it will grow back. They are not aggressive, and they are patient even during shearing and do not fight the process. The shepherd takes good care of them, finding them the best pastures, and even sleeps with them at night to protect them from predators or robbers.

"Compare them to goats that scamper about and get themselves into dangerous or awkward places. They often fight each other and are independent. They eat all kinds of brambles and plants by tearing and uprooting them. They eat anything, even old cloth or shoes, thistles and weeds, without care for their well-being. They are despoilers. Therefore, if a farmer owns them, they must be tied up or they are useless to him. Yet they have their value as they also were created by Abba Elah.

"So, look around you, there are all kinds of personalities among us. Think about it and ask yourself. Are you more like a sheep or a goat?"

Everyone looked around and began to point to their friend or family member and regard their neighbor as one or the other. This caused a roar of laughter and teasing among the participants.

Jesus continued, "He truly is our Creator and as such our Abba. He desires a relationship with you, a closer personal relationship with Him. But as you are all different as the sheep and goats, so are your relationships with your Abba Elah.

"Even though we are all different, Elah created you lovingly from Himself and hoped in your differences you would find life fascinating, rubbing against each other and developing each of your characters more fully. Life can be so stimulating through our differences. In this way Elah created an interesting and exciting world. What do you think?

"The sun shines on the good and the bad. But remember the lesson here. Can Elah protect those of you whose nature is more like a goat? If you obstinately follow your own desires and leave a trail of destruction behind you, how can Elah protect you? Those of you with this nature must try harder every day to make your heart more in line with your creator so He can help you."

One man stood and asked Jesus, "But what if a person who has the sheep's character makes a mistake, will Abba abandon him?

Jesus answered, addressing the crowd, "What does a shepherd do when he notices one of his sheep is missing? You know that he will leave his flock and search the whole night until the single sheep is found. So it is with Abba, as not even sheep can avoid doing wrong or making mistakes. Be assured that your Abba Elah will immediately respond to its bleating and rescue it no matter how long or how much difficulty is involved. And so it is with you and the Kingdom of Heaven, the Kingdom of Elah."

Several shouted at the same time with great curiosity, "What is this place, the Kingdom of Elah?"

Jesus answered back, "The Kingdom of Elah is not a physical place! Not on an altar and not in the sky. The Kingdom of Elah is within you, around you, or in another's heart. It is a state of heart and mind. When you are in this state, Elah is in your head and directs everything you do and all your life.

"If you can empty yourself of selfish desires, hatred, jealousy, greed, vindictiveness, and desire for retribution, you will be able to experience Elah's love and generosity, caring for your neighbor at the expense of your own self."

A woman shouted out, "Why don't our rabbis tell us this?"

Jesus answered, "Because I alone have seen Abba Elah and through Him perceived the laws of existence and the reasons and manner in which He created this world. The world in which we live is devoid of Elah's presence, but that is why I am here. I am here to bring Him back into this world. You were born to be His sons and daughters. However, ignorance is all around you and when you focus on the pleasures of earthly things, you unknowingly ignore your own Elah-given nature."

Another asked, "Then how do we enter the Kingdom of Elah?"

Jesus responded, "First you must recognize and repent for your lack of love, and your selfish thoughts and deeds and actively work to get rid of them. It is then that you will begin to see goodness and joy surround you.

"Abba does not want us to seek for Him through antiquated rules or laws. He wants us to feel Him in here, deep in the center of our being." He pointed to his chest and expressed sincerely, "He wants us to yearn for him and to make Him the center of our daily lives. If you do this, you will begin to feel connected to Him and connected to the world around you. You will begin to sense the suffering around you, and desire to do your best, at your expense, to love and serve your community and relieve those who are suffering. In order for this change in our perception to happen, we should make ourselves open and receptive to Him like children.

"We already know that Elah prepared our nation for thousands of years. What has He prepared us for?"

Jesus waited for a response, but no one offered an answer. Thus, Jesus answered his own question, "It is so that we can receive the prophesied Anointed One whom we all are presently awaiting. Is this not true?"

It seemed to Mary that, compared to other sermons he had given, Jesus was having more difficulty getting the crowd to respond to him. Nevertheless, he continued, "The prophecy is spoken about all around you. Surely you have heard and felt that this is an auspicious time."

Suddenly, a woman eagerly shouted a response, "Yes!"

Jesus answered and pointed to the woman, "Yes! I am excited like you and believe as you do that in our lifetime, we will receive the Anointed One. I tell you He is surely coming!"

Abruptly, a rabbi stepped forward and asked a question, "If the Messiah is near, then where is Elijah the prophet whom Malachi prophesied to precede the Messiah?"

Mary thought with pride, *He is the husband of Miriam, my guest that I met at the well. What a good and important question!*

Immediately Jesus exclaimed, "Ah! now we have a sincere question." Jesus responded, "Yes, Elijah has already come!"

"Yes! Where is Elijah?" Mary whispered, eager to hear his answer.

Suddenly, Jesus was interrupted by another rabbi with a totally different question. And then a flood of insincere questions came from other arrogant rabbis. Mary realized that they were only interested in testing Jesus' knowledge of scripture. She wondered if they just wanted to cast doubt in their public by questioning Jesus' authority.

Deep in thought and frustrated by the discourteous interjections, Mary made a mental note to ask Rabboni later about Elijah. But she let that thought go and listened to Jesus' perfect enunciation of Hebrew, albeit with a charming Galilean accent. She also appreciated his insightful and refreshing explanations of the scriptures that they shouted out at him.

At the same time, Mary realized that the commoners' lack of knowledge of Hebrew, including all of his disciples, made it difficult for them to appreciate the depth and nuances of Rabbi Jesus' answers in the Hebraic discussion with the rabbis. She was happy when Jesus began to translate into Aramaic what they were asking. At last, the villagers could understand Jesus and the rabbis' exchanges.

Turning to the villagers, he shouted in their common dialect, "All of you!" He pointed toward the crowd, "More important for you is hearing news of Elah sending His Anointed One. Isn't it?"

"Yes," they replied in an uproar of enthusiasm. Mary noticed the change in the atmosphere as they were happy to be included in the discourse.

Continuing, Jesus walked up and humbly squatted near the front row of people. He noticed an attentive family of five seated in the front and he placed a hand on the shoulder of the father, "I assure you that this is the time. I ask you to listen and believe in what I tell you. Absolutely the time is at hand," Jesus proclaimed emphatically.

Mary was surprised by Rabboni's personal touch, and it moved her to tears. She whispered a prayer, *Yes, Abba Elah, please speak to our hearts. We are open and prepared.*

Finally, after the religious leaders had lost Jesus' attention they began to leave, all the while making a scene by shaking their heads as a sign of their disapproval. Their desire was to influence and discourage their simple congregants.

Jesus called to them in a loud voice as they were leaving, "You search the scriptures, because you think that in them you have eternal life. It is they that bear witness to me, yet you refuse to listen to me that you may have life."

Without a pause, Jesus continued praying with the families who came up to him to ask questions and to ask for his blessing. He spoke and prayed until darkness began to descend and the people started to leave. Finally, Jesus ended his sermon with a prayer.

Chapter 10

Mary Finding Her Place

Therefore, I tell you, do not worry about your life,
what you will eat or drink;
or about your body, what you will wear.
Is not life more than food, and the body more than clothes?
(Matt. 6:25)

Simon found a place to set up camp for the night. After the chores were done, Mary sat on her pallet reviewing her witnessing experiences and Rabboni's responses and sermon. Then, she quietly walked past the campfire and her sleeping brothers. Earlier she had noticed Jesus walking toward a secluded area a distance away from everyone. She knew he was going to commune with his Abba, but she boldly made a secret plan for herself to attend and support him during his prayers at night. Keeping a discrete distance, she would pray quietly.

She chose a spot next to a small embankment, just close enough to hear his prayers. She heard his positive resolve and promise to Abba Elah that he would never give up. And then she heard his anxious begging of Abba to give him ideas on how to break through the calcitrant religious leaders.

She determined from this time forth to attend him in silent prayer and always keep it her secret. Tonight, hearing his sobs broke her heart. It was hard not to cry. On the other hand, hearing his hope gave her so much courage.

This was not the first time Mary had stayed awake to support him. She saw a difference in Jesus' public character to that in his personal time with his Elah. When the moon was full, she saw his serene and tender expression. There were desperate moments as well. She heard him plead for Elah to give him ideas on how to move the hearts and minds of the religious leaders. He also prayed for each of his disciples that they would quickly come to understand his heart and separate from their ingrained prejudices.

She came to understand how much grief his illiterate disciples caused him. Nevertheless, Rabboni prayed for each man by name and implored Elah's help that he could find a way to help them try harder to grasp his meaning. He prayed that what little they understood of Judaism they would let go and adopt his words.

Mary remembered how he often poured out answers to his disciples while dripping with perspiration. There were times when he answered the same questions asked in different ways many times over. The same was true with the rabbis. This is how he had come to understand how difficult his mission would be.

At times Mary wanted to help him with the rabbis, but she forced herself to remain silent. She knew it would be utterly scandalous if she uttered even one word. It was totally unacceptable for women to be erudite and converse with men in public, much less in formal Hebrew.

She thought about Jesus' recent request of her, being his assistant. She already carried several watered wineskins and extra food, knowing his habit of long and sometimes grueling discussions lasting from morning to night. She served him enthusiastically, anticipating what he needed for his comfort.

Her fellow disciples recognized her hard work and appreciated Mary's kind assistance to Jesus. They watched her as she attended him with enthusiasm and joy, often serving long hours and finding only short periods of time to sleep. Eventually she was spending more time with him than anyone else.

During this time, Jesus recognized Mary's unusual perspicacity for his mission. With her youthful and pliant spirit, she did not have to struggle with old habits. She was like malleable clay. And due to her past suffering experiences, she was also compassionate and thoughtful.

It became common for Jesus to ask her to pray before meals and meetings. Elder Simon, who was always protective of his position as chief assistant, at times felt that she was encroaching. Mary noticed that it was difficult for Elder Simon and some of the more traditionally minded men to accept a woman having such prominence. However, James often stepped in and chided them for their offended male sensitivities.

Jesus knew that his senior follower struggled, but left him to work out his preconceptions. He prayed for them and hoped they would realize that her helpfulness far outweighed their intolerance and stubbornly fixed ideas. Also, Mary overheard Jesus pray for her to remain humble and to be able to withstand the social pressure they furtively exerted toward her.

Often, during their study, they had no choice but to rely on Mary's translation of the Hebrew scriptures. Soon enough, and mostly because of her humility, they accepted and appreciated her ability, though reservedly and still with a tinge of chauvinism. She knew that Elder Simon's conscience understood that she was needed. He understood that Jesus could not do all the translating. Therefore, he knew how undeniably necessary her mission was to Rabboni Jesus. Nevertheless, it still was not easy for the traditionally minded Simon to accept.

Mary also recognized the reality of her situation. *As a woman,* she thought, *I must govern myself when asked to assist Jesus. I don't want to damage his reputation and bring a scandal, causing him more trouble.* Therefore, she was always aware of keeping enough distance and formal attitude when receiving his direction. She prayed that Simon could overcome his prejudice and distaste, though she felt his unresolved antipathy toward her still.

Simon, always vigilant, knew that the integrity of their relationship was straightforward and that their nearness was beyond reproach. He trusted Jesus, but he also genuinely wondered how long it would be before it became a public scandal. He could not imagine anything good coming from it, but in the meantime, he admitted Mary's value to their mission. It was a difficult problem for Simon to resolve.

Within the first six months of beginning his mission, especially since coming to northern Galilee, Rabbi Jesus became a household conversation. Word traveled, reaching the eastern and western shores of the Sea of Galilee. It began to be whispered among many of the humble people that he was possibly the Anointed One, or at least a new prophet. Tales of his miraculous healings made him even more intriguing to all strata of Galilean society.

Families pursued him with their sick and disabled. The people of Galilee were eager to meet him and hear his inspirational anecdotes about Elah, whom he called Abba. Rumors grew that that he might be the long-awaited Messiah.

There were other reasons the common people sought out Jesus. They were disillusioned and uninspired with what they heard in the synagogues. They began to question their inability to understand the Hebraic dissertations and grew tired of the incessant tithing demands. They realized that the religious autocracy had little interest in finding solutions for their many problems. However, they were greatly inspired by Jesus and felt his concern, thereby finding a renewed hope and zeal for Elah, whom they learned was really their Abba.

All over Galilee, from the northern towns surrounding the Sea of Galilee to the western and eastern shores and into the hill country, Jesus gathered large crowds, sometimes numbering hundreds. There was a resurgence of their faith in Abba. His new understanding about the Almighty filled their hearts. And Rabbi Jesus became a folk hero to many as he stood up against the corrupt heartless rabbinate. Those within the walls of the synagogues were the last to catch this flow of information.

Jesus' sermons, refreshing natural lessons about bettering their relationships, inspired those who listened sincerely. Jesus spoke directly to them about their need to care for neighbors and that the Creator Elah intended to have a personal relationship with each person and family. This inspired them.

However, the real depth of love the people felt for Jesus was because of his personal attention to them. For hours he prayed for each of their requests. After his short lessons, he spent most of his time going to individual families and couples, laying on his hands and praying their requests directly to Abba the Creator of all. Or he simply went from person to person, family to family, asking about their individual problems and bringing it all to Abba Elah in prayer.

Jesus looked directly into each person's eyes and asked genuinely, "Can I pray with you and your family? What is your name? Is there something I can ask for you personally from Elah, our Abba in Heaven?" Poignantly touching a hand or holding a shoulder, placing his hands on the head of a child, or touching the infirm as he empathetically called out their name, he brought people to tears in each situation.

The needy people, many longing for a renewal of their spirituality, felt revived when they took Jesus' advice seriously. They recognized at last that Elah truly cared for them. Worshipers stood patiently for hours, waiting to have their own personal prayer requests heard.

Jesus never tired as he spent hours with these individuals and families. During these times there were many physical and emotional healings, after which Jesus commissioned them, "Go forth now, understanding that it is not what you take for yourself or your family but what you give to others." Mary realized that this was what he considered his most important message to help them.

Though the priests and rabbis tried to ignore the growth of Jesus' popularity, especially among their young congregants, the decrease in their weekly Sabbath attendance and tithing could not be ignored. These leaders of faith knew that they would suffer eventually, especially when the Chief Priest found their coffers lacking the funds required by Rome.

Therefore, they began to send spies to investigate the Nazarene. They joined the crowds on the hillside and fields, judging his sermons, looking for specific statements that would declare him a heretic, a crime punishable by death. These educated priests and rabbis were not there to understand and learn. They were deviously compiling evidence to put an end to him.

Others investigated his qualifications and pedigree, and found Jesus to be without credentials and with no formal training as a rabbi. Their shrewd minds heard only what they wanted to hear and reported back that he preached against the Hebraic Law and the Prophets. They also classified Jesus as a disrupter of society as he boldly accused the rabbis and priests of habitually following the law without caring about the present needs of the people.

They found many offenses against Jesus for not following the divine law and reported them disparagingly. They reported healing on the Sabbath, cavorting with sinners and tax collectors, and, even worse, his disregard for the laws of kashrut, the dietary regulations defining the kosher foods that may be consumed. The most extreme was a report that said he put himself above the Sanhedrin in challenging the interpretation of the ancient laws and scriptures.

Truly, these inflexible rabbis were not open to Jesus' words.

At a recent gathering Jesus had proclaimed, "Elah, our Abba, sees the suffering of His children. Part of my mission is to solve the problems. I am here to reveal Elah's love for you, not His punishment. He does not punish anyone. You suffer, not because of Abba, but by your own selfish actions."

Jesus paused and Mary assumed he was in prayer, deeply searching for a meaningful connection to Abba.

"Listen!" He spread his arms enthusiastically, pointing to the rocky hills around them and the distant view of the lake, "Look at the sheep and goats wandering around grazing on grass, think of fish in the lake or birds of the air. Each species has everything that it needs to live. The female cares for her offspring even at the risk of her life. Abba deliberately created all things to live in harmony.

"Look at the environment, everything has a purpose in one way or another. They give comfort to our eyes, food for our stomach, material for our homes. Think about it, every individual being is protected, nourished, and their needs are met. And Abba, the Creator, wonderfully fashioned everything in the universe to reproduce through procreation.

"Therefore, do not covet what you have. Do not cling to your possessions. Know that Abba created the world to multiply goodness and joy. And thus, to be like Him, we must multiply goodness and joy.

"We find ourselves in need, or ill, or destitute when we fail to appreciate others and give to others as our Creator gives to us. When you live for the sake of others you actually bring blessings to yourselves.

"From now on, take notice of your actions. You will realize that when you hold back or take for your own pleasure, you will find yourself growing unhappy, or anxious, or angry. These emotions pull your spirit down and cause you to become sick, or even cause others pain or sorrow. Our sorrow, our illness, and our unhappiness are not because Elah punishes us but because we have lost our natural innocence." Emphatically, Jesus repeated, "Elah does not punish! When you recognize that Elah lives within you and only wants your own good, then you will want to rid yourself of selfishness and insensitivity."

He asked the crowd, "You know the law says the Sabbath is the day to worship Elah and all labor should cease, right?" Everyone answered emphatically, "Yes!"

Jesus then posed a question, "If someone is suffering on the Sabbath, should we give or not give comfort to him on that day?"

There was murmuring throughout the congregants. No one voiced an answer.

Jesus answered, "Can you decide not to get sick or injured on the Sabbath? Of course not! Therefore, we must give care at any time, whether it is on a holy day or the Sabbath. The commandments and laws are meant to guide all of Abba's children. But these rules are not meant to take away our humanity and concern for others. All human beings are Elah's children."

Later that day, Mary followed Jesus as he went from person to person to pray. She witnessed his prayers mostly in Aramaic, "Abba, hear this man's plea for his family. Ezra and his wife here have a dozen children. Their oldest is of marrying age, please help them find a complimentary partner. And Sarah, Ezra's wife has a hard time feeding and clothing her family. Please grant the family abundance and joy, that he and his wife can see their family grow in Your love every day."

That moment of Jesus' tender individual care brought grateful and hopeful tears to the family and even to the disciples in attendance. Families close by were encouraged by his sincerity and the power of his prayer. With excitement and anticipation, they lined up waiting with their loved ones to receive his prayer. Hours were filled with prayers for every individual who asked. He went from person to person and prayed over them. His genuine concern never waned, and he never refused a single request.

Often, Mary noticed the rabbis standing around gawking. Dressed in their traditional tasseled garb and head dress they loudly and haughtily gossiped among themselves. They deliberately exhibited their annoyance with Jesus' conspicuous affection toward their congregants. They were blatantly disrespectful, taunting the families and individuals, clearly showing their disdain for Jesus' behavior.

From these experiences, Mary realized that Jesus was right. His plan to visit synagogues and religious establishments was necessary, though difficult. Nevertheless, he had to confront and challenge their understanding with his new perspective.

She also remembered the importance of Jesus' warning, "Unless you empty yourself of old wine and make your consciousness like a new wineskin, you will not understand my concepts. Otherwise, everything I preach will be misunderstood or only half appreciated."

At the same time, she realized how important and helpful her knowledge of scripture would be in witnessing to religious leaders. But she promised herself that she would never allow her education in the scriptures to interfere with Jesus' new words of hope. Therefore, she determined to pray daily to refresh her heart and mind.

Mary watched the aggressive rabbis purposely address Jesus in Hebrew with many questions and an aloof attitude. She believed it was their intent to influence the common folk, who were watching and listening, with a propensity to defer to their educated leaders. And, as expected, these belligerent men fired question after question at Jesus, testing his knowledge of scripture.

She knew that most questions from these educated elite were meant only to test him so that they could find fault with his message. Mary recognized that the religious leaders were interested in a mental debate only to give themselves a sense of superiority over him and their congregants. They were not open to his message.

Chapter 11

The Galilee Campaign

Truly, truly, I say to you, unless one is born anew,
you cannot see the kingdom of God.
(John 3:3)

Mary became accustomed to their itinerant routine. She calculated the number of sandals she had changed and figured her time in Jesus' presence was now a whole season. She had visited many interesting villages and towns and viewed the beautiful vistas of her country surrounding the Sea of Galilee. She was in awe of her countrymen and the crowds flocking to see Jesus.

She was reassured every day that she and her brothers and sisters were really helping him spread his good news. Mostly everyone was friendly, and they were enthusiastic that one of their own countrymen was spreading good will and speaking about Elah in their own language.

Jesus' message was always refreshing, heart-warming, but revolutionary. Mary and all her new family of disciples witnessed Jesus' popularity increase. He was certainly creating a stir, especially with the idealistic young men and families whose daily lives were a struggle. It was a sign to Mary, and to many, that things were changing for the better. Stories of his compassionate deeds and the mercy of his healings, and even some of his sayings, refreshing words about Elah, preceded him. Many were inspired, and word began to spread that he was the prophesied Messiah.

Mary still had not been able to ask Jesus her many questions. There was no time. During their tour of the villages around Galilee they scarcely had time to sleep. They rose early and slept late. All their efforts were focused on reaching as many towns as possible during the mild weather.

The religious elite more and more began to take notice of the young, unorthodox rabbi. Many members of their community came to them with questions about their faith that had been inspired by Jesus' sermons.

Mary remembered the bright, sunny day in the town of Caesarea Philippi. There were more hecklers than usual as she listened to Jesus speak candidly of his Abba Elah, "I tell you that Abba is in me and I am in Abba. Unless you become one with me, you cannot see or enter the Kingdom of Heaven."

Out of a few hundred townspeople, one man stepped forward and addressed Jesus sarcastically. He bellowed, "I am a man. Is it not absurd to think that I must become one with you?" The crowd laughed. "And if a woman is married, how can she become one with you?" he continued.

"Yes!" another man shouted, in the same challenging manner. "Are you suggesting that all women marry you?" Again, the crowd roared in laughter. And he added, jokingly, "You would become very busy."

The crowd began to hum with all kinds of comments. Mary suspected that the orthodox rabbis were responsible for initiating the heckling. Standing within a few feet of Jesus, she watched and prayed. But she witnessed Jesus taking the comments with ease.

He related a story about engrafting trees that simple farmers and laborers could understand. Choosing to speak about nature brought home his message more vividly, "If you have a beautiful and productive olive tree and you have a large number of wild olive trees that produce inferior fruit, you need to engraft each of the wild trees with a small branch from the healthy one. Is that so?" Jesus asked.

The crowd answered loudly, "Yes!"

Jesus went on, "Then all of your olive trees will produce abundant and tasty fruit? Yes?" The people understood and responded enthusiastically.

Jesus continued quickly to keep their attention, "If you have uncluttered minds and open ears to hear, you know this to be true." Many guessed that Jesus was purposefully provoking the rabbis who were present and trying to get them to think deeper.

"In the same way, I am the healthy olive tree and all of you are wild olive trees. If you engraft yourself with my branches, then you will become the same as me. Can you understand my meaning?"

The idea was thought-provoking, and the simple, rustic folk clearly understood. They enjoyed the analogy and expressed their enthusiasm with rousing, clamoring voices.

In amongst the hum of realizations, from the center of the crowd a man's voice rang out, in their dialect though with a strong Hebrew accent, "How do you presume to speak with such arrogance and audacity to these uneducated people? They do not know the scriptures and can be confused." He then repeated his question in Hebrew, thereby exhibiting his authority over the simple and uneducated.

Jesus answered the educated man respectfully and kindly, but with strong conviction. He went back to the common dialect, "I have been ordained by Elah Abba, and must follow His bidding."

Reacting to Jesus' answer and feeling challenged, the official stepped forward out of the midst of the crowd. Everyone recognized him as one of the most influential and well-known rabbis in their district. With the weight of his authority to negatively influence the crowd he continued in an authoritative voice, "As Israelites, we are already of a special lineage because of our common ancestor Abraham. We are given a special status in front of Adonai Elohim, so says the Talmud and the Holy Scriptures given to us by Moses. We are already the true olive trees; perhaps *you* need to be engrafted to us," the man taunted.

Unmoved, and with absolute confidence and unrelenting resolve, Jesus continued to answer the rabbi, "I tell you that I am the reason that Abraham was even born. It is for me that Abraham's lineage was chosen. Through me, with you in me and I in you, all mankind will come to truly honor and worship Abba Elah and become part of His lineage, not the lineage of Satan. Not just one person but whole families."

Explaining further with an even more contentious supposition, Jesus continued in Aramaic, "You are from the false lineage of Adam and Eve. Before Elah's blessing they were thrown outside the Garden of Eden and began the

— 111 —

human lineage without their Creator's blessing. You, as their descendants, inherited their sin. Here I stand before you and have the authority from Abba Elah to forgive this ancient sin right now. This is why you must come to me and engraft yourself to me, for I am the true olive tree!"

The rabbi gasped. The crowd, siding with Jesus, roared gleefully, obviously not impressed by the educated religious heckler. Mary saw their expressions turn to wonder and awe, and even some displayed rebellious righteousness toward the rabbi.

In another town, Jesus spoke with the same zeal and his speech was not any less controversial than previous ones. She noticed the concerned expressions of a few of the disciples, who feared for his safety. She remembered the first time she heard this sermon, *This is the one where I prayed so desperately to understand him. It brought tears to my eyes.* Today she whispered during his whole discourse, *Elah, I pray You will help all of us to understand.*

Jesus decreed in Aramaic, "In order to go to the Kingdom of Heaven, you must become one with my blood and one with my body. You must be born again through me. In fact, unless you are reborn through me, you cannot enter the Kingdom. Blood is the symbol of life, so unless you come to me you cannot have life or Elah's love. Your heart must be one with my heart and one with my love.

"I will even go further to say that if you love the world around you, your parents, or even if you love your husband or wife or children more than you love me, you cannot enter into the Kingdom. Unless you love me first, you cannot love others properly."

Many of the earnest believers in the crowd expressed consternation, asking many questions. But, like Mary, they wanted to believe him, so they continued to listen.

However, there were those who were offended and shocked. One of them shouted, "How can you arrogantly put forth these ideas? You are speaking against the holy commandments of Moses! Are you telling us to turn away from our families? This is a hard saying which is against our society!"

Another outraged, obviously educated, priest bellowed, "How can I, as a man, be reborn from you? You are not even married!"

Shocked by such words, true or not, many of those in the gathering became discouraged and walked away. Mary recognized that this comment was most controversial of all, *This is true and one of the biggest reasons Jesus is not taken seriously. A man of faith without a woman and family is odd.* She desperately whispered a prayer, *Abba Elah, please help Rabboni to find a wife.*

In most of the towns Mary witnessed moments like this but she prayed each time, *Come back. Those are unfair and false accusations! Please, Jesus, please be careful.*

Jesus continued as if he had overheard her unspoken concern, "I know that my discourse is hard to understand. I did not come to you to say things you already know. I don't speak things that you will immediately agree with or like to hear. But you must know that I come to free you from the bondage of your false parent, Satan, present, past, and future. You must pray and ask Abba Elah if what I am telling you is right.

"This is the reason I speak to you in stories and symbols, because when I speak to you directly of the truth, you can hardly bear the truth or under-stand it. The day is coming when I will be able to speak to you plainly and clearly the truth of Elah.

"If you don't know Elah's desire for you and His design for you, how can you live properly? He wants you to know Him. Just as a human parent, He is all loving and all forgiving and all caring. You know that as parents you feel this way toward your children, your family, because Elah feels that way. That is why I refer to Him as Abba."

Every day there were more Sadducees, religious leaders, dispersed in the crowd accusing and taunting him, "Heretic!" Many officials stood and cov-ered their ears trying not to hear Jesus' words. With each sermon it seemed that the authorities were becoming exceedingly more desperate, screaming out, "This man, Jesus, equates himself with Elah. For the sake of your eternal soul do not believe him. He is a charlatan and is using the power of Satan to mesmerize you." After each intense sermon, Jesus retreated into the solitude of nature.

Presently Jesus was leading them back to Capernaum. They began their return before daybreak and used the light of the campfire to adjust their belongings in the wagon. Mary admittedly felt physically and emotionally exhausted after her review of their recent experiences. As she and her sisters wearily walked behind the wagon she contemplated, *We began this journey weeks ago, united together with Jesus our Lord, and we are finally returning to Capernaum.*

I know we're all tired, and though it has been difficult I hope that we are all deeply enriched. It seems that every week the hecklers increase, fomenting bad will against Jesus. I wish that someday soon someone will step forward and chastise these rabbis and priests on Jesus' behalf; that they all will begin to take Jesus seriously and realize the truth of his words.

Anyway, I'm glad that Simon chose this more direct route along this more comfortable and modern Roman stone paved roadway, Mary thought wearily.

As the road curved around a rather large bluff, she noticed a flat rock jutting out from the hillside and a wide, open cave-like area under it. Suddenly she spied a movement inside the darkness. At the same time Phillip, walking in the lead beside Jesus, called a halt.

Focusing her vision, Mary beheld a group of individuals hiding under the stone shelter. Unexpectedly, one emerged. The sudden brightness of the sun caused him to squint, quickly covering his face with a horrifically festered hand. Except for his hand, he was covered from head to toe in tattered, dirty, and blood-stained clothing. Mary was close enough to notice a rancid odor coming from him and his companions. His squinting eyes were all that identified him as human, until he began to talk. At the same time Mary heard painful moaning coming from under the rock.

Phillip immediately became defensive and commanded the man to stop. But Jesus, noticeably distressed by his gruesome appearance, went around Phillip and began questioning the man, "Who are you and all of your companions? I can see that you need help!"

"We are lepers, outcast by society. Could you spare some food and water for us?" the feeble and pitiful spokesman begged.

Compassionately, Jesus motioned with an outstretched hand and immediately called Simon to bring food and water. As they waited for the food and wineskins, Jesus instructed to the sick man, "Tell all your companions to come out into the light."

Obediently, one by one they slowly emerged. One, lying on a tattered blanket, had to be pulled out by three weak women. Jesus and his disciples stared in disbelief at their deplorable condition. Before them were seven diseased and emaciated beings. It was hard to believe that they were people. Only their eyes gave them away as human.

"Quickly!" Jesus demanded, unabashedly grief stricken, "bring the nourishment, the food and wine." He shocked everyone as he disregarded their contagious condition and knelt directly beside the woman who was lying on the blanket, so weak that she could not lift her head. Fearlessly, he supported her head as flies buzzed around her eyes and maggots crawled on her uncovered wounds.

It was the most abhorrent experience ever witnessed by the group. And for Mary, who was standing next to Jesus, it was the most tender action that she had ever witnessed. She could no longer hold back her anguish and sadness. Remembering her own healing, she prayed aloud. "Abba Elah, please help these unfortunate people!"

James, John, and Joanna arrived and hastily doled out the provisions to Jesus and all the other disciples. Jesus took a wineskin and piece of bread and instructed, "Quickly, hand out the watered-wine first. They are thirsty. Give them only small amounts of food as they may not have eaten in a while. Too much food will make them vomit."

No one dared touch them. Jesus patiently showed them what to do. Holding the helpless woman's head with one hand, he gently pulled a pus-filled cloth away from her mouth and carefully poured the liquid drop by drop into her mouth and slowly fed her small pieces of bread.

James and Andrew overcame their revulsion and followed Jesus' instructions, giving the wine and bread to the other invalids.

Mary and Martha watched Rabboni as he lovingly gazed into the eyes of the untouchable woman. It was a cathartic moment causing everyone to weep. Mary noticed that even Andrew and Simon, men hardened by life's ups and downs, were overwhelmed and immobilized. But she and Martha followed Jesus' example and fearlessly approached the other disease-ridden people and gave out the food.

When all had taken their fill, Jesus stood and offered a simple prayer, "Abba, these children of Yours have been deemed incurable and hopeless outcasts by all the leaders of society and left to die. As Your son I ask You, Abba Elah, to restore their health."

They all witnessed the visible wounds suddenly drying up and healing. Jesus instructed the lepers to remove their head cloths and pull up their sleeves and robes. As the early morning sun bathed the uncovered parts of their bodies, they were healed.

Mary rushed over to the woman lying on the blanket and helped her stand up by holding her clean hand. Though she was only skin and bones, the woman was able to stand on her own along with all her companions.

Then Jesus announced, "Now that you are healed, go and live your remaining lives for others. Use your experience to develop your heart and soul. Give to others and do not expect anything in return."

He bowed politely to the now healed men and women. Then Jesus humbly gave instruction to Simon to head on toward their destination. Overwhelmed and astonished, the unfortunate outcasts observed themselves and each other, laughing and dancing.

Suddenly, their spokesman overcame his shock and noticed that the healer Jesus was moving unpretentiously down the road. He and his companions immediately ran to Jesus and bowed to the ground, thanking him. Jesus humbly acknowledged them and continued on as if nothing extraordinary had happened.

For the remainder of their trip to Capernaum, Jesus and his disciples walked in silence. The experience was beyond words. Yes, they had witnessed other healings, including Mary's, but none was as poignant as that one.

While walking, Mary reviewed the incident and silently prayed, *Abba, Jesus is truly a gift to our homeland. More and more we can see that the Messiah, Your anointed son, is here. I am a witness to his miraculous power of love. He is using every waking moment to revive this chosen land. Thank you for allowing me to walk with him on this quest.*

Then she remembered the words of the prophet Isaiah and whispered them,

Every valley shall be raised up
and every mountain and hill made low.
The rough ground shall become level
and the rugged places a plain.
And the glory of the Lord will be revealed,
and all people will see it together.

The last line she repeated loudly in their own dialect, causing everyone to turn and look at her. Mary laughed and joyously sang out the famous line again and again. She imagined that Jesus heard her and was smiling.

Chapter 12

A Test of Faith

Take my yoke upon you, and learn from me
(Matt 11:29)

As their month-long journey came to an end, Mary realized that the experience with the lepers had motivated and invigorated everyone. With a spirit of accomplishment, everyone entered Capernaum's outer perimeter with a renewed determination to unite with Rabboni and help him bring the Kingdom of Heaven as quickly as possible.

Mary's last prayer before arriving at Simon's home was, *Abba Elah, it was a good day's work and a successful trip. Let us fill the nation with great hope and joyous expectations!*

The morning after their return Jesus announced, "We will take a break to renew and refresh our spirits. I will bring Simon, James, and Mary with me into the hills. Andrew will take a boat out to fish. Joanna and Martha need this time to rest. This is a time for each of you to take individual time for yourselves in prayer or visiting relatives. When we come back together, we will offer our work to our Heavenly Father and celebrate.

Surprised and proud to be chosen to attend Rabboni directly, Mary quickly and enthusiastically prepared for all his personal needs. She rushed to the kitchen and, with the help of the servants, packed double amounts of watered wineskins, bread, and dried fish. When all was set, Jesus led the appointed three into the hills north of the city.

They climbed uphill along a goat path. As they reached a distance from the lakeside town, the rugged countryside, with scatterings of acacia trees and wild olive trees, became a welcome peaceful reprieve. Boulders here and there seemed to hold the soil on the slopes. As they climbed, Mary felt the weight of the packages, but the weight on her mind and spirit was lightening. Each deep breath she took was refreshing and peaceful. She prayed that Rabboni was also feeling relief.

After some time, she turned to view the valley. She could no longer see the town clearly and the air, though warm, was lighter and fresher than below. She rewrapped her scarf.

She had to hurry to rejoin her companions, being careful not to step in any of the many ruts along the uneven path. The sparse yellowish-brown vegetation, stubby and dry, was patched with green growth. Rocks, covered in lichen, jutted out here and there. Small marmots and rabbits scampered in different directions away from the sound of their footsteps. Mary noticed a magnificent ibex standing gallantly atop a giant rock in the distance.

She also noticed different herbs. She bent down and picked the ones close to her path, sniffing their scent and stuffing them in her bag to bring back to camp. Coriander, dill, and sage were all tasty and healthy to use in their diet. She even saw the Felty Germander herb her mother used to burn during her bouts of illness, but she left it, glad that she no longer needed it.

No one spoke, and it seemed that they were all deep in thought and perhaps in prayer. Jesus led their group at a quick pace. After weeks of walking, they were all accustomed to the exercise and Mary felt joy in each step.

When the sun was on the horizon in the west, Jesus stopped and turned around to view the whole valley. Mary could tell he was deep in thought. The quiet filled her with peace and contentment.

Jesus spoke, pointing, "There is a cave up ahead. I would like to withdraw from you for a while. Simon, please find a good place to camp. Light a fire and use this time to rest but also to meditate and pray with me. We can thank Abba Elah for His protection and love. And consider what to do and where to go from now. This will help us prepare for the next few months."

The two men went to work. Mary ran to catch up with Jesus and offered him his watered wineskin and bread. Jesus refused the bread but took the water with a nod and, without a word, turned toward his destination.

Mary went back to their campsite and gave Simon and James their wineskins and bread. They worked together to start a fire and prepare the pallets that each carried. James had brought one for Mary as well.

Mary was happy to serve her brothers, but as the darkness surrounded them she took her pallet halfway up the hillside between the campfire and the cave and prepared to rest and pray. Admittedly she was tired, but energized that Jesus had asked her to go with them. Surprisingly, she was refreshed by the climb and being in nature. She slept quickly but was awakened by the cry of a wild animal in the distance.

She was not frightened, but she was ashamed to have fallen asleep. The rest of the night she thought and prayed, wondering about Jesus. She also thanked Abba for this time that Jesus could rest and rejuvenate and commune with Him.

As morning light filled the hillside, Mary noted the difference in temperature, thinking, *It's a bit cooler up here. This is yet another experience to share with Jesus.*

Thinking of her brothers, she quickly gathered her things and picked up some wood from around her to replenish the campfire. The men were still sleeping, and she sat next to the warm fire and continued her prayers to support Rabboni. The peacefulness and quiet were exceptional, and her prayer reflected her consciousness, contemplating the pristine surroundings and cool fresh air.

After a while, the fuel began to run out, so she went in search of more wood. She wanted it to be warm for her brothers and Jesus when he returned, and she filled the fireplace with wood.

After Simon and James awoke, Simon offered a prayer and the three of them prepared to share a simple meal. James thanked Mary for bringing the nourishment. Surprised to feel accepted by them, and especially Elder Simon, she realized that working together made a difference. This was the first time she had felt a genuine connection to her brethren. They had shared so much over the last few months, and especially the healing experience of the lepers certainly added to their comradery.

Elder Simon, who hardly spoke when she was around, commented, "I wonder how Rabboni is doing. I am happy he is taking time to rest and refresh. He hardly ever sleeps and is always trying to inspire us and push us forward. Let us wait here for his return."

Together they broke their fast with a meager meal of dried fish and bread. "Mary, thank you for bringing the wineskins and food," Simon remarked quietly, without making eye contact.

Mary straightened up the fireplace and the few items they had brought and then went further up the hill alone. She went closer to the cave that she thought Jesus might be in and sat down on a large flat rock. Throughout the day, Mary prayed and continued replenishing their firewood. She also collected more herbs and watched the small animals scurrying around.

The second day faded into night and still Jesus did not emerge from the cave. Mary remained on the rock, and from her vantage point she watched the stars that were even clearer than from her roof at home. They were brighter, and it seemed like there were seas of stars. Some were in clusters and some even made patterns. She picked a star that she deemed the brightest.

Still Jesus did not emerge from the cave. They spent a second night on the hill. Not much was said as the three waited for their master's return, and the night went much like the night before.

Mary returned to her spot, as if guarding the cave where Jesus was. As dawn broke on the third day, Rabboni surprised her as he emerged from the cave and greeted her. She immediately noticed Jesus' glowing and peaceful visage, even though she knew he had fasted for two days. Together they walked down the hill and woke the men.

As they shared the remaining dried fish and bread with Rabboni, he shared his experience with his Abba, "I felt His energizing and loving embrace. He showed me how He exists in all things; in the heavens, in the waters and land, and everything alive. He created everything to reflect His nature, which is both masculine and feminine, assertive and recessive, giving and receiving. He created all kinds of living beings, from small creatures like a fly to the largest animal, and His children, masculine and feminine. Every single creation was made with an individual purpose. And He gave them the ability to procreate, to protect their kind, individual ways to nourish and heal themselves, and females having the nature to nurture their offspring.

"Abba is always loving. Abba's nature is seen easily in the animal world. Take for example a bird. Everything exists in individual separateness, while at the same time coming together to procreate. In some cases, the male bird makes the nest and the female bird sits in the nest on her eggs. Then their whole life is spent finding and bringing food to the offspring. The mother bird, in some cases, helps the chicks learn to fly and once they have learned and are gone from the nest, the adult birds begin the process all over again. Animals reflect Abba the creator's nature.

"Abba encouraged me, saying that soon His ultimate plan will be realized and restored by His dearest creation, humankind. Through me, all humankind will accomplish their real purpose as Lords of Creation through Elah's unconditional love.

"Through these visions He reminded me that this is our mission, to announce and spread His simple message to all of Israel. I will bring all humankind out of ignorance of their Heavenly Parent. All it will take are those who have ears to hear and understand Abba's true heart and nature; they will find the proper way of living and serving Abba. And these first men with ears to hear will need to spread it by their example and effort.

"But let me remind you," Rabboni emphasized, staring directly at Simon, "the old idea that Abba punishes and destroys life is totally false. Giving to others with a sincere heart of love, no matter how difficult, is the only way to achieve His will. In fact, a person who wishes ill upon another doesn't hurt them but rather hurts himself with their ill wish.

"Abba is proud of our ministry and encourages us. Each step forward is a step closer to the Kingdom of Heaven. Abba Elah wants this relationship, not just with me but also with you. It is as natural as our communication."

Mary noticed his bright countenance as, standing up, he instructed them, "Let us now bring this message back to our brethren and to all of Galilee." On the third day he led them down and back to Simon's home.

After three days and not a word from Jesus, everyone expressed relief that there was obviously no unpleasant incident which they had assumed had kept them away. They noticed that the respite was good, because Jesus and his ensemble looked healthy and refreshed. Joyfully they gathered, hoping to hear from Rabboni, who expressed his appreciation for their dedication to Abba and himself.

"Are you strengthened by your rest and refreshed?" Rabboni asked them lovingly. "You may wonder at times, saying to yourselves, why am I following this man?" as he pointed to himself. "But our Abba Elah is proud of you and your incredible faith and sacrifice for Him and me. Are you aware that we are the culmination of all prophecies, prayers, and yearnings of our ancestors?"

Jesus continued with an announcement, "This is harvest time and almost a full year has passed since many of you began this odyssey with me. Martha and Joanna, I have not forgotten your commitment to your families. Your help has given power to my mission. Without you, the large numbers of people of our nation would not have had the chance to hear Abba's essential words of compassion and love.

"Tonight, we will celebrate all of our work together. And then, tomorrow, we will bid you farewell for a time. I pray that, with Elah's help, you will be able to return when your responsibility to your families is fulfilled."

Mary realized that she would really miss them. She prayed, "Dear Abba, please guide them to return and I pray that other women will join us."

Jesus continued, "Your commitment to me over the last year has warmed the heart of Abba Elah. Through me, the spearhead, and with your help we shook the heart and soul of our nation. I appreciate and notice all your silent sacrifices and your practical accomplishments for Abba." Pausing, Jesus went up to each of the disciples, Simon, Andrew, James, John, Thomas, Matthew, Nathaniel, and Phillip, and to Martha, Joanna, and Mary. placing his hands on their shoulders and personally looked directly into their eyes, blessing each one of them.

Everything became still. Mary felt emotion swelling in her heart, and when he came over to her she noticed tears welling in his eyes. Suddenly Martha, standing next to her, burst into tears and fell to her knees. This precipitated a flow of tears from everyone, even from the toughest fisherman, Simon.

Jesus faced everyone, himself weeping, "Let us offer these tears to Elah Abba. This water binds us to memories we will never forget and propels us into tomorrow. I promise you that we will witness even greater feats than we've already seen, with the help of Abba Elah. Remember to love one another as Abba loves you. And fight the tendency to give in to your selfish desires.

"Let us dry our tears and prepare a celebration of joy this evening. Those of you who remain will continue on with me tomorrow. However, let us prepare to enjoy this evening, inviting Abba to join us."

Mary's heart felt wrenched and uncertain. Already she felt lonely for her sisters' companionship. They had worked so well together and taught her so much. They were leaving at dawn and she wanted to spend as much of the remaining time that they had with them. She prayed for their speedy return.

Everyone began milling around to accomplish the different tasks given by Simon and Perpetua. Mary noticed Rabboni leave from the back of the house to his customary prayer place upon a knoll overlooking the great lake. For the celebration and their next trip, Simon instructed the women to go into town and procure the food and wine and water, "Matthew will lead the wagon and carry the purse."

As Mary prepared to receive direction from Martha, a surprising change of plans came from Jesus as he returned from his prayer, "Simon, I changed my plan. I will need Phillip and Mary to accompany me to the nearby village synagogue to speak with the rabbi."

Immediately, Simon deferred to his master, calling to Phillip and Mary, "As you heard, prepare yourselves to go with Jesus and leave your responsibilities to the others."

Surprised, Mary felt excited that she was again asked to accompany Jesus with only one other brother. She quickly changed her scarf and tunic, embraced Martha and Joanna, and went to the kitchen to prepare wineskins and some fruit and nuts. When they were ready, with the skins strapped to her shoulder, Phillip, as security, led the way.

Although short in stature, Phillip was stocky and strongly built. Lately he had a sword hanging at his side, as Jesus' reputation for making controversial statements preceded him. His radical message had begun to reverberate in the religious establishment. Jesus was not naïve and knew that he needed protection.

Mary marveled at Rabboni's energy and determination, always pushing himself beyond his own personal needs. However, he did not neglect to show his appreciation to his followers. Nevertheless, he wasted no time when there were so many of his countrymen still needing to hear Elah's new words of hope. As they walked, Jesus seemed to be deep in thought and prayer.

Mary strode energetically behind Jesus and Phillip and recalled all the questions from the past weeks that she truly wanted to ask Jesus. She hoped that soon she would get the opportunity. But she knew now was not the right time. Hence, onward they marched in silence.

The synagogue was on the eastern side of Capernaum, but not all the way to Bethsaida. It was one that he had not visited before. Jesus paused before entering the simple adobe building that was not nearly as large as Simon's compound. They sincerely prayed together, "Abba open the hearts of those we meet."

Rabboni instructed Phillip and Mary, "Stay alert and pray that my words will move the hearts of these traditional men."

Phillip remained outside keeping watch. After handing Phillip a water-skin, Mary entered the vestibule where she remained, because women were not allowed to enter the inner sanctuary. She felt important to have been chosen by Jesus for such a mission and thought proudly, *Maybe I can help him with my knowledge of the language and scriptures.*

Seriously, Mary endeavored to aid Jesus through a strong prayer. After placing her packages down in the dark and dank inner room, she stood attentively near the opening to the inner sanctum. It was a thrilling moment. As she listened, she estimated that there were at least three different men conversing with Jesus in Hebrew. Thus far, the voices were respectful. She strained to listen, but was unable to catch any words. The voices fluctuated, high and low, softly and forcefully, but no matter how hard she tried she could not hear a distinct phrase or single word.

After a while, Mary gave up trying to follow their discourse and reminded herself that her mission was to assist Jesus through prayer. So, she paced back and forth in the small dim space. Sincerely focusing on her words and heart, she prayed, *Abba inspire Rabboni with your love and open the hearts and minds of the religious leaders.* Over and over, she prayed these words.

As time passed, Mary's high expectations began to wane. Due to the discomfort of the hot and airless room, she found it difficult to pray and remain focused. Her expectation of directly attending Jesus began to go awry, and negative feelings and disappointment slowly captured her consciousness. Pacing the ten steps from wall to wall helped keep her alert, until she decided unwisely to have a seat on the single wooden bench. Boredom, feeling overheated, and the lack of fresh air made her sleepy.

Try as she might to keep praying, she became distracted by the mumbling voices, the words growing louder and then fading, that interrupted her focus. When there was silence in the inner room she wondered if Jesus was leaving, so she stood up. But then they continued.

She decided to walk faster, back and forth. This helped momentarily. But then her discomfort and the voices distracted her and she could not keep a single prayer going. The voices subsided, and Mary thought perhaps the conversation was over and gave a sigh of relief, but suddenly they continued again. She chided herself, *My prayer is insufficient and I'm not doing a good job.*

Hours passed, and Mary guessed it was late afternoon, but she kept up the spiritual battle, forcing herself to pray with more feeling, dramatically and desperately pounding her arms and legs. Going to the outside entrance, Mary peeked outside and saw that the sun was still high in the sky. *It's still early,* she thought.

Back inside she continued walking, but off and on she sat despondently on the uncomfortable wooden bench. Suddenly feeling her head jerk she realized that she had nearly fallen asleep. Her conscience reminded her of Rabboni's request, *Stay alert and pray that my words will move the hearts of these traditional men.* Catching herself, she jumped up from the seat and continued pacing.

She stood up and sat down, desperate not to fall asleep, until she was tempted to go outside into the fresh air and a shaded area. However, her conscience reminded her that she could not give up, *I dare not leave. I must force myself to endure.* Abruptly she remembered her waterskin and poured water on her palm and splashed it onto her face and neck and then took a long drink.

Suddenly the voices became noticeably louder and sharper but still incomprehensible. Mary scolded herself, *Rabboni is having a hard time because of me.* She prayed harder.

Sitting again on the uncomfortable wooden bench, dozing off she bumped her head against the hard, grey stone wall, waking herself up. Quickly she stood up and continued walking the ten steps from wall to wall. Grabbing her water, again she sipped and splashed it on her face and neck. *How long have we been in here?* she wondered, thinking that Jesus was probably thirsty as well.

Finally, hours after they arrived, Jesus exited unexpectedly. Shouting, strained, angry voices followed him to the doorway. Mary noticed his crimson and perspiring face. She had never seen him so frustrated. She felt totally ashamed, feeling that she had failed her mission.

Mary turned and quickly donned her scarf, which she had removed because of the heat, and bowed respectfully. She wanted to help him more, but she could only wordlessly offer him the waterskin, which he shoved back at her. Humbly, she followed him out of the building.

Phillip, standing guard outside, respectfully bowed as Jesus emerged. Both Mary and Phillip stood waiting for direction.

One of the rabbis followed Jesus out of the synagogue and abruptly and disrespectfully asked a prying question, "Who is this woman?"

With a reserved but frustrated expression, Jesus answered, "She is my servant."

Unsatisfied with Jesus' response, the rabbi continued to examine Mary with disdain, ogling her with lascivious eyes. It was obvious to him that she was dressed as a single woman and in an inappropriate place without a guardian.

Though Mary was dressed modestly she felt humiliated and blushed. Quickly she grabbed the edge of her scarf, covering her nose and mouth and lowered her eyes.

Jesus responded, loudly and sarcastically to the impertinent man, "As a man of ha-Elohim, your attitude is outrageous and uncalled for."

Then with an agonized expression, Mary looked up at Jesus. She was surprised to see his anger and offended expression, one that she had never seen before. Without further comment, he commanded them, "Let's leave!"

Jesus, nevertheless, bowed respectfully to the rabbi and turned and led them away. As the three began their hike back to the compound there were no words, but for Mary there was much to think and pray about. With Phillip in the lead, they trekked back to camp. It was a good time to collect her thoughts and examine her unusual feelings of disappointment in herself. She admitted that it was certainly a difficult day and her first real challenging responsibility.

Mary repented that she had not done a good enough job supporting Jesus. She even had to admit that she felt shame over the word Jesus had used toward her. *I assumed that Jesus would ask me to assist in the conversation with the rabbi. When I couldn't even hear their conversation, it disappointed me and rather than praying more diligently, I thought too much about my physical discomfort. The priest's scrutinizing inspection of me left me feeling embarrassed as he examined me salaciously.* The memory lingered in her psyche as she plodded along behind Jesus. *Why? There were other times when people said hurtful things, but it didn't disturb my confidence and composure.*

Finally, Mary owned up to the real reason she felt morose, *It is my guilty feeling for falling asleep and not focusing my prayers and wanting to be a part of their conversation to support Jesus as he conversed with the rabbis. And feeling superfluous. Oh Abba Elah, I am so sorry that I have such a selfish nature. Please help me never forget that I must remain humble and grateful for any assignment.*

She suddenly felt drained and barely able to walk. Each step was a struggle to keep up. *This is the first time since I met Jesus that I feel downhearted and humiliated and exhausted. Abba, I am so sorry that I didn't do my best. And that I'm thinking about myself instead of Rabboni's disappointing experience.*

Then she suddenly realized that she had felt disparaged when Jesus identified her as his "servant." The word reverberated in her mind and bit into her soul. Finally, facing her own conceited ego she admitted, *The pain in my heart is that I felt insulted by Rabboni when he called me his servant, servant, servant.* The word resounded in her consciousness because it felt so menial rather than the higher position of assistant.

She admitted all her failings as she stumbled along the dirt path, looking down and barely able to keep up with their pace. She repented that for the first time since her healing she was thinking only of herself and that she had failed. *I am no longer thinking of Rabboni's difficulty even though he also looked unusually bothered.*

Understanding her despondent attitude and her lost confidence, she could not get past failing her duty. Weakly she prayed for enough strength to make it back to camp. The idea that she might collapse and need to be carried gave her enough strength to keep going. With sheer willpower, and choosing to remember happier times, she could make it back.

At the same time, unknown to Mary, as Jesus led them through Capernaum's paved streets, he was aware of her struggle and prayed for her to conquer her disappointment that he had called her his servant. He prayed that for the sake of her own personal growth, the demeaning experience would deepen her heart, not diminish it. Confidently praying that her own spirit would be strengthened and that she would soon regain her pure-hearted innocence, he understood her surprise and that it would take time for her to digest it in her heart and mind.

As they rounded the last turn in the road, Mary spotted Simon's welcoming home and reflected, *I never appreciated this abode as much as I do in this moment. She felt the sensation of her mother's arms wrapping around her, soothing and totally accepting.* After the weariness of the day, it was a comforting sight. Even so, her unresolved consternation still pestered her conscience.

Perpetua and her staff greeted them warmly. The simple cold water splashing her feet helped clear her head. *It is truly good to be home,* she sighed.

She took notice of the other members returning from shopping and other chores. They, too, enjoyed the foot wash after the long day of physical labor. They were laughing and happy, even splashing each other with water. She doubted that anyone felt as heavy as she did.

Sitting with all her companions and appreciating each man and woman, she thought, *After today's humiliation, I appreciate their companionship like never before.* Her experience helped her appreciate that their faith and belief in Rabboni was much deeper than hers. She noticed in their expressions undeniable innocence. There was no strain or worry, or concern for self.

She remembered those days of arduous work and her guiltless and satisfied accomplishments. Then, she began to understand that their joy came from a simple and humble desire to serve Jesus and the whole group. They held no individual distinction. She reminisced about how she also had followed faithfully and humbly.

But this morning, when Jesus unexpectantly chose her to go with him, she recognized her unexposed haughty attitude. Her expectation was completely different this time. She recognized that she had felt elevated in status getting to travel again with Jesus, imagining that standing next to Jesus while he spoke with the rabbis would be easy. Admittedly, she even thought that the special assignment meant that she was special. As she stared into the abyss, it became clear what had actually happened to her. Caught by a flood of emotion and before she broke into tears, she rushed out of the room, not daring to look at anyone.

Mary found a water basin and splashed her face with cool water as she sobbed and repented. Finally, she gained control over her thoughts. Willing herself to overcome her emotions, she decided to return to the celebration. *This is Martha and Joanna's farewell dinner!*

Back in the hall, Mary tried to participate. The aroma of the prepared food was wonderful, though she ate only a few bites. Fatigue, and her unresolved disappointment in herself, caused her to become unusually reticent.

After the meal was cleared away, thinking that Simon might ask her to share as was the custom, she self-effacingly went over to Martha and Joanna, "Thank you for taking care of all of us. I will miss you so please come back as soon as you can. Thank you for all your support and love for all of us." Then she abruptly excused herself.

Before leaving the room, she respectfully asked Rabboni if there was anything else she could do for him. He shook his head without a word or a glance at her and thus she found her way behind the house to the moonlit slope that had a view of the lake.

As Mary watched the light sparkling on the waves ebbing and flowing and rocking the boats tied to the docks, she prayed, *Oh, Elah, please help me face my shame and failure that is causing me much pain in my heart. I fear that Rabboni is also surprised. I am so tired.*

Struggling and perplexed, she thought, *This is the last day for Joanna and Martha. Rabboni also needs my support and everyone's oneness of heart. He, too, had a rough day and needs our unity of spirit. I just can't help him in my state of mind. I must figure out what is really bothering me! Or I can't help anyone.*

Sitting alone on the earth, she again reviewed the day, *My only job was to be supportive. Oh Abba, I am so sorry for allowing my physical discomfort to distract me! And to allow my vanity to push me away from Jesus and my sisters on this their last night with us.*

No, her conscience answered suddenly. She remembered Rabboni's words, "She is my servant." And she realized her hidden vanity. *I am fortunate to be helpful to him as his personal servant.* The words shook her. *My arrogance shames me! From this time forward, I must remember that I am here to serve him and help in any way I can. My knowledge and ability do not make me any better than anyone. I must apologize to Jesus and everyone!*

Shamefully, she wept and repented. The tears cleared her conscience and gave her relief. It all became clear. Then she prayed, *Dear Abba Elah! please forgive my pride and smugness. I hope Jesus and my brothers and sisters will forgive my misdeeds and absence from the celebration. I promise to be more committed and serious if I ever have this mission again. I will not allow the physical circumstance to control my prayers.* Overwhelmed with shame and overcome by fatigue she lay down on the ground and fell asleep.

Joanna called Mary from her sleep. She opened her eyes in darkness. She blinked and remembered her last thought before falling asleep. It seemed later than it was. Ashamed still, she asked her kind sister standing over her, "Oh, I am so sorry! How long have I been asleep?"

Joanna responded, "Not long, we are waiting for you. Elder Simon requests that you come back to the celebration. Can you join us?"

Humbly, Mary stood up. She straightened her clothing and followed her elder sister back to the gathering. She stretched her limbs and felt surprisingly revived. No longer did she hold on to the selfish emotions. She promised to adopt her fellow companion's humility and dedication. Remembering the afternoon's struggle, however, gave her a new perspective. With gratitude she renewed her commitment to Rabboni and was happy to welcome another chance to be his humble servant.

Mary humbly addressed her elder sister, "Thank you for calling me to share this important festivity. I will miss you and I will pray for your happiness. I will also pray that Elah will make a way for you to return to us."

Joanna nodded with a smile and responded, "I will not forget our wonderful experience together and with Lord Jesus. Of course, I plan to come back as soon as I can."

It was good to return and see Rabboni and his disciples enjoying each other's company after the long and arduous tour of Galilee. Jesus ate and shared his food with Simon and Andrew. Everyone was enjoying friendly discussion. As Mary neared, she heard Simon telling Jesus one of his many fishing stories. She looked around at everyone engaging in some sort of merriment. Perpetua and her servants were all huddled around Martha, laughing at a funny experience that had happened to her in one of the towns.

Jesus looked up and saw Mary. He stood and announced, "Now that we are all here, let us continue our celebration of experiences with Abba during the past season. Please offer something from your heart, a testimony, a song, or playing a musical instrument."

Mary went to her customary place in the circle next to Martha and Joanna. Perpetua placed a small table of food in front of her and Jesus invited her to eat. Though she was embarrassed for her obviously unhappy disposition and delaying the festivity, she nonetheless ate heartily.

Rabboni called upon Martha first. She improvised playing her lyre as she recited David's Psalm 121:

> *I will lift up mine eyes unto the hills, from whence cometh my help.*
> *My help cometh from the Lord, which made heaven and earth.*

The music and the words were beautiful and soothed Mary's soul. It reminded her of her own yearning for Abba Elah.

Martha and Joanna had prepared a statement together and Martha recited it, "It is with gratitude to Elah that we were permitted to meet our Lord Jesus. Thank you for accepting our request to travel with you and assist you in your mission. We promise to return as quickly as possible, Abba Elah willing."

Jesus stood and proclaimed that he was very proud of all their efforts, "Your outreach and witnessing made an incredible difference. The Galilean people are moved. They are beginning to ask questions and notice that all nature reflects the living Abba. They are also realizing that Abba Elah is all loving. We had some difficulties, but we are waking the people and stimulating their awareness. This is Elah's desire.

"My plan is that we take our experience to Judea and into the very heart of Jerusalem. But while we are here in Galilee, we have to do our best to reach as many inhabitants as we can. Each one of you has your own individual personality and abilities. Your faith in Abba Elah and trust in me is very comforting and I am very grateful for your sacrifices to be here.

"It is a harvest time in this physical world but also harvest time in the spiritual life of our country. With the new year beginning, those of you who are leaving us, we hope you will return as soon as you can. We will miss you and will pray for you and your families. I hope you will continue to remember us in your prayers as we continue to bring the truth of Abba to all who will listen."

Pausing, Jesus requested tenderly, "Mary, could you sing for us?"

"Yes, Rabboni," she answered spontaneously with humility. Her spirit was revived. With the struggles resolved, she sang with all her heart:

> *Baruch Haba, B'shem Adonai,*
> *Baruch Haba,*
> *Blessed is He Who comes*
> *Baruch Haba, B'shem Adonai,*
> *Who comes in the Name of the Lord?*
> *Now arise, O Lord*

Come to your resting place,
You and the Ark of Your might
Then we will rejoice, as we're clothed with
Your righteousness and celebrate the love.
Baruch Haba, B'shem Adonai
Blessed is He who comes.

Jesus stood smiling broadly, which helped Mary to let go of her guilt and heaviness. He repeated that he was very proud of everyone's efforts and added, "I can see that we are causing ripples in the strongly held, ancient, and impersonal religious dogma. It may feel difficult to you with all the experiences, incidents, and responses, but this means that we are waking the people. Abba is pleased.

"It is difficult work but let's continue, putting one foot in front of the other, and soon we will reach our destination which is the fulfillment of Abba's providential plan.

"Finally, my hope is to eventually leave the north with a good foundation of believers and carry our momentum to Judea and ultimately Jerusalem. But we still have much to do here in Galilee, and many villages yet to visit. With your help, I am determined to reach as many receptive inhabitants as is possible."

Chapter 13

The Beatitudes

I will speak to you in parables.
I will explain things hidden,
Since the creation of the world.
(Matt 13:35)

Shortly after sunrise Martha and Joanna readied to say goodbye. Martha tearfully bowed before Jesus and bid him and all her companions farewell with a promise, "I will only be away for the time being but I will return after my responsibilities are completed."

Joanna could hardly face Jesus as she turned to hide her tears. She also promised him, "I will rejoin you as soon as my husband grants me permission."

Everyone prayed together for their safe journeys home. There were tearful well wishes and farewells from everyone, and then they walked to the shore together.

Standing a few meters from Andrew's fishing vessel, Simon stoically offered his thoughts, "I believe I speak for everyone. You will be missed, and you clearly added so much to Master's mission. Andrew has arranged for a fellow fisherman to sail you to the port of Tiberius. From there Joanna will travel westward to her home in Sepphoris, while Martha's brother, Lazarus, will meet her and they will travel southward to Bethany together."

As the women sailed slowly away, Mary felt the emptiness in her heart and the loss of their support. She already missed their companionship, but she was consoled by knowing that they intended to return.

Meanwhile, Simon had prepared his boat as well. Jesus announced, "We will sail to the Gennesaret region and arrange a gathering. It is only an hour away by boat." To Mary's surprise all the supplies were already prepared.

On board, Mary sat in the stern remembering the different experiences together with her sisters. It was bittersweet. *I will miss you, sisters!* she whispered. *Elah be with you.*

She recalled their conversation from the night before. Martha had said encouragingly, "Rabboni told me that he may come to Judea sooner than planned. You will certainly visit us in Bethany. I look forward to seeing you soon."

Mary's thoughts were interrupted as the ship made its approach to a small dock in a coastal village on the northwestern shore. Jesus instructed, "Pair up and announce that I will give a sermon tomorrow morning. We will meet back here before dark."

Mary and John went together to Mary's customary spot, the common well. She explained to John, "I think everyone is relaxed and open there with their families. The women enjoy chatting and finding out gossip and other news. Their husbands are usually enjoying conversations with friends as well. It's a good place to capture their attention."

John agreed with her and, since he was familiar with the town, led the way straight there. Mary excused herself and went to a quiet place next to a corner of a building to pray. She asked Elah to help her find the residents in the village ready to hear Rabboni's words.

Then, boldly she walked over to a middle-aged woman drawing water, "Have you ever heard of Rabbi Jesus?"

Surprised, the woman looked up at her as she pulled her bucket, full of water, out of the well. "Yes, I have," she said smiling curiously. "You know him?"

Nodding, Mary explained proudly with enthusiasm, loud and clear, "Rabbi Jesus will speak in the village meeting place tomorrow morning. Please tell your neighbors."

From experience Mary knew that others would be listening as everyone was eager for news. Gossip and unusual news spread like a wildfire. Good or bad would be broadcast and carried even to other smaller communities.

Then Mary and John walked a short distance to the market and did the same. There they ran into James, and they greeted each other affably, happy to meet and share their experiences. It was the hottest time of the day, so they found a shaded stoop of a building out of the heat and shared their best testimonies while they ate their lunch.

John explained to James, "So far, the people are positive, and some had already heard of Jesus' love for Elah. This fishing port has a good feeling about it. The people are friendly and seem open to new ideas. Some expressed to me their eagerness to see and hear Rabbi Jesus. One man even asked if Jesus would pray for him and his family."

"Yes, to me too," Mary interjected. "Many women already heard fascinating news of his compassion and healings. While I was speaking with one lady another one came up to me and expressed her desire to meet Jesus. There is certainly much interest to see and hear him and they promised they would bring their husbands and families."

James was happy to hear their news and explained that Rabboni had asked him to go around and check how the witnessing was going with everyone. "I will relay your exciting news to Master and I'm sure he will be encouraged.

"Also tell the people where Rabboni will hold his sermon. It is on a wide-open green valley between two hills north of here, called the Korazim Plateau. It is within walking distance, and is a well-known meeting place for the residents in this region. Announce it to the people. They will know where it is and will spread the particulars by word of mouth. Also, this evening we will meet near the boat and discuss plans for tomorrow."

James was in a hurry to get the information out to everyone witnessing so he stood and bowed respectfully and prepared to leave, "Go with Abba. Let us continue. There are lots of people here now and everyone must get Rabboni's message and a chance to meet him."

John walked toward the other side of the market and Mary focused on women standing around, chatting to each other. She no longer felt shy or fearful about addressing the people.

Standing by herself momentarily, she had a lonely thought of Joanna and Martha. She truly missed them and wished that they were still with them.

They would be amazed at how Jesus' persona already preceded us. And that people are even inviting themselves. There is really an aura of excitement all around.

Interrupting Mary's thoughts, a woman came over to her and introduced herself, "I am Esther and heard from my friend that you are with the healer who is going to speak tomorrow. I am excited to meet him. Where and when will he speak?"

Encouraged, Mary answered with a broad smile, "He will speak tomorrow morning, in the valley north of town. Are you familiar with it?" she asked.

"Yes!" Esther answered sadly, adding, "I heard about a traveling healer. I think he must be the one. You see my husband recently lost his eyesight." Mary then understood the woman's desperation.

"He is in the prime of life and a boat builder. He is distraught that he can no longer take care of our family. I want to bring my husband to this Rabbi Jesus. Do you think he can heal him? Is it also true that Rabbi Jesus is a fellow Galilean and a compassionate man of Elah?"

Mary explained sympathetically, "What you've heard is true! Rabbi Jesus is reviving the faith of many and healing the faithful and helping the despondent and incurable. I hope you will come in the morning!"

They parted and Mary continued meeting many other enthusiastic people. As the sun entered the western sky, she and John headed back to their meeting place at the boat. Simon led the witnessers to their campsite on the plateau where Jesus would speak.

It was dusk and the campfire was a welcome site. Though she was tired, she went directly to the wagon where customarily the food was prepared. Phillip was already preparing dried fish and bread. Mary carried the food along with the wineskins to the campfire and laid it out for everyone to eat, all the while missing her sisters.

Simon commanded, "Eat quickly so that we can sleep and get up early, before the sun rises, to prepare for the early morning meeting and Rabboni's speech."

Jesus was not present, and Mary knew that he was already praying and preparing his mind and spirit in communion with Abba Elah.

After the quiet meal everyone took their leave and slept. Simon pointed out Mary's bedroll and after her prayers of gratitude, she slept.

The morning was a rush. After waking and taking care of her own hygiene, combing and braiding her hair, and splashing her face with cool water, Mary hurried to their communal area.

Jesus led them in prayer, "Abba Elah, we are preparing to give Your message to the people of this region. Most of all I want to convey Your love to each of Your children. Their souls are longing for You, longing for hope and healing. I pray that their hearts are prepared to receive Your message though me, Your humble son." Then Jesus told his disciples, "Let us give love and care to all who walk in a spiritual desert, longing for the Anointed One."

Everyone ate quickly. Mary prepared the wineskins that Jesus would need during his speech. Then Simon called all the disciples, "Let us go to the natural entrances to this valley and welcome the people."

As Rabboni's assistant, Mary stayed close by him as he prayed, but paced around looking out toward the empty field as the sun began to rise. She noticed the sparkling dew upon the emerald grass, *The thick grass will provide a natural softness for everyone to place their pallets and blankets.*

Standing on the hillside, Mary spied throngs of people beginning to fill up the huge field. Some were trying to get as close as they could to where Jesus was supposed to speak. She whispered, "The sun is hardly even visible. Its rays are just appearing on the other side of the lake and already the field is filling with people. Everyone seems enthusiastic and eager to get close to the famous Galilean."

Mary decided to climb to the top of a hill and, astounded, she counted hundreds of people coming from many different directions and entering the field. Already throngs of people sat upon their blankets on the cushion of green grass. She caught sight of Jesus and the other disciples not too far away on the hill, and she ran over to join them. Mary exclaimed, "Oh my! If only Martha and Joanna could see this amazing crowd."

As they all met up with Jesus, Simon proclaimed, "This is truly an astonishing and optimistic moment, Rabboni." Jesus was smiling.

Yes, this is the largest crowd, Mary thought jubilantly. *Thank you, Abba,*

for helping us bring such a great number of people for Jesus to give Your message.
She imagined how happy Jesus was. *Thank you, Abba! That I can be a witness to this exciting moment. It is the result of Jesus and his disciples' year-long tribulations. Their long-suffering work is, at last, coming to fruition.*

Standing with the disciples, she watched Jesus pointing from left to right toward the furthest arriving people. He gave direction to Simon to help organize everyone, "Go and make sure all the space is used. Direct everyone to move forward and choose some of our members to go to the entrance of each path into the field and cordially direct the people where to sit." Then Jesus added to Simon, "I will continue to pray up here."

Mary was happy to see Jesus was inspired and even a bit surprised. But she also recognized his extraordinary modesty.

Finally, when the sun was not yet mid sky, Jesus returned. Simon humbly informed his master that there were at least five thousand people, adding, "They are excited and enthusiastically waiting to meet you and hear your words about Abba Elah. Several asked if you will heal their relative. One man even spoke to me using your term for Elohim as Abba Elah. It seems the people are hearing about your new understanding of Elah."

Finally, Jesus went atop a large flat rock and began to speak. The large crowd quickly became silent and attentive, with the exception of children's voices here and there.

Mary stood in attendance to Jesus on his right side as she was instructed by Simon. James arranged beside her a parcel of several skins of watered wine and bread, her usual supplies for Jesus.

She watched Rabboni humbly address the crowd of thousands. She made a mental picture of his ecru, flaxen robe gently flowing in the comfortable breeze. His hair, tied back from his face with a rolled scarf, flowed in the gentle breeze. Above him were billowing white clouds gliding across the sky, sometimes casting shade upon him and the crowd. All in all, the weather was not too hot. It was comfortable for everyone.

As Jesus projected his voice as loudly as he could, the massive crowd hushed, "Where do you think Elah is, right now, as we come together?" He pointed above him. "Is He in the sky?" he asked facetiously.

Everyone considered his question in total silence.

Jesus asked. "Are you trying to recall lessons from your rabbis, scriptures, or sermons? Ideas that they taught you about the 'Almighty' so that you can give me an honest answer? I would like to ask you to put aside your concepts, your ideas of all you have learned about Elah in your lifetime. I want to give you a new perspective about our Abba Elah that will help you prosper and find fulfillment. Will you follow my request?"

"Yes!" the crowd roared enthusiastically, eager to hear his ideas. It was clear that the massive assembly of Galileans were open and ready for his words, as they waited in hushed expectation.

"So, ponder this. Elah, our Abba, does not live in the sky. He is the creator of everything and is also within everything. In order for each individual plant, animal, or human to live, Elah created the means for all life to grow and live freely in the sky, land, or sea. He gave nourishment, protection, healing, growth, an innate affectionate intelligence, and a will to survive. There is rhythm and law and order in all of Elah's creation.

"Look at the flowers in the field. They are nourished through the soil, the rain, and the sun. And the bees that find nectar in the flowers to produce honey. The bee also carries pollen from plant to plant. Honey then becomes food for animals and sweet treats for humans.

"Look at the bodies of the animals. Fur, feathers, and hair provide comfort and protection. Think of all the animals, from the smallest to the largest, all those you've seen throughout all of nature. Some of you have seen them nurturing their kind. Do all of these behaviors happen by chance? Think about it.

"I tell you no! It is not by chance. These are clear examples of Elah's forethought, His plan, and his desire for all His creations.

"Think of a mother's love. It is common not only in humans but in a whole array of animals, where the females nurture, feed, and protect their young, sometimes at the risk of their own life. This in its entirety is the most obvious description of Elah's everlasting care for all things.

"Now you, His sons and daughters, He provides for the same as He does for all of creation, but also, He gave you the propensity to experience joy, happiness, and even to be co-creators with Him. Elah gave you a mind, an awareness, to perceive every aspect of life with intelligence so you can be stewards of all that you see. Through all things you can become aware of the Creator Himself."

Jesus paused and scanned the crowd. The people became quiet. Jesus sensitively connected to their hearts, allowing them time to think about all he had introduced to them.

"Though like you, I don't see the joy and happiness part. For like most of Abba Elah's children, I see that you are weighed down and weary. As you age, your tasks grow heavier, your bellies are often empty, your clothes are threadbare, people make you angry, and you feel there is no end to your trouble and heaviness of spirit and responsibility.

"Is it true that from the moment you wake in the morning that you are often plagued by the anxiety of good and evil? Do you actually expect these bad things to happen to you sometime during your day?"

Many responded enthusiastically by nodding or shouting, "Yes!"

"I must tell you that your ignorance of how you perceive good and evil obscures all that the Abba has in store for you. You are truly the master of your life, but good and evil thoughts that are attracted to your lives and minds are expressed through your physical body. Also, most of us have memories of pain or hardship in our past. Do you agree?"

"Yes," the crowd agreed.

Jesus continued, "By allowing and bringing those thoughts and feelings into the present, we are inviting that pain and difficulty to become our everyday experience. Think about this. You can now begin to perceive that it is you that enslaves yourself. These experiences of resentment and pain, over and over, day by day, you believe and accept that they are normal and are your burden to tolerate.

"However, listen to what I tell you! If you change your belief instead to Abba's love, and reject fear, and begin to imagine and expect abundance, protection, good health, and happiness, the Creator will begin to supply you with all things necessary for your health and well-being. The more you believe and practice this, the more that Abba Elah's abundant life and love will live within you.

"Therefore, you need to heal your beliefs and reject your past negative thinking! Bring your thoughts in line with the Abba's true intention for you, and your wrong thinking will dissolve like the mist in the sun.

"When I perform a healing, I reject any skeptical thought and ask the Father's Will to be done. My desire is to allow only Abba's goodness and compassion to heal to enter my mind."

One man stood and asked, "Isn't illness punishment for the sin we commit?"

Immediately Jesus answered emphatically, "No! Absolutely not! And thank you for asking that question." Jesus continued, "How can Elah be both good and evil? This is not possible. It is only in your mind that you perceive of Elah's need for retribution. These thoughts have nothing to do with the Abba within you. Abba is ready to bring you abundance and fulfillment when you, His child, merely ask.

"I want to emphasize it is the struggle between good and evil in the human mind and heart that brings illness and unhappiness. Remember what I teach you this morning. The Kingdom of Heaven is found within you. Put aside all those old destructive ideas.

"I know that you were taught from a young age to believe in Elah the punisher. And that only blood sacrifices of innocent animals in the temple will save you. These concepts make you the heir of misfortune, sickness, poverty, and misery. These happen to you because your own ill trained mind attracts them, the very things you do not want.

"Remember these simple words. What you believe is what you will get. Believe in punishment, then it is punishment that you will get. Believe in killing and destruction as a way to reach Elah, as in animal sacrifices, and that is what you will experience, killing and destruction.

"Blessed are you if you hunger and thirst for goodness and the experience of Elah, then you will be filled up a hundred times.

"Blessed are you when you are caught up in conflict, yet you resist the conflict toward your brethren and thus become a peacemaker. It is then that you will carry the love of Abba in your heart, and you will truly become the child of Abba.

"Blessed are you when you are deeply wronged by another and yet forgive and show mercy, denying your urge to seek retribution or need to persecute. You are putting yourself in harmony with the love of Elah within you, and you will be spared in times of trouble.

"Most blessed are those of you with pure hearts. Those who have rid themselves of anger, hatred, vindictiveness, unkindness, envy, and hardness of heart. You can stand before the world as love made visible. And then you will know the reality that the Abba is within you.

"Blessed are those who find the Kingdom of Abba that is within you. Instead of tears, fears, hunger, and sickness, you will find peace, joy, plenty, and health. With this state of mind, no negativity can touch you. Contrary to your present way of thinking, this internal awareness brings harmony, beauty, and kindness.

"However, the first thing you all have to deal with is the self. Why? Because out of your desire to defend and promote your own personal good comes your selfish thoughts, words, and actions, which can be at odds with your neighbor.

"Abba Elah is the creative mind, and as such He bestowed the same on His sons and daughters. Within your own minds and hearts, you create and make plans for your own lives. But what if your plans are at odds with your family or neighbor?

"Presently, you are taught and believe in an eye for eye, which means if someone does something that hurts you, you are allowed to seek similar retribution. You believe that since it is human nature to hurt others, you can retaliate, make wars on every level, between families, neighbors, and even between nations. However, that cycle will never end. Therefore, cease the retributions and those things will cease toward you. Only then will you be able to see the Abba at work in your mind, heart, and body."

It was already afternoon, with the sun in the west. Mary thought that the people had been fascinated and mesmerized by his words and concepts for hours. She noticed children receiving food from their parents, but wondered about the thousands of people who did not bring enough to eat.

Interrupting Mary's thoughts, a man stood and shouted, "Teacher, I have never heard such interesting words before. But my heart tells me, these are truthful words. Why have we not heard our spiritual leaders explain them in this way to us?"

Jesus smiled and responded, "Because, I alone have seen Abba. Abba Elah has sent me to you and anyone else who willingly listens. Blessed is your humility and open mindedness, for you can hear and understand the truth of the Kingdom of Abba Elah."

Another man shouted excitedly, "But what is the Kingdom of Elah? What is it?"

The crowd responded, "Yes!" they yelled, "What is it?"

"The Kingdom of Elah or Heaven is around and within you. It is a state of mind and a heart of sensitivity, becoming one with the Abba."

Another man inquired anxiously, "How can I, a sinful man, know Elah like you?"

Jesus responded, "It is possible when you empty yourself of selfish desires, hatred, grudges, jealousy, vindictiveness, and greed. Then in your mind and heart, Elah can lead you."

A woman, close by, spoke, "What will happen then?" Her sweet and innocent voice was barely audible, but Jesus heard her and so did Mary.

Jesus, pointing out the woman, repeated her question, "This woman asked, 'What will happen then?'" Jesus laughed with joy and said, "What a precious question, she asks!" He answered her, "You will enter a state of closeness to Abba Elah. It is altogether beautiful and glorious, feeling emotions of love, generosity, peace, caring for others, rejecting to judge others, and knowing that you are Abba's child and in His care."

"How can we enter the Kingdom of Heaven?" another asked.

Jesus explained, "Repent by taking your selfishness to Abba, sincerely asking for forgiveness. Cleanse yourself of selfish thoughts, words, and deeds. Then you will surely realize the Kingdom of Abba Elah. You will notice that your attitude toward others changes. And then Abba will do His loving work within you. He will satisfy your every need. Like I said before, you do not need to offer animal sacrifices. Elah is not interested in their blood and death. He is interested only in the living!"

Then a woman hollered, echoing the thoughts and feelings of nearly everyone, "I have a need, right now, Master, I am hungry!"

The crowd around her roared with laughter. Her words were carried by people behind her and people behind them. Laughter reverberated gradually throughout the whole outdoor arena.

Jesus realized the truth of the woman's comment and felt sympathetic toward the whole sea of humanity in front of him. He turned toward his disciples and requested, "Bring me all the food we have. They will faint on the way home if they do not eat."

Simon went to gather whatever they had. There were only seven loaves of bread and a few small dried fish that he brought to Jesus. Then Jesus asked his disciples to announce to the whole crowd that they should arrange themselves into groups and everyone should sit down.

Jesus prayed over the food and his disciples, with the help of others, carried the baskets from group to group. As Jesus' orders were carried out, Mary and the disciples witnessed with astonishment that every mouth was fed by their loaves of bread and fishes. By the end of the afternoon, all five thousand people had enjoyed the humble but satisfying food.

Mary exclaimed, "This is a miracle! And there are baskets of food left over."

Two days passed and still Jesus spoke, and the people remained. They wanted to remain in Jesus' presence. Each day Jesus spoke, and the people listened. Some went home and returned. Some people left and others joined, but everyone was deeply moved.

At night, when everyone slept, Rabboni went down to a knoll overlooking the Sea of Galilee. Alone he stood in communion with Abba. Mary followed at a distance but close enough to hear his passionate prayers. She witnessed him standing nearly the whole night. He spoke as if Elah was standing in front of him. Sometimes he asked questions and at other times his words were inaudible. Mary imagined that he was listening to Elah's answers.

She tried to stay awake, but sleep overwhelmed her as she laid her head upon a rock. Both mornings, John called her to wake up. The sky was brightening as she stood and stretched. Tidying her braid and clothing, she walked back to the fireside. Some of the brothers went into town and purchased food and replenished their water supply.

On the third day, Rabboni accepted the people's requests to heal the sick and maimed. Hundreds of people were brought to him, and Mary and the other disciples assisted. Mary was happy when the woman she had witnessed to brought her blind husband. As everyone watched, the man's sight was restored.

With each healing, Jesus encouraged them to change their thinking, "Remember, do not allow evil, self-centered thoughts to rule your life. Examine your thoughts every day and earnestly repent to the Abba for your misgivings and never give up!

"Soon you will notice that you are becoming an admired citizen. Your friends will trust you and even confide in you. There will be abundance in your life."

Finally, as his sermons and communing with the people came to an end, Jesus prayed over the remaining crowd, beseeching Elah's blessing on all. Many wept, as did Mary, who was reminded of her own healing now nearly a year before. She earnestly prayed that the whole nation would recognize and accept Jesus as the Anointed One of Elah.

Before sailing back to Capernaum, Rabboni gathered his disciples together and they reviewed all that had taken place over the past few days. Everyone was elated and rejoiced over the successful experience.

Simon spoke, "After all these months following the direction of Rabboni, we see now how the hearts of our countrymen are as enriched and accepting as we are. As we continue, we now have a vision of the greatness that Jesus' influence has on our countrymen. When at last we travel to Jerusalem, we will have a good foundation. It is unimaginable that here there were only a few rabble rousers, during the whole three days of speaking."

Mary asked for permission to speak, "Do you think that was because of the huge, enthusiastic crowd and we, your disciples were united, one in heart with you?"

Jesus nodded and emphasized the word 'united,' "This is very important. Thank you, Sister. All of your unity with me brought this about. And then because of you, the crowd was united with us.

"Of course, we will have disagreements as we all have different perspectives in our creative minds, given to us by Abba. However, on any main decision, you should follow my direction completely. Always unity will lead us forward."

Jesus emphatically reminded Simon, "Your heart and mind must always be united with mine at all times."

"Yes, Master," Simon answered humbly, bowing,

Jesus concluded, "It was a wonderful meeting but do not allow your expectations to consider that our path will get easier or that I will be easily received. We still have a long way to go. We cannot relax. More of the traditional and stubborn religious leaders will attend and try to disrupt future sermons. They will continue to question and challenge us. Only through our unity will we prevail."

Jesus warned his disciples, "We must meet every person, positive or negative, with kindness and compassion, never in anger or malevolence. And do not become complacent."

Jesus rose and told Simon, "Let us prepare to board the boat and head back."

John and James approached Jesus and asked about their mother, "Rabboni, the last time we were home our mother, Salome, asked if she could join us. Since our sisters left, Mary is alone without other female companionship. Would you permit us to bring our mother to join us?"

Jesus closed his eyes in prayer, "Yes, that is a good idea. John, you may leave from here to bring your mother. Return to us in Capernaum by tomorrow evening."

John bowed respectfully and headed south along the shore toward his home. Everyone else boarded the boat and sailed for home.

Chapter 14

John the Baptist and Elijah

Lo, I will send you the prophet Elijah
before the great and terrible day of the Lord comes.
(Mal. 4:5)

The wind blowing and the waves splashing against the hull of the ship gave Mary a feeling of unrest, but she shook off the negative thoughts, assuming it was because of fatigue. *There is so much to be excited about after our huge gathering in Gennesaret and so many of our countrymen receiving Jesus with open minds and hearts throughout the three days.*

Sailing back to home port in the afternoon of the fourth day, Jesus expressed gratitude to his disciples for their unified work in orchestrating such a successful assembly, "It was a tremendous success for Abba Elah. Though you must be exhausted, let's remember this event and use the experience for even greater result in our next gathering." His words buoyed and energized everyone's spirit.

Uplifted and full of ideas, after having dismissed her apprehension, Mary now imagined that anything was possible. *Surely our future gatherings will increase as soon as our Master's hopeful words and new concepts multiply by word of mouth throughout the communities. Jesus' fresh understanding of Elah is truly extraordinary.*

Interrupting Mary's reflection, Jesus announced, "After dinner I want to put together another plan immediately for a gathering in the eastern hills around Bethsaida. Enjoy your celebration dinner and then quickly join me on the veranda."

Upon their entrance into the vestibule of Simon's home, Perpetua immediately welcomed everyone. Mary instantly missed Martha and Joanna. Taking a deep breath and trying to stay optimistic she decided, *I will make a good relationship with Perpetua and the female servants. And I really long for a bath and a home cooked meal.*

She asked Perpetua, "Have you heard that John and James' mother, Salome, is coming to join us?"

"Yes!" Perpetua answered. "John will bring her tomorrow. I know you will be more comfortable with another woman, especially when you spend so much time away from here." Mary nodded, appreciating her understanding and kindness.

As they prepared for Salome's arrival, cleaning the room and setting out fresh bedding, Mary told Simon's wife all about the last few days, "There were thousands of people, mostly families, all together sitting on rugs and blankets or on just the green grass in a huge field. Master Jesus stood on a hill overlooking the field. I think his voice carried better there, but the people were resourceful and echoed his words aloud so that everyone could understand."

Mary paused remembering the amazing day and then continued, "Lots of people interrupted Rabboni with good and respectful questions, unlike our experience on other occasions when most of the questions were disrespectful and provoking arguments.

"This time the crowd's attention hung on Rabboni's every word. There were moments when he caused the multitude to roar with laughter at some of the comments or questions asked by people in the audience. Yet most of the time the crowd listened quietly to his every word, thoughtfully. Many people stayed for two or three days, or left and returned the next day.

"I have never seen so many people in one place. From the questions they asked Rabboni, I could tell that they were inspired and interested in his message, and that some truly understood him to be a great teacher. There was much pride in the fact that he is Galilean.

"Perpetua, you should come with us to the next speech. You will be inspired," Mary suggested, noticing Perpetua's earnest attention.

Mary added, "On the boat sailing home, I know it's hard to believe but

Rabboni was already making plans for another speech and this one is in Bethsaida. He wants us to set it up within a few days in an even larger space. He expects the crowd to be even bigger as we have so many contacts around here and in the Bethsaida area. Simon and James are making plans and giving ideas of possible arenas."

After the room was prepared, she and Perpetua went to the kitchen to check on the preparation for the dinner to celebrate their successful venture. Unexpectedly, a servant rushed up to Perpetua and told her that visitors had arrived from Judea carrying an urgent message and had requested to give it personally to Rabbi Jesus without delay. Mary and Perpetua looked at each other, asking simultaneously, "Who could they be?"

Without being asked, Mary set off to inform Rabboni of the visitors, overhearing Perpetua instruct the servant to take the guests to the bath to wash their feet, as was the usual custom for guests.

Walking past the entrance, Mary quickly glanced at the formally dressed, bearded men standing in the portico. She guessed from their clothing that they were Judean. She had first observed men dressed like that in Tiberius when her uncle had pointed them out to her.

Three of them wore white linen ankle length tunics while the leader stood out rather noticeably. It was not only the way he carried himself, but his attire was the most elaborate and formal, a white tunic with blue striped edges and white tassels along the edges of the garment tied with a leather belt. He also wore an ornately colored scarf wrapped around his head over a skull cap. The heads of the others were uncovered, with their dark hair tied in a top knot. They all wore loose-fitting sleeveless mantles covering their tunics.

Mary proceeded to the back of the house and announced the guests. Moments later, Jesus entered the room with Simon, Andrew, James, Matthew, and Thomas, with Mary in the rear. From Mary's perspective, their spokesman appeared anxious and urgent. He was perspiring profusely, but he nodded his head properly in greeting.

Straightaway he explained his purpose in Hebrew, "We are followers of John the Baptist. Our leader sent us to you with an urgent message. He introduced himself, "I am Judas Iscariot, tasked to lead this expedition.

"Our leader ordered us to carry this urgent message from him to you. We traveled three days after meeting with him in prison, making only short stops in order to reach you as expeditiously as possible. Notwithstanding our exhaustion, we as his most devoted assistants fear for his life."

Noting their anxious demeanor, Jesus invited them into the receiving room. With concern for their comfort, he had them sit upon cushions. He instructed Mary to translate and she remained standing on the right side of the disciples. At the same time, Simon requested Perpetua to bring drinks and dinner for everyone.

The leader, Judas Iscariot, seemed anxious to fulfill his task. He formally took a knee with his right fist upon his chest, demonstrating deference toward Jesus. Then, standing again, he waited respectfully for Rabbi Jesus' acknowledgement and permission to speak.

Jesus nodded, "I am gladdened that John is contacting me. I have been praying for this moment. It seems that your message is urgent. Therefore, be at ease and proceed."

He turned to Mary and asked her to translate Judas' Hebrew into Aramaic. Caught by surprise, the newcomers gasped in astonishment at a Galilean woman knowing Hebrew. They did not hide their expressions of surprise and disapproval. Nevertheless, no one dared interrupt the solemn moment.

Judas began. "We are regretful that at this, our first meeting, we bring you ominous news. However, we must do so at the behest of our leader nonetheless. Permit me to explain his situation and then I will read his message.

"Surely you know that the Baptist was arrested nearly two years ago by Herod. He has been held in Machaerus palace dungeon on the top of a desolate mountain. It is located in the middle of the desert on the eastern side of the Dead Sea." The man paused as if formulating his speech, taking time to wet his dry throat with watered wine from his goblet.

Judas explained the reason for his master's imprisonment, with notable pride for his leader's action, "John righteously accused Herod's wife, Herodias, of adultery, a sin against Elohim's law. She took offense and pleaded with Herod for his arrest. Admittedly John's insult was audacious, but actually it was but a mere flash point in an already growing tension between our ministry and the Sanhedrin."

He continued, "The truth of the matter is that the Baptist drew large crowds, which made the Sadducees and Pharisees angry. Their congregations throughout the Jordan Valley and into Galilee shrank due to his charismatic preaching, as he attracted many of their young and old congregants.

"Herod relies on traditional dogmatic religious leaders to keep the people under tight control. You surely know that the priests and rabbis are his frontline in preventing revolts, insurrections, and more practically in keeping the coffers full in order to appease the Roman magistrate.

"There is no doubt that many young commoners' faith in Elohim has been revived by the Baptist's sermons and baptisms. John believes that we are surely the generation to receive the long prophesied Anointed One. They humbly came in droves, bringing their families, eager to be baptized and purified to be prepared to receive the One."

Judas continued eloquently, "You may ask why the religious leaders have not come to John's defense since he is the son of a notable high priest. It is because of their jealousy that they blindly ignore John's incarceration and refuse to officially register their dissent."

As Judas related this information to Jesus, Mary wondered what had caused John to seek him out. *Is Jesus' ministry becoming that widely recognized in Judea, as well? How did they hear of Jesus and did they expect him to intervene?*

From Judas' authoritative manner of speaking Mary deduced, *He is a Judean from the orthodox, educated class.* His manicured beard and unusually ornate scarf tied around his head gave him a dignified appearance. She guessed that he and Jesus were about the same age.

Pausing quickly to take another drink of the prepared beverage, Judas continued, "Now, I will explain why we have come to you." Turning to acknowledge his companions, he said, "We recently visited the Baptist in prison."

Then he reached inside his mantle and brought out a scroll. "Our Master gave us this handwritten scroll and commissioned us to bring it to you. The letter is personally addressed for your attention and sealed with wax."

Judas handed it to Jesus, who opened and read it, quickly understanding its message.

He handed the scroll back to Judas and asked him to read it aloud, again requesting Mary to translate the Hebrew into Aramaic.

Judas humbly bowed his head and unrolled the scroll and began to read, "Ever since I met you, Brother, in the Jordan River, I have been curious about you and truthfully have not been able to forget the moment we first met and the extraordinary event that took place. Admittedly, I dismissed the experience, honestly believing that I had been overcome by the heat of that day.

"Truthfully though, as I languish in this dismal place, curious thoughts come to mind that we, our missions, are connected. Also, that we are connected through what my parents revealed to me about my life's mission. I am speaking specifically about the prophecy my parents revealed to me and reminded me about throughout my childhood.

"The revelation given to my father goes like this: That I would go before the Anointed One in the spirit and power of Elijah and turn the hearts of the fathers to their children, and the disobedient and incredulous and unpersuadable to the wisdom of the upright, in order to prepare a path for the Lord and His people.

"As I sit here in prison, having only thoughts and memories to dwell on, I recall your baptism and its exceptional nature. Could it be that you truly are the Anointed One of Elohim, the Messiah that we are to expect? Or shall we wait for another?"

Neither Jesus' or John's disciples had any idea of the depth and meaning of the cryptic message. There was total silence as Judas rewound the scroll and handed it over to Jesus. Even Judas was unable to conceal his surprise at its content.

Surprisingly, Jesus handed the scroll back to Judas and asked that the inkwell and pen be given to him. "Judas, write my answer, word for word. Make sure you get every word that I say correctly. What I tell you is very important. I trust that you will record precisely my response." Explaining his intention to Judas, "I speak to you as if I am speaking to John, face to face."

Mary continued to translate into Aramaic, mirroring Jesus' commanding

Hebrew and using his extraordinarily solemn manner. Interestingly enough, and unknown to everyone, Mary quickly deduced what was going on.

Speaking in Hebrew, Jesus' voice and carriage was loud and powerful in the relatively small room. It reminded Mary of his voice and carriage when he had spoken a few days before to thousands of people. He surprised everyone. She wondered if Jesus was speaking to the visitors as if they represented the whole nation.

"John, your father, the Chief Priest, was one of the few who had the extraordinary honor and responsibility to attend El Shaddai in the Holy of Holies in the temple. Your father told you and others about your miraculous birth and the prophecy given by the angel.

"You correctly remember the prophecy. It was most certainly about your mission, which was that you would precede the Anointed One in the spirit and power of Elijah. In that way you would make ready a people prepared to receive the Anointed One.

"Yes, your inspiration is correct, but its usefulness is negated since you publicly denied that you are Elijah. Yes! It is I, Jesus, your brother, just as you ask through this letter. I am the One that you and our whole nation await.

"Why do you have to ask such a question now? Elohim needs only that you speak out what you know is true. He is awaiting your faithfulness. You clearly know this and just now admit that you know. You missed a very momentous occasion. Now you are confined and helpless to undo your lack of faith.

"I tell you this, that while you sit in prison those who are sick are healed, those who are blind receive their sight, and the deaf are made to hear. The poor have good news preached to them.

"However, because of your arrogance or stubbornness in being unwilling to support me, I now must redo your mission, going village to village preaching much the same as you, in order to begin my public mission given to me by Abba El Shaddai."

Jesus' countenance became crimson, dripping with perspiration, and there was anguish in his voice, "Blessed are the countryfolk who hear and believe me while you, the most prepared man of our faith, did not." He paused as if holding back deep-seated emotion.

"Further I ask you. Why did you go into the desert? What did you go there to do? Did you go there to find a person dressed in fine clothing? That is not where you go if you are looking for nice things. You find those things in the palaces of kings. So, what did you go into the desert to look for?

"John, you went to the desert because you knew that you were a prophet, more than a prophet, you are the return of Elijah, the one to proclaim directly to me, the Anointed One. You could have walked a straight path toward me. Our whole nation would have taken both of us seriously and all would have accepted and believed us.

"The truth is that, among all men who were ever born there is no one greater than you, John, yet he who is the least in the Kingdom of Heaven is greater than you."

Then Jesus confidently continued even more emphatically, "There is still time. I remind you, John, you *are* the returning Elijah! You are to give testimony to me. Your mission is to bring all of Israel to me. This is Elah's will. The whole nation is waiting and looking for you, the spirit of Elijah, to show them who the Anointed One is! Together, through our unity, we can bring the Kingdom of Abba Elah, now!"

This information was news to everyone. Jesus' disciples realized his seriousness more than ever before, and they began to shake as they understood John's true role. They began to experience the spirit of Elah and immense hope.

Judas, more than anyone else, immediately understood the profound implication of Jesus' words. He knew the Malachi prophecy which John himself had explained to him. As he wrote, he whispered it, *Elohim would send Elijah the prophet before the great and terrible day of the Lord!*

Now Rabboni chose to speak in Aramaic to his disciples. He wanted them to glean understanding and the importance of his relationship with John the Baptist. And Jesus demanded Mary to translate further in Hebrew to clarify for John's followers. "John the Baptist was born to introduce me to the religious establishment. His orthodoxically prepared father, a Chief

Priest, received that revelation before John's birth, just as I dictated to Judas. It was the main reason John went into the desert and chose to live such an ascetic life."

As Jesus spoke, Mary remembered meeting the prophet those many years ago as he stood in the cold waters of the great lake, calling everyone to be baptized. She thought, *He certainly was a humble man.* But for Mary this was the answer to the question she had entertained from several months ago. The depth of her understanding was profound as she whispered, *John is the return of Elijah!*

She already knew from her religious study that Elijah was to return, and also, she remembered the prayer her mother prayed every Passover dinner, calling Elijah the prophet to return and announce the Anointed One, longed for over the centuries. She whispered, *To make straight His way, a people prepared. That is why the religious people ask, "Where is Elijah?"*

She had been contemplating this for months since Jesus referred to Elijah's coming in his sermons. Now she realized the significance of John the Baptist. Now she comprehended, *The Baptist is Elijah for whom everyone is waiting!*

After translating Rabboni's words, Mary shocked everyone as she became filled with the spirit of Elah and shouted, "Elah Abba!" She fell on her knees and prayed in wonderment.

Everyone gaped at the woman's bizarre reaction. Mary forgot all dignity and composure as she became overwhelmed, praising this holy and profound moment. She forgot her position, decorum, and how she might appear to others. She began to cry in repentance and then joy, prostrating herself at Jesus' feet. She remembered her shameful reaction toward Jesus, when he called her his servant. She repented for being so slow to recognize Jesus' value.

Then, oblivious to everyone's reaction and still filled with the spirit, she requested, "Pardon me, Rabboni! Permit me to speak!"

Jesus answered her, "Mary, you are a blessed one. Speak openly, for your heart is more directed to heaven than any of your brothers."

Mary looked at Simon and explained her realization, trying to help him and everyone understand the powerful implications of Jesus' answer, "Elder

Simon, remember the prayer at Passover and that we set an extra plate out for Elijah, waiting for his return?"

Unsure of why she called his name familiarly in public, Simon's face turned scarlet from the breach of decorum. He was embarrassed and uncomfortable with the attention, as he felt all eyes on him. He did not really understand the significance of Jesus' answer, though he surely felt he should. Nevertheless, Mary made him the center of attention and everyone waited for his response. He nodded, but awkwardly admitted that he did not understand.

Mary continued, "In the scripture, the prophet Malachi predicts that Elijah will come first, shortly before the Messiah appears, announcing him to the nation. This is why all the educated religious men, who know the prophecy, ask about Elijah. Now we know that Elijah is already here."

Mary became ecstatic and proclaimed aloud, "Oh! my Elah Abba! Elijah has come! Rabboni, you are the Anointed One!" She was overwhelmed with joy and exclaimed as one finding a treasure, "How great is this day, that we are the first to witness and believe!"

Silent, everyone was more shocked at the woman than what she was proclaiming. Especially shocked were the followers of the Baptist, because they never imagined a woman would act in such an unconstrained manner, like one possessed by the devil. And she spoke excellent Hebrew, quoting the Holy Scriptures.

Scandalized and aghast they questioned, "How could this woman be so wildly arrogant and emotional?" They were distracted by her demonstration, which was hard on their eyes.

The depth of her respect and love for Jesus overflowed. Again, filled with the spirit Mary mutely knelt before him, gazing at him in ecstasy.

Jesus smiled at the innocence of the woman and praised her in front of all the men, "Mary, always feel free to speak openly and don't be afraid, for your heart truly understands. This awareness is a blessing to you and for us all. You are truly prepared by Abba Elah!"

Thus, because of Jesus' acceptance and praise of the woman, the men stoically tried to understand her. Since they were in shock, Jesus knew that it would take most of them time to truly appreciate the revelation about John.

Then he made an even more astonishing announcement, "I am related to your leader, John. His father is Zechariah, a chief priest in Bethlehem, and his wife, Elizabeth, is the sister of my mother's mother." He astonished everyone, including Mary, causing them to murmur among themselves.

Rabboni is related to John? Mary savored another revelation.

Jesus went on to explain the importance of his disclosure, "John was born six months earlier than me. If John understands his very important position, then together we will move the hearts of all the leaders of Israel and all the religious factions of Israel to understand Elohim's auspicious timing. Let's pray that John will be released from prison imminently."

He added, "However, without him and his support it will be very difficult for Jerusalem to receive me. I need… Elohim needs, the understanding and acceptance of the leaders of Israel. Otherwise, reaching the entire nation of Israel will take too much time, especially dealing with the inflexibility of the religious class.

"Our countrymen are taught to follow the leaders of their faith and John has the pedigree to be a respected leader, though he is unconventional. He has the people's attention."

Speaking strongly to Judas and his group, "Now do you understand his importance and how crucial his testimony is? Do you truly grasp its significance?"

Mary noticed the astonished expressions of the newcomers. Much like Simon earlier, some were red faced, others pale. She knew they needed time to appreciate the afternoon's fantastic revelation.

However, Jesus gave them no time. He instructed the devotees of John, "Rest well and go with haste at first light." Looking directly at Judas he commanded, "You must swiftly bring the scroll back to your mentor! There is no time to waste." Jesus added, "Tell him that I still have hope that we can work together."

Rabboni brought the meeting to a conclusion, asking, "Let us pray."

"Abba Elah, at John's conception You prophesied that he would make straight the way of Your Anointed One. The prophecy even said that he would come in the spirit and power of Elijah. I pray that John's response to this forthcoming message will be that of acceptance and that his timely action will follow. We have no time to lose. After all, John's entire adult life has been in preparation for this moment. I pray that John will never forget our meeting at the Jordan River."

Finally, Jesus added, "I pray that John, firstly and humbly, beseeches Your guidance."

Chapter 15

Jesus' Testimony

You are my beloved Son, whom I love,
With whom I am well pleased and find delight.
(Mark 1:11)

Jesus quietly left the meeting. Mary knew he craved communion alone with his Abba. She also felt compelled to follow him as he went out to a bluff overlooking the Sea of Galilee.

"Rabboni, this is Mary," she humbly announced her presence, not sure if he would approve.

Jesus turned and saw her standing about twenty steps away. He did not seem surprised or averse to her being there.

She relaxed and asked, "If it pleases you, I would like to support you with prayer, at a distance."

"Yes, Mary, but come over here," he called to her. He pointed to the sand about ten steps away from him, indicating that she should stand there. They prayed separately for about an hour until twilight.

Then Jesus invited her to sit upon a flat rock near enough for her to listen to him. The darkness gradually enveloped them. Jesus spoke to her, "I am grateful to speak to you. From now, I must make changes to my plan, and I would appreciate your consideration and any inspiration that you might have."

Mary blushed and nodded in the darkness, praying that she could empty herself and be a humble object. She was always ready to serve him any way she possibly could.

Jesus began to recount additional parts of his experience with John, "I am recollecting the day, two years ago, when I asked John to baptize me. It seems like yesterday. I went up to him to be baptized after searching for him a long time.

"John stood in the Jordan River. I waded through the water toward him and met him in the middle, boldly asking him to baptize me. He complied and submerged me in the river, probably exactly as he was used to doing with everyone, and baptized me.

"As he brought me up out of the water, he saw the spirit of a dove upon my shoulder. It was then that we heard Elah speak to me, 'You are My beloved Son and in you I am well pleased!' We were both shocked and incredulous.

"But just moments later, not knowing what to expect and myself totally flabbergasted, I noticed consternation in John's expression. Without explanation, he left me standing there in the water. But now since reading his letter, I don't doubt that he is haunted by our intense experience. Even now he contemplates its significance."

Mary listened, captivated by Rabboni's words.

Jesus continued after a time of silence, changing the subject as he pondered aloud, "Truthfully speaking, when I was young, I rebelled against my mother's strict adherence to Judaism. As long as I can remember, she repeatedly told me that I was a messiah. I didn't understand what that meant, and admittedly I was a mischievous son.

"She taught me to read and write, but I could not tolerate studying the religious scrolls because she could not answer any of my questions. So much of the scripture made no sense to me.

"When I was twelve, she took me to Jerusalem for religious training, but they rejected me for asking too many questions. The teachers determined that I was too obstinate and headstrong. This greatly disappointed her. After that she did her best to discipline me at home, which only made me more obstinate and resentful of her attempts to control me.

"I also refused to learn a trade. I was much more interested in hanging out in town, talking to simple people in my village. We often indulged in conversations that denigrated the sanctimonious and insincere religious leaders. All afternoon we would talk about how easy it was for the self-righteous leaders to stand in judgment of us, the lower stratum of society.

"I enjoyed speaking with characters like myself. We drank together and enjoyed talking and laughing. Whenever I needed money, I just worked in an orchard for the day and made enough to support my leisurely lifestyle. I was unruly and rebellious, but I felt free and happy.

"As I matured, I found myself arguing with my mother often, every day. I taunted her with different unjust situations. I threw in her face the hypocritical actions of the religious leaders and how they looked down on our family.

"I was not afraid to question her intractable faith, though I knew it pained her heart. There was one question that I was adamant about and not afraid to asked her, 'If Elah created us without the ability to take care of our loved ones, then what kind of Elah is He?'

"I frightened her because she thought Elah would punish me. She scolded me for questioning Elohim. This kind of thinking truly frightened her, which caused her to pray all day for me that I would not bring down Elah's wrath upon me or our family.

"At the same time, I was unhappy with myself for hurting her feelings. But I could not tolerate her blind and unquestioning acceptance of religious dogma. Therefore, I purposely escaped my home and roamed around the village, meeting and speaking with the common people, those who agreed with me.

"I began to think that self-preservative actions were natural and were not necessarily sinful. If a family had no food to feed their children or even themselves, how could they tithe?

"In my social interactions I observed that everyone looked for pleasure and happiness. Religious taboos were not strong enough to deter a person's desire for happiness. For most of society, self needs were all they knew throughout their lives. I surmised that if Elah created humans to seek for pleasure, even in the basest of ways, then it was not a human fault.

"Often, though, my conscience was heavy and uncomfortable because of the way I treated my mother and family. I knew that my mother heard gossip about me, lazing around and associating with despicable people, like drunkards and society's castaways. But I had no answer for my guilty conscience.

"Finally, in my early twenties, I began yearning for something more. I walked the countryside alone and there I found peace and freedom in the natural world, with no need to rebel. I came to deeply desire to know and understand what was true in this world. Someone, or something, had created the natural world. As I observed it, I wanted to understand it in my deepest heart. Also, I thought, 'What is the point of life if I am not happy?'

"I found in the hills and valleys, the streams and lakes, places where I could let go of my angst. There I felt peace, simplicity, and freedom without judgement and finally I began to feel content. There I could think clearly.

"I examined my anger toward the Jewish Elohim and pointless Jewish condemnations. I also began to feel ashamed of my disrespect and selfish behavior that hurt my mother and family. The emotions welled up in my heart as well as shame for my past behavior.

"While deep in thought, I remembered hearing tales of the untraditional and unorthodox preacher, John the Baptist. Impulsively, I decided to go in search of him, to possibly be baptized. Without a plan or even informing my mother, I set off.

"The possibility of meeting a radical preacher inspired me. The idea of making a new start was exciting. That day I went on my quest without returning home. I had no idea that my journey would take so long and be so difficult. My only intention was to find a way to help others, the pitiful people whom I had grown to love. I also hoped that through my experience I would return home with love for my mother and siblings.

"I left the hills around Nazareth unprepared, without money or provisions. With only a wineskin, I journeyed south to Judea.

"It was not easy finding John, as he was an iterant preacher and did not stay in one place long. By word of mouth, I tracked his path from town to town, moving all over Judea. In order to eat, I found temporary jobs, harvesting figs, olives, or grain, or anything that had no strings attached. At last, after several months, I finally found his most recent trail.

"During my long trek, I examined myself and the people that I had failed, like my mother and brothers and sisters. I realized that I was a useless individual. Also, I recognized my bitter disappointment toward my mother when she failed to arrange my marriage. I decided to resolve my antagonism and disappointments. I decided to use my trip to find answers and make a new beginning.

"Finally, I saw John standing in the Jordan River. For the first time since I began my quest, I took notice of how I looked, weatherworn and shabby. However, I was anxious to cleanse myself and be relieved of my anguish and bitterness. Without announcing myself, I waded through the water toward the Baptizer.

"As I came close to John, he was looking downward into the surface of the water, and he saw my reflection. Suddenly, surprised, he looked up at me and stuttered, 'Your reflection… you remind me… You look like my dead father.' He blinked and rubbed his eyes as though he had seen an apparition.

"As our eyes met, I wondered why I surprised him so. Uncannily, I felt and heard John's reaction to me, immediately feeling his disdain toward me, at first a stranger. But he knew me to be his cousin. This was my first realization. Then he thought vehemently, *The one whom I never wanted to meet.* Sensing his intense emotions, everything around us seemed to freeze in time and I felt his painful heart. It was as if I stood inside John's body and mind.

"John's cold heart shocked me. I felt his repressed resentments, his hateful loathing, his unforgiving judgement and accusation toward his father, Zechariah; hidden and unresolved feelings. Then I saw and felt John as a child.

"It all flashed before me: His strong and righteous nature as a child. The whispered rumors of his father's deceitful infidelity. His character naturally and vehemently reacted against his hypocritical father. This critical heart and unresolved disappointment drove him away from his home and orthodoxy and into the wilderness, physically and spiritually.

"His nature compelled him to be acutely judgmental. His parents knew this tendency and feared their son, because of their own secret. Therefore, when he finally learned the truth of his own father's sin of adultery, he responded passionately and broke his relationship with him and set out into the wilderness.

"When he was young, he was proud of his father, the honorable Chief Priest. Thus, he became a scholar of the sacred scriptures from an early age. He learned all about the vengefulness of Elah and how Elah hated sin. Thereby he became what he was taught, and there was no room for forgiveness or hypocrisy.

"John's whole persona was built on pride at being born into the tribe of Levi, the priestly family. He believed that his family was perfect beyond reproof. His childhood, until his twelfth year, was idyllic. However, his fervent but naive life changed abruptly in his thirteenth year. That was when he overheard the rumors of his father's secret, his other son by his mother's niece.

"From that moment, his life was thrown into chaos. For years he tried to ignore the shocking truth about his father, living in denial, afraid to face the truth. At first, because of his staunch unforgiving character and his pride, he refused to believe the sinful rumors.

"However, as John matured, his scrupulous nature drove him to ask his mother, Elizabeth. Shocked that he had discovered their secret, and knowing her son's righteous nature, she denied it. But John would not let it go. Finally, after his father's death, he got her to tell him the truth.

"Completely devastated and disillusioned, John remembered his mother's explanation of the scandalous truth. What made it worse was that she accepted the infidelity as being inspired by Elohim.

Revolted, John thought, *How could my father have done such a thing? Was he totally out of his mind? As an honored priest of the tribe of Levi, he knew the commandments of Moses. Did he not fear Elohim? Did he not love his family and know that he risked losing everything? How could he stand before the people as a hypocrite and preach the Mosaic Law, knowing he did such a thing?*

"He cursed and hated his father. Filled with cynicism, he left his home and his inheritance and he never resolved that resentment or disappointment. He hiked into the wilderness of southern Israel near the Dead Sea, where a fundamental and fanatical sect of Judaism, known as the Essenes, lived. He was attracted to them because they sought purification from all hypocrisy, living a stark life of poverty. He rejected all of his past, his patrimony, even forgoing his inheritance of following in his father's footsteps to become High Priest.

"Though the lifestyle was harsh, he followed the strict countercultural society. But even his daily self-castigation did not help him escape his hatred. John adhered to their lifestyle for a while but then went his own way."

Jesus stopped speaking and glanced at Mary to see if she was listening. Because of the full moon he could see her in the darkness. All was silent except for the sound of the crickets and the water washing ashore. He turned and walked toward the edge of the hill with his back to her.

"Mary, I appreciate you listening. Because of your uncommon understanding of scripture and especially your profound appreciation for the prophecy regarding John, you are the only one at this time to understand my heart and the seriousness of the moment. There is more but I don't want to burden you. Would you like to go back inside? Are you tired?"

Mary appreciated Jesus's concern but nevertheless she wanted him to use her as a sounding board to unburden himself and work out this complicated relationship. She was willing to help him. "No, my Rabboni. I am not tired, and I am here to support you," Mary answered, hoping that he was relieved enough to find a solution to this problem.

Going back to his previous position, Jesus sat upon the earth. The darkness enveloped them, but with the moments of fleeting light from the moon Mary could see the glistening of tears in his eyes.

Jesus continued where he had left off, "I was aware that John tried to hide his reaction to me, but oddly enough I was in his head. This was his most feared moment, meeting me face to face. He knew, without a doubt, that I was his half-brother and that he was being forced to accept the reality. *Yes,* John thought, *you do resemble my father, even more than I do!* He could no longer deny the rumor. He knew without a doubt that the story was true. Finally, he accepted the reality, and admitted, *This man is the son of my father and my mother's niece.*

"Acknowledging the reality helped open up his consciousness and suppressed emotions, the hatred along with the adulteration of all that he believed. Divided in mind, heart, and reality, he, the great purifier, almost lost his composure. Even though the situation was forcing him to confront his demons, the rigidity of his personality and arrogance would not let him. He could not imagine an acceptable point of view and humble himself."

Jesus paused. In the silence, Mary heard him sobbing. He stood and walked a distance away, stumbling in the darkness.

Mary did not know what to do. She could not console Rabboni physically, so she prayed for him and repented for John. She realized a personal lesson, *My stubbornness prevents me from recognizing my sins.* Thus, she prayed, *Please Abba Elah, help me to recognize my imperfect peculiarities and change them, that I may be more useful to Jesus and to You!*

After a while, assuming that Jesus wanted to be alone, Mary started to get up and go back to the house, but Jesus returned and requested her to stay, "I am sorry for keeping you so long. I know you are tired."

Mary responded, "No, my Rabboni. I am happy to wait upon you if I can lighten your weariness. If you will permit me, I would like to stay."

"Thank you, Mary. As always, I am inspired by your humble mindfulness. Speaking this through helps me formulate a plan to go forward. Abba needs me to go forward, but I must make the plan."

Jesus continued, "Experiencing John's emotions was almost more than I could stand. I tried to clear my thoughts and emotions of his, but it was not easy. At the same time, I was struggling with myself. I was immature and indignant. I had little patience in those days for arrogant religious fools. I had had enough of his insolence and almost gave up. However, my nagging conscience stopped me from leaving and, now that I think of it, Elah was reminding me that I was there to make a new beginning. Therefore, I remained standing before him.

"I did regret the pain I caused him, and it was very painful to me as well. But nonetheless, spurred on by something more than my own will, I continued with my request. 'Baptize me,' I demanded.

"My words seem to shatter the silence and his spirit. My demanding attitude surprised him and initially when he tried to speak he was mute. But, after he cleared his throat, in a shaky and barely audible voice, he denied my wish. 'I cannot baptize you,' he said, as if rebelling against his own principles.

"I was shocked by his response. However, I surprised myself when I did not turn away from him. I stood still with an expression of determination. I did not budge. He was about to turn away, when out of nowhere I snapped out words that I did not understand at the time, 'You must baptize me, as it is the will of El Shaddai Elohim that you pass on the inheritance of our nation to me.' It stunned me and John looked as though I had slapped him in the face.

"He was astounded, but understood my request. The words reminded him of his original destiny and the prophecy at his birth. His spiritual turmoil became obvious. He threw back his head and covered his ears as if trying to ignore the words gnawing deep in his psyche, his father's words, *You will go before the Lord to make a people prepared. You will go forth in the spirit and power of Elijah.*

"John squirmed and wrestled with his self-centered consciousness. Again questioning, *How can this illegitimate man tell me what I should or shouldn't do? How does he know about my destiny? This vile…he cannot possibly be the anointed one of Elohim! This is not the one I am expecting.*

"Minutes went by as John searched for an excuse not to baptize me. However, the words I had spoken jolted him back into the physical reality, reminding him of the dozens of eager believers standing on the shore witnessing his actions.

"Caught in the impossible situation he deliberated, *The crowd is waiting for me to baptize them! I am chosen by Elohim to purify the people of this nation. I must continue with them and not be distracted by this degenerate man, who comes out of nowhere.*

"He realized everything he did was on display for all to see. He knew they were watching his every movement and as yet he hoped that they had not noticed his struggle.

"To get on with his duty, John breathed in deeply and forced himself to regain his composure and dignity as 'The Baptist.' And thus, because of the multitude of witnesses, he insincerely and irreverently relented. 'Yes, of course!' he nodded and agreed, though he could not look me in the eyes. 'I will baptize you,' he announced. And in a dramatic and audacious manner, John loudly explained to me what he was going to do.

"I knew that it was taking all the willpower he could muster. Playing to his faithful audience, he made the motions. Admittedly, I was becoming impatient with his pompous attitude. But again, I reminded myself of the reason that I was there, to make a new start. I remained humble to him, although it was very difficult.

"Finally, he lowered me dramatically into the water. But as John lifted me up out of the waters, I saw the Heavens open and a light, bright as the sun, shine down upon us. The spirit of Elah, like a dove, descended upon me and spoke, 'You are My beloved Son and in you I am well pleased.'

"I stood stunned in silence, and noticed that John was likewise speechless and in shock. I watched him standing in the water, staring at me in awe and displaying a completely changed mien of unbelievable deference toward me. My ears were deaf for a moment, while everything was frozen around me.

"Though I could tell that John had also perceived something like what I had experienced, I could no longer hear or feel his thinking. He seemed to be having trouble breathing and stood in silence. He grabbed his chest as if in pain and stepped backward in the water. Dazed he spoke the words, 'You are the one that I am waiting to proclaim, aren't you?'

"At that time, I had no idea what he was talking about. It seemed that he believed his own words and became overpowered by emotion. He fell on his knees in the water and proclaimed loudly for his audience to hear, 'I saw the Spirit descend as a dove upon this man and heard *Behold the Anointed One!*' He bowed his head in deference to me.

"Many on the shore, upon hearing John's words fell on their knees modeling John. There were clamors of awe and wonder. Those who caught the moment explained what they saw to the rest of the witnesses, who understood the majestic moment as they roared in praise.

"John loudly reiterated, 'This is the Anointed One! The one that we have all been awaiting. The one that you have heard me predict. The one whose sandals I am not fit to untie.' The whole crowd was spellbound. The scene was a mix of joy and confusion.

"When I heard all the turmoil and saw John's reaction and change of heart, I was confused and stunned myself. This intense experience was a new one for me! I was not able to think clearly, and I became emotional. But then I remembered, I had come to be baptized by John to make a new start. I knew that the words I perceived and spoke during the whole experience with John did not come from my consciousness. It truly was a new beginning, but I did not know what to do next.

"John turned and returned to his followers, leaving me alone in the water. I also was stunned as I stumbled back through the water to the shore, and I decided to find a place of solitude to think everything through. I wanted to examine and understand the whole experience so that I would not forget it.

"Also, the awareness of John's hatred and perception of me weighed heavily on my mind and soul. Nevertheless, I felt compassion toward him. I also began to feel regret for the anguish I had caused my mother and family. I truly wanted to figure out how to restore my relationship with them.

"But also, in the moment the words and the whole experience were very powerful in my consciousness. I needed to analyze the experience. I knew that in its meaning I would find my new beginning. Without a plan, I let my legs carry me out of the water and onto a dirt path, though I did not know or care where I was going. All the while I was hearing the words, playing over and over in my consciousness, *You are My beloved Son and in you I am well pleased.*

"From there I walked, remembering the euphoric feeling and thinking of the words and the meaning of The Being who spoke to me. It must have been the Almighty Elah. I realized that my experience had little to do with an angry and vengeful Elah, for if it had I would have been struck dead. I recognized that even though I had lived a life causing heartache for a lot of people, there was no expectation of payment for those misdeeds but rather a welcoming parental like embrace. The love that I felt, without any condition, no anger or rancor, is what inspired me to want to change.

"As I walked, I was aware that I was walking into an arid land without provisions, but I did not care. I felt that I was being led, leaning only on Elah's care and guidance, as we walked together."

Jesus paused. The cloudless night was quiet and it was late. Mary waited and prayed, *I am humbled that my Lord trusts me enough to tell me his astonishing account of his experience with John the Baptist. I will treasure this in my heart and never forget it.*

Finally, Rabboni stood facing away from her, and asked her to return to the house. He thanked her for her attention and support and added, "I will remain here a while longer. Abba be with you."

Mary retired to her room.

Chapter 16

Respite

You prepare a table before me in the presence of my enemies.
You anoint my head with oil, my cup overflows.
(Psalm 23:5)

The day after the Baptist's men left, John arrived with his mother, Salome. After greeting Jesus and his fellow Friends, he explained, "My father, Zebedee, brought us in his fishing boat. This is how we could come here so quickly."

Immediately, Mother Salome approached Jesus and prostrated herself in front of him, respectfully and with a bright countenance. Mary noticed and mused, *Unknown to this woman, she has brought a brightness and eagerness of spirit that, like fresh air, has cleared away the intensity of yesterday's visit by the Baptist's followers. She has also brought another feminine hand to assist our Lord, for which I thank You Abba.*

Salome became emotionally overwhelmed, expressing her gratitude with tears of joy, "Dear Rabboni Jesus, thank you for allowing this humble woman to do all I can to serve you. From all that my son John reported to me, and all he has done since I last saw him, I can see that you are preparing this land to receive the Anointed One.

"I am grateful to attend you. I am also proud that my sons want to support you and I have encouraged them to be your most responsible associates. They believe you are certainly doing the will of Elah, as do I! Praise be to Him," as she pointed upward indicating Elah. "I believe we are witnessing Elah's promise that our countrymen have long awaited! Even though I am only a humble woman, I am proud to have this opportunity and I will do my best to serve you and not hold you back."

Quickly she grabbed her sleeve and dabbed away the tears of gratitude that spilled over her cheeks. Then she reached into a large pocket under her sleeve and pulled out a bag full of coins, "My husband and I proudly offer this to you." She bowed her head and extended her hand in humble offering.

Immediately, Jesus rose and helped the matron to stand. With the genuine heart of a mother, Salome placed the gift into his hands. Surprised, Jesus expressed his appreciation, "We have received much love from Elah today, especially through your wonderful family. This gift comes in a timely manner and we are grateful! Salome, we are inspired by your humility and generosity. Also, I believe sister Mary appreciates your company as well. I know that everyone is grateful for your willingness to help in our effort.

"Mother Salome, I want you to know that I have given your sons a title. We call them the Sons of Thunder because of their passionate and enthusiastic energy. I now see where they get their notable characters. Let us celebrate your arrival!" Jesus declared.

Mary noticed that Jesus' spirit was refreshed from the previous day, *I don't see a bit of hopelessness or anxiety.*

Then Rabboni invited Mother Salome, "Come and participate with us in our morning meal." He motioned to Mary to begin serving everyone from the platter of fresh bread and cheese.

John was happy to be back with his brothers, and reported, "Rabboni, thank you for permitting my mother to join us. She's been praying to join us and be a part of our work for a long time. When I reached home and asked her if she would like to come, she immediately rejoiced, 'Son, you know my answer. You know I wanted to come even sooner.'"

He explained, "This has been her wish since the time you came to dinner, nearly two years ago. She planned and prepared for my father's approval. Ahead of time she arranged much food for him. Thus, it only took her an afternoon to prepare to leave home."

"I see how Abba Elah has prepared your whole family to participate with me at this significant time," Jesus exclaimed.

After breakfast, Jesus announced that he planned to go to the lake side for the morning, "Simon, organize everything and let us leave as soon as possible."

Simon began doling out responsibilities, "Mary, settle Salome's personal things and as you prepare our supplies for the whole day, introduce Salome to the kitchen staff and Perpetua. Don't take long."

Eager to help Salome and make her feel comfortable, Mary introduced her to Perpetua and her staff. But at the same time, she also was aware of Rabboni's plan to leave as quickly as possible. Mary guessed that Jesus wanted to have a chance to let everyone relax one more day after their campaign in Gennesaret. Therefore, Mary focused on her responsibility and turned to Salome, "Mother Salome, let me show you to our room."

John brought Salome's bag and Mary noticed her expression of admiration toward her son. It reminded her of her own mother's expression when she left her home. With a fleeting thought she wondered, *Maybe, one of these days when we travel near Magdala, I will get to visit her.* Taking a deep breath, Mary remembered her responsibility and thought to herself, *I will have lots of time to think about that later.*

Salome, a talkative woman not at all shy upon meeting all the strangers, went on and on about Rabboni Jesus, "He is very warm, isn't he? I can't believe I am finally here. Though I am middle-aged, I am strong, and I pray I will be helpful and not become a burden to him."

Happy for her company but a bit distracted, Mary tried to stay focused on their schedule. She knew that Simon would be calling them soon. They quickly arranged Salome's modest possessions and then proceeded to the kitchen to prepare the supplies needed for their outing.

With motherly warmth, Salome continued, "Mary, as the only woman disciple, you must be overwhelmed with all your responsibilities. Please, teach me everything you know, and I will gladly share your burden. I promise to catch on quickly even though I am older. I want to receive your instruction. Let me assist you."

While Mary prepared the food and drink, she went over their responsibilities, "I usually prepare Rabboni's two skins, one with watered wine and the other with only water, a bag of food and a bag with extra sandals and a towel. Perpetua helps me with the rest, all the wineskins and food for each brother.

"Finally, when all is prepared, I carry Rabboni's wine and waterskins and my drinks and personal bag. Brother Phillip carries the heavy communal food parcel and Rabboni's personal bag. Each brother carries his own wine and waterskins and a personal bag. This is our usual practice on short trips, but if it is a long one then we usually load a wagon," Mary explained, all the while hastily preparing everything. "Today, I prepared an allotment of bread and cheese for fourteen. Each trip is different, though, depending on who is going, where we go, and the variety of food provided by Perpetua."

Salome was amazed at Mary's organization and also the amount that she carried. "I see that I can be of help to you, Mary, my dear. You are so young and yet you carry so much responsibility. Let me carry some of those skins."

Mary answered her, "Yes, I am very grateful for your help! Martha and Joanna taught me everything. They had to go back to their homes, but they plan to return. I'm also very lonely for womanly companionship. I'm grateful you are here!"

James entered the kitchen, "Mary, is everything prepared? Simon is calling for everyone to come together." He smiled at his mom, bowing respectfully, "Mother, I imagine that Mary is happy you joined us. Did she introduce you to Perpetua, the staff, and our lifestyle?

"Yes, son. She is a very good teacher and I feel we can help each other. I am so glad I came. Thank you!" Salome said vivaciously, not at all showing her age of over forty years.

Jesus led his disciples to a grassy knoll overlooking the Sea of Galilee. Facing toward the south, Jesus pointed, "Ahead of us, both physically and metaphorically, is the land of Judea." He continued, "Let us have a restful day for we have much work ahead of us. Abba Elah has great expectations for us and He is proud of our work together for His providence. Take a deep breath and know that Elah is with us."

After a brief silence, he turned his followers' attention to the many skiffs sailing far and near. Together they watched the fishing vessels coming and going to and from the docks. Everyone delighted in the gentle breeze and their bird's-eye panoramic view of the distant eastern and western shores.

The tops of the mountains to the west were shrouded in mist but all around them the waters were fresh and clear. Some of the shoreline below was a smooth beige sand while other areas were mottled with grayish brown rocks. Yellow and green flora growing along the shallow water defined the shore and the beginning of the land. Seagulls flew over them, squawking and scavenging for food.

Mary took in the energy of the nature around them. The sensation was invigorating and mesmerizing as gentle breezes wafted off the water. As she gazed at the azure waters, an occasional gust of wind caught her scarf, whipping it to and fro, and she noticed the sea breeze rippling upon the surface of the water. Everyone listened to the comforting the ebb and flow of the waters, the birds calling above, and the sound of sudden gusts of wind. It was very relaxing.

Mary prayed, *Thank you, Abba for giving us this special time together. We can experience Your peace and calm together with Rabboni and make a new beginning with him. Let us offer all our recent experiences to You, our Gennesaret campaign and the visit of the Baptist's men and the new arrival of Mother Salome.* Then she added, *Dear Abba, let this moment soothe Jesus' mind and heart as he is greatly concerned for John and Your providence.*

She noticed that Rabboni's steady and calm appearance and his attention to everyone was no different today than any other day, but she was sure that John's failure was a major concern of his. Nevertheless, she guessed that Jesus did not hold a grudge and would want to find a way to get John released from prison. She watched him as he engaged each man tirelessly, giving and giving, one by one, pointing out the beauty of the scenery and the fishing boats below. He continued giving goodwill, encouragement, and compassion to everyone.

This was a good time for Mary to review all her many experiences from the past weeks, *So many experiences…witnessing… bringing the unexpected cascade of thousands of humble people to meet and hear Jesus speak truth. Rabboni's astounding miracle. …multiplying food for the hungry people. Lines of people begging Rabboni to be healed. And my dear sisters, Martha and Joanna, leaving and now the arrival of Salome.*

My favorite memory, though, was accompanying Jesus as he walked among the people after his speech. Watching him generously spend hours going person to person, family to family, praying with them…interviewing every person and family that approached him. After he understood their needs… placing his hands upon their heads, shoulders, backs, or even touching their diseased bodies, all the while sincerely and compassionately praying for each individual's concerns.

Overwhelmed with emotion, Mary found a rock to the side away from everyone where she could sit in peace. Listening to the soothing sounds of waves gently lapping against the sandy coast below, she recalled Rabboni's testimony to her the previous night. Her heart was so full that she had to fight the release of brimming tears.

Suddenly she heard a hearty laugh from Jesus that diverted her emotion. Smiling, Mary glanced over at him and watched his mannerisms while he talked and laughed with James and the other fishermen. Rabboni's light-hearted voice brought Mary out of herself and back to the present. She watched him standing in the midst of his men, commenting and pointing to a particular fishing boat. She made a personal note to herself never to forget this joyful moment.

"There, over there," Jesus enthusiastically shouted, "That seining one! Am I right?" as he pointed to the nearest craft. Everyone's attention went to the craft bringing in its catch. Animated and youthful, Jesus continued demonstrating the knowledge of fishing that he had gleaned from his teachers, the fishermen standing around him. Mary understood, *He is truly seeking a bond with them, in their environment.*

Again, Jesus shouted enthusiastically and pointed. Mary, feeling lighter now, continued taking in the moment. *He's like an excited and youthful adolescent.*

"Look, that vessel is leaning to the starboard side. It must be full. Am I correct, Elder Simon?" He asked the expert fisherman, Simon, standing stoically beside him. Mary was surprised to see a half smile from the fisherman, showing his apparent enjoyment. She noticed Simon's unassuming smile, *Oh! how he controls his strict character!*

Jesus yelled over the loud wind gusts and splashing waves, "Is that why they are preparing to return to port?" Again, Mary noticed Rabboni's desire to show off his knowledge and interest in fishing to his men.

The elder nodded, but to Mary it seemed as if he was trying to maintain his strict facade, "Yes, Rabboni. You warm my heart with your genuine love for the sea! It seems that you have learned a lot about our craft. Thank you for honoring and demonstrating your sincere appreciation for our humble profession."

Mary was overcome by emotion when she suddenly realized how much Simon longed to be upon his skiff, *It is truly his sacrifice. He surrendered everything for his love of Rabboni.* At the same time, she appreciated all the men and women standing together, sharing the same oneness of heart and determination for Jesus' mission. She suddenly grasped the realization and importance of her life, living and walking with Jesus. She proudly reaffirmed her service toward this man, the Anointed One.

It was about noon and the hot sun was beating down upon their head coverings, which helped to deflect the heat. Mary continued observing everyone relaxing and enjoying each other. Just as Jesus had intended, it was an unforgettable moment allowing everyone to release the tension of the past few days.

Finally, Jesus turned and gathered everyone together near the path back to Simon's home and asked, "Do you feel refreshed?"

Everyone in unison shouted joyfully in agreement, lifting their hands in jubilation. John, overcome with joy, suddenly shouted, "Rabboni, we treasure this precious time spent with you!"

Jesus concluded by turning their joy toward the Creator, "After gazing out at Abba's creation, we are refreshed. The gentle sea breezes, the tranquil waters, and even the hardworking fishermen honing their skills are the reflection of the harmony of the Creator's consciousness. It is His way of relieving us of our anxiety and tension, giving back to us solace, healing, and courage."

Closing his eyes and taking a deep breath of the sea air as if to hold it in his memory, Jesus turned to Mary, "Let's have a meal together."

Mary, Salome, and Phillip brought out the wineskins and food for all to share. Mary respectfully handed Rabboni his bread and cheese and his wineskin. She and Salome took a place beside the circle, to Jesus' right side, and enjoyed their meal. Mary noticed everyone's refreshed demeanor, and it felt much more personable and direct than any other time together.

Jesus spoke, "Together we worked hard and gave our utmost effort to bring Abba's love and new understanding to these chosen people. Abba prepared for centuries for this very moment that we live in. Because of your efforts many of our countrymen are hopeful and inspired for their future.

"We still have so much more to do here in Galilee. I planned to speak in Bethsaida, but we must go to the south to support the Baptist instead. Afterwards we will return to Galilee. Let us carry the momentum of our success with us and bring the light of Abba Elah's love to Judea. After we are able to help the Baptist, with Abba's help, we will return. As usual, Abba will open a way.

"Therefore, we will leave as soon as our preparation is complete, by this evening but hopefully sooner. We must support John and his disciples.

"As most of you know, in Judea there are differences in customs and language. However, whether Judean or Galilean, we are all of one family, children of Abraham. Let's use our experiences here in Galilee and expand the good news to every village and town in our whole nation of Israel."

Chapter 17

James' Testimony

*The vineyard of the Lord Almighty is the nation of Israel
and the people of Judah are the vines He delighted in.*
(Isaiah 5:7)

Jesus gave instructions to Elder Simon but spoke for everyone to hear, "Organize the preparations and include the wagon and both mules to carry everything because we may be there a while."

On the walk back home, Simon began allocating responsibilities. He assigned Mary, James, and Salome as a team to shop for supplies in the Capernaum marketplace. He handed the bag of money that Salome had given Rabboni earlier into James' hands, adding strictly, "Be frugal with the money. We don't know how long we will be away."

The three were pleased with the arrangement and set to work loading the empty water and wine urns and food baskets. The two women quickly prepared their own personal belongings while James readied the mules and wagon.

When they came back together, James announced, "We will go to the public well first and then to the market." Mary could see how overjoyed Salome was to work with her son. As they began their trip to the market, James asked his mother to sit upon the top board of the wagon. Seeing she was about to refuse, James gave her a look that both of them understood. Salome accepted his direction without further discussion.

Leading the mules, James and Mary set forth along the road. Though it had been nearly a year since Mary joined their group, she and James had never had a chance to speak about their first meeting. Mary thought, *Perhaps we will have an opportunity to catch up on all that we've experienced since then. I remember James told me a short time after I first joined them that he wanted to tell me his testimony of how he met Jesus.* She looked forward to hearing it as they both kept an eye on Salome sitting on the top board.

The clippity-clop of the mules along the dirt road gave a nice rhythm to their steps. With brotherly enthusiasm James began, "Sister Mary, I'm happy that you joined us and I'm amazed that your health is so resilient. Elah is good to have brought you to us and Rabboni. Do you know that everyone recognizes your importance to Rabboni and to all of us?"

Mary blushed from his remark and noticed his quirky way of expression especially while talking. He hadn't changed a bit since their first meeting. He punctuated each phrase by waving his hands and arms, expressing almost everything passionately, as if his words could not emphasize his meaning enough, and he hardly took a breath between ideas.

She noticed that both James and his mother used the same mannerisms in slightly different ways. Mary recognized the similarity in Salome and James' personalities, both garrulous and vivacious. They never seemed to tire and were always full of spunk, both in energy and words. *Now I see why Jesus calls James and his brother Sons of Thunder.* She smiled thinking, *I love having this opportunity and time together. It is a good time to get to know him. He is like the brother I never had.*

He continued, "…without you, things would be difficult, I will even say, impossible! Thanks to you, we can actually fully understand when someone speaks in Hebrew. Thanks for all you do, especially assisting Jesus and taking care of all of us. And let me repeat, translating Hebrew. Though most of us understand some words, you help us to understand completely. And thank you for helping us with scriptures and explaining the value of John the Baptist and his historic role, as well." James finally took a deep breath and enthusiastically shouted, "Elah bless you!"

Amused, Mary thought, *Finally, he took a breath!* They both looked back at Salome, who was happily looking around at the countryside.

Mary responded, "I am grateful for your support also. There are times when I lose my confidence because, as a woman, I sometimes feel out of place. I get the feeling that most of the time Elder Simon does not know what to think of me."

James answered, obviously understanding about Elder Simon's barely tolerant attitude toward her, "Sister Mary, thank you for being frank with me. I understand what you mean and I will happily come to your aid, anytime."

As they walked toward the town, there was a lull in their conversation. Mary listened to the creaking sound of the wagon wheels and the rhythm of the mule hooves hitting the ground. She glanced up at Salome and noticed her clinging to the side rail due to the constant unexpected jolting as the wooden wheels hit rocks or rolled over holes in the road.

Then James boldly broke the silence, "By the way, Mary, so much happened to me shortly after first meeting you. My whole life changed."

Not wanting to interrupt him, Mary helplessly remembered that horrific time after she met him and thought, *Brother James, my life changed also. But you have no idea how Elah used our acquaintance to keep me alive during all those long and hopeless years.* She nodded though, indicating that she was interested to hear his story. Truthfully, she wondered what he remembered about her.

James began his tale, "Do you remember that preacher who called the people to enter the water to repent and be baptized? That was John the Baptist! Do you realize that?"

"Yes!" Mary nodded, picturing the preacher's bizarre performance and clothing. *It was my first time hearing the word, Repent! That word confounded me so. I struggled with it intensely.* Immediately it took her back to the days of misery. *It was the first time I realized that even Hebrews needed to repent.*

Then she recalled the first time she cried out to her mother, *Please forgive me! I have caused you so much pain.* Now tears of gratitude came to her eyes and she shivered, remembering her past tortured life, her arrogance, and at last her contrition. Walking in silence, Mary took deep breaths which helped relieve her misery from those times. After a few minutes of noticeable silence except for the sound of hooves hitting the dirt path, Mary resolutely pushed the painful memories away. Finally, she commented to James, "We were young then and many years have passed. I've learned so much since then, haven't you?"

He nodded in agreement, noticing a change in her usual positive nature. After a few moments of uncomfortable silence, James changed the subject and began his story.

"A few days after I met you, my brother, John, told me that after listening to the preacher he got really inspired. He nagged me to go with him the next day to 'have a listen' to the Baptist. He was unusually excited, so much so that he piqued my interest. You know John, he's pretty cool headed. Right? Well, that got my attention and then he whispered to me, 'The Messiah is coming, soon!'"

Mary almost laughed at James' amusing characterization. He was actually a good story teller, and that helped to lighten up her spirit.

"John explained to me that he went into the water to be baptized because the Baptist said everyone had to be baptized or cleansed, in order to recognize the Anointed One. It was because of John's unusual enthusiasm that I became interested. He actually reminded me of my mother talking about 'the coming of the Anointed One' nearly every day during our childhood.

"Therefore, we went together and I was ready to be baptized. Well, to make the story short, we both became so inspired and excited about the Anointed One that we decided to drop everything and follow him.

"Not surprisingly, our mother also got baptized and caught up in the spirit. Like I said, she always believed that the Messiah would come in her lifetime. Deeply inspired, she gave us her blessing and encouraged us to go and find the Messiah. She told us, 'If you find him, come back and tell me!' She also got our father to give us his blessing and permission to leave home to follow the Baptist.

"So…. we traveled with John around the Sea of Galilee and then south to Judea. There, for the next year or so, John focused on the Jordan River valley. We traveled from town to town in Judea, drawing large crowds of people, and we lent a hand to help John baptize. Mostly our job was to manage the crowds. At first, it was really exciting."

James comically began impersonating the Baptist holding his hand in the air and pontificating, "The Messiah is mightier than I! Repent and cleanse your soul. Make yourself ready for His coming! For I am not even worthy to untie his sandals!"

Mary laughed at James as she remembered her own experience witnessing the Baptist's unusual gestures.

"I was twenty then. Though our life was ascetic and often uncomfortable, it was thrilling. We felt free and often filled with the spirit. However, after time went by, about nine months or so, and still no Messiah, we began to get restless and disillusioned. Thereafter, slowly we lost our enthusiasm and began to doubt John's postulation. Impatiently, we began to consider going home.

"Then one day, as we performed our usual duties preparing the supplicants for baptism and keeping orderly lines, we noticed a shabbily dressed man coming from upstream. I thought, *He's out of line. How could he be so bold, approaching the Baptist without going through us and waiting his turn like everyone else!*

"It was our duty to stop any rabble-rousers, but it all happened so fast as he made his through the water that we did not have time to stop him. I ran into the water to protect the Baptist. But I noticed that they were speaking together as if acquainted with each other. So, I relaxed and went back to the bank of the river.

"They conversed for an unusual amount of time, a lot more time than anyone else would spend with John. We could not catch all their words clearly because everyone in line was complaining and angry that the man got ahead of them.

"However, at one point, it appeared that John got angry and actually refused to baptize him. I couldn't believe what I heard. Why would John hesitate to perform the ritual? It surprised me as he was always eager to carry out the ceremony. We never saw him turn anyone away. I became really curious. And I wondered what they were talking about.

"However, after a while, John glanced over at us, as if to check if we were watching. Then he turned quickly back to the man. He made his usual gestures, but this time more dramatic than usual, like he was performing for all of us on the riverside. Then, he lowered the man into the water."

James paused, contemplating the whole memory, "As I said, we could not hear their words, but when the man came up out of the water, the most unusual thing happened. The Baptist's expression completely changed to astonishment. His countenance beamed with exuberance, as he proclaimed loudly, 'Behold the Lamb of Elohim!'

"My brother and I both heard his words clearly. We looked at each other and were stunned! Believe it or not, many on the shore did not hear John's words as clearly as we did. So, my brother and I had to repeat the words over again to everyone standing around. It surprised us all. We all shouted in joy!

"Caught by emotion and not knowing what to do, my brother and I ran into the river. But before we could reach them, we were even more astonished when the Baptist turned and left Jesus standing there. He waded past us in a daze and into the crowd on the bank. I don't think he was even aware of us.

"Turning toward everyone, he announced to us, kind of nonchalantly, 'The Spirit that led me to baptize with water told me to watch and wait. It said that I would know the One who baptizes with the Holy Spirit. The one whom I would not be worthy to untie his sandals!' He continued, 'As I was baptizing him, the heavens opened and a white dove descended and remained upon him.'

"What John did next contradicted his glorious testimony. He sat down on a log and continued to mumble, completely disconnected from all of us standing around him. He ordered me, in a confused and irritated manner, 'Bring me my wineskin. Perhaps I am sun struck.' And mumbling almost incoherently under his breath, 'I certainly saw a white dove.' Then the Baptist made another aside comment, 'But he is not the one whom I expected.'

"Immediately, there was great confusion with all the faithful hearing this while waiting for their own baptism. Whispers of dissent, doubt, and wariness arose. John became annoyed with the faithless voices around him, and told me to cancel the rest of the day's baptisms. Of course, we complied, though it caused many to complain. All those standing in line left, upset and disappointed. Unbelievably confused, John and I wondered what to do.

"The Baptist turned to us, his faithful disciples, and can you believe this? He repeated his complaint, 'I feel lightheaded after being out in the hot sun all morning, I need to take a rest.'

"We were shocked, because if his words were true then why would he feel despondent. We surmised that something had gone radically wrong and were unbelievably disappointed. From that time on John and I made a plan to leave. It was a bizarre experience. My brother questioned, 'If that man was the Lamb of Elohim, as the Baptist announced and even confirmed to our faces…'" James stopped speaking.

Mary understood how terribly distraught he was that the Baptist did not accept Jesus! Then James added, "After yesterday's meeting with John's disciples and hearing about the Baptist, I am not surprised." He stopped walking and suggested, "Let's take a break." Obviously, he felt the weight of the memory and was overcome with emotion. He sat down on a rock, staring into space with a lost expression.

Mary distinctly understood his anguish, but even more so hearing James' direct experience a day after hearing Rabboni's testimony about the same incident. Now she had the whole story in her heart and mind. Pondering the two testimonies, deep in thought she seriously wondered how she could help Jesus more, *What can we do to help the Baptist to testify properly to Jesus? If not, how will the nation accept the Messiah without the testimony of Elijah?*

Interrupted by James as he cleared his throat and shook his head, Mary continued to listen.

"For me, I was completely disappointed. We had waited all that time for the Messiah and followed John during those years of incredible sacrifice and persecution. Do you know how unpopular we were among the Sadducees and Pharisees? How much grief we got from them?" Oddly speechless, James stood up and they continued on slowly down the road.

After a long silence, except for the rhythmic steps of the mules, James continued, "The Baptist persisted the next day baptizing as if nothing had happened. He continued to preach as if the mystical experience had never happened. He carried on proclaiming that the Messiah was coming and that everyone needed to repent. My brother and I no longer had a reason to stay with John. We were totally disillusioned. We excused ourselves and told John we had to return home.

"You know what?" James asked. "Like I said before, most of the Baptist's followers did not even hear John's testimony." Shaking his head, he sighed, "I don't know how they missed it. Regardless, my brother and I left Judea and returned home. We were very disappointed. But before we left, we asked the Baptist again about the whole incident.

"He answered simply, 'My mission is separate from that man Jesus.'" And James added cynically, using John's voice, "The one he called the 'Lamb of Elohim.' Mystifying John and I, he also admitted to us that Jesus' popularity would increase and his would decrease."

James sighed as they continued walking, "Bewildered, we returned to Galilee and to our home. Of course, our parents received us with joy, though after we explained what had happened, our mother, understanding our hearts, told us wisely, 'Do not give up. The Anointed One is coming. Do not despair.' She turned our depression into hope, saying, 'John may have missed the moment, but you were there to hear John declare the Lamb of Elohim! Now we just have to find that Lamb of Elah!'"

James paused and dropped the straps pulling the mules and the wagon stopped. He was not finished with his story. Gesturing with his arms and hands, he continued, "Just imagine what would have happened if John had followed Jesus!" James kept talking but picked up the reins and they continued on to their destination.

"So yesterday we learned of John's imprisonment. It sounds like it was not long after we left. If only he had welcomed Jesus. Can you imagine if the two could work together? They would be able to stand against any and all opposition. Especially with John's prestige, he only needs to claim that he is preaching in the spirit of Elijah, as was prophesied at his birth."

James chided himself, "We're almost at the market, so I really have to finish my story. I'll be brief. We fished with our father while trying to decide what to do. But it was not easy, enduring long days spent on the quiet water. We could not ignore our unfulfilled hopes and dreams and were too restless.

"Then, about three months after we returned to Galilee, Rabboni walked close by our boat. I just happened to be there and recognized him from the baptisms, but not as the one John announced. Excited to see a familiar face from those days, I jumped out of our boat and walked over to him. I asked him, awkwardly but straightforwardly, 'I think I witnessed you being baptized by John the Baptist, a few months ago?'

"Surprised to be remembered, Jesus smiled and humbly answered, 'Yes, I was. You were there?' Thrilled that we shared similar experiences, we spoke like old acquaintances. Then my brother John came over and suddenly he remembered that Jesus was the one that the Baptist proclaimed as the Lamb of Elah!

"Stunned, I couldn't take my eyes off him. *The Lamb of Elah!* I thought. And both John and I fell down on our knees. Rabbi Jesus felt our sincerity but quickly and humbly pulled us up. 'Please, no,' he exclaimed, 'I am your brother. We are all sons of Elah, we are brothers and friends.'

"That day was amazing. We conversed warmly together like we were family. My brother and I excitedly showed him our boat. We were thrilled when he asked to go fishing with us and we spent the whole day together on the water. Of course, we told Jesus of our time with John, which was still foremost in our minds. He was proud of us for our contribution to the Baptist and all the work of salvation that we had done.

"Of course, we could not wait to introduce him to our mother. We told him that she never gave up believing that we would one day meet the Anointed One. He accepted our invitation to share an evening meal together with our parents. For me, it was the best experience of my whole life and I thanked Elah that we could finally meet and speak with Jesus, whom we truly believed was the Anointed One.

"After dinner that evening, in the dark except for the moon and stars, we sat outside on the beach. I remember feeling a bit uncomfortable because it was so quiet. I tried to think of what to ask Jesus. But nothing came to mind and I hoped that my brother would speak, but I knew he was not a talker. I realized that Jesus had listened to me all afternoon with only nods and smiles and a word here and there.

"Then, for the first time he spoke, 'Are you happy as fishermen? You know that the Kingdom of Heaven is at hand? Why do you spend time fishing? Come with me and I will make you fishers of men.'" James' voice choked up from emotion as tears flowed from his eyes uncontrollably. Ashamed of his unmanly reaction, he quickly turned away wiping them away with his sleeve.

Pausing to control himself, he cleared his throat and took a deep breath, "Here I am. My brother and I have been assisting him ever since. We know that he is the Messiah. Right?"

His tears were contagious, and Mary also wiped away tears as they were truly kindred spirits, contemplating, *Even though we met years ago, in totally different situations, we had no way of knowing how intertwined our lives would be. Now we both share the same commitment to Rabboni. Perhaps this common thread came because of the longing prayers of our families to find the Messiah?*

Finally, after James' emotional conclusion, he picked up the pace. They continued on toward their destination.

Chapter 18

Winds of Change

Trust in the Lord with all your heart
and do not lean on your own understanding.
...and he will make straight your paths.
(Prov. 3:5-6)

As they entered the busy market midafternoon, it was crowded with townspeople going to and fro. Alongside the road were women with urns upon their heads and children tailing them. It became noisier the closer they got to the well. Even though the street was wide, James had a hard time maneuvering, especially because of the children darting across from the side paths.

All roads led to the well at the center of town as it was an important stop for everyone. As in all Galilean villages it was a place to congregate, a place where news and gossip were exchanged. Mary smiled as she watched the women laughing at each other's stories. She caught snippets about husbands... children...holy days. Some were solemnly sharing stories of their lives, and as they passed by Mary heard only single words here and there, like death...sickness...taxes...tithings. She also heard conversations about religious announcements and national news.

Then suddenly Mary's attention was piqued by someone using the word, 'Baptist.' She moved closer to that conversation. A woman was whispering, "The reason you haven't heard about him lately is because I heard the Baptist was arrested over a year ago. The authorities said that he caused them great concern. They were afraid that he was starting insurrections against the temple. Others said that he accused Herod of adultery. No one really knows but he was always spouting off all kinds of nonsense and attracting followers with his fanatical message."

Mary realized that she was becoming distracted. She caught her wandering mind and refocused on their responsibility. She mentioned to James what she had heard, but they realized they had to speed up their undertaking. They knew that everyone was waiting for them, and time was of the essence.

Trying to conserve time and money, Mary went ahead to buy sacks of flour, spelt, and wheat. James continued to have difficulty guiding the wagon through the market and navigating around people, wagons, and animals. He filled three clay containers with water and lifted them onto the wagon and pushed them up against the back of the top board where Mother Salome was sitting. Then he proceeded onward to the wine cellar as quickly as the mules could pull the load. There, he purchased three vats of the least expensive wine.

At last, James found Mary waiting and hurriedly lifted the sacks she had bought onto the wagon. They continued on to buy the least expensive cheeses and dried fish. Mary saw a good deal on a container of olives and bought them as well.

They worked through Elder Simon's list until the wagon was full. It was then that they realized that their pace maneuvering the mules would be much slower on the return journey than when the wagon was empty. Their innocent miscalculation of time meant that they would be late returning to Elder Simon's house.

Mary chided herself for losing her focus, *It is my fault. I am irresponsible and I lost track of time because of his story. My, he certainly has a talkative nature! I should have been mindful of the importance of our mission and kept better track of time. I know that Rabbi is in a rush to support the Baptist. I am sorry!*

Because of her own shame, Mary became uncharacteristically curt and not at all womanly as she retorted, "I think we are really late. Can we walk faster." Immediately, she realized that she was out of order and put her hand over her mouth.

James looked at her with a surprised expression.

The second the strident words had left her mouth, she felt bad and wished she could take them back. *After our wonderful time together…It is not his fault that the wagon is heavy and the animals' pace is slow!* "Brother James, I am so sorry to speak to you that way. Please forgive my rash manner!"

James laughed out his answer, "Honestly, I got so caught up in talking. I confess that I, also, did not realize we were going to be late until it took me so long to guide the mules and the heavy wagon through the market." The young man admitted, "I kind of talked a lot, right? I forgot about time, being engrossed in my experience. I will tell Elder Simon it is my fault."

"No, it was also my fault. I will stand with you in front of Elder Simon. We can face his wrath together." They laughed nervously with Mary adding, "Also, I want to apologize to Rabboni."

As they silently, slowly, and guiltily entered camp, it was already evening. They anticipated facing their impatient and stern manager. But to their surprise, without any comment on their lateness, Simon inspected and approved the bounty. He seemed to be too busy to care that it took them so long. Then he ordered them to get their personal things ready for their long trip.

Mary helped Salome down from the wagon and turning to James gave him a big smile. All was forgiven, and with relief they hurried in different directions to make ready their leave.

At last, Simon informed Rabboni that all was prepared. The group stood waiting for direction. Jesus explained that they would stay with Martha and her family when they arrived in Bethany, "Our haste is necessary as John is languishing in prison. After we arrive in Bethany, I hope to visit him as soon as possible." Finally, Jesus called everyone together and asked for a sincere prayer in unison. Everyone prayed earnestly.

As Mary prayed, she could not help overhearing Jesus' desperate prayer in Hebrew. He tearfully appealed to Abba Elah that John would remember what was foreseen for him. That his essential mission was, and still is, that of the prophet Elijah announcing the Anointed One. Jesus included John's messengers, that they would hastily relay his answer to John's question.

Mary was sorry to hear him repent for walking away from John after his baptism and losing the moment to help John resolve his hatred and resentment toward him. He repented for not being humble to him.

Also, he prayed quietly, "I am sorry that I have such a small foundation. I promise You, my Abba, that I will work diligently to make my mission successful. Don't be concerned about our situation. John and I will work it out. Thank you for the men and women who are willing to give up the comfort of their homes to support me. Please bless them and give them Your love."

Rabboni became very emotional as he whispered in desperation. Hardly believing what she heard, she opened her eyes and gazed at his visage. Tears poured from his closed eyes as he repented that he had not yet made a foundation to take a bride. It seemed as though he was trying to console Abba's heart. He promised that he would work with every part of his being to make the foundation to further Abba Elah's providence.

Jesus continued, "The nation and religion of Israel are filled with very faithful people. While they are loyal to their rabbis and the law, don't worry about this nation and Your foundation. I know that they will live up to Your expectations and that they will be able to help me take Your love throughout the whole world." Jesus ended the prayer loudly, "Amen, Abba Elah."

"Are we prepared? I know this direction was unexpected, but we always need to be ready to follow Elah's guidance at a moment's notice." Jesus thanked Elder Simon and James for all their work and led them to the entrance of the house.

Suddenly and unexpectedly, he instructed Mary to bring him a basin of water. Directing everyone to stand before him, his announcement surprised everyone, "I will wash your feet. I want to show you by example. We must be willing to care for all people starting from the lowest position." It shocked everyone because only servants did that.

Rabboni would wash our feet? Mary thought, as she carried the basin and set it before Rabboni. "Sit, Elder Simon," Jesus commanded.

"Rabboni, I cannot allow you to take such a lowly position!" Simon exclaimed.

Nevertheless, without words, Jesus knelt down and dipped the sponge into the basin, and holding Simon's foot he proceeded to scrub it. As he did to Simon, he followed diligently scrubbing the feet of all nine men, and then the women.

Jesus explained to everyone, "I want to show this by my example of forgetting my self-centered dignity by loving and serving you as if I am serving all humankind. I come to serve you and all humankind, and you must follow my example. If you wish to be close to me, you, too, must be humble and willing to serve and give Elah's love substantially to all humankind forgetting your pride. I know it is against custom, but I am showing you Elah's way."

His followers were overwhelmed by Jesus' humility and compassion. For Mary it was an unforgettable moment.

Before taking the first step on their way to Judea, Jesus added, "And for those of you who felt painful persecution during witnessing, remember the best way to leave a good impression is by humbling yourself to others regardless of how they treat you. In this way you will touch something in their heart that they may not be aware of right away. But someday later they will remember your kindness."

Jesus stood facing Simon, who was standing at the front of the line, with everyone looking at Jesus' face. Rabboni placed his hands upon the elder's shoulders and spoke, "Seeing and feeling the practice of love is like laying a seed that someday will sprout love and then that love can be given to others."

Mary realized that even though he spoke to Simon as one man, Jesus was using him as a surrogate through whom we could multiply His love, thus multiplying himself from one man to every individual present.

Rabboni spoke again, "I truly want to show my appreciation. I may not have told you of my gratitude, but I want to demonstrate it to you now. I am aware that you would prefer to go home and work at your own craft or labor, but instead you follow me and Abba Elah."

Finally, he thanked everyone in Elder Simon's household for their loving service to him and to everyone. He promised to return as soon as they possibly could. And to Perpetua he promised, "I will bring your husband home as soon as I can."

Jesus led the way southwest along the coast of the Sea of Galilee toward the main fishing port of Tiberius. As the path ahead curved, Mary got a glimpse of Rabboni walking with vigor and determination. Choosing not to wear the customary ornate garments of rabbis or priests, his clothes and head-scarf were those of a simple Galilean fisherman, made of homespun muslin. Today, his hair was tied at the top of his head with a piece of cloth. His head scarf laid across his shoulders and his carriage was proud and straight.

Mary was assigned to walk beside the wagon as Mother Salome rode on the top board. Before leaving, Mary had checked the seat and added a woolen blanket for her comfort, and also gave her a waterskin. She prayed silently, *Abba Elah, please help us make a speedy and safe trip*, as she strolled along.

She remembered Simon and the men discussing their intended path. "Without problems," they had said, "it will probably take us about a week." Since it would be a long hike, she had prepared several pairs of sandals for Jesus and two extra for herself.

As they neared the edge of the village of Capernaum, someone began singing a traditional Galilean hiking song and they all joined in. The sun was low on the horizon to their right. They would walk until sunset.

Along the way, they picked up precious pieces of wood and dried animal dung for the fireplace. Mary had learned about the valuable kindling during their last witnessing tour. And from experience, she knew where to find it. She enjoyed the splendid fresh air of the countryside, different than the stale air of the towns. *How wonderful it is to breathe freely!* she praised Abba Elah once again, in gratitude for her good health.

Mary glanced up at Salome, bouncing around and holding on tight. The woman was a slight figure, covered mostly with her scarf and robe. Mary guessed that the devout woman was deep in prayer. Salome must have felt Mary's glance because she turned and met her eyes. She returned Mary's attention with a broad smile, making her face appear even younger that it really was.

Mary thought, *She's an amazing woman, so late in life enduring our uncomfortable situation. She must be at least twenty years my senior.*

She was walking behind Thomas, one of the brothers she hardly knew, as he led the two mules pulling the wagon. Thomas turned his head and asked her, "How are you doing back there?" He mentioned that it was nice to be on the move again. This was the first time Thomas had ever spoken to her.

"I feel good, and the walk is invigorating," Mary answered, as they walked on.

Then, again he commented, shortly, "I don't like sitting still."

As they walked, Mary was happy to receive even a few words from him because she realized that, like most of the brothers, he was not comfortable speaking to a woman. But to her surprise, after a long pause, he spoke again, "I actually like a healthy discussion with most of the townspeople. Even if the words become controversial, I feel eager to stir their minds and make them think."

After another period of silence, he continued, "Some of them are looking for a colorful and majestic Messiah. They expect the Messiah to be wrapped in golden robes with a crown of jewels on his head. Some men think a magical event should certainly happen before they believe. Those stiff-necked men love to ask about Elijah. I've gotten scolded for not knowing about that prophet. Do you know? They like to make fun of ignorance. It hurts."

Thomas mimicked the Jews, accusing him, "You mean you do not know about Elijah!" He admitted, "To my detriment, I never liked to study. I was always more interested in fishing with my father. Of course, my parents raised my brothers and sisters and myself with all the religious traditions. We even traveled to Jerusalem for Passover. But I don't remember hearing about Elijah, the prophet. My mother prayed that prayer at Passover in Hebrew, so I did not understand, even from that. I am a man who finds it easier to understand from my heart," the short and stocky Thomas explained about himself.

After walking a couple of hours, the sun set over the hills, and Simon suggested to Jesus, "Rabboni, we are on the outskirts of Magdala, and here is a flat field of grass where we can set up a campsite." Simon indicated the spot.

Mary looked all around. It was hard to think that her mother was only a short distance away and that she would not be able to see her. She knew the right time would come; therefore, she did not request to separate from their central objective. *Perhaps on the way back, there will be time for me to visit,* she hoped.

Much to her surprise, Simon, unusually considerate, called to her and said, "I am sorry that we cannot visit your home. I know that it must be on your mind. But the next time we pass by we will visit," he reassured her.

That night after dinner, they all sat around the glowing embers of the fire and enjoyed relaxing together with Rabboni. He used the time to instruct them in the stories of the Holy Scripture and asked if anyone had a question.

John, son of Salome, asked to hear the story that he had learned about John the Baptist's birth from the Baptist himself.

Matthew called out, "Remind us why Elijah is important."

"Yes!" Thomas and Phillip shouted in agreement with Matthew. Thomas added, "During witnessing, I have been asked many times if you are the prophet, Elijah." Then Phillip, usually very quiet, spoke out, "Some also have asked me, if the Messiah is coming soon then where is Elijah? Rabboni, please tell us why it is so important."

"Of course." Jesus agreed. "I am delighted that you want to know this very timely information! Brother John, your request is also very important. I will first tell you the story of Elijah. Then tomorrow night I will tell you the Baptist's story. Both are important for you to know in your witnessing."

Even though, over the last few days, a lot had been said about Elijah and John the Baptist, the disciples were eager to hear the stories told again. They really wanted to be ready when asked again by those they witnessed to.

Jesus repeated the stories, and Nathaniel still had a question, "Why, if it makes so much sense to us, did the Baptist ask you 'Are you the one or should we look for another?'"

Everyone sitting around the campfire became spirited. They started noisily chiming in their agreement, "Yes, why doesn't he know?"

Jesus answered, "I am happy to see that you understand clearly. In answer to Nathaniel's question, there are many reasons, but one is pride or hidden issues that have not been resolved. No one can see clearly if he is not humble and is not like a new wineskin. Do you understand?" Jesus asked.

Everyone answered with a resounding "Yes!"

Thanking Rabboni, Simon announced, "It is time to rest. We will start out again at first light. Tomorrow we will travel a longer distance." Then Simon gave the closing prayer.

Elder Simon instructed Phillip to wear his sword and keep the first watch. They were in a sparsely traveled area and wild animals were not uncommon, as well as bandits preying on weary travelers between Galilee and Judea.

Mary thought, *As usual, Phillip was chosen as guard first for he is the strongest and most experienced with the sword.* She remembered Martha telling her that when he was young, he fought Roman soldiers as a religious zealot. She said that after he nearly lost his life, a spiritual experience took him away from that violent life and brought him to Jesus. Mary felt safe with him keeping watch.

Mary gave Rabboni his waterskin and asked if she could help him with anything else. He told her to retire to be prepared for their long walk. She lay down on her pallet next to Salome. They were on the opposite side of the wagon, away from the men, who slept on one side of the fireside. The fire dwindled to glowing coals.

Mary noticed that the sky was full of stars. Looking up at her old friends, she felt drowsy. She whispered a short prayer and quickly fell asleep. But she did not sleep well. She tossed and turned because of a frightening dream. She saw a headless body that begged her to find its head. Mary cried because she could not find the head and apologized to the headless being. She woke up in tears from her fretful sleep.

She rose wearily from her bed. The air was chilly as she walked over to the fireside. With a stick she poked the coals for warmth. Sitting beside the fire, Mary said a prayer and tried to shake the memory of the nightmare from her mind.

John, James' brother, whose turn it was to keep watch, saw her rise and told her that he would be waking everyone soon. She nodded and reached for some dried dung, throwing it on the coals. She went to roll up her pallet and filled a basin with water and washed her face, then she brushed her long hair and braided it. She was glad that she had woken early to catch a private moment.

She and John put water on to boil and woke everyone. The stars were fading, as was the crescent moon suspended high above them, and another cloudless dawn emerged on the eastern horizon.

Their expedition was without incident. The weather was favorable and they made good time. For seven days they traveled from morning to evening. At midday they rested in groves shaded from the heat. Jesus' evening sermons were not long because he wanted everyone to be strong for the long and tiring journey.

As the humble travelers neared their destination Mary watched Rabboni for a long while. He appeared focused and strong. She remembered what he once told her: If he got tired walking these relatively short distances, then how could he go to Persia or Rome to bring Elah's salvation to the people of the rest of the world?

It was dark when they finally arrived at the village of Bethany and Lazarus' house. Lazarus and his sisters amicably received the inspired but weary travelers. Lazarus took Jesus to his own personal room while Martha asked the servants to take the men to the bath area.

Martha was overjoyed to see them and embraced Mary, who introduced her to Salome. Noticing the weariness in their smiling faces, Martha took them to their room and the bathing chamber.

Mary looked lovingly at Martha, her big sister, "Let me tell you all about the last few weeks."

Martha answered, "I cannot wait, I missed you. But you must rest." She took them right to the baths and then to their beds.

For Salome and Mary, washing away the dirt and grime was a luxury. They would have loved to spend more time, but they nearly fell asleep in the soothing waters. Mary's last thoughts were about Rabboni's situation. She knew that he would be cared for by Martha and Lazarus, so she allowed herself to fall asleep.

She dreamed the same dream as the night before. The headless man was still searching for his head and screaming at her to find it. Mary explained to the man that she could not find it, though she desperately searched for it. The frightening dream again kept her from a sound sleep. In the middle of the night, she sat up and looking around groggily, she thought, *It was only a dream.* Because it was dark, without more thought, Mary fell back to sleep.

Breakfast was already prepared when Mary stumbled drowsily into the dining hall. Salome followed her. However, when she saw the banquet that had been prepared, she immediately revived and forgot her terrible sleep.

On the tables everything was carefully and elegantly arranged, delicious and lovingly prepared. There were bowls of freshly picked grapes, plump figs, and dates, almonds, and cashews. Pomegranates and melons were cut open and waiting for consumption. Loaves of bread and goat's cheese were all prepared. On a different table were meat dishes and wine goblets which marked every seat.

This exquisite banquet was a first for her. She had never seen such extravagance, and she noticed eucalyptus plants and palms decorating the room. There was even a harpist, playing background music. Jesus and all the brothers had already gathered. It was a meal such as she had never seen and Mary thought that maybe it was the same for Jesus and all their companions. He appeared pleased with the wonderful reception.

Mary was given a seat next to Jesus as she would help translate Hebrew, the Judean's common language. Also, she was expected to keep Jesus' goblets full of wine and water. She was overjoyed to serve him. She noticed how handsome he was with his shining hair and clean clothes.

Mary realized that at last someone with material affluence had received Jesus into his home as he should be received, as the Anointed One. She remembered Martha's story and realized what a remarkable person Lazarus was. He was obviously the lord of the house. His ornate robe was beautiful. His curly hair was short, and his beard was well manicured. He stood to the side of the tables, giving instructions to the servants who were coming and going, refilling emptied platters and pouring homemade wine into emptied goblets.

He appeared to be older than Jesus but not as tall. Very congenial, he greeted everyone as they arrived. Finally, Lazarus asked Jesus to offer a blessing over their meal and then sat down beside Jesus, and everyone ate their fill.

Afterwards, Lazarus stood and bowed respectfully to his honored guest,

Jesus, and then to everyone else. "Welcome to my home, Rabboni, and all of your followers. I hope that you will find this a comfortable setting where I invite you to carry out your mission that you explained to me a while ago. I have even taken the initiative and asked many of my friends to come and meet you in the early afternoon. I hope this will please you."

Mary was fascinated by his elegant discourse. She noticed that she felt more comfortable here than anywhere she had been before. Suddenly she realized that she was distracted by the atmosphere, and redirected her attention to what the host was saying.

Lazarus spoke nobly, "I must say that some of my associates have already heard stories of your work in Galilee, Rabboni. They are interested and open minded, as they have heard good and bad but they are curious to hear you speak to them."

Lazarus took a sip of his wine and continued on about his sister Martha, "I am impressed from her account and time with you. She told me about her witnessing experiences and about each one of you. Thank you for your kindness and your religious and communal education, which she brought back to us." He indicated Martha with his hand, "She came back to us wanting to serve and love us and with a maturity that is beautiful." Lazarus ended with a toast to Rabboni.

Jesus stood and spoke, "Thank you, Lazarus, for this unexpected and gracious reception. I am impressed by your foresight and look forward to meeting with your friends as you have arranged. I know that Abba Elah is very happy with your plan. But as I indicated in my message that preceded us, I also intend to visit John the Baptist in prison, as early as tomorrow, if that can be arranged?"

Lazarus nodded and stood up, addressing Jesus' question, "I have sent an envoy to the magistrate and requested that you, Rabboni, be allowed to see him. And the answer was affirmative." Hope and joy filled the gathering.

Finally, Jesus asked, "Mary of Magdala," addressing her formally, "sing for us and Martha accompany her with her lyre."

Happy to please him, Mary stood and announced she would sing a psalm of David. Martha sat with her lyre and waited to hear the melody and then began strumming.

> *Blessed is he who comes.*
> *Who comes in the Name of the Lord,*
> *Blessed is he who comes.*
> *Come, come Lord.*
> *For the Lord Elohim is Almighty,*
> *For the Lord Elohim is Almighty.*

The celebration concluded as Rabboni asked everyone to pray with him.

In the afternoon, about fifty dignified men from the Bethany area came to meet the famous preacher. Jesus told the story of Elijah and John the Baptist. He explained forthrightly, "John is the prophesied Elijah. It is crucial for John and myself to unite together in a singular effort."

The guests, already prepared by Lazarus, were receptive and approachable. They were noticeably surprised, but curious about Jesus' account of John the Baptist being Elijah. The bond that they had with Lazarus certainly helped them to easily accept Rabbi Jesus' proposition.

Some respectful questions were asked. One man mentioned, without malice, "I already asked the Baptist if he was Elijah or even the Messiah. He denied being either. Why?"

Jesus answered, "John could not accept Elohim's revelation because he could not accept me. I want the chance to meet with him to help him understand his true mission." Even so, Jesus repeated his affirmation to everyone, "He is indeed! He preaches with the spirit of Elijah."

After the speech, Jesus announced, "I will travel to the prison in Machaerus at daybreak along with my followers to meet with John."

Chapter 19

The Baptist's Demise

With the spirit and power of Elijah he will go before him…
to make a people prepared for the Lord.
(Luke 1:17)

The day dawned after a restful and dreamless sleep and Mary was grateful that she would be ready for their long journey to visit John in prison. On her way with Salome to their morning meeting she prayed that Rabboni also was well rested.

With Lazarus and all the disciples gathered together, Jesus prayed for Abba Elah's guidance and protection, "As this new day begins, I beseech Your presence Abba Adonai. We are a part of Your great design.

"From the beginning of time, You, Abba envisioned the unity seen last night and your guests' willingness to consider that Elijah is indeed here. You need those with influence to recognize what You are doing in our nation at this time. Their support will be the bulwark upon which John and I can stand. Surely the day is coming when John as the Elijah will fulfill his mission and announce to this prepared nation that I am the Anointed One.

"This is truly a hopeful morning. Responsibilities have been assigned. Soon I will leave to meet with John. Let us sincerely pray that John will finally see Your perspective.

Rabboni prayed with his arms outstretched as everyone present offered their communion of prayers, echoing loudly and beseeching Elah's presence and guidance.

Mary, feeling bright and optimistic after the success of last evening's gathering, prayed, "Abba Elah, it was a comfortable experience to meet dynamic and successful men who listened respectfully to our Rabboni and asked sincere questions. From this experience, everyone realizes the importance of Lazarus' influence. It is in this same way that John's acceptance of Jesus will also influence his followers. Truly it will be a straight path for the nation to receive Jesus as the Anointed One."

Overcome with hopeful anticipation and emotion, Mary wept aloud. Her sincere yearning caused the same passionate pleading among all the others. It proliferated throughout the room causing an eruption of tears. Everyone sensed the desperately pivotal moment.

While they prayed, Jesus walked around the room placing his hands in a blessing upon each head and shoulder of his flock. He prayed with them, adding to their words, entreating Elah's protection upon their mission. The multiplication of all their prayers together became a shared cathartic wailing. Mary felt that perhaps every ancestor was present and praying with them.

Jesus concluded with a resounding, "Amen."

Without losing any time, Jesus gathered Simon, James, John, and Mary together and prepared to embark on the arduous journey to Machaerus prison. They were packed and ready for a two-day journey.

Unexpectedly there was a loud commotion at the gates of the compound. Strongly demanding voices outside the gate were begging to speak immediately with Rabbi Jesus. Four men, one of whom was dressed in official priestly regalia of tassels and thin blue stripes edging his robe, were led into the compound, breathless, disheveled, and anxious. Their darkened, fearful eyes chilled Mary's heart and soul, *What news do these visitors bring?*

James ran to receive the men, who were obviously overheated and out of breath, and escorted them to Rabboni. It was then that Mary recognized them from their previous visit in Capernaum as the followers of the Baptist. Observing their desperate physical and emotional state, she ran to the kitchen for water as it was a hot morning and they were sweating profusely.

When she returned with the water pitcher and mugs, all were

muted and somber. As she served the men, she noticed that everyone was dumfounded. And then she heard Jesus' tremulous voice, questioning in disbelief their shocking news, "John was executed, two days ago! Beheaded! No, this cannot be!"

Reflexively, she gasped aloud at her Rabboni's words. Gripped in terror, she was hardly able to breath, *No! It cannot be. This cannot be so!* The announcement was so painful that Mary cried aloud, uncontrollably, "Dear Abba Elah! No! No!" and collapsed on her knees.

The pale messengers, affected by her emotional reaction, began to tremble themselves. Their wailing cascaded throughout the hall. The hopeful day seemed to turn to hellish night.

It took only moments for everyone to grasp the unbelievable news. The ramifications were eternal. It was like a fist to the gut. Finally, when there were no more tears to shed, everyone remained on their knees waiting in supplication for direction. The shock was hard hitting and due to the emotional pain, no one moved, and even their breathing was shallow. Except for Mary's continued weeping, there was cold silence.

Judas, the spokesman, whom Mary remembered, fell to his knees, begging Rabboni to forgive him for bringing such devastating news. He tried to continue his report, but the reality had struck the Baptist's man so deeply that he was hardly able to continue.

With slumped and trembling shoulders and a despondent expression, he explained in an emotionless monotone, "Though he was imprisoned for two years, John reassured us that his detention was only temporary. When we last saw him, we gave him your answer to his question. However, before we returned for his response, he was martyred."

Judas continued with downcast eyes in a miserable manner, "Last Sabbath, Herod's wife, who had continued pressing her grievance against John for calling her an adulterer, finally achieved her passionate appeal for his beheading. It took her two long years of petitioning her husband.

"Herod, who basically knew the strong loving and trusting sentiment of the people for John, did not want to bring the wrath of the people against himself. He gave John numerous opportunities to recant his statement. He thought the time in prison would wear him down and he would concede and apologize. But John remained stubborn and obstinate until the very end.

"Finally, with additional pressure from the Sadducees, Herod relented. That religious organization had its own grievance against John for disrupting society and for other things like the decreasing tithing. After John was beheaded, his head was taken to Herod."

His last words trailed off in their consciousness. Again, a morbid silence fell over the compound. It was suddenly broken by one of John's followers. He exclaimed in tears, praising his leader, "Israel has lost a great prophet!"

The awkward words lingered in the air. *Absolutely not!* Mary believed, knowing that his was a useless death, with no victory. Then she looked up at Jesus. His face went scarlet as if he had been slapped. He ignored their praise of John and turned away from the zealous followers.

Mary quietly shifted to Jesus' side, on the other side of the room. He stood with his back to everyone. He was still as a statue looking out toward the olive orchard. His face was composed but solemn. The room, warm and stuffy from the mid-morning sun, was partially responsible for the perspiration pouring down his brow.

Suddenly Mary remembered her dream. She shuddered in fright, but not wanting to trouble Jesus, she swiftly left the room. Finding a quiet spot in a garden in the back of the house where she could think and pray, she recalled her gruesome dream of the man screaming to find his head, *This was John! Now I realize it.* "Dear Elah!" she exclaimed aloud. "Was the dream a warning? Could I have prevented it from happening?" As she sobbed uncontrollably, Mary felt totally alone for the first time since joining Jesus' mission.

The sisters, who were helping in the kitchen and unaware of the messenger, heard Mary's tearful outburst and ran to her, asking, "What's wrong, Mary?"

"Oh Abba Elah! The Baptist is dead," Mary wailed. "Herod beheaded him."

Stunned, Martha and Salome received the news. The three women held each other.

Martha cried, "Why did Herod do that? John was known and loved by all the people of Israel. My Abba Elohim, his father was a High Priest. How could that happen?"

An announcement came to the sisters that Jesus had changed his plans and decided to stay in Bethany another day. He asked that everyone take the afternoon to pray for the soul of John, and for Abba's changing providence.

Throughout the quiet and morbid afternoon, Mary felt uncomfortable, neither lying down in her room nor sitting on the veranda. Even though the veranda overlooked the peaceful and comforting view of the olive groves surrounding the house, she could not shake her restlessness.

The large manor was totally silent. An immense heaviness pervaded the hearts and minds of the whole household. Martha brought out lentil soup and bread. But only a few empty bowls were left on the side.

Mary looked for Jesus, but he was not in any of his usual prayer places. She imagined that he had gone into the hills to seek Elah's direction.

At twilight after everyone, emotionally exhausted from the day, had retired for the night, Mary went back into the lonesome quiet hall, where she expected Jesus to be; but he was not. She went outside searching for him. Finally, out of the corner of her eye she saw him moving in the grove. She followed him and stopped at the edge of the orchard at her usual distance, and knelt upon the rough, rocky ground to support him in earnest prayer.

Jesus stood amidst the trees, facing toward the hills. She noticed that after a day of great restlessness, she finally felt calm to be close to him. She watched and heard his passionate prayer and sensed his powerful spirit. His conversation with Elah was a mixture of fervent words in Aramaic and Hebrew.

Jesus tenderly whispered "Abba," like a son trying to comfort His abba's grieving heart. She caught a few chilling words. "...plan has gone awry, but don't worry."

Shivering she understood, *He consoles Elah and tells Him not to feel undue concern as he entreats Abba about how he should go on from here.* She became aware of warm tears spilling down her cheeks. *Abba,* she whispered, *please show me how to best serve Your son.*

Patchy bands of clouds passing across the sky sporadically interrupted the moonlight. The stillness embraced them, and the atmosphere provided contemplative communication with the Creator.

Mary witnessed Jesus' fortitude as he prayed the whole night while everyone else slept. She also stayed there all night. Several times she fell asleep curled up on her knees, and caught herself nearly falling over. She pushed herself to stay awake. Her mind was active with many questions, but admittedly she was physically and emotionally exhausted.

She recollected the many scriptural warnings to the people to prepare for the coming of the Messiah. And the baffling the word she had heard John use long ago, Repent! As she prayed in the darkness, she begged Elah for understanding, "If only the Baptist had overcome his pride and openly pointed out Jesus as the Anointed one."

She recalled James' explanation of seeing and hearing the Baptist's reaction, *This is the Lamb of Elah! I saw the dove rest upon his shoulder.* "If only John had spoken to Jesus about his revelation. If only he had had more time, even one more day, to admit that Jesus was the Anointed One," she whispered.

Mary sighed, lamenting and confounded by many unanswered questions. Because of her intense focus and anguish in her heart, she did not notice her physical discomfort kneeling upon the firm, unyielding earth and the chilly late-night temperature. Tears flowed without comfort or answers, *What do we do now? He is dead. He never attested to Jesus. He even denied that he was the prophesied Elijah. Now, without John's affirmation, who are the people to believe?* Mary concluded, *John shamefully misled his countrymen.*

As the sun rose above the horizon, Mary watched Rabboni return to the villa. She was amazed to see from his countenance, *He doesn't appear to be tired or worried or hopeless after his all-night prayer.*

She made her way back to her room to freshen up for the new day.

Salome was not there and Mary guessed she was in the kitchen. Thinking she would lay down for a brief moment, she fell asleep.

"Mary, wake up. Rabboni is calling for everyone to join him for breakfast." Salome gently shook her. She opened her eyes and sat up, realizing that she had unintentionally slept, and apologized, "Salome, I am sorry. I fell asleep. Is breakfast over?"

"No, dear. Rabboni is asking for everyone to join him," she answered and then asked, "Where were you last night?"

Mary responded, "I couldn't sleep. I was praying."

Salome smiled and praised the young woman, "You are a special person, Mary of Magdala. Because of your youth, you are strong. Elah bless you. But let's go to break our fast with Rabboni and our brothers."

Chapter 20

Setting a New Course

The harvest is plentiful, but the laborers are few,
Therefore, pray earnestly for the Lord of the harvest
to send out laborers into his harvest.
(Matt 9:37-38)

As Jesus gathered his small group of downhearted followers, Mary wondered, *With this small number of workers, what can we do with no Elijah?* She assumed that everyone was thinking the same way.

Enthusiastically, Jesus announced, "Do not let yourself doubt Abba Elah for even one minute. Abba is with us and we are with Him. There is nothing we cannot do. I have a plan."

As he took a breath about to explain it, a servant ran into the hall with yet another surprising announcement. The group of men from yesterday had requested another meeting with Master Jesus. Jesus nodded and motioned for them to be admitted. Mary recognized them as the followers of the Baptist, including the honorable and dignified spokesman and apparent scholar, Judas Iscariot.

Judas formally reintroduced himself and reminded Jesus of their previous two meetings. Bowing respectfully to Jesus he explained their purpose, "I followed the Baptist from shortly after he began his mission. I did so because I believed he had a special mission to revive our nation in preparation for the great awakening, the much-anticipated advent of the Anointed One.

"Yesterday as I grieved his loss, I asked myself how could I return to the stilted traditional religious practices and formal worship of Elohim? When I was with John I witnessed every day the authentic rebirth of our countrymen, renewed and inspired to worship Adonai, Elohim. I heard John call you the Lamb of ha Elohim and that you would increase. I would like to continue reviving our country with you. If you will have me."

Judas indicated the three other men, "We have talked, and we all have the same desire. I am exceedingly sorry that we did not reach John in time to obtain his response to your question. My allegiance to John has been severed by his untimely death. If you will have us, we pledge our allegiance to you."

Judas turned to his associates, and they affirmed in unison, "We agree with Judas. We sincerely pledge our allegiance to you."

Standing beside his companions, together they knelt in humble submission, with their right fists over their hearts and heads bowed, petitioning, "Would you accept us, Master Jesus?"

The atmosphere in the room went from melancholic to exhilaration within seconds. Everyone held their breath and regarded Jesus as they waited for his response. Mary could not read Jesus' expression. She, like everyone, anxiously awaited his decision.

However, Jesus, sitting cross-legged on the floor, said nothing but motioned to them, "Come here to be seated in front of me." Jesus then asked the women to bring water, basins, and towels. While the men waited curiously there was silence. Jesus remained prayerful and waited with his eyes closed.

Mary brought the requested items and placed them in front of him on the floor. Jesus called Judas first to stand and instructed him, "Place your right foot in the basin."

Surprised by the request, Judas started to object, but observing Master Jesus' emphatically defined expression, he awkwardly submitted. Lifting his foot, he placed it into the wooden bowl. Jesus motioned for Mary to pour the water over Judas' foot. Then one by one, Jesus washed his feet and dried them, followed by the feet of his companions.

Elder Simon and the disciples, familiar with the action, watched. When Jesus had finished, he motioned for everyone, his disciples and the Baptist's former disciples, to sit on the floor surrounding him and taught them, "I know what you are thinking. Washing my feet! How can this man defile himself by touching my dirty feet?"

After a short passage of time, he continued with tears in his eyes, "Unless I show you how to serve and care for others, you will never understand what love is. It is through selfless and humble disregard for our own pride that you come to understand what love and compassion are. As I washed your feet you likewise should wash the feet of others. You must love people at your own expense, without concern for yourself and how it might benefit you."

Jesus gave time for the men to consider his words. Then he asked them, "Introduce yourselves."

"Master Jesus, I am Judas Iscariot," the leader said. Then he motioned to his brethren to introduce themselves. "I am Thaddeus Alphaeus. I am James Alphaeus. I am Simon Cananean."

Jesus invited each to give a testimony of his life of faith.

Judas spoke in Hebrew as it was his first language, and it was obvious to all that he was well educated. "I am from southern Israel and I was a loyal confidant of John for nearly three years. Our relationship goes back to our childhood. We were educated together in the temple school in Jerusalem and became close friends. After school, though, we lost contact with each other.

"I continued on as a scribe, assisting Sadducee priests in the temple. After a few years, we began to hear curious news of a so-called holy man using crazy antics and giving fiery sermons on the banks of the Jordan River. I was assigned to go and investigate him.

"After days of searching, I found him near Jericho on the shore of the Jordan River. I was surprised to see that the bizarrely dressed man was none other than my old friend. Right away I was mystified and wondered how it was that this son of a Levite priest became so eccentric?

"Well, to make a long story short, we met together. Though I remained skeptical, I listened to his sermon and watched the ritual he performed but did not participate in it. Stunned by his sharp change of character, I did remember that he had always been confrontational in school. Still, I wondered why he became so crazed, so extreme, knowing that he was so well connected through his priestly father.

"Regretfully, I did not speak long with him because I saw him as too extreme. I left, shaking my head, not wanting anything more to do with him. A few days later, back in the temple office, a priest came in with a list of grievances and his main complaint was John the Baptist. Well, of course, after seeing John, I knew that the traditional establishment of Judaism was heading for a major clash and John was their focus.

"I decided to travel again to John and warn him. In that meeting, I was won over to his simple but passionate cause. After a long discussion, I agreed that in fact our religious tradition did need a change, and I saw John as the instrument of Elohim with a holy mission and I wanted to be on his side.

"I never reported back to the temple. Instead, I dropped everything and became his disciple. I committed my future to him and enthusiastically participated in his work. I witnessed the resurrection of multitudes. His greatness was apparent. He truly was similar to the prophets of old. John absolutely knew that he was preparing the people for the coming of the Anointed One. Now I am devastated by John's death, but I cannot go back to my old life. Therefore, I decided to continue with you, Master Jesus, if you would have me?"

Jesus listened earnestly and then spoke, "I appreciate your incredible sacrifice of power and position. You are well trained and with Elah's help you can fortify our ministry."

Jesus stood and motioned for Simon to stand. Jesus introduced him, "This is Simon, my chief assistant. He will introduce you to everyone and to our routine."

The introductions continued. Thaddeus and James Alpheus, sons of Mary of Clopas, stood and introduced themselves. Thaddeus explained in Aramaic, "We, my brother and I, are from Paneas in northern Galilee, near Caesarea Philippi. We met John only a few months before he was taken to Jerusalem and put on trial. We were attracted to his rebellious actions and his vision to prepare for the Anointed One whose coming we believe is imminent."

Then his brother James added, also in the same dialect as Jesus, "We proudly and humbly offer our lives to your service, if you will have us. We know that John proclaimed you the Lamb of Elah. Please teach us that we may know and serve you with great vigor and devotion." Both men bowed respectfully to Jesus.

Mary noticed Rabboni's eyes were wet with emotion and knew that he was moved by their humility.

Lastly was the young man, Simon Cananean, another Galilean with an exceedingly candid character. He introduced himself with an unusually strong and deep voice but with the same accent as Jesus. Passionately he continued. "I followed the Baptist only a short time because soon after John baptized me, he was arrested by Herod's sycophants. I see no other hope for our nation. Therefore, I devote my life to your mission. Please, allow me to join you!"

Surprised at his loud voice and strong physique, Mary was moved by his sincerity. She watched as he energetically knelt before Jesus.

Then he stood and continued, speaking passionately, "I am opposed to our religious leaders defiling our faith. They allow the pagan Romans into our holy city of Jerusalem without even a challenge. They are responsible and should be held accountable for putting our faith second to those pagan legions of death! I will do anything you ask of me. I am determined to give my life, if need be, and to confront the priests and rabbis for their hypocrisy."

Ending his testimony, Simon admitted, "Honestly, I was not sure of committing myself to you Rabbi Jesus. But when you washed my feet, I realized you are not just talk, but you are a humble man actualizing what you preach. At that moment, I realized you were not another corrupt religious leader but truly a man of Elah. Lord, you have my allegiance!"

Mary felt his fiery passion and determination. She thought again with tears, *His fervor inspires us all!*

Encouraged, Jesus proclaimed, "It is Abba Elah who reclaims you from John's foundation. We welcome you."

Jesus turned to Judas and asked him to stand, "I am grateful that you as an educated man will be able to help me reach the clerics and possibly the very leaders of all Hebraism. I imagine that the Baptist trained you in humility, which is also an exceptional quality for a man of your stature. I hope you are the first of many educated men to learn from me and follow my direction.

With your help, we can reach the top strata of society and thereby influence the nation much quicker. Judas, would you agree?" The man nodded.

Jesus added unexpectedly, "Though, I must first re-educate you. Do you accept this challenge?"

Judas answered earnestly and loudly, "Yes, my Master Jesus!"

"We also need someone to manage our purse. Can you accept this as your first responsibility?"

"Yes, I would be honored to serve you in this way," Judas said with notable respect.

"Simon, please work with Judas. Your unity will be important."

Jesus became realistic and solemn. Taking a deep breath, he added, "Unfortunately, with John's untimely death his historic role as Elijah was left unverified. He failed to announce and accept me publicly as the Anointed One. Therefore, do not reveal that I am the Anointed One until the time is right."

Mary understood the seriousness of Jesus' words thinking, *From now on he stands alone to face those who came against John.* A queasy sensation came over her. Perspiration slid down the side of her flushed face. Taking a deep breath, she whispered her rededication, *I will go with you wherever you lead, my Rabboni!*

Jesus looked directly at her, as if he heard her words. Mary caught his eye and felt comforted by his resolve.

Then Elder Simon, recognizing the end of the meeting, shouted, "I will help!" This instigated the binding of all the disciples, old and new, to register their determination together with loud shouts, "I will help!"

Jesus explained his newly formed plan, "Immediately, I must take on the necessary position of Elijah. Once that foundation is made, I will then announce myself as Elah's promised one. Several of you witnessed John's proclamation that I am the Anointed One. You are already trained to announce me to the nation. I am confident of your absolute commitment. Unity and oneness of heart with me is crucial!" Jesus paused and repeated with emphasis, "Unity and oneness of heart and mind! Don't forget this important ingredient for our success. Our new path will not be easy. We have a lot of work ahead of us. But together, without concern for our own selves, all things are possible with Elah's help."

Then, Jesus asked, "When should we begin?" To which everyone again shouted, "Today!"

Not long after noon Salome and Martha brought the midday meal and placed it before the community of believers. The food was greatly appreciated. Everyone was hungry from not eating since they heard the news yesterday.

Mary guessed that they would leave Lazarus' home soon and begin the long trek back to their base in Capernaum. She wondered how things would change. *But no matter what, Rabboni is still the same and his commitment is still the same,* she reassured herself and her commitment.

Jesus asked Martha to play her lyre and Mary to sing as the brothers ate their meal. The new personalities and friendships brought a freshness to the atmosphere. However, Mary felt there was an underlying mood of uncertainty still lingering.

Jesus spoke after all the food was cleared away, "We have much to do. I would like to begin this new start with my first lesson. I want you all to understand with unequivocal clarity what John's mission was. Though he is gone, people are still waiting for the return of Elijah and some think that the prophet will actually return on a cloud, as the prophecy states.

"Truly you cannot find Elah until you let go of your self-centered desires. This is what Abba Elohim taught me in the desert. Therefore, let us work with strong conviction to overcome our selfish thoughts and wishes, and demonstrate this simple, heavenly secret through our actions. We must magnify Elah's love in this world.

"Let me give you an example of this kind of love. Look at mothers of all kinds, animals and humans. They sacrifice themselves to give birth, to nurture and to protect their young. This is what love is. Men cannot understand the feeling of mothers, but simply put, it is to give and do for others at the expense of oneself. That is love and Abba is love.

"From the beginning of time, Abba wanted His children to understand this. However, they gave into their lower nature, generation after generation. Therefore, Abba, out of His unchanging and magnanimous love, quietly and painfully worked through time to prepare for and send His son of His direct lineage.

"But His son cannot save this nation alone. This foundation is now disrupted. Therefore, I must basically reestablish John the Baptist's position and on that foundation our countrymen will eventually realize that I am the Anointed One."

Jesus stared directly at Simon Cananean the Zealot, his new disciple, "I feel that you are filled with a passionate fire of righteousness. Do you understand? I cannot do this alone but with your desire and hard work, we will continue that fire of faith that we all started. Once we are successful in finding those who are ready to understand, then finally Abba Elah's design will be accepted by His people and thus the nation prepared for the Anointed One.

"Ignorance causes suffering. I will teach the Good News that dispels ignorance and thereby promote healing and happiness. You represent Abba's chosen nation. Without you, Elah is helpless. Taking the Good News, you, as the purified clouds that Daniel prophesied about, are cleansed and changed and thus you will bring all to receive Elah's True Son.

"The nation is full of leaders who know only to live for self-interest and misguided tradition. They will come against us and want to destroy us in order to keep the status quo. However, we speak the truth. Through our selfless giving, our example, we must help them understand that the time of their rebirth is at hand."

Jesus felt some uncertainty. So as usual he used a story to clarify his meaning with symbols, "You will go out as lambs among wolves. You must be humble and serving, but you also must also be wise as serpents. If you encounter people who readily accept you, then give them the blessing of Elah; but if you encounter opposition, leave that home or town. If someone strikes you, do not fight back; just walk away and pray for them. Harbor no ill will for that is what you will get!"

Jesus continued, "Do not be afraid. Believe that Elah is with you from this day forward. Look at how Elah takes care of the simple things of creation like the birds of the air. How much more will He take care of you, His children.

"Do not be afraid of losing your life. Ponder this riddle. If you seek to gain your life for your own sake, you will lose it. However, if you freely give your life to proclaim the glory of Abba Elah to help others, then you will surely gain your life."

Mary watched his expression. Momentarily she drifted off in her own hopeful thoughts, *Rabboni is thirty-two years old. He is in the prime of his life as we all are. We share the same heart, hopes, and the same great expectations. We will see the Kingdom of Heaven in our lifetime!*

Suddenly, Jesus' voice interrupted Mary's distracted thoughts, "We will return to Galilee. On our way, I want to visit the temple in Jerusalem. It is but days before Sukkot and there will be much activity there."

Elder Simon stood to receive direction from Jesus. Mary admired his willing heart.

Finally, Jesus turned to Lazarus, "Your kindness and hospitality have been a great comfort to us at this unexpectedly serious time. Abba Elah will never forget how you cared for us. We will take our leave."

Unexpectedly, Martha came forward and knelt before Jesus. "Rabboni, please allow me to join and serve you again," she begged.

Jesus, happily surprised, looked at Lazarus and asked, "Will you allow your sister to join us? We welcome her!"

Lazarus was not surprised and nodded, "Martha already asked my permission yesterday. Yes, my brother, she goes with my blessing!"

Lazarus went to Martha and handed her a bag of money, "Sister, please place this into the hand of our Rabboni, that he may use it to accomplish Elohim's work. I want to join you, but I send you in my place!"

The unexpected generosity overwhelmed Jesus. He went to Lazarus and Martha and wrapped his arms around their shoulders, one on his right and the other on the left, "Your blessings will be great!"

After everything was loaded onto the wagon and goodbyes had been said, Jesus led his disciples out of the compound and onto the northwestern road to Jerusalem.

Before leaving, Jesus directed Simon, "Help Judas Iscariot and his brethren, Simon the Zealot and Thaddeus and James, sons of Alphaeus, become acquainted with our routine and customs. Because they are familiar with a lifestyle like ours, I am confident that they will quickly adjust." Then he called to Judas and handed him the money bag that Martha had given him.

Judas received respectfully the money with his right hand, humbly saying, "I will do my best to safeguard and handle this money diligently."

"Elder Simon," Jesus called, "this evening when we make camp we will gather together for dinner and get to know each other." Everyone understood and humbly bowed at Rabboni's request.

Standing in front of the mules, Jesus prayed aloud for Elah's protection and blessing, "Abba Elah, we are taking our first steps in this new direction. We sense Your protection, guidance, and inspiration in our new endeavor. Let us always reflect Your divine loving and caring nature to each other and all Your children waiting to hear the Good News."

Walking next to Martha, with Salome on the top board of the wagon, Mary reflected on all that had recently transpired, praying always for her Rabboni.

PART III

Chapter 21

A New Resolution

You cannot make wedding guests fast
while the bridegroom is with them, can you?
(Luke 5:34)

Jesus knew that he needed to reassemble the spiritual foundation of John the Baptist's ministry. Since John's death, all of Abba Elah's foundation was lost and Jesus faced the nation alone. Thus, he planned a return to Galilee where he had a foundation and following of his own.

While everyone prepared for the trip, Jesus took James and Mary aside and explained his change of plans, "I want to take a small group and make a necessary diversion into Jerusalem. As you know this is the week of Sukkot (Feast of Tabernacles). There are many worshipers inside the temple walls. Their hearts are prayerful and open. I want to use this opportunity to speak to them about my refreshing experience with Abba Elah."

Jesus continued, "Therefore, I want to go as close to the temple as I can and draw a group of people and speak with them. I want you two, and also John, to go with me. Simon and the others will make camp for the night. Mary, your knowledge of Hebrew will help me assess the mood of the people. You will be a big help to me. James, ask John to come with us. I will speak with Simon. Everyone else will wait outside of the city gates with the wagon and make camp."

Mary and James answered, respectfully, "As you wish."

In the early morning, Jesus led his followers out of Lazarus' compound. The wagon followed their humble procession. As she walked next to the wagon, Mary thought, *I'm glad to leave the disappointment behind us and make a new start.* Though uncertainty lingered in her thoughts, she felt happy to return to the countryside, *Sincerity and openness are more prevalent here.*

Jesus' idea inspired her. Reassured she thought, *Rabboni will find a way to pick up where we left off in Galilee. The country people are moved by his compassion. Their innocence allows them to listen openly, and his down-to-earth parables are easier for them to understand and learn how to make Elah real in their lives.*

Mary had a fleeting thought of curiosity, *I wonder how Rabboni will be received among the staunchly orthodox clerics and conservative pilgrims today. Hopefully they will be surprised by his wisdom and compassion and be drawn to him as are those in Galilee.* Distracted by the unfamiliar countryside, she relaxed as she walked along and accepted her mission.

Not long after they left Bethany, their pace slowed due to the many travelers converging on the main road to the temple. It was a required pilgrimage for every Hebrew family to properly practice their faith and give their offerings.

"How can large families manage the expense?" She wondered, since it was her first time to attend a holiday in Jerusalem. *Experiencing it is a lot different from hearing about it.* She remembered her mother's words, "…a full year is necessary to set aside denarii and coppers for our three mandatory celebrations, Pesach (Passover), Shavuot (Pentecost), and Sukkot (Feast of Tabernacle). Of course, we would attend if you were healthy.

"But many families have only meager resources. Any extra money, if there is any, is set aside for expenses needed for each trip. They need to bring food for the whole family and enough money to make offerings, as they also need to buy an animal to sacrifice at the temple. It's truly a great expense.

"Mary, it is a stretch for a family of four, but even more so for the larger families. In addition, we must pay our taxes and tithes throughout the year. As you can imagine, everyone struggles to survive."

Mary realized she had not fully understood her mother's words. But now, experiencing the crowds of pilgrims, she appreciated the wisdom of her mother. Most of the folks traveled on foot, with a mule or a wagon carrying their supplies. They came from the whole region, north, south, east, and west. The fortunate were those living in the area who had to make only a short journey. The local residents were obvious as they carried only light bags, while their children skipped along or played with each other. These families seemed happier and less weary or burdened.

As Martha and Salome rode on the top board of their wagon pulled by two mules, they also watched the pilgrims. Mary walked beside them and listened to their experiences and talk about the holiday.

Salome explained to Martha her gratitude to be a part of Jesus' mission, "Since I married a fisherman and lived next to the sea it was easy for me to feel the spirit of Elah. Surrounded by nature, it was easy to feel close to the Creator. I guess my sons caught that inclination as well."

Then Salome continued, "Yes, as a family we made the pilgrimage for the holidays. It was required to be in good standing with our rabbi. We never missed one, even when I was pregnant."

"How about you?" she asked Martha and Mary.

Martha nodded, "Living close by we were able to go to the temple for the worship and offering, but we celebrated the holiday comfortably at home."

Mary interjected, "Today will be my first day to see the temple. From early childhood I was too ill to travel. My mother told me that after my father died, she accompanied her brother and sisters to observe the holiday. She carried me on her back as I was not even a year old. However, when I became too ill, she feared for my life to make such a trip. Our rabbi gave her a dispensation to abstain from the journey.

"My mother and grandmother, however, always made wonderful celebrations. Passover was my favorite holiday." These thoughts of the past brought pangs of sadness. But her fortune to be walking with Jesus now easily pushed the uncomfortable feeling away.

Salome and Martha understood her remorse, because they knew about her past. They continued on in silence as they approached Jerusalem.

As the great city of King David came into view, Mary stared awestruck at the expansive wall. *Such an impressive fortress.* Comparing it to Tiberius, the largest city she had ever visited, she thought, *Tiberius is small compared to this!*

"The wall is too high to see the top and too far to see the end, both to the north and to the west!" Mary exclaimed in wonderment to her sisters.

Martha and Salome laughed at her childish astonishment and answered, "Mary, all that we can see is only half of the immense structure. It surrounds the whole city!" The women chatted on as the wagon moved a few feet and then the line paused.

Leading in the front, Jesus unexpectedly guided them out of the line to the side of the road to allow the other pilgrims behind them to proceed onward. "From here," Jesus informed Simon, "as we planned last night, we will continue on to Galilee at first light tomorrow morning. Find a campsite nearby for tonight. I will take James, John, and Mary into the city with me and when I'm finished, we'll join you. Make sure everything is prepared. We have a long journey home and will start out early tomorrow morning."

Together with James, John, and Mary, Jesus continued on through the throngs of wayfarers and entered the crowded city. Since this was Mary's first time to visit the famous city, she was engrossed by all the sights and sounds. As they walked through the eastern entrance, suddenly she became aware of the stale and fetid stench of animals and humans. It was so strong that it brought tears to her eyes and she felt like retching. Reflexively she grabbed her scarf to cover her nose and mouth.

She thought of the how old the city was, *It has been enclosed for so long that the smell is the unintended consequence. How can the people stand it?* She noticed Jesus, James, and John had also covered their nose and mouth with their scarves.

There are so many new sights, she mused as they walked along. Upon entering, they walked under a large black and white striped canopy. To her right, the sound of animals caught her attention as she got a brief glimpse of the stockyards in the distance. *That is one of the reasons for the rancid odor,* she inferred. Between the stockyard and where they stood there were two-story buildings lining both sides of the granite paved roadway.

Used to the countryside, Mary examined all the new sights, noticing the unusual order and architecture of the capital. The road was uncommonly straight, and each structure was made with exceptionally square angles. Most of the dwellings were light brown adobe with reddish-brown adobe roofs. Some had awning-covered patios in front of their entrances. *They look like family residences,* she thought. *But they are orderly and detailed, much different than Galilean homes.*

As they walked toward the temple, Mary continued noticing the modern design. The roads crossed at straight right angles and the smooth stone paved streets were relatively clean. She was relieved that she no longer noticed the stench, or else she was just used to it.

She heard clear voices and conversations coming from the wide-open windows of the residences. She guessed that the wooden panels that were folded back were used at night or during bad weather. Delicious aromas of food being cooked filled the air and caused Mary's stomach to rumble, reminding her of home.

Finally, they arrived at the Temple Mount and in awe she whispered, *Another wall, it looks as high as the wall surrounding the city.* She exclaimed aloud, "It is huge!" James turned and smiled at her youthful amazement.

Leaving John at the entrance for possible protection, Jesus, James, and Mary continued on into the courtyard. As Jesus had expected, there were many people within the outdoor assembly area. Dozens of people were congregating. Since it was the first day of the holiday there were actually fewer than the normal number of people.

Jesus stared up at the massive parapet that surrounded the city. Mary knew he was praying in preparation for his sermon. She understood his plan, *Of course, everyone's hearts are naturally open and waiting for inspiration in this holy place. It is a perfect time and place for Rabboni to teach them his new understanding of the Divine.*

She breathed, "It is awesome standing here!" Tears of gratitude spilled over her cheeks as she felt deeply and prayerfully contemplative and imagined how all the pilgrims felt, and Rabboni as well. *No matter whether it's the first time or a lifetime of visits, this edifice's majestic history and immense structure are eternally awe inspiring. What an experience to participate in the celebrations, praying and meditating and being immersed in this highly spiritual atmosphere,* Mary reflected.

Then, after taking a few obvious deep breaths, Jesus turned and began speaking to the person nearest to him, not in a soft voice but a strong echoing voice as if he was speaking to many. "We are standing in an edifice that glorifies El Shaddai Adonai, doesn't it?" Jesus' voice surprised the stranger next to him. Surprised, but with courtesy, he nodded shyly in agreement. Other worshipers turned, also nodding in agreement as he was verbalizing their own thoughts. Others, however, wondered why the audacious man was breaking the meditative atmosphere.

Continuing, he elaborated, "I ask you, what is the purpose of the long prophesied Anointed One? He must be sent by Adonai for a divine purpose. Wouldn't you agree?"

The words 'Anointed One' grabbed their attention and the small crowd answered affirmatively, "Yes."

"The Creator is the Abba of all life. Did it ever occur to you that He deeply loves His children and creation? Did you know that He wants you to experience Him with that understanding? As Abba El Shaddai gives you this life to enjoy and share with others, He freely gives you sustenance for yourself and others as well. He wishes that you do the same, that you give to others. In doing so, you receive life and progress in your life. Do you understand?

"However, often out of frustration or anger, we create situations that take away Abba Elohim's life force. For example, our hatred toward others, revenge or payback, eye for eye, tooth for tooth, all these attitudes that you've been taught throughout your life actually take away from your life. Can you think about this and reject those seemingly normal responses?

"But I tell you, those base reactions, common in society, are accepted because of ignorance. I am teaching you that those reactions actually hurt you and cause the life of Elohim to dissipate from you. Through those base responses, we lose life elements from Abba and unknowingly open ourselves and our families up to illness and misfortune. And likewise, the negative reaction of another toward you causes them illness as well. Without realizing the cause of our sorrow, how can we find solutions to our problems?" Jesus added compassionately.

"We are told by our rabbis that it is because Elohim is angry with you and wants to keep you in line, but that is untrue. Abba Elohim does not act as humans do. He is the benevolent creator and source of life and loves His creation! I am telling you that when you are kind and compassionate toward your neighbors you will notice the same action comes back to you. And your life, free of misfortune, will be filled with joy and prosperity."

Mary noticed that Rabboni's refreshing message relaxed the travelers and mesmerized them with his novel concepts.

"Therefore, you must be born again in order to truly set your life on a course that brings blessings rather than curses. You must change your old ways!"

Looking around at the accepting and enthralled expressions on their innocent faces brought tears to Mary's eyes. Most were simple commoners. There was one man standing behind them, an official of some type, Mary guessed. *The cleric is listening with an unusually positive and attentive expression.* It was so unusual that she continued to pay attention to him. *He is captivated by Rabboni's refreshing words. It seemed he is uncommonly openminded.*

Jesus was about to continue his discourse when suddenly from behind him, menacingly heavy steps were heard pounding on the granite floor as a swarm of guards surrounded him. Their leader inquired, "Why are you interrupting the silent prayer and meditation of these holy pilgrims? It is a place of reverence, a respected and solemn courtyard, and a preparation for entering the holy areas."

Immediately, fear came over the people and everyone scattered!

Boldly, Jesus stood his ground and announced, "I am Jesus of Nazareth. I am inspired to speak the truth of Elohim to all His people. There is no other place more appropriate, and you would do well if you had ears to hear as well!"

He continued with confidence, "We are living in a time of great change. Whether it is a zenith or whether it is an abyss is totally up to the human response to the one Elohim has sent. That is why I am teaching that humankind must be reborn."

The lowly official, caught unprepared by Jesus' confidence and strong spirit, found himself flummoxed. As he stood trying to make a decision, another magistrate appeared and demanded, "Who are you?"

Jesus repeated his name. Surprised, the official exhibited recognition of his name. He squinted his eyes, challenging Jesus, "What credentials do you have to speak here? With no authorization, you must leave. If you do not, you will be arrested on the spot and charged as a disrupter of society!"

As the guards started to advance, James jumped in front of Jesus preparing for a confrontation. Suddenly, the dignified man who had caught Mary's attention earlier stepped forward and proceeded to ease the tension. His magnificently flowing white robe edged with black stripes, and phylactery sitting atop his forehead, gave him all the obvious authority needed to overrule the official and the soldiers. With dignity he addressed the leader of the guards, "I am Nicodemus, a Pharisee of the ruling council here in the temple," showing them his large golden ring as confirmation.

The guards and the official immediately stood down as the Pharisee projected his authority, "I have this under control. You may leave now." Clearly this cleric had clout. Without further discussion they withdrew and the four stood alone in silence, the loud cadence of marching steps fading into the distance.

Cautiously, he cleared his throat, "Let me introduce myself. I am Nicodemus and as you can see, I am priest, and a Pharisee." He paused and seemed uncertain. Looking around nervously and lowering his voice he admitted, "I have some questions, but this is not the place to ask. Could I meet you this evening, somewhere we can speak candidly?"

Without hesitation Jesus answered, "Yes!"

Though he was of the establishment, the Pharisee was uncommonly humble. His reserved but benevolent demeanor reminded Mary of her uncle.

Jesus, James, and Mary walked together with Nicodemus to the East Gate where they found John. Nicodemus kept up his pretentious demeanor as an official ushering them out, as they were not sure who or if anyone was watching. As he bowed respectfully in a customary and official farewell, he whispered, "Can you meet me after dark in the Kidron Valley outside the city? There is a discrete and private olive grove near its summit."

"Yes!" Jesus answered, and quickly Nicodemus turned and left.

Without further discussion Jesus and his three followers continued at a fast-paced walk back to their encampment.

Mary chided herself for becoming distracted by the fascinating city, *I should have prayed and focused more for Rabboni's success.* She reviewed all that had happened during the day, *This whole incident was a chance for Rabboni to make a new beginning! He found the best place and certainly found innocent and open-minded countrymen in the heart of the temple. His short sermon was refreshing and inspiring. It was the first time these people heard such ideas. This was truly a great day. And Rabboni met the Elder Nicodemus!*

Arriving at the campsite, Jesus did not rest but began organizing everything with Simon. Mary went to Martha to bring a light meal to Jesus. Martha followed, handing out food to everyone. After eating quickly, the same three left again with Jesus.

Jesus led them down an embankment eastward from the campsite into the Kidron Valley. It was dark but John and James carried torches, illuminating the path. The valley was between Jerusalem on one side and the Mount of Olives on the other side. At this time of night, it would be a quiet and private place for a meeting. Ascending the slopes amidst a grove of olive trees, Mary thought, *It is certainly a desolate place.* There were large edifices that looked like tombs.

Jesus stopped and took one of the torches and looked around. Turning to James and John he instructed, "Stay here while I go further into the grove nearer the summit. The cleric will be here soon."

Mary followed to support him in prayer. She explained to the brothers that she needed a quiet place to pray. As she began her prayer, she became distracted by Rabboni's intense prayer, "Abba Elah! I know that if I have more time, I can reach the nation. This Pharisee was indeed moved by my sermon and so interested that he is willing to risk his reputation to meet me. It is a good place to begin. From one, I promise there will be others. I know that You are with me as I make this my new beginning.

"...With only my few dedicated disciples, I reassure you Oh Abba Elah! that I will rectify my lost foundation! You saw those inspired worshipers today. I have hope and will make a clearer plan. I want to relieve your frustration with your stubborn children, Abba Elah. However, if I need to sacrifice myself even more to gain the spiritual momentum, I will. I want to inspire you with my determination to overcome the obstacles. I promise with my life!"

Mary heard his strongly articulated prayer and felt his emotional determination. She determined herself to walk with him, even if it became more difficult.

As expected, soon Nicodemus walked out of the darkness and into the light of the torch. Jesus walked up to him and announced himself. Mary stood a few steps away but out of the light. The tall, stately gentleman was not wearing his official robes. Although he was dressed as a commoner, he nonetheless had a distinguished air about him. He was as tall as Jesus but much older, with short, curly silver hair. Nicodemus' attitude was noticeably more respectful than any of the other religious leaders she had met. His dispassionate expression was hard to read but when he bowed to Jesus, his respect and earnestness were apparent.

Jesus spoke first, "Thank you for meeting with me. You have questions?"

Nicodemus nodded and said, "From what I heard and saw today I am convinced that you are a teacher inspired by Elohim Adonai. I, myself, have for a long time felt uncomfortable with the constant bantering of a vengeful Elohim. In many ways our religion has become more and more like the pagan religions surrounding our nation. Your concern and care for our countrymen, especially the poor and downtrodden, is what caught my attention. What I heard today can only come from one who is inspired by Adonai. I am curious about this rebirth you spoke about today."

Boldly, Jesus answered him, "As I said today, you must be born again to see the Kingdom of Elohim."

Nicodemus thought for a moment about the unusual statement, and then asked sincerely, "How can I be born again when I am old? Must I enter my mother's womb a second time and be reborn?"

Jesus explained, "No, you cannot be born again in your mother's womb, but your spirit and consciousness must be reborn. Originally given life by

Elohim, His children chose a different master. This evil master became the father of all humankind. Thus, they are servants of the servant Lucifer. In order to become children of Elohim, all humankind must be reborn, through me. I am effectively the second Adam."

Jesus boldly but desperately explained, "From the beginning of time, humankind disobeyed Elohim the Creator. Instead, they obeyed a different master, the servant. And because of that, human beings see the world from a servant's perspective. The Creator Elohim is our true parent. Therefore, we must be reborn as children of our original Creator in order to clearly understand our relationship with Him. Mistakenly, human beings, including the current Hebraic theology, created Elohim from the viewpoint of a servant.

No one can serve two masters. Either you will hate the one and love the other or you will be devoted to one and despise the other. You cannot serve both God and mammon.

"We are living at a very special time, as I am sure you are aware. And, as such, Elohim revealed Himself and His creation to me." Jesus' statement obviously astounded the religious man, but Jesus knew that he understood, "Yes! You got it!"

Determined not to let the incredible realization be lost, Jesus explained, pointing to himself, "Then Abba Elohim sent me to proclaim His truth and give rebirth to all His children. By following me and uniting your heart with mine, I will guide you through the process of rebirth."

"But how is one reborn?" Nicodemus asked again.

Jesus continued purposefully, "You speak of things we know and have seen, but you do not understand my explanation? Think about it. You, as a religious teacher, recognize how the word of Elohim can resurrect a man's soul. Am I correct?" Jesus asked, and paused as the cleric was obviously pondering his words.

"Nicodemus," Jesus spoke directly, "you realize who I am. But your physical intellect continues to argue. Your spirit perceives the truth of what I say but your pragmatic mind fights this awareness. Am I not correct? If I tell you about physical things and you do not believe, then how will you accept or understand spiritual things? No one has ever truly understood the Creator, Elohim, except His true son. If you believe in His son, you will be reborn.

"It is time for humankind to find the truth of Elohim Adonai, you admit it yourself. I am the first son of man to experience the light of Elohim, that He is my Abba. Through me, all can come out of the darkness and into the light and become sons and daughters of Elohim hayyim."

Nicodemus' face changed. It relaxed, and to Mary he even looked younger. He listened with serious intent and humble attention. He understood and then earnestly responded, "Lord, you have enlightened me. How can I be of help to you?"

Jesus was moved to see his open mind and heart and said, "Nicodemus, you are one of the first to be fortunate enough to understand. You must pray and gather like-minded associates. Elohim will inspire you as you are a valuable leader and know my heart.

"I will go back to Galilee where I have a foundation. When the time is right, I will return to Jerusalem, the seat of our faith. Please remain here in Jerusalem until I return. Please pray for my mission, that Elohim's will be done. And gather those as open hearted as you."

The scholar, obviously bright with the new revelation, nodded and expressed his commitment, "I will pray in the temple every day for your success!" Then he respectfully bowed to Jesus with his fist over his heart, signifying his commitment and allegiance.

As Nicodemus left, Jesus offered a prayer, speaking to Abba as if He was standing right in front of them. He asked for the cleric's protection, "The man is blessed and prepared to have an open heart and dares to seek the truth."

Mary saw how Nicodemus' capacity to understand gave Rabboni hope. She realized that this was the first religious official who showed appreciation for Jesus. She had never seen an educated cleric so open and receptive. She too felt great hope from this unexpected experience.

They returned to the camp and gathered everyone together to end their successful day in prayer. After the uplifting meeting with Nicodemus, Jesus was empowered. Mary reflected, *It is like a weight has been lifted off his shoulders.* Even after the long eventful day, he continued on as his usual congenial and warmly gracious self. Filled with hope and enthusiasm, Jesus went to each of his companions and prayed with them individually.

He prayed an unusually strong prayer with Simon the Zealot, and asked him to give a testimony of something about his life.

Simon explained, "Before joining the Baptist, I was inspired by Judas of Gamala. I am passionate about our Elohim-centered nation. The pagan Romans are contaminating this nation. However, following the Baptist taught me to prepare for the Anointed One. There I learned repentance and humility and I think that helped me to find you. Lord Jesus, I am proud to follow and help you. There are many calling you the Anointed One. I want to understand and accept you. I promise my allegiance to you."

Mary saw Jesus' approval, though he said to Simon, "Do not tell anyone what you believe. It is not yet the right time. However, I appreciate your heart and honesty."

Jesus turned to Judas Iscariot. He stood still, gazing into Judas' eyes for an unusual amount of time. So long that it obviously made Judas uncomfortable, shifting his weight as he continued looking into Jesus' eyes. Then Jesus bowed his head and prayed a strong prayer, "Abba Elohim, thank you for bringing us eager men who want to participate in your providence. I am grateful for this humble educated man, Judas. I pray that he will walk beside me and assist me as we meet together the leaders of our faith." Jesus ended with a loud "Amen."

"Tell me more about yourself," Jesus inquired.

Judas bowed, looked around and said, "I've noticed that I am the only Judean here. While I come from a different culture, I feel I can be of assistance to you, Lord. Regardless of my previous allegiances, I am ready to assist you and everyone to the best of my ability."

Mary noticed Judas' brownish eyes and felt his sincerity, but also noticed a hint of superciliousness. She prayed that he and his three associates would develop a strong allegiance to Rabboni.

It was late and darkness enveloped them and the fires in other campsites were going out. A breeze sent sparks from the fire sporadically through the air as Jesus sat next to Simon. He leaned over and asked, "Is dinner ready?"

Simon answered affirmatively. He turned to Mary and requested, "Can you ask Martha and Salome to bring the food?"

Moments later, Mary returned with Martha and Salome, carrying baskets filled with freshly made flat bread. There were baskets of cheese and of dried fish and walnuts. And as Martha announced that Salome had made her famous lentil soup, Mary handed out platters and bowls and spoons. Everyone had their own wineskins. The baskets were passed around.

Mary went to Rabboni's side and presented him with the warm soup and filled his platter. She knew he was hungry. She bowed to him and went back to join her sisters. Everyone ate heartily and there was a friendly atmosphere of sharing.

After the delicious food, Mary suddenly felt exhausted and overwhelmed with emotion. She tried her best to help clean up and converse with her sisters, but she asked to retire. Listlessly, she went to her sleeping place. As she sat on her bedroll, the memories of the whole week flooded her mind as did tears from her eyes. She allowed the release of repressed emotions from all the changes and events of the last few days.

She prayed, *Thank you, Abba Elah. Such extremes happened these last few days. And the whole time Rabboni remained constantly encouraging. Even though he was disappointed in losing the Baptist, he did not give up. And from his determination to speak in the temple, he attracted the cleric Nicodemus. I am greatly inspired.* She tried to continue, but overwhelmed by emotion she cried herself to sleep.

Chapter 22

Education and Foundation

I am the vine and you are the branches.
If you remain in me and I in you,
You will bear much fruit.
Apart from me you can do nothing.
(John 15:5)

As Mary and Martha walked beside the wagon on their way to Jericho, the first stop on their way back to Galilee, Mary explained about meeting the Pharisee, Nicodemus, to her sisters. "He initiated the meeting and was very receptive with good questions. He made it clear to Jesus that he wanted to help him and would await his direction."

Martha commented, "This is encouraging. It is clear that Rabboni is making an impact even here in Judea. There are also many people who respect the Baptist and who are open and longing for the Messiah, aren't there?"

Salome listened, sitting on the top board of the wagon, happy to hear about yesterday's meeting. But Mary noticed herself feeling uncomfortable and regretful, *Maybe I should not have spoken about the temple occurrence. Maybe it's not my place to speak about such things. If Rabboni wants everyone to know about it, he will explain it.* She thereby determined to keep his confidence in the future.

During the journey back to Galilee, Mary felt the depth of Rabboni's resolution. She realized that in each solemn prayer and every word he spoke, he followed his plan. Jesus became more serious with all his disciples. He became stricter in their routine, and he stressed unity. Each morning he spoke about the importance of compassion and willingness to have consideration for one another.

There was a lot of time to think as they walked. Mary recalled Rabboni's sermon that morning. He reminded them to look at nature, "Look at the birds of the air and the lilies in the field, Abba Elah has arranged for the fulfillment of their every need. And all the creatures running around in the fields and mountains. And thus, as His children we are not different to Abba Elah. Do not worry! Abba Elah knows and fulfills our every need, as well.

"We must seek first His goodness and compassion and then all things will be given to us as they are needed. Take encouragement from these words and hold them strongly in your hearts."

Inspired and greatly encouraged by his every word, Mary noticed that the spirit of hope was gradually returning to everyone and also to the newcomers, except for Judas. He seemed stiff, a bit pompous, and a cautious man. *I guess his heart is still connected to the Baptist and hasn't gotten over it yet. Still, he's very concerned for our safety, ordering everyone to stay alert to possible dangers ahead, even requesting a sentry posted every night when they camped.*

Jesus advised him, "All that is fine but more important is our unity, sincerity, and diligent work. This will foster Elah's protection."

Jesus used Mary as an example and explained to Judas, "She has an open heart and quickly conceptualizes my meaning with a humble attitude. This is my hope for you, Judas, that you do the same. Lay aside your scholarly and worldly concepts and receive my new concept of Elohim in your heart. Remember what I have told you. Human beings have created a false Elah that acts and looks like a human being; an Elah that resents and retaliates, that hates and takes revenge, and so on. I am presenting a new paradigm for humankind."

Jesus explained, "As I explained this morning, I cannot say enough times that Elohim is the Abba of all creation. Abba Elohim created out of love for all He created. To each individual kind He gave the ability to nourish itself and its offspring. Everything, from the smallest gnat to the largest tiger, He caused to grow, know how to protect, seek comfort, to heal, to procreate, and thus fulfill all of its needs.

"To humankind, His direct children, He gave all the above. But, He also He gave them a unique position, as His children. He gave His own nature with the sensibility to love and care for the whole creation. He purposed them to be guardians of this tangible world. There is nothing in the Creator that even resembles hatred or revenge." Then Jesus emphatically remarked, "Elah does not seek punishment."

Observing Judas' stoic expression, Mary hoped that he grasped Jesus' meaning. After a few minutes of thought, Judas asked, "Then how does El Shaddai keep man from sinning. From what I see, without the fear of Elohim and punishment, humankind would become animals."

Patiently Jesus answered. "That is a very good question, Judas! An excellent question! What you just asked is at the heart of all that needs to change in the world and in you."

Let me explain, "I, the Son of Man, also come from this society that created these false concepts. However, through my experience in the desert, I came to know the reality of this world. The new ideal that I am teaching refutes that false concept. Our whole way of thinking has to change, our hearts need to change, and the way that we live must change.

"Elohim meant for His children to have a life of joy and happiness, comfort, and good will. This is the meaning of the Kingdom of Heaven. It is not a place. It is a change of heart!"

He went on, "This is one example of why your old way of thinking must change. If you seek revenge toward another, revenge will be what you get. If you take for yourself, things will be taken from you. Joy and happiness will not be possible for you."

Trying to reach Judas' heart, Jesus repeated compassionately, "However, the reverse is true. If you give to others freely, others will give to you. If you comfort others or go out of your way to help others, then you will be comforted, and others will go out of their way to help you in your time of need. Elah showed me the truth of all existence. Everything is created to flow through giving and receiving. My responsibility is to help people in all levels of society to understand this and change. Can you help me?"

Mary noticed that Judas' expression seemed unmoved. She prayed that soon he would be able to understand.

Their caravan arrived in the surrounding hills of Jericho at dusk. The men worked together to set up the camp while the three women prepared dinner and brought out all the food.

"Rabboni, I would like to give a testimony," Mary requested.

Jesus nodded, "Please teach us, dear sister. Your heart is very close to mine."

Mary began, "When I first heard the Baptist speaking of repentance for all people including the Hebrews, I was surprised at the concept of repentance and confused by it. It took me a long time to reconcile the idea. But after much anguish and disrespect toward my mother, I recognized my need to repent from seeing how I hurt her and others. I truly felt relief when I did!

"Then one time you gave a simple sermon about a full cup of water representing a person's consciousness. You said that if a person wants more water, first he must empty the cup in order to make space to receive more water. That meant a lot to me. I realized the cup represented my mind and water represented ideas." I also thought, "What good are my old ideas, if I cannot help someone or solve a problem. Therefore, I want to be an empty vessel, ready to receive new ideas."

Jesus responded, "Yes, Mary, thank you for this testimony. It is essential for everyone to empty themselves in order to hear correctly and clearly a new concept." Jesus then suggested, "One must be like a child to enter the Kingdom of Heaven. Why?" he asked.

Phillip answered, but seemed unsure that his answer would be correct, "Because a child begins the world without any concepts, like the empty cup?"

Jesus praised him for his answer, "Yes, that is why a child learns quickly."

The second night, the travelers stopped along the Jordan River on their way northward. After dinner they sat around the campfire and Jesus asked if anyone had a question. Mary sat quietly listening to the conversations.

Judas asked another question, "Rabbi, when will we see the Kingdom of Heaven? Will it happen in our lifetime?"

Again, Mary sensed Judas' impatience and frustration, *Perhaps he is tired of this nomadic life and wants to put down roots, to have a family?* she thought.

Jesus nodded and answered frankly, "It is a fair question, one that I am sure is on everyone's mind. With the change created by John's death, you have realized that much more time and effort will be needed. Then you consider your own personal desires and that your goals may need to be put off indefinitely. And you are asking yourself, is this all worth it?"

"What do you think Simon? Is this true?" Jesus asked.

Simon was not accustomed to Jesus' attention. He hesitated.

Jesus challenged him to speak, "Then, how do you think Perpetua will think, when you tell her your mission may last for many years?"

Simon blushed and answered honestly, "She asked me that very question the last time I was home. She was concerned that I would not be coming home to stay anytime soon. But I told her, that it would not be too much longer."

Jesus went on, "What about all you bachelors. Isn't it your goal to have a family?"

Straightforward questions, Mary thought.

Jesus kept probing, "Some of you are questioning about personal goals you gave up for Elah and our nation. I imagine your most desired goal in life is to be a husband and father. Am I correct?

"This is natural. And frankly I also have the same desire, which is natural because this is Elah's desire for all of us." Jesus stood up as if to change the atmosphere of personal reflections. He spoke loudly, but hopefully to inspire them, "We are living in an auspicious time. The Kingdom of Elah, long dreamed of, is now at hand. However, it must be created. It must be built with our sacrifice of blood, sweat, and tears. Just as our ancestors created this nation, they had to expend themselves unselfishly and sacrifice their immediate desires for the future. All of you, whether with John or with me, were inspired by Elah.

"You believed in John's message that pointed to me, and you gave your all for his mission. You willingly gave up everything to see it accomplished. Therefore, you are great men and women of Elah. I invite you to continue giving your all. The Kingdom of Heaven is knowing that Abba Elah fulfills completely your every need. It is not a place, but it is a state of mind, with the awareness of perfect fulfillment of joy, happiness, love, compassion, and a creative healing process. In here," Jesus pointed to his chest.

"Listen, I myself had to learn that selfish desire leads to destruction. I realized that I had to rid myself of old prejudices, old beliefs, and attitudes. It did not come easy for me but because of Elah's love and confidence in me, I felt a renewed concept of the world. I also realized that no one really understands Abba Elah so I learned to forgive.

"My desire is to help you deepen your faith and regain our momentum before returning to Judea. With the foundation we have in the north, my plan is to influence the center of the temple, the rabbis and priests. It became clear to me in Jerusalem that the establishment will surely be hearing about me. I made my first uproar in Jerusalem. Remember we were recognized by some of the worshipers. News of my sermons, and what they call miraculous events, actually preceded us.

"Already news of our campaign has reached the notice of the Pharisees, the leading members of the religious council. I met with an admittedly curious cleric just the other day, and after our conversation he told me he was willing to help in our cause. This was a very hopeful sign for me."

Jesus concluded, "Therefore, let us not lose our vision. The events of the last week caused a ripple in the providence, but as long as we remain single-minded, unite, and support each other, we will be successful. Elah's plan must be and will be fulfilled."

Then Jesus turned his attention back to Judas and compassionately continued his answer, "You believed in John, and you know who I am, right? Did he not tell you that I am the one the nation is expecting? He was a shining light, and you were willing to follow him. But what I have to give is greater than John. My message is from the Abba who sent me. Can you understand?"

Judas nodded and with reassurance he replied, "What you say is true, Rabbi. I give you my total allegiance!"

Jesus stood up and began to pace back and forth, "Everyone, listen. This is very important for you to understand. When we go out and speak with the people, the curious will ask you questions relating to what I am about to proclaim.

"John the Baptist was asked if he was the Anointed One and he replied that he was not. He was asked if he was Elijah the prophet, to which he also replied that he was not. Isn't this true?" Jesus asked everyone, but directly to Judas.

"Yes, Rabbi, he did, and I understand you," Judas said.

"He died without correcting his mistaken answers. Isn't this true?" Jesus asked and waited for Judas to answer.

Judas thought and added, "Because of that mistake, he cast aspersions upon you and left you standing alone." Jesus saw that Judas understood, and nodded.

Unexpectedly Mary asked, "How will those looking for Elijah know that you are the Anointed One?"

"Exactly, yes!" Jesus said, pleased that she understood. "Therefore, I am unable to fulfill my true mission at this time. I have to first take the position of Elijah." Jesus continued, "I admit that this is frustrating, but it is necessary, especially for the educated who follow the scriptures word for word. Therefore, do not tell anyone at this time that I am the Anointed One. It can't be announced because there is no foundation."

Jesus added compassionately, "Remember that Elah understands your heart, even as you begin to understand His. Abba Elah is aiding us to move the influential people much more quickly. Religious leaders are slowly becoming curious in a positive way toward me. Therefore, please do not give up because we will see and experience the Kingdom of Heaven in our lifetime."

Jesus defined their new objective, "Eventually, I will go back to Jerusalem and speak in the Sanhedrin. On the basis of our good deeds, and with numbers of purified believers, upon that foundation a proclamation of the arrival of the Anointed One will be made! Everything we do from now on will be for this purpose."

Mary watched and understood and was greatly encouraged. With hope, she vowed with renewed dedication to remain steadfast in her attendance and unity with Rabboni.

Throughout the trip back to Galilee, Jesus used every opportunity to teach, to inspire, and to prepare his disciples for their mission ahead. The evening meal was the best opportunity. He poured out his heart, answering questions and explaining important scriptures that they needed to know, always teaching about the living and vibrant Abba Elah.

Mary witnessed his sincerity and unyielding effort. He never stopped speaking, serving, and giving. As his designated personal assistant, she was responsible to encourage him to eat and drink. She knew that he hardly slept. Nevertheless, he was vibrantly full of energy.

Nearly every night, after sending the disciples to rest, Jesus chose to educate Mary and Judas further. In the darkness, with only the firelight and the moon, he continued. Night after night, speaking in Hebrew, he prepared them to face the staunch clerics by broadening their scope of Elah's providence. He even revealed unknown secrets, trusting that it would strengthen and enliven their spirit.

He encouraged them, "You two are my vanguard. We will be the spearhead and contact the educated religious leaders. But first, I want to arm you with Elohim's truth and clarify some misinterpretations of scripture. Elohim's manner is completely different from Judaism. I will fortify you with Heaven's understanding." Therefore, every night, he gave profound guidance to the two late into the night.

Chapter 23

Secrets Revealed

I have spoken to you in figures of speech
but the time is coming
when I will speak to you plainly of the Father.
(John 16:25)

On the first night of their in-depth education, Jesus clarified his own personal history to Mary and Judas. He knew there would be questions brought up about his personal life so he wanted to prepare them. He began with the most sensitive truth about his life, "John and I are brothers. Our father was Zechariah, a temple priest in Jerusalem. Zechariah's wife, Elizabeth, is my mother's aunt."

Jesus paused to give Judas a moment to consider the implications. It was not news to Mary because he had already explained the reason for John's reaction to him while they were at Lazarus' home. Nevertheless, tears stung her eyes regarding the unusual nature of their relationship. She noticed that Jesus had spotted her reaction and paused. However, she was surprised at Judas' stoic demeanor, as he interrupted Jesus with a surprising disclosure.

In his typical educated Hebrew, Judas stated, "During my studies in the temple, I associated with many priests. The exclusive Levite tribe see their responsibility to procreate for the sake of the nation. It is perceived as a patriotic duty, a means of increasing the venerated priestly class. I am not surprised by your story, because in my early days as a scribe in the temple I overheard several cases similar to yours that were never openly acknowledged. There were cases of adopted sons."

After a brief pause, and without further explanation, Jesus continued, "This is the story my mother Mary told me. My mother was raised in a temple where she lived an austere life of faith and prayer. Her grandfather, a priest himself, brought her to his home as a baby after her mother was killed. They were direct descendants of David, and he secretly arranged for her to be cared for and protected from Herod's pogroms.

"At fourteen years of age, before she married her betrothed, she received an unusual spiritual request from Elohim. A messenger informed her that Elohim had chosen her to give birth to the Anointed One and asked if she would accept Elohim's request. Innocently, she answered without question, 'May Elohim's will be done to me.' Not long after that experience, she received a request for help from her mother's sister, who was in her sixth month of pregnancy and older than most women to have her first child. That child would be John.

"My mother willingly traveled to the hill country of Judea to help her aunt. It was there, in the household of Zechariah, that my mother conceived me. It was Elohim's hope that together with my aunt and uncle, she would raise me with their son.

"This couple, the High Priest Zechariah and his wife Elizabeth, had also had a revelation that their son would carry out the role of Elijah in preparing the way for the Anointed One. You can imagine their joyful expectation.

"When my mother entered her household, to her surprise, Elizabeth proclaimed that she had received a revelation about her young niece standing in front of her. She exclaimed with joy and proclaimed it guilelessly, 'You will give birth to the prophesied Anointed One.'

"Elizabeth immediately told her husband of the revelation. However, months later when Elizabeth learned that Mary had conceived, she had forgotten the revelation and turned against my mother. And my father would not admit responsibility either for the pregnancy. Truly, everyone turned against my mother, including the parents of Joseph, her betrothed, my stepfather.

"Had it not been for Joseph, who himself surely wrestled with the infidelity of my mother, she would certainly have been punished by stoning. He alone stood between life and death for both of us.

"Zechariah died denying the revelation and his action in creating my life. He never accepted me as his son. My mother never revealed him as my father to her husband Joseph or to anyone. Because of this abandonment by Zechariah and Joseph's families, the course of my life took a different turn. My mother and her new husband were sent back to Nazareth without concern for our welfare.

"If Zechariah and his wife had followed the revelation and taken responsibility for his action, he could have officially adopted me as his son and I would thereby have received formal education in the temple. John and I would have grown up as brothers. It would have been natural for John to realize my value and I his, especially with the tutelage of our father. He would have taught both of us the revelations at our birth.

"That was not how it turned out, however. When I was born, do you think my parents were joyful newlyweds? No, actually my mother struggled every day thereafter with her premature motherhood and illegitimate son. They had no family support. As outcasts, they began their life together." Jesus added, "I know that this is not easy to understand, but I ask you to see this situation from Elohim's point of view. I entrust to you this story of my life and ask you to pray for understanding."

Jesus sighed, "It is late, and you need to rest. We have a few more evenings that I hope to give you a broader perspective of Elohim's providence. It will help you realize Elohim's hand in our lives."

Bowing his head in prayer, he entreated Elohim's grace and support, "We are determined to further Your plan during this providential time. With a clear purpose and with Your inspiration we will bring about Your heavenly kingdom. Your ways are not yet known to humankind. I will correct their misunderstanding and bring Your truth to this harsh world, even if I have to shed my blood doing it."

After another day's slow journey through the Galilean countryside, in the evening Jesus brought all his disciples together. Mary felt Rabboni's resoluteness and his concern for the quick passing of time. He did not want to waste a moment. So, he gave up sleep to teach them all that he had learned in his life and the knowledge he had gained during his time in the desert.

Jesus began, "I want to clarify some misunderstandings in Judaism. Mistakes are not iniquities, rather they are an inevitable process needed for men and women to learn. They are unavoidable because we come into the world knowing nothing.

"Another wrong concept is that a misfortunate person is being judged by Elah. Abba Elah never judges His children. He does not seek revenge. A person becomes wise when he learns from his mistakes and puts that acquired knowledge into action. The deepest thing one may learn is the connection of heart though care and compassion for others. This is the hope of the Creator. With this understanding, a man brings Elah into this world and becomes the physical hands of the Creator. Thus, he creates harmony, joy, health, and happiness in all that he touches and inspires those who witness his actions to do the same.

"When I was young, I was rebellious and resisted my mother's insistence that I was a messiah. When I was twelve, she took me to the temple in Jerusalem to attend their Religious School but they rejected me for asking too many questions and being too obstinate. Extremely disheartened, she traveled back toward Nazareth, thinking that I was in the caravan. When she couldn't find me, she desperately returned to Jerusalem. Three days later she found me still in the temple, conversing and arguing with the clerics.

"After she took me home, she tried her best to teach me her own attitude toward her faith. But I was rebellious and nonconforming. I hated the self-righteous attitude of the religious leaders. The suffering and misery of people in my neighborhood really bothered me. And when I was forced to go to the temple and hear that tithing came first, before relief of starving families, it incensed me. It did not make sense to me that those who professed belief in Elah were often the cruelest toward the downtrodden.

"I refused to believe that a just Elah judged those most unstable in daily living. I did not want to believe in an Elah who took revenge or punished or condemned those who disobeyed the Law. For, after all, people were just doing whatever their human nature urged them to do.

"My nature was outgoing and gregarious and very emotional, but at home the rigidity stifled me, so I escaped. I found unruly types like myself, gadabouts whom I could laugh and joke and drink with. I would find day work to make money in order to be independent from my family. However, when I passed a miserable human being begging for help or food or money, I was reminded of my anger toward Elah. I felt helpless and depressed.

"This went on for some time, until I decided to go to the hills to find quiet and harmony in nature. I reasoned that if there was ha Elohim who created the natural world with such beauty and peace, why were humans tied to ideas of hate and indifference which didn't help anyone. I noticed that even the little marmot female created a lair of comfort to protect and nourish her offspring. I began to feel the heart behind all nature and wondered about the Creator of this simple animal. I began to think that humans had the wrong idea. It was not long after this that I set out to find John the Baptist. I heard people talking about his audacious activities and I was curious." Jesus finished for the night and requested Mary to pray.

As was her custom when asked to pray, she prayed in both Hebrew and Aramaic, thanking Abba Elah, and asking for a peaceful rest for everyone.

It was late at night when their meeting ended. As Mary left, she was surprised to see Elder Simon obviously waiting to speak with Jesus. She thought that he was waiting for Rabboni's direction and plans for the coming day, but he looked annoyed.

She considered sympathetically, *Could he be feeling left out? Recently Jesus started speaking in Hebrew more often. And Jesus has been sharing with Judas and me, speaking for hours in Hebrew.* Nevertheless, she bowed to him respectfully and went to her lean-to.

Mary lay awake thanking Elah for all that Rabboni had confided to them. She also prayed for Simon that he would not allow himself to become jealous. She knew he felt ignored, but also, she knew that Jesus would always respect Simon and consider him his assistant.

The next morning while preparing to continue their trek, Mary overheard Simon complaining again to Rabboni in a low voice, "I don't like having to ask Judas for denarii and accounting to him for every little thing. You have always trusted my judgement. Am I not your captain? He and his band of newcomers have only been with us for a short time. Why do you place so much trust in him?"

Simon was not trying to conceal his frustration as he addressed Jesus. Mary thought that he feared losing Rabboni's confidence. And again, he asked, "Why are you giving him so much attention?" She noticed how Simon's attitude was influencing the others. This had begun after her first meeting with Jesus and Judas. She knew that they simply felt a loss of attention even though they were his first disciples.

She began to notice them gossiping together, and Simon as their spokesman boldly asked Jesus, "Rabboni, why is Judas becoming so influential?" Not long after this rift started, Simon brazenly complained about Mary being too close to Judas and Rabboni, "She is only a woman and should not be seen conversing with men, especially late at night. Many will question what is so important for a woman to be up so late with men." Mary overheard the whole conversation.

Rashly he asked, "Why do you love Mary so much?"

Jesus, surprised at Simon's question, closed his eyes and answered him using an analogy, "In the dark a blind man and one with vision are no different, but when light comes the man with sight sees the light while the blind man remains in darkness."

It was a hard truth for Simon. However, it made him think realistically. The reality was apparent, but this was not the first time that Jesus had commented thus. Jesus continued, "Truly her sincerity is apparent, and her actions are innocent. You know this to be so and cannot argue."

Simon refrained from questioning further, but his brooding did not end. Mary knew that Rabboni reminded Simon often of her helpfulness and thus denied his concern. Simon, however, would not drop his distaste for their close though platonic relationship. When Simon overheard gossip about the two, he did not speak up on their behalf even though he knew that their relationship was irreproachable.

On the other hand, Simon truly loved his master and eventually his conscience guided him to inform Jesus of the rumors. Without quelling them himself, he suggested that they send Mary away for a while to let the scandalous talk die down. Jesus, not concerned by Simon's report, asked him pointedly to examine his own wrongdoings, his prejudice, and jealousy. "Let us put an end to this nonsense," Jesus insisted strongly, reminding Simon, "Disunity is the first ingress to destruction."

Jesus convened everyone and reminded them that self-centered thoughts were destructive to their undertaking, "Your frailties, your accusations, and other unseemly struggles in your mind must be addressed by each of you." Jesus nodded directly to Simon, "Stay alert to your thoughts, are they self-centered or are they altruistic? Do not gossip among yourselves. Mary is our sister. You know how very valuable she is to us and to Elah. This is a test of your unity with me. Don't doubt me. Use this to strengthen your resolve as my disciples. Tests of your loyalty and commitment to my mission are coming. Be careful.

"As we travel, let your prayers and concerns be to bring my Good News of Elah's heart and love to our countrymen as quickly as possible. We have an uphill task, but we will prevail if you remain steadfastly united with me!"

Jesus continued his nightly meetings, bequeathing his understanding to all his disciples and sometimes to his two most prepared disciples. Night after night, he desperately poured out his heart without regard for the length of their meetings. They came to understand that every hour was treasured time with Jesus.

One rainy night, under a lean-to canvas, Jesus revealed another event in his life that was unexpectedly significant to Mary. "The time my mother took me to the temple in Jerusalem, she first stopped to make a request of my birth father, Zechariah. She asked him to use his influence with the Hebrew school authorities to grant my acceptance there. He refused.

"She also asked him to perform the ceremonial blessing upon me becoming an adult. Her excuse to Joseph and myself was because of his high status as a high priest. She insisted that it was best and appropriate for him to perform the ritual. However, my mother told us that Zechariah referred us to the attending priest to perform the ceremony in his place. It was an acceptable practice and it saved our honor, but my mother never forgot his cold indifference."

Jesus reminisced, "I remember that day so clearly. When the servant answered the door, she went to announce us to Elizabeth, but her aunt refused to meet us. However, while we stood waiting, I noticed a young girl watching us from the atrium. I knew right away that she was Zechariah's daughter. I looked into her eyes and never forgot her gaze. Intuitively, I knew there was something special about her.

"For many years, I forgot about her until my mother announced that she had begun to look for a spouse for me. I remembered the girl and confidently told my mother that Heaven intended her to be my spouse. My mother was shocked and refused to hear me out. Now I realize that there was too much resentment in my mother's heart as she had been shunned by them, along with the rest of her family. On top of her subtle feelings of abandonment by Elah, she had little fortitude to arrange any match and she dismissed my request entirely. My stepfather Joseph made attempts when I was about sixteen, but by that time I was known as a rebellious and disobedient son. Together with the rumors that Joseph was not my real father, it was hard to find a willing betrothal. After Joseph died, alone without a husband and with no confidence to continue to search for a wife for me, my mother postponed the search for a match.

"From that time, I spent time in the taverns and the streets, talking with marginalized people like myself. I hardly went home, finding company with those on the edge of society. I was more comfortable with derelicts and prostitutes, who I believed knew more about life than my family. We shared our disenchantment with religion and society. I enjoyed besmirching the pompous, hypocritical religious clerics, as did my companions.

"But after the passing of time my conscience began to bother me. I knew the torment that I was causing my mother and family. Gossip spread and they were well aware of my galivanting lifestyle. My mother was horrified, and I knew it.

"In my mid-twenties, in order to find solace and quell my conscience, I went into the hills. I walked and observed the simplicity of nature. There I could think, and there I came to understand many lessons of truth. I could question everything without judgement."

Jesus paused. Mary perceived that he had endured yet another disappointment, and reached for the wineskin to offer him a drink. After a few moments, Mary prompted, "How did your mother fare after that rebuke when you were twelve?"

Jesus answered, "I am sure it was a bitter experience for her. She never attempted to see Zechariah or Elizabeth again. On our way back to Nazareth, we passed through Jerusalem and went to the temple for me to be consecrated as a man and made offerings and prayers. After I was rejected for being too outspoken and argumentative, she left for Nazareth totally disheartened and dazed from the lost opportunity. She assumed that I was in the caravan.

"However, I continued discussing with the scribes and priests to learn from them. I did not find any answers, especially after questioning them about their own experience with Elah. They found me naive, and told me that they believed they could not possibly relate to Elah in a personal way. They also did not like my probing questions that put them on the spot. When it was time to leave, I found that it was dusk. I realized that I had lost my sense of time, and that I was separated from my parents. I knew they would come back so I waited for them outside the temple.

"After a day or two of traveling, my mother realized that I was not in the caravan. In a fog of disillusionment and heartbreak, she had finally started looking for me and found that I was absent. So she and Joseph returned to Jerusalem in search of me. When they finally found me, she scolded me for getting lost. I told her that I was not lost and that she should have known that I was searching for answers. Due to her confusion and disappointment, she could not understand what I was talking about. I realized her state of mind, and I pitied her.

"My mother still does not understand. I think she even lost the memory of her original revelation. While the revelation was a great experience for her, it became nothing more than a dream."

Jesus completed his message for the night and indicated that it was time to retire. Then standing, Rabboni took hold of Judas' left hand and Mary's right hand and requested, "Let us pray." By the time his prayer was over, tears were spilling over Mary's cheeks for she understood the great sadness of Rabboni's life and why he was not married. All was quiet. There were no words left to be said as they bowed and left for their tents.

Mary's physical body was tired, but her heart was filled. She did not know if she could sleep. After she washed up and lay down, she stared into the darkness. Everything was much more serious. She treasured the privileged and personal understanding of Rabboni's life. One thought occurred to her, *What would have happened if his father and his aunt had remembered their revelations about Jesus?*

Her next thought was waking to a beam of sunlight coming through the tent's opening and being called to rise.

Chapter 24

Samaria

But whoever drinks the water that I give, will never thirst.
(John 4:14)

Following Rabboni's desire to reach Capernaum within a week, Simon laid out a plan choosing the well-worn path northward out of Jericho. It was more comfortable and easier for everyone, especially the mules pulling the wagon.

In the evening they stopped not far from the beautiful Jordan River, on a hill overlooking the life-giving waters. The plan was to go through Samaria to Jacob's well, two days journey north, reaching there in the afternoon. By then they would need to refill their water containers. The route followed a gradual uphill clay path through the hills and then down into the valley to the town of Sychar.

At dawn Jesus called, "Simon, prepare to leave." Simon respectfully bowed and led the group back to the road that followed the ancient route returning to Galilee. Their next stop was to replenish supplies. In order to save time, Jesus, Mary, James, and John were to detour to the southwest into the hills toward Mt. Gerizim with one mule and the wagon and go directly to Jacob's well. Simon, Martha, Salome, and the rest were to go into the town of Sychar with the other mule to procure food and supplies, with all meeting up at the well at dusk.

As they walked, Mary still felt the newness of her life, though she also felt the maturity of her faith. Tears came to her eyes as she again felt the need to thank Elah for meeting Rabboni. She loved to see the different people during their journeys. As they passed through Samaria, she noticed the different styles of clothing and listened to their different dialect.

The people are more contemporary here, adopting a more western-style culture. The men with short hair and shaven faces look like Roman soldiers. Mary remembered one of her mother's reports about the Samaritans, *They seem to adapt more to the customs of their conquerors and are not a rigid people. They are a culturally mixed people, yielding more easily than Hebrews.*

Mary noticed that the elderly men and women were dressed much like Hebrews. Some of the men wore caps or thin strips of cloth tied around their heads as Jewish men did. *I wonder if they share some Jewish traditions.*

Also, Mary noticed that the Samaritans were very much aware of them. They watched the foreigners with sidelong glances as they made their way toward the public well. The ancient well was open to all and because water was so important it was a central meeting place outside of the Samaritan town.

As they neared the well, Mary enjoyed watching playful children running around chasing each other and their personal goats. Women filled their urns and carried them on their heads back to their homes. As the water sloshed around in the urns, some spilled on the ground, scattering the dust and creating muddy spots. It was an interesting place.

Mary observed how the Samaritans instinctively knew that the Jewish travelers required their own space and thus they accommodated them in a distant way, humbly moving to one side of the well. It was customary for Samaritans to allow the strictly religious people a time at the well alone. And they expected to be ignored by orthodox men who customarily avoided eye contact with infidels.

Mary thought, *Here is the well that our common forefather Jacob dug, but we have no relationship between us. Brothers and sisters we are, but neither of us wants to recognize that fact, just because of our prejudice and ignorance. How odd!"*

Rabboni walked up to the well and sat down on its stone ledge. Mary sat under a small shade tree, within hearing distance. To her surprise, he began talking to a woman who was purposefully keeping her distance, drawing water on the other side of the well. "Will you give me a drink?" Rabboni asked the woman. "What is your name?"

Surprised, the woman looked around and realized he was talking to her. She was aghast and asked, "Are you speaking to me? I am Susanna." She cleared her throat and continued, "Why do you ask water from me? You know I am not orthodox, yet you speak to me and ask me for water from my cup? You are Hebrew, aren't you?" The woman's manner was mischievous, and her eyes were dancing with glee. She was genuinely interested in this handsome and brazen Jew.

Rabboni replied, himself a bit mischievous, "Why wouldn't I ask for water from you, Susanna? You have a cup, and I don't."

Now the woman was really curious, "Surely you are aware of the prejudice between our people. Your strict laws prohibit you from breaking kosher and drinking after me."

Jesus answered, "I am thirsty and so I ask for water. But do you know that I already have water to give you that if you drink of it, you will never thirst?" Jesus began to speak about her personal life, "You, in fact, must thirst greatly, for you have known many men and have had many husbands. Do you know that you are really thirsting for true love but have yet to find it?"

Mary, enjoying their interaction, watched the woman's astonished face. *She certainly feels something special about Jesus, but she doesn't know quite what it is.*

Jesus continued, "I am the vessel and bringer of Elah's love and if you receive my water, you will thirst no longer. I can give you the blessing of true love, which all are seeking."

Susanna listened earnestly to the stranger, for he had touched a sensitive and private part of her heart. "How do you know my longing? I have no words to express it, yet without forenotice, you come to me and detail it so simply!" she asked, almost in tears.

Fascinated and envious, Mary watched and thought, *Rabboni is so wonderfully free of the rigid Jewish rules. He speaks with anyone. I, too, have no concept of that feeling in my heart. Yet I know it is lingering there. I hope that he will give me the life-giving water that he speaks so freely of and that I can live with him forever.* Now that he had clarified that mysterious feeling, she yearned for it.

Susanna became excited and asked, "Are you a prophet?" She gave her cup of water to Jesus and watched him drink and was captivated, her eyes wide open with excitement. Then she excused herself. Within moments she returned with many of the local inhabitants who wanted to meet the prophet and Holy One.

Mary was filled with awe as the people filed around the well to take a look at him. Jesus rose to greet each person warmly, reaching for their hands, touching their shoulders, and even embracing the elderly. Mary stood and walked nearer to her master to help greet the townspeople, there were so many. Rabboni hugged them as if they were his closest friends. Mesmerized, Mary thought, *Touching the untouchable.*

Jesus said to Mary in Hebrew, "These people receive my words easily, more than my own people. They are closer to my heart and to Elah's heart because of humility. In this day it is better to know nothing than to have read and memorized all the scriptures."

Then he spoke to the Samaritans in Aramaic, a dialect most could understand more deeply than Hebrew. The late afternoon heat had subsided and the people sat out in the open, on the ground and around the well wall. Some of the women held their babies, nursing them at times while the little children played on the outer edge of the crowd. Young and old were eager to hear Rabboni's words. They felt from Jesus an openness of love and truth. Mary's eyes filled with tears when she saw their meekness. They were truly just like curious and guileless children.

Every word that Jesus spoke was with authority and confidence. His love for Elah and humankind was contagious. Unpretentiously he told them that Elah was their parent, "Abba of all things is pure love. And because of our common parent Jacob, we are all tied together as brothers and sisters."

"What is sin?" Jesus asked. "Sin is not really due to moral ignorance but is more the manifestation of imbalance in the soul. When human beings lost skin touch with Elah, we lost everything and became unbalanced. I come to you as Elah's son to help you realign yourself with Him. If you become engrafted to me, then you will become a part of me, and through me you will be able to connect to Elah's heart as your True Abba.

"Just because I, a Jew, may follow the tenets laid out by the temple and the scriptures, do you think this makes me closer to our Abba Elah? No, these rules made by humans reflect their imperfect thinking. Because love, self-sacrifice, and giving without seeking a return are not appreciated, their Elohim does not reflect these attributes.

"I met Elah, the Abba, and was shown the reality of this world. I am here to reveal to you a deeper realization of Elah. Abba is the parent of all things and human beings are His children. Does this make sense to you?" Jesus looked around and into the eyes of each person.

"If you have ears to hear, then know that my words are true and that through me you can know Elah's love which is life-giving, like water." Jesus looked over at the woman he had a conversation with.

Everyone was enthralled. A loud murmur of voices rose as people nodded and spoke to each other, "This is the Messiah! We are hearing and seeing the Messiah in our midst."

Realizing that she was holding her breath, Mary inhaled deeply. She was mesmerized by the truth and peace that were tangible in this moment.

Just then, as the sun neared the evening horizon, Elder Simon and the other followers arrived. Simon was shocked to see Jesus sitting with and speaking to a large number of Samaritans.

"How can he speak with these infidels, these heathens?" Simon said under his breath to James and John with disgust. "They know little about Elah, and their lives are certainly too immoral compared to the Hebrews. If word of this gets out that he is mingling with the sinners there will be great shunning and criticism from our people. We Jews are the only ones prepared and purified enough to understand this Holy Man." John and James said not a word.

Simon paused and walked over to Mary, who was still sitting under the tree. He noticed that Mary was as mesmerized as everyone else. He whispered to her, "What is happening here? You should have kept the Rabboni away from these Gentiles. It is not appropriate for Jews to have contact with them. When the rabbis and other Jewish leaders hear about this, they may hold this against us and make our work harder." Mary listened to Simon's comment but said nothing so as not to interrupt Jesus, who was only a few steps away.

Just about that time a young Samaritan child ran up to Jesus and offered him a drink of water that his mother had given him from Jacob's well. Jesus took it and ceremoniously drank it as if he had overheard Simon. Those in the crowd were amazed. The rumor was true!

Simon's jaw dropped. He whispered with revulsion, "Jesus is drinking from their dirty, non-kosher dish!"

Jesus continued speaking to the crowd, "Do you know that Jewish people cannot eat or drink with infidels?" Rabboni spoke rather playfully, as if pretending that it was a little-known fact. Everyone laughed because, of course, everyone knew of the prohibition. Elder Simon blushed purple. Then Jesus facetiously asked, "What is the name of this well?"

Everyone answered in unison, "Jacob's well."

Jesus said, "Jacob was my forefather. How about you? Was he your forefather?" He laughed and said, "This is becoming fun." And the audience joined in his glee. "Of course, he is our forefather. After all, this is our hometown. If Jacob is my forefather and he is your forefather, then we must be brothers."

"Right! Yes!" everyone shouted in a joyful cheer.

Rabboni glanced over at Simon with a big smile and a wink. It seemed to wash away any ill feelings that Simon had, especially since Jesus seemed to be making fun of him in front of all the people, but in a respectful manner.

Rabboni called Susanna to come up to the front of the crowd. He thanked her in front of her fellow townspeople and announced, "You will be remembered forever for welcoming me and serving me water from this well, for you knew in your humble heart, unlike many of my people, the moment of your visitation." Jesus spoke confidently, "If only all of Elah's work could be this easy. Many have prayed to welcome this moment throughout the ages, but unfortunately few have appreciated it like you have. Let us pray.

"Heavenly Abba, thank you for this joyful meeting. We have shared Your heart and love with each other as Your children. As brothers we have missed each other for many years, but now we are reunited, and we are truly grateful. We are sorry for the misunderstandings of our ancestors over the ages, but we hope to overcome the prejudices of the past in our generation. Please renew our hearts with Your parental love.

"Jacob is our forefather, but we know that You, Abba, are Jacob's father. In fact, You are the father of all people, so we all must be brothers. Open our hearts to Your love and to love one another. In the names of Abraham, Isaac, and Jacob, I ask this prayer. Amen."

As Jesus finished the prayer, the townspeople ran up thanking him and bowing to him unpretentiously. Many invited him to stay with them in their home, as it was getting late. Jesus agreed and he and his disciples stayed in Sychar another day. All the while Jesus spoke with them and joined in a celebration that they prepared for him. Finally, in the late afternoon of the second day, he and his disciples bid them farewell. They promised not to forget Jesus and invited him to return. Mary noticed Susanna standing quietly in the crowd with tears in her eyes.

Jesus instructed Simon to change course for Nazareth, "Let us pray that we will find the hearts of the people in my hometown as open as these meek Samaritans."

After refilling the urns and skins with water their little band set off. Jesus waved a last time to the crowd of believers. It was a bittersweet farewell for Mary, and she imagined also for Rabboni.

Chapter 25

Nazareth and the Synagogue

But the truth is, there were many widows
in Israel in the time of Elijah…
Yet Elijah was sent to none of them except to
a widow at Zarephath in Sidon."
(Luke 4:25-26)

Their experience in Samaria was refreshing for everyone. The travelers had time to ponder their previous prejudices based on their narrow-minded religious upbringing. Most of Jesus' disciples realized how wrong they had been. Now they looked forward to more positive receptions during the next leg of their journey.

After this impressive experience, Jesus decided to go to his own hometown. Most of his past success had come in the northern Galilean towns, but that was before the death of the Baptist. Now that he was creating Elijah's foundation, he had hope that he could one day be recognized as the Anointed One.

Mary was happy with their new start. She recognized from what Jesus told them that they all must all learn the Good News he taught of Elah's love and embody it. As she plodded along, she reviewed how, with the people supporting him, Rabboni would go to Jerusalem, ready to give the blessing to all of Elah's chosen people, the nation of Israel.

She reflected on their recent experience. *Samaria was a wonderful new beginning. Elder Simon made a major breakthrough. His prejudice was so strong that when he was able to sit and eat with Gentiles, it was really an incredible moment of transformation. If he can be transformed, then others can also.*

She remembered what Jesus had told Simon, *It is not what you put into your mouth that defiles you; it is what comes out of your mouth that defiles you.* During the Samarian celebration, she had watched Elder Simon relax his staunch religious views, realizing that love was more important. And she had witnessed how happy that made Jesus.

Our hearts are growing, as we follow Rabboni's example, Mary reflected. *And we're learning to embrace all people, even the foreign people. Our prejudices are dissolved within seconds. That is the magic of Elah's love introduced by Rabboni and spread by us. His example of love and compassion teaches us that humanity can change in the twinkling of an eye, just as Simon did.*

To Mary, as the day came to an end it seemed like a silvery light had been guiding their path since leaving Sychar. Elder Simon led the mules to the end of the camp area and motioned for everyone to set up camp. They normally would have felt tired from the long day's trek, but instead they were energized by their experience in Samaria.

Mary helped prepare dinner. Afterward, they shared testimonies and songs around the campfire. Elder Simon even sang a fishing song in his gruff voice. Others joined in and there was laughing and many joyful tales. James juggled a few apples, and then Jesus sang a song in Aramaic and one in Hebrew.

Mary sang one of the psalms in her lilting soprano voice with Martha playing her lyre. Their femininity reminded everyone of their loved ones— their mothers, sisters, and wives. They could hardly wait to see their families and tell them about their travels. Tears mixed with laughter as Rabboni ended the evening with prayer.

Sleep came quickly for everyone, except Jesus. He disappeared into the darkness and went up on the nearby rocky cliff. In the moonlight Mary saw his silhouette in his usual prayer stance. She tried to stay up with him, but she found herself dozing several times.

The howl of a nearby jackal awakened her. It was late in the night and the air was chilly. Mary rubbed her eyes and could not believe that she could see

Rabboni was still praying. She knew he must be cold. She climbed the rocks to give him a blanket. As she neared him, he looked down at her, and even though it was dark she could see his wet, swollen eyes.

"Rabboni, would you like a blanket? I am sorry to disturb you," Mary said respectfully.

"Thank you, Mary, for your kindness. I will take the blanket and soon go to bed. Please go back and rest; we will get an early start."

As Mary went back, she noticed Phillip keeping watch a short distance away. His sword was at his side in readiness for any wild animal.

She returned to her pallet and went to sleep. She had a dream in which she was standing in the midst of her countrymen. They were lifting their fists in the air and screaming, "Blasphemer!" Mary was trying to convince them that they were mistaken, but she could not change their minds and felt frustrated.

Suddenly she heard her name being called. Martha was calling her to wake up, "Everyone is ready to leave." Mary felt embarrassed and rose quickly, rolling her bedding and carrying it to the pack mule.

"I let you sleep a while longer since you were up late during the night," Martha said, and Mary realized that she had stayed awake as well. Martha added, "Those jackals were close last night."

Mary understood that, like herself, Martha and everyone also loved and had concern for Rabboni. Martha's faith had grown since the last witnessing campaign, and the experience in Samaria had boosted her spirit as well.

The distance from Sychar to Nazareth was about 40 kilometers. It would be a three-day journey, and each night Jesus shared his life-giving words. Every night he gave a chance for questions.

One evening Elder Simon, who was not one for asking theological questions, asked unexpectedly, "What is sin in the world? It's a question that people ask me when I am witnessing."

Mary was surprised that Simon's asked such a question, *It seems that he is beginning to look earnestly for answers.* She understood that as a fisherman it was not natural for him to think from his heart, but now he was really trying to understand. She recognized it was a good question and would help others to search for the internal spirituality of love.

Jesus stood and considered Simon's question, "What is the meaning of sin? Is it sin or simply a mistake? There is a difference. A mistake is making the wrong decision between two choices. This is due to your lack of knowledge and or experience. This is one of the best ways of learning in life, as after the repercussions of a mistaken decision you are actually wiser from it. The next time you come up to that quandary, or a similar one, if you learned from the previous mistake, you will usually make a better decision. Don't you think?

"But sin is making self-centered decisions based on self-gratification or self-interest. Sin began when the first man and woman turned their hearts away from their Abba Elah and acted in their own self-interest. From that beginning, humans lost the knowledge of Abba's purpose for them. Selfish love replaced altruistic love. Only human beings experience enmity, anger, jealousy, greed, and murder because of selfishness. And from the beginning this has become a never-ending cycle.

"I come to light a fire of truth upon this earth to change man's consciousness from selfishness to unselfishness. This can be done completely only when the evil lineage of man is changed back to Abba's lineage through me. That is why I am constantly repeating the need for rebirth through me. No one can go to Abba except through me."

Jesus looked earnestly at Simon, "Simon, do you understand? You must try to understand more with your heart than with your head."

Simon asked sincerely, "Why don't the Rabbis tell us about this?" Other disciples also agreed with Simon. Nathaniel was obviously moved and spoke out, "Yes, Rabboni, I long to hear your answer."

Jesus nodded and said with a smile, "Because I alone have seen Abba, during my time in the desert. He showed me how the world was created and the laws which He set in place. His design reflects Him and everything He created had a purpose. Each being from the lowest to His final masterpiece, humankind, was conceived in proper order, with the ability to grow, develop, be nourished, regenerate, heal, protect, and seek fulfillment of their needs through spiritual and physical laws.

"We, as humans, are born as Abba's children and His heirs. In other words, His plan for us was that we become His co-creators and stewards of this physical world. We were born to appreciate all that Abba created, experiencing the same joy as Abba. But instead, humankind became distracted by the physical world from the beginning and looked only for immediate pleasures, selfish and short-sighted needs. As they while away their life, they find that they are no closer to the Kingdom of Heaven than the day before."

"Rabboni, how do we find the Kingdom of Heaven?" Judas shouted, overcome by emotion.

Jesus felt his fervor and continued, "You find it when you realize your deepest self-centered desires and take these base impulses, thoughts, words, and deeds to Abba in prayer. It is when you recognize them and claim responsibility for them, and then sincerely ask for forgiveness and for the strength to overcome them. It is your choice to recognize them and change. It is then that you will find the Kingdom of Heaven. Those evil desires are chains that make you a prisoner, but when you overcome them, you will experience that Abba will fulfill your every need."

By sunset on the third day, the idea of arriving in Nazareth was exciting. They set up camp on the outskirts to prepare to enter in the morning. Water was scarce, but Mary took water in a bowl to Jesus for his use. Simon erected a lean-to so that Jesus could wash himself in privacy. Mary joined the women to bathe herself with the small portion of water that they were given.

She recalled her dream and wanted to tell Jesus about it. From her experience with her dream about the Baptist, she wanted to inform him of the possibility that this new dream could be another premonition. Jesus was preparing to pray when she went up to him, "Rabboni, may I speak openly with you?"

Jesus said, "Mary, please speak freely and do not fear. I will tell you anything you want to know."

Mary asked her question, "What does it mean when one dreams? Are these dreams to be taken seriously?"

Jesus answered, "Sometimes, if someone is prayerful and humble, Abba may send messages to that person through dreams. It may take time to understand what a dream means. Remember Joseph, the son of Jacob. He was able to interpret dreams. Those dreams were sent to him from Abba, messages from Abba Elah. He was able to predict the future and save lives."

Mary then told him about her dream about the Baptist and the one she had just had the other night. Jesus told her that the dream could help them prepare for the day. "However, let's be hopeful that going to Nazareth will be as much a success as we had in Samaria. On the other hand, it is also possible that Abba is warning us about possible problems. I will inform Simon and Judas to stay alert so that if there is trouble, we will be expecting it. Thank you, Mary. This is very helpful and necessary," Jesus responded, smiling.

Mary left, hoping that her dream was just a dream, and that Nazareth would be a happy homecoming for Rabboni. She was excited to meet his mother, brothers, and sisters and expected that his home would be the first stop. However, to Mary's surprise, Jesus went directly to the synagogue. He was focused on meeting the leaders of his hometown.

When he walked into the synagogue, many of the old leaders recognized him and greeted him. Though they remembered his mischievousness as a boy and young man, they received him warmly, expressing their happiness to see him again. They also noticed the strangers accompanying him and greeted them as well.

A few of the elders remembered him asking many questions and initially commented positively with pride, "He was obedient but very inquisitive." However, a few remembered that his questions probed them like burrs, sticking them sharply. Nevertheless, they welcomed him and all of his friends. As usual they began with a prayer. Mary heard Jesus' whispered prayer that they would allow him to take them to a higher spiritual level; right to the heart of Elah.

When his time came to read, Jesus stood and received the scroll of Isaiah from the head rabbi. Jesus chose a passage and read it with great authority and confidence. There was no doubt that he implied in voice and demeanor that he was the one it was referring to:

"The Spirit of the Lord is on *me,* because he has anointed *me* to preach good news to the poor. He has sent *me* to proclaim freedom for the prisoners and recovery of sight for the blind, to release the oppressed, to proclaim the year of the Lord's favor."

At first, the teachers began to make comments among themselves. Their hushed voices began to grow louder, like a hissing sound gradually becoming louder and louder as they began to focus on his audacity. Their hissing voices became a roar, with some even shouting out.

One voice that Mary heard echoed above the rest was, "Are you blaspheming and implying that you are the fulfillment of this prophecy? How dare you presume that the verses in Isaiah are speaking directly of you! They are certainly not fulfilled by the likes you!"

Another exasperated cleric screamed in retaliation, "We know of you and your family. We remember. We watched you grow up and we taught you the Holy Scripture. From where you come from, you can never hope to understand the Creator fully."

They screamed in frustration, "The best we can do is have faith without question and live according to the Law of Moses."

Another man reiterated, "You cannot presume to say that this passage refers to you. How dare you! This passage, in fact, refers to what the Anointed One will say when he comes."

Jesus answered brazenly, which did not surprise them, "The law is meant to guide man until it becomes a hindrance. We are all Elohim's children. And the world that Elohim created was meant to give joy to Him."

Mary could hardly believe their retaliation and obvious prejudice toward him. Jesus continued audaciously with forceful words that made them furious, "Before you worry about following the law, you must worry about how you are to become a son of Abba Elohim. Moses gave the law, but I am standing in front of you as the culmination of the law. Before Abraham was, I am.

It is I whom all of the creation is waiting for. Come to me and I will teach you about your Father in heaven who loves you. Never mind the old laws!"

Their faces, covered in perspiration, grew bright crimson with anger. The rabbis had never experienced such a challenge. They could only think to scream the worst word they knew, which was "Blasphemer!"

Complete mayhem broke out as the most educated men of Nazareth found themselves screaming in unison. How quickly their innocent welcome became an offended dismissal!

At that moment Mary, who was watching from the vestibule, remembered her dream. Just as in her dream, no one tried to take the young man seriously.

The angriest and most senior rabbi spewed out what he knew of Jesus' family and the scandal to do with Jesus' birth. He even brought up Jesus' own life as a gadabout. Consequently, everyone was appalled at his audacity to claim himself as the Anointed One.

As pandemonium broke out, they grabbed Jesus and his followers standing next to him by the collars of their robes and threw them out of the sanctuary. They tried to carry Jesus to a nearby precipice and throw him over.

Because of Mary's premonition, though, Elder Simon and Phillip were posted outside the building, and they grabbed Rabboni and the other followers from the roaring mob and rushed them away before any damage could be done. There was a lot of shoving and pushing, but Jesus was protected from injury.

"Get out of here and do not come back until you are willing to apologize to us for this act of disrespect and blasphemy!" the elder rabbi shouted as they escaped.

Suddenly, a young man ran up to Jesus. They looked at each other and embraced in haste. As his followers hustled him away, Jesus spoke to him familiarly but unexpectedly, "It's good to see you, brother James, but I don't think we have time to talk."

Mary, who was pressed near to Jesus in the crowd, curiously watched the man following their retreat. Even though there was much commotion, she heard his familiarity with Jesus and his surprising jest, "What's happening here? Are you up to your old habits? Did you ask the rabbis another question they could not answer?"

Jesus spoke seriously to his brother, "No, I spoke the truth. I told them that they should recognize me as the one that they are waiting for, that they may see the fulfillment of Elah's promise. Elah wants to renew their faith, but with this action they have missed the time of their visitation."

The shouts from the religious leaders were all around. The young man continued, "We should get out of here. Come on, let's go home!" It was only logical that the young man thought Jesus would certainly visit his home and his mother.

Jesus surprised even Mary when he responded, "No, I must go to a place that is prepared and ready to receive me. Truly, I say to you that it will be more bearable for the towns of Sodom and Gomorrah on the Day of Judgment than it will be for this town." Jesus spoke so sharply to brother James that his countenance paled at the callous words.

His brother stopped walking. Jesus said farewell and left without even looking back, leaving his followers trailing after him in bewilderment.

Chapter 26

Who Are My Mother and Brothers?

For God sent the Son into the world not to condemn the world,
but that the world might be saved through him.
(John 3:17)

A couple of days after the encounter in Nazareth, Jesus held a speech not too far from his home. It was a particularly hot and muggy day in the village of Nain, located southeast of Nazareth. About an hour after noon Jesus finished his sermon, which had begun at daybreak. Humble male villagers who had arrived early eagerly had filled the meeting hall's front two rows squatting, kneeling, and sitting cross legged. They were able to acquire those prestigious spots because they had arrived before daylight. A handful of cavalier clerics and rabbis took standing room only places behind the early arrivers, and, in the very back, stood his disciples. The door was kept open for fresh air and to release the heat generated by the crowd in the adobe building.

As usual, Rabboni's presentation was inspiring to the humble but challenging to the traditional theology of the educated. And as usual the clerics and rabbis stood around deliberating with him, picking at his words, and all the while missing his point. There was an ongoing debate, with the usual air of skepticism and arrogance as they competed with Jesus.

Standing at the very back next to the door jam, Mary watched as they tried to catch him in falsehoods or blasphemy, rather than trying to understand him. She knew from experience that their minds were already filled up and they had little room in their hearts for the speaker's new concepts. She, however, prayed for Jesus to find something to stimulate their curiosity. This was rarely seen with the educated, though she hoped and believed that one day the holy men would catch his meaning.

This day Jesus patiently listened and responded with clear explanations to their questions, although he did not allow them to goad him into an argument. While Mary had witnessed steamy exchanges in the past, he was more relaxed and caring this day. She prayed silently for a breakthrough, or that at least someone would grasp his genuineness. However, the religious men held to their stodgy and unquestioning belief in their own definitive scriptural understanding. Their discussions were superficial and frustrating.

Their expressions of incredulity struck Mary when Jesus repeated a familiar concept from his sermons, like Elohim was not far off in the sky somewhere, but rather was present living with us and in us. Jesus criticized their thinking, "Your teachings are based on human concepts and are completely opposite to the truth of Elohim's world that I bring to you."

Behind her there was a small crowd of curious bystanders coming and going. Suddenly unexpected scuffling and shouting caught her attention. Turning toward the commotion she was surprised to see the familiar face of James, Jesus' brother. He was the one causing the fuss, as he tried to press through the gawkers to get in and speak with Jesus. She also noticed three women near James who seemed to be with him.

She introduced herself, boldly and informally calling him by his given name, "James, I am Mary, one of Jesus' followers. We met the other day."

Mary saw his surprise that she knew his name and he was shocked at her assertiveness. She reminded him, "We met recently on our way out of Nazareth. You may not remember me, because we were leaving Nazareth in haste." She showed her tenaciousness, asking, "Can I help you?"

She saw from James' expression that he recognized her as being a part of the synagogue incident. However, unaccustomed to conversing with an unfamiliar young woman he quickly lowered his eyes and changed his attitude. Clearing his throat, he explained humbly, indicating the women behind him, "My mother came here to Nain to speak with her son. She heard gossip about the incident in Nazareth. Though that's not unusual because she often hears gossip about him. Although we are accustomed to his social disruptions even as a youth, she wants to speak with him. She wants to tell him to stop his fight with society. She is worried for his life, and she begs him to come home. She wants him to stop his blasphemy, which is embarrassing to our family."

Mary noticed his condescending attitude but also his frustration, though she was caught off guard by his disrespect toward his own older brother. Immediately, her natural protective instinct caused her to display a wary expression.

James' countenance flushed bright red as he felt her judgement of him. He tried to justify his impertinence. Clearing his throat again he cajoled, "Pardon my rudeness, as I am speaking for my mother. As I said before, my brother has been an embarrassment to my mother and our whole family for many years. He is always seeking attention."

Mary realized his ignorance about Jesus and felt pity for him, though she was stunned by his cynicism and disdain toward his brother. Nevertheless, she respectfully addressed him, "Brother James."

Surprisingly, he winced at her use of the word 'brother.' Ignoring his attitude, she asked him kindly to wait at the doorway. Then she went through the crowd to explain to Jesus that his family was outside.

The heated debate that was now in its eighth hour was continuing without resolution, but she waited respectfully to speak with Jesus. After a few minutes, Jesus motioned for her to come to him.

Because as a woman she had to keep her distance, she had to project a whispered notification to him about his family in Hebrew, "Your mother and brother and sisters are outside asking to speak with you." The whole room heard her message and many in the crowd turned to see who they were.

Surprisingly, Jesus abruptly changed the subject of his current conversation and answered her back loudly, as if he was speaking to multitudes. Reverting to his mother tongue for all to hear, including his family, he shouted uncharacteristically in a seemingly sarcastic fashion, "Who are my mother, brothers, and sisters? Who is my family?"

After horrified gasps there was a hush in the room. Everyone was caught off guard by his cold statement about family and hardly believed the harshness of his words. Silence fell over the room as even his close disciples were stunned and felt uncomfortable.

Jesus expounded, "I say this to you and to them. Those of you who are following and attending me are my true mother, brothers, and sisters. Elah's desire is for you all to listen and believe in him whom He has sent. You must become one with me in heart. Do not take me for a fool.

"In fact, I say even more, that your love for me must be greater than your love for your mother and father, your sister and brother, and even your spouse and children. This serious attitude of commitment is the only way that the Kingdom of Heaven will be able to come quickly."

His abrupt words were severe, especially in their culture. Family was sacrosanct and Jesus' words caused a mighty roar in the crowd. Some spoke in Hebrew while others declared in Aramaic, but there was great consternation within the room and outside it.

Jesus' words toward his family struck at the very heart of their society. The disciples held their breath in fear of what might happen next. *Master Jesus' words struck directly at the center of one of the Ten Commandments.*

Some of the rabbis received a report from their followers that Jesus' own mother was outside. They began shouting and criticizing Jesus' lack of respect and callous spirit. One of the most respected rabbis turned on Jesus, "What is this? Your own mother is here, and you spurn her. Do you make yourself greater than the Law? Are you set to destroy our nation? If you take away family, then we have no nation!"

Influenced by the senior rabbi, the rest of the religious clerics lost confidence in staying any longer. Tempers flared and the disciples feared that a fight might break out. The clerics, also, took notice of the time and realized they were tired of the sparring back and forth. Mumbling on their way out, "Eight hours is long enough!"

Even as they exited the room, Jesus continued his dialogue to his followers, speaking as if to a large crowd, "Do you think I come from Elah to say nice things to you? I come to change this world from a world of self-interest to Elah's world of love and compassion even at my own expense. I come to encourage you to give up your old selves and make yourselves new, to be reborn as Elah Abba's children, at last. This should not be so hard to understand as you and your forefathers have been prepared for centuries to understand these things I speak about."

Mary knew that Rabboni's family heard his harsh words and that they were certainly hurt and insulted. She imagined that they had no idea of his purpose or why Jesus would act and speak as he did. She recognized his mother's lack of understanding of her son's true mission. Earnestly, Mary thought, *Jesus' comment certainly reinforces their negative presumption of him. How can we help them understand and appreciate the value that Elah has given him?*

That evening after dinner, while taking shelter in the house of one believer, Mary had an idea. She took it to Jesus and asked, "Rabboni, your mother does not understand you. She only hears rumors that are perhaps terribly exaggerated slights and insults about you." She offered a simple solution, "Please let me visit your mother for a few days. Maybe I can help her understand you."

Jesus spoke quietly as if to himself in Hebrew, but his words were for Mary to hear, "My mother had her own revelations from Elah, but she forgot them. In any case she has become a hindrance to my mission. It is because of her that I am not married and that I had no relationship with John. Time is short. I cannot be concerned with my family at this point. I must save this nation first, all the people and families!"

But after a few moments of prayerful deliberation, Jesus answered Mary, "Mary, I am happy that you have the inspiration and desire to help my family. I think you have a good idea. Please go, but don't spend a long time there. Return to us in three days." Jesus spoke with gratitude, "I will ask Simon to arrange an entourage to accompany you."

He brought his disciples together. They prayed and Jesus explained his plan for Mary to visit his family.

Chapter 27

The Woman Behind the Veil

It is not good that the man should be alone;
I will make him a helper as his partner.
(Gen. 2:18)

With plans set with Simon for the next day's return to Capernaum, Jesus went out to the hills surrounding Nain. As was her custom, Mary followed to support him in prayer, remaining a respectful distance to allow for his solitude.

After the tension of the day's events, Mary inhaled deeply as the night's cooling freshness and stillness immediately soothed and relaxed her. Free now, her prayer expressed her love and gratitude to Abba Elah for their protection. She also thought and prayed about her own journey to Nazareth. The beauty of the evening, the star-lit sky and full moon illuminating the countryside, and a pleasant breeze further stilled her heart.

She was about to close her eyes in prayer when the flapping of Jesus' robe caught her attention. He was standing silhouetted in the moonlight with the high grasses around him swaying in the breeze. Mary thought, *He is in communion with Abba Elah. If only his mother could see him now! She would be so proud of him.*

Although Mary had silently prayed a short distance from Jesus many nights during the past year, tonight she caught herself thinking in a most uncommonly sensual manner, noticing his manly appearance. *The breeze caresses his hair and tugs at his robe. How strong he appears!* She suddenly felt her cheeks burning as she embarrassed herself thinking of Jesus so personally.

Shaking off her distraction and concentrating her thoughts, she began to pray, *Abba Elah, it is not hard to pray in such a comfortable atmosphere. I am grateful that Rabboni was happy with my idea to visit his family. Dear Abba Elah please help me find a way to comfort his mother's heart.*

Not long after she began her prayer in earnest, she heard footsteps coming toward her. Opening her eyes, she looked up into Jesus' glistening eyes and smiling visage. Embarrassed and ashamed for distracting Jesus, she immediately whispered, "Rabboni, please forgive me. I became distracted and made too much noise, interrupting your prayers."

Tingling with agape love for Rabboni, she quickly looked away. To her surprise he took her right hand and held it in his warm hands, prompting her to look at him directly. Demurely she stared into his eyes. She felt her cheeks flush and burn and the thumping in her chest embarrassed her. Trying to ignore the thrill of emotion, her extraordinary sensations, she swallowed and gave Jesus her full attention.

Her thoughts and her heart were racing, *Should I hide my emotions or show him how I really feel? I am overwhelmed. How should I respond? Should I say something? What can he mean by this?* As she stood in his shadow, she hoped that the darkness would hide her struggle.

Suddenly she became aware that he was speaking to her and responded awkwardly, "Um, yes, Rabboni. Ca-can I help you?" He did not respond, rather he stood calmly, smiling and gazing into her eyes.

He's holding my hand. She thought dizzily because she could hardly breathe. Stunned, she stood staring back at him, feeling his warm hands while tears moistened her eyes. Then she felt embarrassed for allowing herself to accept his attention, though admittedly thrilled by it. She allowed a conscious thought, *He is so handsome.*

She reached for her scarf out of habit. Jesus pushed her hand away and the scarf. Then with the same hand she touched her burning face. *It is, indeed, fiery hot!* Then she demurely smiled back.

Jesus stepped closer, and intentionally catching her gaze with his eyes, he spoke to her in a much different manner than ever before, "Mary, do you know that you are a great source of inspiration to me? You always understand my ways and directions even without explanation. Over the many months we have traveled and worked together, Abba has also watched you. He is inspired by your faith and loyalty, your naturally selfless giving and constant support for me. Your allegiance to me helps me remain on my course.

"While others come and go, you humbly remain and continue serving. I have noticed the many nights you've stayed awake with me praying and supporting me. You are intelligent and selfless. Often you need to be reminded to eat and you are always the last to sleep. I notice that consistently you deny yourself comfort and I know of your unseen preparations and care. Because of this you make all our lives easier." Jesus paused, watching Mary's expression.

Mary could hardly breathe and felt that she might faint.

"Mary, what do you think my purpose is? Who do you think I am? Do you ever wonder what exactly Abba wants me to do to liberate his chosen people?" Jesus asked, pausing for her to answer.

Mary, astonished that he wanted to know what she thought, caught herself staring into his eyes longer than was customary for a woman to a man, and she quickly looked away. But she noticed that he waited for her answer. She cleared her throat and replied, "You are the one that Elah has chosen to bring the Kingdom of Heaven, the Messiah. You teach us that you are bringing us new life, teaching us love and compassion for our fellow men and women. If we believe and follow your teachings, then we will truly see the Kingdom of Heaven on earth!"

Jesus nodded and said, "You are correct but how? What is the kingdom? Is it in the sky? Can we find it here as we live and breathe, or do we expect it only after death? Mary, we human beings are not meant to live this life alone. Abba desires that men and women marry, and their togetherness is meant to bring them joy as it brings Abba joy. As Abba gives us life, so we then give life to our children and thereby experience the same love that Abba experiences.

"But why do we not see that joy in families today? Because of the fall of Adam and Eve. Abba Elah saw His first son and first daughter turn away from Him. They began a family without Him. Because of that, from the beginning, human beings never understood their real value and purpose. Because of their shame, they never asked their Creator. Living without connection or understanding of their Creator, they made many mistakes and thereby brought suffering and sadness into this world. Blind to their real Creator, they have no answers.

"However, Abba Elah, the Creator, never gave up His ultimate goal for His children. He always worked throughout history to reestablish His lineage and thereby end His children's suffering due to their selfishness and ignorance. My conception and birth were unusual, but according to Elah's plan. I am the only one born since Adam with the lineage of Elah. From me, Elah hopes to see His sons and daughters, a new lineage, begin and live in this world at last. From me, all of humankind who follow me can be reborn into Elah's lineage. Do you understand, Mary?" Jesus asked gently.

Mary nodded and breathlessly responded, "Yes, I understand. I am surprised by what you tell me but that the greatness of Elah in you is clear to me." She exclaimed, "I praise Abba Elah for sending you, His son, to this confused world."

Jesus took both of her hands in his. Breathless and with eyes filled with tears, she looked into his eyes. She desired to embrace him. The warmth of his hands caused her to move closer to him. She felt his breath on her forehead as she waited, unable to take a breath, all the while treasuring the experience in her heart.

Jesus continued, "Therefore, Mary, I must marry. I am a bridegroom searching for a bride. Already Elah has prepared one woman to fulfill this position with absolute dedication and resolve."

Jesus paused. Motionless and hardly able to breathe from anticipation, Mary waited for him. Time stood still as he looked down directly at her, searching her expression. Then he continued, "Mary, you are this woman."

Mary heard the word 'bride' and her consciousness and emotions were spinning, *Is he asking me to marry him? Am I to be his wife? Is this really happening, is this a dream? Pay attention!* she scolded herself, as she tried to concentrate and calm the beating of her heart.

She caught the end of a phrase, "…it is not to be taken lightly. Elah knows that there will be many difficulties along our path." Jesus was continuing, "This position is the one that Eve held but betrayed and lost. No woman has ever restored her failure, the position of Adam's wife and Elah's daughter. Much sacrifice will be asked of the first woman taking that role. A woman who takes on this marriage proposal will have to be a woman of great faith."

Jesus continued gently and lovingly, "Mary, Abba told me that you are this woman. Throughout your whole life He secretly raised you for this purpose. You have proven your great love and respect for me time and again and developed your love for Elah as well. Since that day you were healed your love and character have blossomed. You have laid a strong foundation to inherit this position as my bride." He paused and added, "You give me great joy!"

Filled with unbelievable delight, Mary wanted to cover her blushing face. Thoughts were flooding her mind, *I never imagined that I would marry. It never occurred to me to be possible. I do not care about my situation, but I am concerned for Jesus' comfort and provision. I truly love this man, and there is nothing I want more than to become his wife and bear his children.* Finally, Mary gazed passionately with her whole heart and without reservation into Jesus' eyes.

"How do you feel about me and what I tell you?" Jesus asked meekly.

Mary was surprised by his humility toward her. Her expression and tears of joy gave him his answer. With dignity and formality her words sealed her acceptance, "Yes, my lord, although I am unworthy, I accept your request. I am honored to be your wife."

Mary saw Jesus' joy like never before. He embraced her, pulling her close to his chest. Mary's senses were stimulated, and she breathed in his scent and became profoundly elated.

"Now that you accept my plea, and with Abba Elah's help, I plan to hold our marriage after Passover and bring joy to Elah and all the creation."

Mary watched and listened. She noticed his strong eyebrows and his aquiline nose and well-formed lips and how they curved up at the corners. She had never looked so closely into his face before, at his features, *They are handsomely symmetrical and strong.* She felt a desire to reach up and touch his eyes and nose and mouth, but resisted.

Oh! How much I love this man, she thought. He truly was the whole reason for her life. Nothing else mattered in the world. She felt warm and comfortable in his arms, but she wanted to kneel before him or dance around him. Her emotion was hard to control but she knew she must. Finally, she fell to her knees and buried her face on his feet, "You are my lord, today and forever!" Mary spoke with joy, "I am unworthy, but you will not regret this request of me."

Jesus reached down to Mary and raised her up to stand before him. This time his expression changed to serious consideration for her, "We will go forward together to bring Abba Elah's dream to fruition." They stood together and Jesus did not speak for some time. He continued to gaze into her eyes and their faces came close. Mary felt his warm embrace; however, they held back from any further physical demonstration of love.

They wanted Elah first to bless their love, for the sake of all humankind's liberation, not just for themselves. Nevertheless, Jesus breathed in her fragrant scent and caressed her face with his eyes. With joy and tears in his eyes he said, "At last Elah has shown me my bride to be."

Lovingly, Jesus told her, "I want to make this announcement as soon as possible, but I will wait until Passover. At that time, we will go to Jerusalem to gather support from the Pharisee priests and rabbis. After speaking with those leaders, I will announce Abba Elah's blessing on our marriage."

He explained his plan, "With the support of the Galilean and Judean people, the priests like Nicodemus and others he will influence, and the rabbis, will surely listen to me. Simon, James, John, Judas, and all my disciples will come with me. Their foundation of absolute faith and support will allow me to go directly to the heart of Israel. This can be very dangerous, but with Elah's guidance, your support, and all my disciples, this foundation will stand strong and evil will not prevail.

"I must have the support of the Pharisees and through them the whole nation of Israel. Judea and Galilee will become one, as in the days of David the King. Then Elah will be able to claim the whole chosen nation. Without the Pharisees and Sadducees, I feel like only half of Elah's chosen nation would be liberated."

As Jesus spoke informing Mary of his plan, she realized that he also did not want this intimate moment to end. He added lovingly, "From here, rebirth can begin with our family and progress to all the disciples and then the whole nation and then the world."

He continued, "Mary do not speak to anyone of this. We must pray earnestly that Elah be liberated and finally that He stand as Abba to us all, His sons and daughters. This is His dream since the beginning of time. In fact, this is the whole reason that He created this universe in the first place. Do you realize this?

"And incidentally, thank you for your idea and desire to teach and love my family. As we planned earlier, you will visit my family in Nazareth and then return to Capernaum. I will take Simon, James, and John to Mount Hermon in Caesarea Philippi, where we will pray and prepare for a new course of action."

Mary agreed to keep this precious moment secret. Her heart was beating like never before and her spirit was soaring, but she managed to control herself and show Jesus her composure so that he would be proud of her. As she gazed into his glistening eyes and he into hers, each felt an explosion of love which they would never forget.

It was late when they parted. She whispered a prayer to remain focused and serene. Tomorrow they would separate, Jesus and the disciples heading to Capernaum and beyond, and she would return to Nazareth.

Chapter 28

The Marys Meet

In an outburst of anger, I hid my face from you for a moment.
But with everlasting loving kindness I will have compassion on you.
(Isaiah 54:8)

Wispy clouds filled the sky as Mary and two companions made their way from Nain to Nazareth. They headed north by northwest along trails through the hills of Galilee.

Jesus had chosen the brothers Thaddeus and James Alphaeus to accompany her. Parting at sunrise, he instructed the two young devotees to follow Mary's guidance. Jesus gazed at Mary as they all stood together in a circle after prayer. Mary wanted to return his silent regard, but she dared not. She realized that this would be their longest separation since she had become a follower.

Mary felt her face glowing red and glanced over at Simon. He was obviously astonished when Jesus explained that she would go to his family for a few days. She also noticed Judas standing next to Simon. He was clearly surprised as well and seemed to notice her blush. However, when he felt her eyes upon him, he quickly averted his gaze.

Mary assumed that they were surprised that Jesus would give her such a mission and thought, *They cannot understand why Jesus would send me, a woman alone without a formal introduction. Oh Elah, how their concepts must change. They saw the exchange yesterday between Jesus' brother and me. Certainly, they will pray for my success and not assume that a woman cannot lead this mission. Dear Abba, please help them appreciate my small attempt to resolve difficulties with Rabboni's family and help us to be successful.*

That was all. Jesus bowed to the three travelers showing his appreciation and without further words turned stoically away, leading his disciples in an easterly direction toward the Sea of Galilee and then on to Capernaum.

As Mary and her spiritual brothers walked in single file along the well-worn paths, the men led the way carrying Mary's belongings and theirs. The brothers chatted back and forth with each other ahead of Mary, as the three watched their steps to avoid rocks and the uneven ground.

This was good for Mary because she had a lot to think about. Last night was foremost in her mind. As she thought of it, she realized she could not wipe the smile off her face. Seeing Jesus in a new light this morning made her blush and constantly cover her face with her scarf. Even Martha noticed something different. She commented on how happy Mary looked, remarking that she must have had another one of her pleasant dreams.

Mary chided herself, *I dare not look at Jesus.* She sought protection, preparing food for all of their long journey ahead until it was time to leave, and then she had to join everyone in a send-off prayer. On the one hand it almost seemed like a dream, but she thought, *My heart is singing and most of all I want to announce my joy to the world. But I dare not.* Then the thought came, *How difficult it is that I will not see Jesus for a few days.*

However, she realized it was a blessing. *These few days ahead will give me time to consider all that happened last night and to internalize the seriousness of my future. The other blessing is getting to know Jesus' mother and family.* There was also an insightful thought, *Some day to be my own. Presently I must focus and pray that I will be able to explain to Jesus' mother properly and help her understand her son's mission.*

It was difficult not to drift back into last night's dreamlike experience. She tried to control her thoughts and emotions, as Jesus' smiling expression came to her mind's eye. She covered her mouth with her scarf to conceal her euphoria. *If the brothers catch my expression they will wonder and might ask me what I am thinking about.*

Mary was so deep in thought that before she knew it, they were standing near Jesus' home. Mary asked the brothers if they would like to say a prayer. Thaddeus prayed, "Abba Elah let us bring the joyful news about Jesus to his mother and family. Let us find a way to open their hearts and give them hopeful understanding. Amen."

Because of her initial encounter with James, Jesus' brother, the day before, Mary was surprised to see that his expression upon opening the door was kind though curious. He even looked around, seeming to think that Jesus might have come as well. However, when he saw that the three of them were the only visitors, he nonetheless received them warmly, "Peace be upon you. Welcome to our humble abode. Give me a moment to bring the head of our house, my mother, to greet you as well."

Within only moments, his mother came to the door, also humbly bowing and welcoming the strangers with surprise and curiosity. Mother Mary immediately recognized the younger Mary as one of her son's friends from the day before.

The two Marys assessed each other. Mary of Magdala noted Mother Mary was a slender, elderly woman, similar to her own mother. Her humble clothing was also like her own mother's. But there was an uncommon air of nobility or restraint that the younger Mary had seldom felt in other Galilean women, and she also noted her reserved kindness. She became curious and encouraged to become acquainted with Jesus' mother.

From previous comments Jesus had made about his mother, she read the woman's age lines and thought that some at least were from her disappointed expectations for her eldest son. Mary knew that at the very least she would try her best to allay his mother's fears.

Mary, Thaddeus, and James Alphaeus introduced themselves. Mother Mary turned to her son James and formally asked him to invite them in, immediately serving them warm goat's milk. The custom reminded Mary of her home; it was truly a Galilean tradition.

Mary explained, "We are disciples of Rabboni Jesus, and he wants us to bring to you his love and a message."

Mary was not surprised when his reserved and formal mother did not directly ask her why she came to visit. She caught the mother glancing curiously at her numerous times and realized she did not want to risk being impolite.

Thus, while sipping her warm milk, having been trained by Jesus, Mary of Magdala began by boldly and enthusiastically giving her testimony, "Rabboni saved my life, and I would like to tell you of his love for Elah and his deep insights about Him. We all would like to share our experiences with him as well," as she motioned to include her brothers. "You will see from our testimonies that your son is truly that which you always believed of him. Maybe not in the way you expected, but truly a dynamic and compassionate man of Elah."

Mother Mary seemed to feel their genuine love for Jesus and accepted Mary and the brothers. She invited them to stay as long as they would like, "Our home is small and humble, but we are grateful that you thought to visit us and tell us all about my son. Thank you for coming."

Mary reached into her bag and offered Jesus' mother a beautiful shawl and headscarf. These gifts were given to her by Lazarus and Martha. They were her most beautiful possessions and she generously presented them to Jesus' mother. Surprised and overcome with emotion, Mother Mary received them. The younger Mary smiled and wished that Jesus was there to give them to her himself.

This thought brought tears to her eyes and a cascade of emotions. Memories from the night before flooded her mind, but she quickly gained control over herself and refocused on the present moment. But not before Mother Mary picked up on her sincerity and began to weep out of longing to embrace her son.

During the following days, Mary served his mother and tried to restore the broken relationship. For the younger Mary it was more personal than she had imagined only a day ago. She came to feel the genuine heart of a daughter toward Jesus' mother and a sister's heart to Jesus' sisters and brothers.

Finally, by the middle of the second day the mother's heart and the rest of the family opened to the younger Mary as she told exciting and positive stories about Jesus. They realized how they truly missed him.

Jesus' younger sister cooked simple traditional Galilean meals, reminding the visitors of their own homes and their own mothers' home-cooked food. After each meal was cleared away, the men went outside to the patio with Jesus' brothers and sisters. Mary of Magdala and Mother Mary remained alone inside in the main room near the hearth.

Mary of Magdala apologized for Jesus' harsh words. Trying to find a simple and compassionate way to explain she began, "Jesus sincerely tries to give his countrymen a deeper understanding about Elah. He tells stories, simple earthy ones, as he speaks to the masses of mostly common people. He tells them of his deep understanding about Elah that he learned through a direct experience with Him in the desert. He told me that this experience with Elah happened a few months after leaving your home a few years ago."

Mary continued but tried to keep the details simple, "He wishes that he could tell you himself, but his mission is to reach all of Israel, and this is a tremendous task. He comes to bring a new understanding of the Creator but our religion, which is centuries old with its deeply ingrained traditions, makes it very hard for him to introduce new concepts.

"He brings the Good News that he believes his countrymen, prepared by Elah, are ready and longing to hear. In fact, he says that Elah is not how the Hebrews picture Him. For example, rather than a vengeful Elah, Jesus explains that Elah is a loving parent." Mary paused taking another sip, and continued, "Jesus himself refers to Elah as Abba Elah."

"We are truly living in an auspicious time, awaiting the arrival of a Messiah. Don't you agree?" Mary bit her lip and paused as she deliberated whether or not she would tell Mother Mary her belief that Jesus was this Messiah. Feeling unsure, she refrained for another day. The women sat silent. The younger Mary guessed that Mother Mary needed time for her own thoughts.

Unexpectedly, Mother Mary drew her chair closer to her visitor and in a faint voice she began to speak, as if revealing a long held personal secret, "I can see that you are a sincere and devoted follower of my son. I am not sure how long you and I have together or if we will ever meet again. Therefore, would you allow me to bare my heart? Things that I have not spoken aloud before. I see that you respect and honor my son and are loyal to him. I feel a need to tell you my long-kept secret, child. One that I furtively kept from everyone…even from my late husband."

Tears came to Mary of Magdala's eyes, as it was her genuine desire to connect to his mother's heart. She knew that this was what Jesus wanted.

Chapter 29

Mother Mary's Story

You prepare a table before me in the presence of my enemies.
You anoint my head with oil, my cup overflows.
(Psalm 23:5)

The two Marys sat in front of the hearth listening to the sound of crackling wood filling the rustic dining room. It took a while for Mother Mary to begin. She seemed to be searching her long-ago hidden memories that she now was ready to reveal. Mary waited patiently.

After some time, Mother Mary began with a sense of heaviness and perhaps shame, "Years ago, we were at a wedding feast given for a family member in Cana, a town north of us. At that time, my son Jesus was in his twenty-seventh year. I asked him to help with a matter at the wedding, but he brashly rebuked me for not finding a bride for him and reprimanded me for being more interested in his cousin's wedding than his own."

Mary gave his mother her full attention and waited for her to continue, *I expected to tell her of the greatness of her son, his love for Elah and all his countrymen, and that in fact he is a Messiah as she always knew, but now I see that actually she has a greater need to speak to me than I do to her.*

After some time, the elder Mary, obviously struggling, opened her heart, beginning with a confession. She whispered so as not to be heard by others in the house, "I know that I made many mistakes with my first son, Jesus." She grabbed her apron and dabbed at the tears spilling from her eyes.

Sitting close together Mother Mary began her surprising story, speaking barely above a whisper. She admitted, "I never tried hard enough to find a wife for my son. I was a coward because our religious laws are so strict regarding blood lineage and marriage. He emphatically begged me to arrange the match with my aunt's daughter in Judea, but I refused. He had no idea of the enmity between our families. It was far too great for me to address."

Mary waited patiently as she observed the obvious pain his mother experienced in telling her story. She guessed, *If she was not able to tell her husband all the years they were married, it must be a seriously difficult story.* So, she waited compassionately. The room was quiet except for the wood settling in the fireplace.

Finally, after a long pause, Mother Mary abruptly asked, "Are you married?"

The unexpected question caught the younger Mary by surprise and caused her face to blush. But she answered reflexively, "No, I'm not." Immediately she felt a need to explain, *Do I need to give her an explanation as to why I am traveling unescorted with men and not married at my age?* But Mary did not want to bring attention to herself, so she left her situation for another time.

As Mother Mary began to speak, she appeared older. Her facial expression went pale, accentuating her furrowed complexion. She was wringing her hands as she struggled. However, Jesus had given Mary some information about his birth, so she waited, somewhat understanding her reticence. She noticed that Mother Mary hardly paid attention to whether she answered her or not. She realized the reason Jesus' mother asked the question, *It is not so much about me, but it is whether or not I can be trusted to understand her.*

Mary was ashamed of her selfishness, *This is about Mother Mary's hidden testimony. It seems like her first time to bare her heart. She is merely trying to protect herself.* As she watched the woman's exhausted expression, Mary silently begged for forgiveness for being so shallow, *It is obviously so difficult for her. I will allow her to feel at ease.* Patiently and prayerfully, Mary waited for her to continue.

Abruptly, Mother Mary began, "You see, my late husband understood that Jesus should marry around the age of sixteen, as is the customary age for young men, but my husband died not long into the search." Using the corner of her apron Mother Mary wiped away escaping tears and sighed. Mary felt the weight she carried.

Mother Mary paused and looked down at the dirt floor and then back to the red coals. Sighing and shaking her head, she began to speak as she again wiped tears away with her apron, "All the responsibility fell on my shoulders, and because of my own personal past experiences, I could not bring myself to follow through with my son's request.

"Jesus was very strong minded. Often and with determination he requested that I ask my aunt's husband for his daughter to marry him. But my son had no idea of our history and the impossibility of such a request. I had had no communication with that family for many years. So, I questioned Jesus, 'Why do you choose her? Why are you so adamant?' He simply told me that Elah guided him.

"I could not face that family. But because of his persistence, I confessed to him a part of my dismal and extraordinary reason for not wanting to speak with them. Now my son is still not married because of me." Mother Mary closed her eyes and groaned.

After a time of silence, she continued, discreetly and humbly, "Mary, I trust that you will try to understand my story. I cannot expect you to understand why I could not grant Jesus' wish, unless I tell you my story. Will you permit me to tell you?" The younger woman nodded.

Mother Mary began, "I was orphaned at three years of age and raised in a northern Galilean temple. I was told by my priest and guardian that my grandfather, a Zadokian High Priest, and my father protected me by hiding me there. Shortly afterwards they were both killed and soon after that my mother died. I don't remember them, but the priests who lovingly cared for me told me their story many times. It was in the days of Herod I's pogroms to eradicate all lineages of David that could claim the right to rule over Israel. Anyone from the line of David was a fugitive."

Mother Mary closed her eyes and took a deep breath before continuing, "I grew up there as a temple virgin, protected and schooled in a pure and sanctified life. I witnessed the flurry of prophecies and spiritual awakenings. Expectations were high that the appearance of the Anointed One prophesied by Isaiah and Micah was imminent. Many spiritual people had dreams and visions proclaiming that the current generation would see him.

"My life changed significantly shortly after my thirteenth birthday when I became a woman. Because I could no longer stay in the temple, I was betrothed to a man from Bethlehem named Joseph. Before I journeyed to meet my husband to be, one morning, while I prayed alone in the temple garden, an extraordinary visitor came to me.

"A young man dressed in white approached me and addressed me directly as if he knew me. His manner surprised me because it was not customary for any of the priests to speak to me, except for my guardian. But he did, though first bowing to me respectfully.

"He spoke with authority. I can never forget his words, 'Hail favored one. You are greatly loved by El Shaddai, like many faithful ancestors before you who chose to live thoughtfully and without concern for self in their actions. Your parents and their parents knew how to live even at the risk of their lives. Therefore, on their foundation, you have attracted the blessing of Elohim. I am Elohim's messenger. Soon you will conceive in your womb a man child who will give life to the world. He will sit upon the throne of David and his governance will be responsible to Elohim. He will be called a wonderful and mighty counselor, an everlasting Father and Prince of Peace. And you shall name him Jesus.'

"Stunned by his presence and words, tears filled my eyes, and I found it hard to speak. But finding words, I asked, 'Sir, how is this possible, I am not yet married?'

"The man answered me, 'Do not be afraid. The Spirit of Elohim will guide you. I also bring you news of your Aunt Elizabeth's own miracle. Though she is of old age and childless, she conceived and is in her sixth month of pregnancy.'

"Those words excited me, and I responded, 'I am exceedingly joyful at this news you brought me. Let this request be done to me as Elohim wills, as I am but a humble maid of the Lord.' The man respectfully bowed again and left."

Surprised at Mother Mary's incredible story, Mary thought, *Her experience was amazing!* She felt her heart pounding. Moments went by and the room became cool and silent.

Suddenly, as Mother Mary realized her responsibility to her family and guests, she interrupted her tale, "Mary dear, it is time for the midday meal. Let us stop and feed everyone. If you permit me, I will continue later."

Mary agreed. If given a choice she would have run out of the room and found a place of solitude to think about the woman's unbelievable tale. However, the two worked together in silence preparing the meal. Then Mother Mary called James and Thaddeus along with Jesus' adult sister, Rebecca, and brother, Simon, to come to the table. Fresh baked bread, cheese, and hummus were placed on the table for six. Though her children were shy and reluctant to eat with the strangers, everyone relaxed and enjoyed the midday meal. The refreshing brew of sweet anise seed tea was an unusual treat for the travelers.

Afterwards, everyone leaned back and rested as was the custom. It seemed a good time for the visitors to introduce themselves to Mother Mary and the family. Thaddeus began, "I am Thaddeus and James is my brother. We are from Paneas, a village in northern Galilee. We originally followed the ascetic, John the Baptist."

Mary noticed the mention of the Baptist seemed to cause Mother Mary to drift away from the present. Her children noticed this, which did not seem to surprise them, and excused themselves, unable to be hospitable to their visitors. Understanding, and out of respect for Mother Mary, Mary asked her fellow travelers to go to the patio.

The two Marys sat quietly for a while. The older woman tried to fight back her tears. At first it seemed that perhaps she would not be able to continue her story, but the younger woman was content to sit and just be there for her whether or not she chose to go on.

Suddenly Mother Mary spoke in her soft voice, "It is hard for me to explain how I felt after the messenger left. I was unaccustomed to feelings of excitement. And the reality of beginning a new life alone outside the sanctuary was truthfully frightening.

"But remembering that Aunt Elizabeth, my late mother's sister, was pregnant was a happy thought. Even though I had never met her, I did respect that she was my mother's sister and my only relative. I had heard news of their family in passing conversations with my teacher and that she was unable to have children. So that was truly good news and it was only natural for me to think of visiting her. I even devised a plan to ask to help her in any way that she would need.

"The man's message was hard for me to understand. I remember feeling special, but I did not think a lot about it. It was like a dream, though a very clear dream. I was confident that Elohim would help me understand its meaning in time.

"Thus, excited and with some trepidation, I left the only home I remembered. I packed up my things and headed south in a one seated wagon pulled by one of the priests from my temple. I was happy to at last meet the closest family I had. Before I left, the temple priest told me about Elizabeth, my mother's older sister. He said that she was the wife of a Levite priest named Zechariah, and was in her sixth month of pregnancy.

"When I arrived, though it was our first meeting, Elizabeth was overjoyed that I came to her, assuming that I would help her during her confinement. She exclaimed loudly in a manner to which I was unaccustomed, 'I am filled with the Spirit of Elohim. Blessed are you, Mary, among women and blessed is the child you will bear!'

"How did she know of the announcement I had received only a week before? She surprised me with her joyful enthusiasm. It was an openness that I was unaccustomed to, after my previous monastic lifestyle.

She continued joyfully, 'But why am I so favored that the mother of my Lord should visit me? And blessed are you that you believed what the Lord proclaimed to you.' Innocently, I answered her unexpected prophecy, 'Though I am only a humble maiden, let it be done to me as the Lord wills.' Humbly I bowed to her trying not to be timid.

"Suddenly, Elizabeth grabbed her abdomen and exclaimed, 'My baby leaps for joy at your words and arrival. My son is excited upon hearing your voice!'

"I believed my aunt to be sincere and genuinely praised her, comparing her to Sarah, Abraham's wife, 'I am reminded of Sarah who was childless and also older when she first birthed Isaac. Likewise, your son will continue your family. Your faith is steadfastly waiting upon Adonai.'

"She continued her excited and familial acceptance of me. 'We are all participants in this great plan of Elohim hayyim,' she remarked with confidence. 'Child have a seat. Let me tell you the revelation my husband received six months ago. While he was praying in the inner sanctuary of the temple, he received an auspicious messenger from ha Elohim. The visitor told him that he would have a son and his son would have a very special mission. The messenger announced to him these words: *You will name your son John and he will go forth with the spirit and power of Elijah declaring to a nation prepared. He will announce and make straight the path of the long-awaited Anointed One.*'

"My aunt's tale surprised me because unknown to her my message was very similar to hers. I thought it exceptional." Mother Mary paused and commented, "Now when I look back on that experience, it seems like a dream. Were it not for my son Jesus, I would have long ago forgotten it."

She was about to continue but she seemed hesitant and offered the younger Mary a cup of anise tea, which she accepted. For a short while they both sipped in silence.

Then, Mother Mary continued, "Late one night, shortly after I arrived, I was awakened from my sleep by a lovingly familiar voice, though at first I could not remember whose. But when He asked me to rise and follow, I remembered it was the voice of the visitor I met in the temple. Then I remembered my promise to him and to Elohim. Innocently, I kept my word and obeyed without question or fear.

"I walked down the quiet dark hall, guided by a light. It stopped at Zechariah's bedroom. Bravely I went in as the voice bid. Zechariah was sleeping on his pallet. My aunt was in her own room since she was six months' pregnant. Zechariah was alone. I lay down next to him as the voice instructed. Zechariah awoke, though very groggy, and felt me lying next to him. It was dark and he took me in his arms. I was unable to see his face, but I felt his spirit. I said not a word. As I lay there, I remembered the voice so clearly in my ear and thought, *I am the Lord's servant. Let this happening be done to me following Adonai's bidding.*

"Afterwards I left his chamber and returned to mine. I felt a blush and warmth on my cheeks. I truly believed that I was participating in Elohim's great plan. However, as I lay in my bed, I began thinking of the reality of what I had done. I wondered if I could marry my betrothed now. Nevertheless, I prayed and clung to the faith that Elohim and His mysterious plan would guide me. I prayed that whatever He willed would be done.

"The memory of my experience with the messenger from Elohim, and his voice as he guided me, came strongly back to my consciousness and I held on to it. I knew that none of this experience had started from my own desire. I truly believed that I was an unquestioning offering that Elohim needed in His mysterious great plan to save the nation.

"Weeks went by and I cared for Elizabeth dutifully, though gradually I began to feel changes taking place in my body. I began to find the sight and smell of food unappealing and even causing me to retch. However, without complaining, I vomited in private each morning and began to wonder if I was indeed with child. Naively I was actually pleased in a dreamy kind of way. I was impatient to see my child, the Messiah, as the messenger had revealed to me.

"I could not wait to share my experience with Elizabeth. I believed that she knew about the plan from the way she had received me at our first meeting, though I did not know how to tell her and Zechariah. I prayed that Elohim would help me announce the coming of His son.

"I prayed every morning for the strength of spirit to tell her, as she was nearing the day of her delivery. I served her every day but never spoke. It was natural for me due to my upbringing. In fact, I was not talkative with anyone, especially since the day I met the messenger of Elohim.

"In my innocent imagination everyone would rejoice once they heard my news. Since it was the will of Elohim and Elizabeth, herself, had predicted that I would bear the Anointed One, I expected that she would be happy to hear my news. I became happier and more excited with each new day.

"A few days before Elizabeth delivered, while lying in bed, she made a comment to me, 'Mary, as I observe you today you seem to be unusually excited and happy.' She praised me, 'Your rosy cheeks have filled out. In fact, you are glowing and becoming more beautiful.'

"I thought that this would be a good time to tell her, after serving her for three months. But as I began to tell Elizabeth my secret, I noticed that her normally reddish face became pale. Her distraught expression caught me off guard. At that moment reality struck me. I realized that over the last few months my imagination of her reaction might have been unrealistic; that I had fantasized a positive response. After all, the fact was that I had had a relationship with her husband.

"As my thoughts raced, I became emotional and began to feel fear for the first time. I swallowed back burning tears. Nevertheless, I continued my explanation, which started to sound outrageous even to me. Burning tears ran down my cheeks. I tried to wipe them away and sobbed desperately. I tried to regain my memory of the initial experience with the visitor.

"Bravely, I remembered her own fascination with me when we met and asked, 'Do you remember when I first entered your home? Your very words were that I would bear a son, your Lord. Do you remember telling me of your miraculous conception and your husband's prophecy of your own unborn child?' She nodded and I noticed that she had begun to wonder why I was crying and what had caused me to become hysterical.

"I frantically reminded her of our joyous meeting, 'Your baby leapt in your womb. You blessed me and called me the mother of your Lord. You indicated to me that my son was to be the Messiah.'

"Surprised, Elizabeth sensed something in my attitude puzzling to her. Slowly her genuine everyday smile became forced into a grave expression. Her eyes' squinted, 'Yes, I do remember your goodness when you arrived and when my child suddenly leapt in my womb. But what are you getting at?'

"My unusual excessive emotion and abrupt change of character caused the soon to be mother to become suspicious. Instinctively, she focused on my words. She paused, trying to remember the conversation of three months ago, and admitted, 'I do not remember you speaking about another child.' She paused and said slowly, 'only mine.'

"Elizabeth's intuition heightened her attention, as her expression changed to curiosity, while positioning herself up on her elbows. Diplomatically she affirmed, 'Yes, Mary, as you said, our family is specially blessed by Elohim. Elohim will also bless you and your womb when the time comes. I understand that.' The older woman said calmly but suspiciously."

Mother Mary paused, and continued, "I saw that she had no idea what I was talking about. I saw her apprehension. As I began to realize my predicament, a feeling of nausea overcome me and I broke into a cold sweat. I took a deep breath and blurted out the truth, 'Aunt, Elohim is using us to give birth to two special sons, as you revealed when I arrived.'

"There was no going back, thus, I announced briskly to her, 'Just as Elohim revealed to me that I would become pregnant with the Messiah, I am confiding this secret to you.' There was cold silence as I waited for her response.

"She scanned me from my head to my feet when suddenly her eyes remained staring at my belly. Suddenly she began to grasp the gravity of my words and began to understand. She asked, 'Please repeat. Do you mean Elohim told you that when you marry you will be the mother of my Lord?'

"'No, Aunt Elizabeth,' I spoke gingerly but directly and respectfully, trying to be brave. 'He told me that I am to be the mother of the Anointed One, whom I am presently holding in my womb.' My words shocked her. In incredulity, Elizabeth could not find her voice and began to gasp desperately for air. Her eyes filled with tears as her comprehension caught her unprepared, and then her complexion visibly went from crimson to pasty white.

"I do not know where I found the stamina but bravely and as gently as possible, I repeated my reality, 'I am pregnant. The seed of the Anointed One grows in my womb.' At that moment, I decided not to speak of my relationship with Zechariah and I simply said, 'I was guided by the Holy Spirit of Elohim and I conceived.' Then I pleaded with her to understand, though the reality of my words lingered in the air. I was so young that I did not know what else to say.

"With difficulty, Elizabeth pushed herself to stand up leaning on the bed with an expression of disbelief. She stammered, 'Y-you were impregnated by the Holy Spirit?' With a sound of mockery in her voice she said, 'Who are you trying to deceive? There is only one male in this household and that is my husband. And you have never left our household. You are without shame? Do you know that is adultery? Adultery is a sin and punishable by death!'

"I simply shook my head because I was frozen in place. Elizabeth wavered and grabbed for a chair. 'I fear that I will fall!' she said as she sat down on the side of the bed. 'How could this happen? Oh!' she moaned, 'my stomach is tightening. I think my time has come. Call for the midwife. I have nothing else to say to you. But I assure you I will speak with Zechariah about you and your pitiful pronouncement!'

"As I stumbled out of the room to find the midwife, I felt horribly empty. I blinked back tears and swallowed hard. Unbelievably naïve and whispering to myself, I prayed, *Dear Elohim, please remind Zechariah and Elizabeth that I am pregnant with Your son.*

"After calling for a servant to alert the midwife, I returned to my chambers feeling queasy and faint. I still remember the feeling that gripped me. It was a cold and empty feeling of doubt. My thoughts were wildly seeking a hopeful conclusion, *What can her response mean? Is it possible that Elizabeth does not understand? Does she not feel or hear Elohim's voice?* Innocently I whispered, *Has she forgotten everything she said? Does she not see this as an act of Elohim?* The thought of all these things filled my mind until all I could do was curl up on my bed and bury my face. I muffled my cries while desperately begging for Elohim's help.

"The next day I was called to Elizabeth's room. She was having minor labor pains and reclining in her bed. Zechariah was sitting in a chair. Only the three of us were present. I remember bravely and assertively reminding them of my experience with Elohim who had asked me to bear His son, 'Even you, Elizabeth, prophesied to me that I would be the mother of the Messiah.'

"The outcome of our dialogue was that they would not take responsibility for their actions; neither the premonition that Elizabeth had, nor the relationship that Zechariah had with me. Zechariah insisted that he did not do such a thing and was totally faultless, denying everything. Elizabeth believed that he was lying and struggled with what to do. She remembered rumors she had heard of other priests having similar affairs due to an obscure liberty given to men of the tribe of Levi encouraging them to have large families. However, Elizabeth felt betrayed and never expected such actions from her husband, especially at their age. From Elizabeth's expression I knew that she did not believe her husband, but without proof I was left with no recourse.

"Zechariah stood and repeated his denial, saying he had nothing else to say about the matter. Insensitively he continued, 'She is your niece and I have no concern for her or her unborn child.' Elizabeth carefully pressed him, mumbling my claim of innocence, 'Mary said that Elohim caused her to conceive. Did you tell her to say that?'

"Zechariah was enraged but continued, 'Absolutely not. Elohim did not tell me about this. I think she is scheming to make an excuse for her loose character. I have nothing further to say.' The priest crossed his arms, emphasizing with his usual motion to his wife that he would have nothing else to say in this matter."

"They told me that as soon as their baby was born, I had to leave their household. Before I was sent to my room, Elizabeth dispassionately explained her plan, 'I only have a day or two before my confinement. I will send a messenger to the family of Joseph and invite them to come for you.' Coldly she whispered, 'I no longer need you nor want you to remain in our household. I will let you tell your story to that family. After that we wash our hands of you. Your life is in their hands.'"

Mother Mary hastened the end of her story, "Joseph and his elderly parents came as requested." She added an aside comment, "Long after this whole incident I realized that Zechariah, for all I know, may not have remembered our encounter. He too may have thought it was a dream.

"When Joseph and his family came, it was my first time to meet them. Without much introduction Elizabeth unabashedly announced that I was pregnant, and then coldly turned me over to them. And my life was then in the hands of strangers.

"Of course, I had to explain the whole ordeal again to them. They were also surprised at my strong insistence that I was guided by the Holy Spirit. And as did my relatives, Joseph's family also failed to see any divine intervention and responded negatively. His father issued a quickly made decision, 'We can trace our royal lineage all the way to King David. We will not allow this stain of infidelity on our family.' Speaking directly to his son Joseph, the father said, 'This girl should be done with according to the Laws of Moses.' Then I was briskly shuffled out to another room to await my sentence.

"I sat calmly on a bench in a quiet room. I had the whole day to review my life and present situation. I still had strong faith and believed that my life was in Elohim's hands. I was not worried, but I was numb. Meals were offered to me by mute servants. I had no appetite, but I ate for my unborn child. Then, without announcement, I was whisked back into a large hall in the residence.

"Zechariah stood and Elizabeth sat stiffly. Joseph, my betrothed, stood beside his parents. At that moment the reality of the moment hit me. My thoughts raced for self-preservation, knowing that I had been betrayed. All were dressed formally and there was an air of coldness in the room. They had stared at me when I walked in. If there were deliberations of what to do with me, I did not know. However, I felt an eerie atmosphere.

"I felt my cheeks burn. Joseph was looking at the floor, while every expression was solemn. I whispered to myself, *Oh Elohim, help me in this moment of need!*

"Stillness and a cold aloofness grabbed everyone in the room. When Joseph's father broke the silence, I jumped reflexively. He decreed, 'Our families were to be united through Joseph and Mary.' He formally indicated my aunt and uncle. 'It would have brought us great happiness. However, with this tawdry news of your sinful condition we are forced to recognize it with abhorrence.' He continued, 'You bring to both families great shame.' Then he delivered the icy judgment, 'As the responsible party under our laws, you must be stoned to death! So be it.'

"I heard the words pronouncing my sentence and managed to hold back my tears. Though I was numb, I felt my body tremble. Joseph's father added, 'You are allowed to say only one thing in your defense.'

"Though I was betrayed and unaided, innocently I stood straight and dignified. I somehow found strength, though my situation was grim, 'I take full responsibility for my actions. As I told you, I followed the Spirit who spoke to me and asked me if I was willing to do Elohim's will, even at the risk of my life, and I answered yes. I know that in your eyes I have sinned. I also know that I am a disappointment to Joseph, my betrothed. I am sorry to cause you such sadness, but Elohim knows that I have followed His will.' Then, I announced defiantly and boldly, 'I told Elohim to let it be done to me as He willed. He made me pregnant by His Holy Spirit.'

"Joseph's father, obviously in disbelief and frustrated by the situation, had no patience. He was clearly angered by my impudence and said, 'I feel no sympathy for you, and I do not believe your story.'

He was about to repeat his determination when suddenly Joseph, who had been mute up to this point, stepped forward and spoke, shocking everyone. This was the first time I took notice of him. He was a mature man much older than me. Though not tall, he looked strong, with broad shoulders and a beard. 'Excuse me,' Joseph interrupted and cleared his throat. At that moment, Joseph displayed his good character."

Jesus' mother was staring into space as if remembering that moment, "Pointing to himself, he spoke boldly and directly to me, disregarding both set of adults, 'As you are my betrothed, I would like to say that I want to marry you despite your condition, and I promise to love and care for you and your child.'"

Mother Mary explained, "Later, he told me about a dream that he had several days before, where Elohim asked him to take care of us under any condition. Elohim told him that his betrothed was to bear a very special child. With uncommon faith and zeal, Joseph stood beside me. Being more mature than me, I felt so grateful for him and his uncommon respect for me. At that moment it did not matter to him who the father was." Mother Mary's voice trembled, and tears flooded her eyes.

Mary realized that it may have been the most thankful moment in her whole life.

Mother Mary continued, "My trembling body relaxed, and I prayed with gratitude to Elohim for protecting me and my unborn son. However, Joseph's father was not going to accept his son's decision. He railed vehemently, 'You will *not* bring this dishonor into our family. You have no idea the future you face with a woman like her. I will not permit my son to do such a thing.' I can still see his face purple with frustration.

"Joseph repeated, defiantly, 'I will continue my betrothal to Mary, and we will marry with or without your support or blessing. You speak of our honorable family's lineage and how we trace our line back to King David. Do you not remember that his own son, Solomon the Wise, was conceived through adultery with Bathsheba? King David himself even ordered the death of his friend and retainer, the husband of Bathsheba. So, in man's eyes where is the honor there?'" Mother Mary added, "Joseph later told me that he never spoke to his father in such a way.

"His father retorted, 'That was a different time and situation. We are only humble Jews, trying every day to follow the Laws of Moses. You cannot allow yourself to believe that this shameful and vulgar situation could be compared to that story.' Joseph's father, with unbelievable coldness, then pronounced his judgment: 'If you choose this woman, you do it alone. We will have nothing to do with you. We can no longer see you as part of our family.' Joseph's mother began to cry. He ignored her demonstration of emotion and without further words or formality they took their leave.

"We stood alone in front of Zechariah and Elizabeth. The disgraceful situation took place in front of Elizabeth as she endured her early labor. She could not lift her face but spoke reservedly to me, 'We can no longer keep you here. You bring disgrace to our home and to your dead parents. We will arrange for you to leave for Galilee where you came from in the next caravan.'

"I noticed that Zechariah stood mutely silent. At that moment I decided to keep the father of my baby secret forever. Since he had not spoken up, I realized Zechariah had relinquished all responsibility. I decided to bear full responsibility.

"The next morning Joseph arrived with all his belongings, as Zechariah had instructed. He had left his home with only what he could carry. Joseph wondered how we would be able to get married. According to custom, the fathers of the bride and groom arranged the marriage ceremony. Since his father had refused to bless us, he was determined to find a way.

"Then suddenly, High Priest Zechariah spoke up surprising us. He cleared his throat and squeaked out an unexpected announcement, 'If you allow me, I will grant you a marriage ceremony to bless your union.' We thanked him for his considerate offer. Thus, without attendants, we were blessed in marriage by Zechariah. Then quickly we were ushered out of the household and taken straight to a caravan departing for Galilee.

"Walking quietly and timidly amid the camels and mules, we moved like we were in a daze. We had no plans, not even where we would make a home. We found a place in the caravan with our meager possessions and a lone mule, an unexpected gift from Zechariah. We had not spoken or even looked at each other. As newlyweds we should have been filled with great expectations and surrounded with an aura of love and joy. Instead, Joseph was helping me escape death. Ironically, however, we carried with us an unseen precious bundle that only Elohim understood."

Mother Mary stirred the hot coals and threw some animal chips into the fire. It was late and the room where the two women sat had become cold and dark.

Because of Jesus' previous description of his family, Mary appreciated the story from his mother's perspective. It gave her an immense respect for the older woman sitting in front of her. Mostly she realized how alone and unsupported Mother Mary's life had been. The younger Mary's only wish, in the last moments of her visit, was to love and serve her with Jesus' heart and in some small way comfort her.

Mother Mary admitted, "I believe I am to blame for my son's difficulties. Elohim meant for me to give my full attention to Jesus his whole young life. I should have doted on him and prepared him more carefully for his intended mission. Elohim wanted me to be Jesus' greatest advocate. Instead, I ignored my intuition."

She sighed. "Joseph and I had four other children. With no family support we were overburdened, and thus Jesus was never cared for as Elohim intended. I did teach him to speak, read, and write the Holy Scriptures. But, more importantly I failed to arrange a proper bride for him."

Mary searched the despondent woman's appearance and thought, *I wish*

Mother Mary could see what a great man he has become. She does not realize how appreciative Elohim is that he is alive because of her. Mary was sure that in Elohim's eyes her true mission was fulfilled a long time ago. And thus, Mary understood and loved her so dearly.

Overwhelmed by Mother Mary's experience, she became speechless. She wanted to comfort her, but could find no words. She also wanted so much to tell her of Jesus' proposal to her but remembered Jesus' request to keep it to herself.

Ending her narrative, Mother Mary stood and nodded. It was late as she simply guided the younger Mary to her room to sleep for the night.

Chapter 30

Facing Resistance

Love your enemies, do good to those who hate you.
(Luke 6:27)

Her departure from Jesus' boyhood home was forever etched into Mary's memory. Mother Mary and her son bid the three of them farewell as they walked down the mule trail leading out of Nazareth. Mary turned one last time, surprised to see the older woman continuing to wave. *We have made a special bond and I have a good report for Rabboni. Thank you, Abba Elah for this precious opportunity.*

The weather was pleasant on their trip back to Capernaum. Thaddeus led and decided to take the quickest route, moving eastward over the hills to the Sea of Galilee and then northward along the coastal plain toward Capernaum. They hoped that by sunset they would meet up with Jesus and their companions.

About midday they climbed the last hill. As they reached the summit, Mary enjoyed the spectacular view of the beautiful lake below. They rested shortly, taking their meal, and then continued on, descending to the fields around Tiberius and onto the sandy shore. Passing by Tiberius, Mary remembered its marketplace with her uncle years before. The memories were no longer painful as happier times had removed the sadness. *It was certainly the beginning of the gateway out of my illness,* she thought gratefully.

Nearing Magdala, she thought of her own mother who lived about an hour away on foot. *It would be natural for me to visit her. I wish I could see her and tell her my many stories and show her how healthy I am. We don't have the time but perhaps when I get the chance to see her, I can introduce Jesus to my mother as my…"*

Thaddeus broke into her thoughts calling to her, "Look up to your left. That trail leads to the village of Magdala. Isn't that where you are from?"

"Yes," Mary answered. "Yes, Magdala is on the other side of that hill. Thank you, brother for remembering I am from there. Of course, I wish I could visit my mother; however, I know that Jesus is waiting for us."

Speaking the name of Rabboni aloud after all that had happened in the last week caused her great excitement. *I'll see him soon. This is the longest time that we have been apart and haven't spoken. But I do have so much to tell him about his mother.* Thrilled with all she had learned she thought, *I hope that someday I will be able to help reconnect their hearts.*

But again, thinking of her own mother, *I promise that one day I will visit with news of his successful mission and surprise her with our marriage.* The thought made her blush and she grabbed her scarf to cover her countenance. Mary added to his acknowledgment of her hometown, directing, "We will not stop this time."

When the three arrived in Capernaum after dark, later than expected, they went directly to Elder Simon's house. Jesus welcomed them back but wasted no time before informing them of his new plan. First, though, he called Simon to arrange a late dinner for the trio.

While they ate bread and cheese, Mary tried to focus on Jesus' plans. She struggled with her own thoughts about his mother and her longing to return to their last conversation the night he proposed to her. Realizing that those thoughts had to wait, she refocused and listened.

Jesus spoke with excitement and hope, "…we will go to Bethsaida where Simon, James, John, and others are preparing. Simon has many contacts there and tells me there is much interest and eagerness in the community to hear my sermon."

Mary was disappointed that no time was given to her to speak to him of his family but … she noticed the excitement in his voice about the event, and she understood.

Jesus continued, "Even though I had to cancel my plans to speak there due to the unexpected news of the Baptist, the people from the whole region are nevertheless gathering with high expectations. We will leave early in the morning."

As Jesus began his prayer to end the day, a messenger arrived from Bethany. The man bowed before Jesus. He appeared anxious and asked to speak, "My master, Lazarus, is gravely ill. He requests that you come to him as soon as you can. He had me travel overnight using the quickest route possible." The unexpected news moved everyone, especially Jesus.

Mary thought, *Lazarus helped Jesus from the beginning of his mission. They are like brothers. His illness must be grave for the servant to come on this long and hasty journey.*

Jesus called to Martha, "Return with this messenger today. I will give my sermon and then we will leave from Bethsaida by ship and get there as soon as we can, hopefully within a couple of days."

That evening Mary forgot her fatigue as she helped Martha prepare for her sudden but necessary departure. Within an hour, Mary and all the disciples stood at the gate of Simon's house, waving goodbye with promises to follow within a day.

Then, Mary attended Rabboni in his nightly prayer. She missed being with him and supporting him. She knelt in one of her usual places, surrounded by rows of tall colorless grass on the sandy ground. From a small embankment she watched him below her. He stood at the water's edge peering out onto the moonlit Sea of Galilee. The light was strong and reflected on his beige robe. He was clearly visible, and she resisted her desire to run to him.

She presumed that he was preparing himself for tomorrow's speech, but felt regretful that he could not immediately leave to help Lazarus, his dear devotee, advocate, and financier. Though Mary felt the pressure of the moment she knew that foremost in Jesus' mind was his communion with his Abba Elah.

Taking a deep breath, she offered her desperate prayer, *Dear Abba Elah, please show me how to alleviate any concerns that Rabboni may have. That I can relieve any situation that may arise on his path. He must be more tired than me.*

I remain committed to him whatever may come our way. Let us all unite and support him.

Kneeling there, she also thanked Abba Elah that she could return to her Rabboni. During her prayer she felt the love Elah had for the people of Galilee and the disciples and for Jesus' success. Tears of gratitude came easily as she prayed, overwhelmed with longing to be near him again. She wept in joy.

She continued her prayer, *Abba Elah, your kindness and greatness is amazing to behold. Right now, it seems only the humble people are longing for Your prophesied Anointed One. We are open and receptive to him. I pray that all of us, Rabboni's disciples, will be completely united with him, especially tomorrow.*

I pray that all the people will know that Jesus brings them Your good news of understanding! His words are meant to liberate our nation and bring all the chosen people back to You. We are ruled by rigid laws causing fearfulness, but Jesus explains that it is time they know You as their loving Father. You want the people to know of Your love!

She prayed for his mother, that she would one day understand her son. She had learned so much about her life's sacrifice, *Thank you for giving me the opportunity to meet her. I hope I made a difference in her attitude toward her son.*

Before she knew it, the moon was nearing the other side of the lake. Jesus walked back to the house, and she followed separately. Their day was over.

With only a few hours of sleep, they woke before sunlight and began walking eastward. Slowly the dimness receded as the light strengthened. Their walk was mostly along the flat tidal plain of the northern Sea of Galilee. James shouted out to everyone to look northward, to their left, "There is the peak of Mt. Tabor." Mary and Salome could barely see anything like a peak, as it was very far away. The women walked together ahead of the mule pulled wagon carrying all their belongings.

News of Lazarus cast a cloud over their previously excited gathering. That being said, they still wanted to love and care for the residents who were coming to hear Jesus. After a year and more following Jesus they were used to last-minute changes.

Mary and Salome talked about Lazarus and together prayed for his recovery. Talking with Salome was wonderful after coming back from Jesus' home.

Salome was more than happy to fill her in on all that had happened since she was gone, "Simon and Judas argue often. My son James tries to smooth out their misunderstandings before they get to Jesus. But there was one time that Jesus had to step in. He took each aside for a personal conversation." Salome's facial expressions as usual added to her tale.

Mary shared a bit about Jesus' mother but only superficially. She guarded his mother's precious privacy.

Salome continued, "You should have seen how elated Simon was about this gathering. After announcing Jesus' coming sermon in Bethsaida to close friends, the word spread like wildfire.

"Yesterday Simon and a few others went ahead earlier to prepare the whole gathering place. It seems that the people of Bethsaida have already heard about the Gennesaret sermon, and they are really excited to hear from Jesus himself.

"We are amazed at how far the tales of Jesus' healings and inspiring sermons have traveled. They have caused great excitement. There are even murmurings of the coming of the Anointed One all over this part of Galilee. It's mostly because of the news spreading of Jesus' words and healings. Simon predicts there will be a large crowd. I never saw Simon so excited."

As Salome took a breath, Mary thought, *It's refreshingly wonderful rejoining Rabboni to once again work to win the hearts of the amicable Galileans.*

As Salome went on with her report about everyone and everything, Mary listened. "They told Simon that even though Jesus was gone for months, they believed he would return to them, and his mystique was kept alive by chatter and gossip at the well and the markets. In this dull world, the talk of miracles and repeated words of Jesus kept them excited and hopeful. They even prayed for his return."

Salome, chatty as usual, continued, "Now that we are back in Galilee, the religious leaders are not at all as happy about Jesus' return as the simple folk are. I heard one day at the well from a friend that the leaders are now concerned and are starting to push back against what they call 'nonsense,' to put it mildly. That's what they say about Jesus and all of us. James reported to Jesus that they have started ostracizing those who do not regularly attend Sabbath services or give their tithings."

She went on, hardly taking a breath, "While you were gone Jesus never stopped planning. He spent a lot of time praying on the shore and in the boats. It was obvious to me that he was waiting for your return to give his speech." Salome smiled at her friend with a wink and a gleam in her eyes.

Surprised by Salome's sudden comment about her, Mary quickly turned away to avoid giving up her secret, whispering, "Oh, how I love my redeemer!" She was glad the sun shone brightly upon her face, giving her a reason for blushing. Because of that comment, Mary realized that she had to be serious not to give away anything between Jesus and herself. "Yes, Salome, now that we are all back together, Jesus is not wasting time."

For two hours they traveled due east in the crisp early morning air. Mary was happy to hear the exciting news that Jesus' plan was taking hold in the hearts and minds of the people of Galilee. The journey was a happy one for Mary and she whispered, *It is good to be home with my Rabboni and family.*

Suddenly, their procession stopped. Up ahead, Mary noticed Jesus talking to someone on the side of their path. "Let's go see what Jesus is doing," Mary suggested to her elder sister.

Jesus was bending over a man who looked like a beggar, but then she realized that he was blind. Jesus was pouring some water from his receptacle onto the dirt. He mixed it with a stick making a paste. He then prayed over the man. Jesus told him, "Your Abba Elah will relieve you of your blindness, if you believe." Jesus took the muddy paste and smeared it gently onto the man's closed eyelids, and then raised the man to a standing position. "Open your eyes," Jesus commanded.

As the man opened his eyes, most of the dried sand fell off and Jesus took the edge of his mantle and kindly wiped the rest of the dirt away. The man blinked and looked into the eyes of his healer. His eyes glistened with tears and then he shouted, "I can see, I can see!" as he looked around for the first time since he went blind.

Jesus told him to go home and show his parents, "Elah made you well because you believed. Now live your life for others." Then Jesus continued on down the road followed by his procession of disciples as if nothing unusual had happened.

As they neared the rallying point, they saw many residents standing around Simon and Andrew. Mary looked up to the grassy hill behind Simon. Surprised, she saw hundreds of people already arranging their places even though it was several hours before Jesus was due to speak. Children lined the outside of the gathering, playing with each other while women stood close enough to keep an eye on them.

Jesus informally went up to the families seated close to the front and asked, "Some of you have heard of my words. Do you remember my lessons? Have you decided to change your attitudes?" He continued, "Have you served your neighbors and loved those who were angry with you? If you have then you must be bringing great joy to others and good fortune to yourself and your family!"

The plan was that when the sun was nearly mid sky, he would begin his sermon. But that did not keep Jesus from visiting the eager people. He went up the slope to individuals and families and listened to their questions and requests for solutions to their problems, praying with each one, sometimes gathering the whole family unit together and placing his hands on their heads or sometimes over their hearts.

Children innocently watched him with awe. Mary saw and felt their genuine love for him. They wanted to stand near him and stopped their playing just to observe the great man whom they had heard their parents speaking about.

Mary and her brethren were greatly encouraged by the people's interest and reception. She noticed that they were not shy. Many were eager to meet Jesus and approached him, though they waited patiently in a line for their turn. Each family wanted to speak individually with the famous Galilean preacher and healer.

Going down to the plain, Mary continued to watch Rabboni on the hill. At about noon, shortly before Jesus came down to give his sermon, she noticed a procession of about twenty rabbis coming toward them along the seashore. They were dressed in their usual regalia and looked unusually serious.

They all wore similar beige long-sleeved tunics tied with white twined linen belts, covered with a white sleeveless robe edged with light blue and tassels attached to the corners of their garments. On their foreheads, or atop their heads, a few wore a tefillin tied with leather straps under their chins.

Mary was accustomed to rabbis attending Jesus' sermons, but in the past, they sat informally and humbly dressed amongst the crowd. She noticed and wondered, *It is unusual that they are coming together en masse and in formal attire.* She remembered the extravagant garb of the leaders in Jerusalem. *They must have heard about the Good News,* Mary thought ingenuously, without concern. She looked for Jesus again and found him far up on the hill, and thought, *He is not aware of their arrival.*

Andrew was about to escort the group further up the hill, but the leader insisted on a front row for their whole entourage. Humbly Andrew guided them to the front and indicated that they should sit in two rows. Their request caused a lot of the early arriving commoners to complain. But out of respect for their priestly positions, Andrew allowed them to stay in the front.

When Jesus came down, Mary went over to him. "Rabboni, a large group of rabbis have arrived, and Andrew seated them in the front row as they requested."

Jesus looked over at them and went to greet them cordially. They were standing and ceremonially bowing and praying, ignoring him.

Simon excitedly rushed over to Jesus to tell him the count, "Rabboni, there are thousands in attendance with lines of people still arriving." In his eagerness he did not notice the group of clerics as he was facing Jesus with his back to the crowd. Then he noticed there was concern in Jesus' expression. Turning to see what Jesus was looking at, he watched the praying religious leaders with skepticism.

Without speaking, Jesus turned to Mary, who was waiting with a water-skin for him. He took it from her and then informed her, "I will begin to speak in about an hour." Then he ordered her strongly, "Prepare in prayer."

Mary understood that the scene right in front of where he would speak was unexpected and unusual, but she believed his prayer would give him poise and confidence. She stepped away to pray as he asked.

By the time Jesus came back, Simon proudly announced that there were at least four thousand people up on the hillside, coming from all around the whole region even as far as Caesarea Philippi.

Mary was reassured as she felt Rabboni's love for the people and saw that his face was calm and relaxed. She felt confidence and thought, *Yes! he's ready to address his fellow countrymen.*

In a loud voice, Jesus began by cordially thanking the people for attending. With his arms open and stretched out he was about to begin his sermon when another unexpected happening occurred. The man whom Jesus had cured of blindness that very morning came forward out of the crowd. Jesus looked at the man and remembered him. He took a deep breath, and with a nod of his head gave the previously blind man time to speak.

"Pardon me sir," the man said loudly but with respect and humility, "I want to thank you and give my testimony to this crowd of worshipers that you are my healer!"

Not at all shy, he turned and shouted in order to get everyone's attention. Gradually the chatter all over the hillside subsided. "I woke up this day, as was the case much of my life, a blind man. I never imagined that I would see. But you, Rabbi Jesus, relieved my blindness and now for the first time in my life I can see!"

The curious crowd of thousands of people became silent instantly as everyone wanted to hear the man. Most of the people saw the bold man speaking, but they could not hear him. They became completely silent in order to hear.

The priests heard well. One of the priests stood and boldly retorted, showing little deference toward Jesus, "I am here with other fellow leaders. We want to see for ourselves your preaching and reported healings." He motioned to his fellow comrades. "And judge whether or not the rumors are true. Is this man your deceptively connived trick to influence the masses?" he asked, waving his hands indicating all the people behind him.

He continued while Jesus remained silent, "This man may say that he was blind, but you have obviously set this up. Another reported healing so that all will praise you for creating miracles." Unabashed he tried to usurp Jesus' position, but Jesus ignored his rudeness. He did not refuse him or tell him to sit down.

Then the rabbi insisted, "I want to ask the supposedly healed man some questions. Where are your parents, that they may confirm that you were indeed blind? We insist on proof, not merely accepting this charade," he continued with a commanding voice.

Startled by the unplanned request of the rabbi, Mary began to feel defensive about the situation. *Is this priest trying to turn the people against Jesus? Is this something he planned before? Have all these priests planned to disrupt Jesus' sermon?*

Jesus called to Mary, snapping her out of her questioning and instructed her, "Translate everything that is said into Aramaic. The people must understand our conversation."

Mary obeyed and shouted out their own dialect for all to hear. The crowd was silent.

At first Jesus shouted also in Aramaic, appearing unaffected by the accusation, "I am willing to meet the priest's demand. But first I would like to welcome you all. I see that the whole region's population must be here. There are so many of you. I have been told that four thousand people are here today.

"Many of you may be curious, but not cynical like these religious leaders in front of me. I believe that many more of you sincerely want to hear my life-giving words about our Abba Elah and about what our relationship should be with Him. Each and every one of you wants to feel the love of Elah. Am I right? Otherwise, you would not have made the effort to come here."

The crowd echoed throughout the immense area, "Yes!" It even caused the rabbis to turn and look at the huge gathering behind them.

"However, first I must answer this rabbi's question," Jesus explained in Aramaic. Continuing in Aramaic, he called out for all to hear, indicating the man he had healed in the morning, "Are the parents of this man here? Let them come forward to confirm that he was indeed blind this morning when he awoke but now can see."

The parents came forward and the father shyly announced, "Master, he was indeed blind yesterday, but he sees today. We do not know how it is that he sees or who restored his sight. You must ask him, as he is old enough to speak for himself."

Mary recognized from their demeanor that the parents felt intimidated. The father spoke with his head bowed, aware of the religious leaders in the front. It seemed to her that they were afraid to speak in Jesus' favor for fear of reprisal from the clerics.

Therefore, the unyielding priest spoke directly to the previously blind man, "Give Elohim praise. We all know you are a sinner!"

The man whose sight was restored answered bravely, "Whether or not I am a sinner I do not know, but I do know that though I was blind this morning I can now see this afternoon."

The priest insisted, "Tell me how he gave your sight back."

"I told you already. Why do you want me to repeat myself?" The man became impatient but courageously continued a bit sarcastically, "Do you want to become Jesus' disciple?"

The question from the lowly man caused the cleric to rebuke him, "I do not want to become this man's disciple. I am a disciple of Moses. I know that Adonai spoke to Moses but to this man, Jesus, I do not know where he comes from or who he speaks to."

Surprisingly, the humble man said impudently, "You do not know where he comes from and yet he opened my eyes. I am an ignorant and sinful man, but I can understand that if this man was not from Elah, he could do nothing."

The priest answered him with disgust, "You were born in utter sin, how is it that you try to teach me?"

Jesus came forward and asked the formerly blind man directly, "Do you believe in the Son of Elah?"

The man spoke honestly, "Who is he so that I may believe in him?"

Jesus said, "You are looking at him, and it is he who speaks to you."

The man replied, "Lord, I believe that you are the Son of Elah." He immediately fell on his knees and worshiped Jesus.

Then Jesus proclaimed, "I came into the world that you all may see. There are some, however, who think they see but they are blind."

The priest snidely retorted, "Am I blind?"

Jesus answered, "If you admit that you are blind you would have no guilt. But now that you insist that you see, your guilt remains."

Jesus then turned away from the priest and began to speak to the multitude, "I am the shepherd and the doorway to the sheepfold. Anyone who tries to come by any other way is a thief. The sheep hear their shepherd's voice and they follow him. The shepherd leads them, and they know his voice and willingly follow. The sheep will not follow a stranger and they will flee from him for they do not know the voice of the stranger."

Jesus saw that the priest did not understand. Therefore, he repeated, "I am the doorway. I am the good shepherd. Any who came before me are thieves and robbers. If anyone enters by me, he will be saved and will go in and out and find pasture abundantly."

Continuing Jesus proclaimed, "The good shepherd lays down his life for the sheep. He will defend his sheep from wolves, while the thief lives only for his own comfort. I have other sheep who are not of this fold, but I also bring them into the fold and they also heed my voice. Therefore, there is one flock and one shepherd. This is why Abba loves me. I am prepared to give my life for my sheep."

The religious leaders felt the sting of rebuke from the whole crowd and stood as one unit, calling Jesus a demon. But the people overwhelmed the rabbis and stood with Jesus, shouting praise for Jesus and repeating Jesus' words. The whole hillside resounded in their applause.

One Galilean resident who had overheard the whole conversation stood and refuted the priest, "If he was a demon he could not or would not give sight to a blind man!" There was great commotion in the crowd of believers.

Earlier, from within the crowd, Simon and James had become aware of the mob of rabbis. Surmising that Jesus needed more support, they called all the disciples who were dispersed among the crowd to join him on the plain. They surrounded Jesus, protecting him. Simon, requested by Jesus previously, had arranged a fishing boat to be anchored offshore. Seeing the seething anger, he signaled for it to come closer to shore.

Jesus boldly continued, "My people know me. They hear my voice. You hear my words, but you do not believe me. I give them eternal life and they will not perish. Abba has given them to me, and no one can snatch them out of my hands.

"You know of John the Baptist. To you John was a lamp and you may have chosen to enjoy his light. But I tell you truly, I give testimony that is more important than John's because I am testifying directly to Abba who sends me. You diligently study the scriptures because in them you think you will find eternal life. These scriptures testify to me, yet you refuse to believe me who can give you eternal life. Still, I want to give it to you abundantly. I come in the Father's name and you do not accept me. If another comes in his own name, will you accept him?"

Jesus reminded them, "Did not David say, 'You are all Elah's. You are all sons of the Most High.' Yes, I am Elah's son. If you do not believe in my words, then believe in my works. I am in the Father and He in me. I tell you truthfully that I can do nothing by myself but only what I see Abba doing. For He loves the son and shows him all He is doing.

"Moreover, unlike your teachings, Abba judges no one but entrusts all judgement to the son. Whoever hears my word and believes will receive eternal life. All authority is granted to the Son of Man from the Father. By myself I can do nothing."

This was the last straw. The religious leaders became enraged upon hearing Jesus' claim of authority from Elah. Hearing the crowd siding with Jesus, they realized that they had lost their influence over the people. They stood and began to leave. Some of the angry leaders screamed "blasphemer," and picked up rocks, throwing them at Jesus and his disciples wanting to hurt them.

Pelted by the stones, Simon ordered them to move as one unit to the boat. The women were protected by Thaddeus and his brother. Aboard the boat they sadly watched the priests and residents leaving. No one could know the pain in Jesus' heart. Mary saw him standing in the stern, his robes blowing in the breeze. It was late afternoon, but it seemed to Mary that darkness enveloped them. Except for the waves everyone remained still, waiting for direction.

After several heavy minutes, Jesus turned and spoke to his followers. "Beware of the leaven of the Pharisees and Sadducees." The disciples became confused thinking Jesus was speaking of bread.

"Oh! you of little faith, I do not talk of bread at this hour. Beware of the leaven of the religious leaders." Then they understood he was speaking to them of the influence the false teachers might have over them.

Jesus continued, "These leaders look to the sky and believe they can tell the weather to be calm or storm, and yet they cannot interpret the signs of the time we live in. This evil and adulterous generation look for signs, but they miss them all. Now no further sign will be given."

Rabboni abruptly changed the subject, presenting a new plan, "I will take Simon, James, and John with me north to the district of Caesarea Philippi. Judas, take the ship back to Simon's house and wait for us there."

Mary watched as the four men jumped off the boat and walked to shore, taking a path northward into the hills. Melancholy and darkness enveloped the boat. Clouds blocked the moonlight, but momentary glints of light helped the sailors navigate the boat back to Capernaum.

Chapter 31

The Long Days
to Ordination

If anyone comes after me, let him deny himself…
For anyone who would save his life will lose it
but whoever loses his life will find it.
(Matt 16:24-25)

After Jesus, Simon, James, and John left and headed north, Judas, following Rabboni's direction, led the rest of Jesus' disciples back to Capernaum. Out on the water, Mary shivered though it was not cold, wondering if her companions also felt the emptiness and loneliness that she felt.

Holding on to the side of the skiff, she reviewed the day's occurrence, the hateful shouting and the violent attack of rocks tossed at Jesus by the rabbis, thinking, *Their vicious physical assault shocked and frightened everyone and I'm sure the inhabitants will never forget it. I'm so sorry Abba Elah! I wonder if Rabboni decided to take the trip to the north because of that or did he plan it earlier? Why?* she asked herself, deeply mourning the absence of her Lord.

Capernaum was a desolate place. Since Jesus had left for Caesarea Philippi in northern Galilee, Mary and her fellow disciples had been glum and bewildered. Judas was in charge but few had patience for his authoritarian manner that was often abrasive and uninspiring. Everyone was on edge and, with Judas' haughty attitude, several arguments and near fist fights broke out.

The difference between Jesus and Judas was extreme. His Judean nature provoked them and proved to be antithetical to the easy-going Galileans.

Mary remembered the empty feeling and uncomfortable silence as Brother Judas led them back to Simon's house. Walking into the comfortable home, Judas responsibly gathered everyone and led them in a prayer before sending everyone to their rooms to rest. Before Mary joined her sisters, Judas called her aside and asked to speak with her. But feeling loneliness for Jesus she declined, using the excuse of not feeling well and went along with Salome. She could not stop thinking of Jesus.

Mary could not sleep and decided to go to her usual station outdoors, where she customarily supported Jesus in prayer. She tried to imagine him further out on the hillside. It was pitch dark with no moon due to the heavy clouds. Instead of praying internally she prayed aloud.

"Abba Elah," she prayed, speaking softly to keep her focus. "What can I do to help Rabboni? Please show me. How can we open the minds of the rigid clergy? Is it even possible? Jesus spoke to the people of Bethsaida that he would give his life for his sheep. But truly I see that the sheep have no power or influence. Today there were thousands of good common people, and even though they understood Jesus' meaning, they had no ability to influence their leaders. Why can't the most educated and supposedly wise see Jesus' sincerity and works and receive his words that can give them new understanding?" she implored desperately.

"Dear Abba!" Mary continued. "Please help us try harder to reach the leaders. Let us find those who may understand and do not fear the reprisal of their leaders. We can try to persuade them to speak out on Jesus' behalf!" Feeling overwhelmed with love for Elah and Jesus, Mary fervently promised aloud, "I commit my life to you, Rabboni!"

Suddenly a male voice interrupted her prayer, causing her to jump from the shock of a man invading her privacy. Stunned, Mary turned toward the dim figure behind her and recognized Judas. *How long has he been there? Was he listening to my prayer?* she wondered, feeling terribly uncomfortable and alone and ashamed to be caught unescorted. She quickly covered her face with her scarf and stood up.

Apologizing, because she thought that maybe her prayer was too loud, Mary stuttered, "I am sorry, I hope I did not interrupt you. I usually pray here while Jesus prays in the field. Pardon me, I will return to my room." As she instinctively turned to go to the women's quarters, Judas nearly blocked her path. She noticed his brazen and smiling expression, feeling it to be indecent. She wanted to run but tried to remain composed and, without a word, walked as quickly and quietly as she could back to her room.

She entered the woman's quarters quietly, trying not to awake Salome. She was trembling from his audacious action. Quickly, trying to shake the uncomfortable feeling, she prepared to sleep, but she found herself just lying there awake with all the events of the day swirling in her head. She could not quiet them, so she just stayed there until first light. She determined not to give any thought to that unusual moment with Judas.

On the first full day of Rabboni's absence, Mary and Salome walked to the shore and saw Thaddeus and James Alpheus picking up and throwing rocks into the water. Mary had an idea and said to her friend, "They are from Caesarea Philippi. Let's ask them how long it takes to travel to that area. Then we will know about how long their trip should take."

Thaddeus the elder brother explained, "The journey to the region is not an easy one. There is a Roman road, but it is mostly uphill. The whole area is rugged and mountainous, rising to the tallest peak, Mt. Hermon, some three thousand meters high. It's nothing like the gentle hills of western Galilee. Some parts of the main road could be washed out. And, depending on where they go, the paths to villages off the main road are even more challenging. It will definitely take time, though returning home could be quicker since it is downhill, assuming there are no problems."

James Alpheus added, "There are many other hazards like wild animals, thieves, and landslides. It is not a safe journey. Let's pray that with Elah's help all goes well. Then, they could possibly return in about five or six days."

Mary and Salome thanked them and returned to the house, where they decided to find chores to do and keep busy. The kitchen was always a bustling place, and their help was always appreciated.

During these six days Mary determined to keep a strong spirit. She saw those with less self-control lazing around and struggling with depression, which brought down the atmosphere. She kept up her prayers at night in her usual place. It was her secret. Everyone else went to their quarters to sleep.

Some days, Mary and Salome walked to the shore together and waded in the waters. Salome often chatted while Mary found her mind wandering and reminiscing about the night Jesus embraced her. She also thought of Martha and her brother and knew they had expected Rabboni days ago. She prayed for Lazarus' recovery and for Jesus to have a fruitful trip, though she wondered curiously why he abruptly changed his plans with all that was going on.

Guessing, she thought, *Maybe Abba Elah told him to go there? Or maybe it was because of the hateful religious leaders that disrupted his sermon? Though he had tried to help them understand his mission they just twisted and disregarded Jesus' words and miracles. As things look,* she whispered, *realistically he stands alone with no notable and respected supporter like John the Baptist, the expected Elijah. Oh, Abba Elah! Jesus' task is truly daunting!*

Salome went back to the kitchen, but Mary told her she needed more time to pray, "I will follow you back soon." Alone, Mary cried out loud toward the gleaming waters of the Sea of Galilee, "Oh! Abba Elah, please give Rabboni an inspiration of how to make a way forward! Please! I beg you! How can I help him more?" She cried desperate tears, falling on her knees upon the wet sands.

After six days of morning prayer meetings led by Judas, tension was rising. His rigid orthodox style and authoritarian manner was very similar to the stilted heartlessness of the rabbis. It was much different from Jesus' loving, compassionate prayers and his constant reminders of Abba's forgiveness.

This morning, Judas quoted words from the scripture of Daniel from memory. Arrogantly he ordered, "Sister Mary translate into Aramaic for your brothers and sisters."

Annoyed by his attitude, she watched him strutting back and forth, pompously waving his hands. This morning he was full of himself and it was obvious that he flaunted his knowledge more than other mornings. He even seemed aware of the unhappiness he was causing and seemed to enjoy it. His Judean aristocratic arrogance was growing and so was his intimidating attitude.

Mary did recognize that for the first few days he had tried to continue Jesus' routine and manner. However, his style gradually took on his own habitual personality, which was strictly traditional, reciting excerpts all morning from scriptures as if everyone knew the verses, even announcing, "This is what we as loyal Jews must do."

As he quoted Daniel 9:3-5, Mary followed his direction and translated, "I prayed to the Lord my Elohim and made confession. Seeking him by prayer and repentance and wearing sackcloth and fasting. Oh! great and terrible Elohim, lover of those who love Him and lover of those who keep His commandments steadfastly. We have sinned and done wrong, rebelled, turning away from your commandments and ordinances."

When Judas asked Thomas to comment on the passage, the man stood and shouted back at Judas, "I cannot stand to listen to your pompous, irritating Judean accent even one minute more! It is because of leaders like you that our master is not here. The stiff-necked stubborn establishment is deaf to our Lord's message! And it seems that so are you!" Without another word the brother stormed out of the room.

The cultural difference between Jesus and Judas became clear to Mary, *Judas, himself, cannot or will not reason like Jesus. And so it is with all the orthodoxy. Whereas the Galilean nature is relaxed and free and able to separate from those bonds, Judas cannot relinquish his past education and upbringing. Though he tries to imitate Jesus, his lower nature emerges. Given this opportunity by Jesus, he continues to side with the strident laws and heartless traditions of the ancient religion and culture, like he has learned nothing. If Jesus is unable to separate the orthodoxy here in Galilee and cannot get Judas to detach from it, how can he reach those in Judea? They are calcitrant and deaf to any new paradigm.*

Thomas' rebellion sparked an uncomfortable atmosphere and Judas' face turned scarlet. It became apparent that he had no supporters to defend him. Everyone began to mumble discontentedly. In an attempt to keep order, Andrew, who was second in command, respectfully addressed Judas, "Thank you for your morning service. We will now go to our assigned chores." Then he expressed his hope, "I expect that very soon Jesus will return. Let's keep our spirits high and ready to welcome Jesus and our brothers back."

Mary continued avoiding Judas, especially because of their interaction the first night and she did not want to cause further ill will. She also felt uncomfortable around him. Therefore, she stayed close to Salome, avoiding any give and take with him.

She prayed for Judas' though, that he would empty his heart of old ideas and accept Jesus' new and compassionate message. She also prayed for Jesus to return before the disciples rebelled totally against Judas' authority. Mary saw confusion and concern in everyone's expressions and the frayed atmosphere worsened each day. Without word from Jesus, everyone was tense and on edge.

Determined to remain positive, Mary remembered what Thaddeus told her, *If there are no accidents Jesus could possibly return in five or six days. This is the sixth day. He must be coming back soon.*

After Andrew released everyone for the rest of the morning, Mary and Salome went into the kitchen. Working helped to while away the hours. Finally, as the evening meal began on the sixth day of Jesus' absence, an excited servant ran into the hall announcing Jesus' return. Jesus, Simon, James, and John were right behind him.

With a feeling of relief, there was a unanimous shout of joyful greeting! Instantly the spirit changed to hope and joy as everyone greeted the travelers. By chance, Mary caught a glimpse of Judas standing behind the crowd surrounding Jesus. His expression was dark and separated from the joy of Jesus' return. Instantly she felt uncomfortable but quickly turned her attention back to Jesus.

Rabboni and his ensemble were happy to be home, but they certainly looked tired and dirty. Mary longed to run up to Jesus as she had done months before but fought the impulse.

After greeting everyone Jesus immediately announced, "We will leave at first light to Bethany, taking the quickest route by boat to the southern shore of the Sea of Galilee. Bring enough food and watered wine to get us to Bethany."

Then Rabboni paused, "Let us pray. Abba Elah, we feel Your tangible love as we are now back together in fellowship where Your love and protection and constant support is real. Our love for each other is also real. This country is prepared and waiting for Your promised Redeemer. Open the eyes and hearts of Your chosen people to receive Your Son. Help me to find a way without the prophesied Elijah!"

Jesus then thanked everyone for holding it together while he was gone and added, "Admittedly it was an abrupt change of plans, but Abba's guidance takes precedence over our limited understanding. As I made the change so did you, and I applaud you. It was not easy for anyone, but we accomplished it through our unity." Mary knew he threw in that reminder of unity on purpose. *Rabboni probably knows what was going on here,* she guessed.

As he looked around the gathering, no one noticed his momentary glance at Mary. It was only an instant in time, but she treasured it silently in her heart.

Jesus expressed his gratitude to everyone, "You are always in my heart. Thank you for remaining steadfast in your prayers. We will need much prayer in the coming days." Abruptly he bowed to everyone and took his leave.

Simon thanked everyone for their prayers, "Time is growing short. We will need to leave very early for Bethany."

Concerned for Jesus' well-being, Mary thought, *Surely, he is exhausted. Has he eaten?*

Simon's commanding voice interrupted her thoughts as he gave instructions to the men. Then he turned to Salome and Mary, "Prepare the food left over from dinner. Fill the wineskins and sleep quickly as we have a long trip ahead of us."

Mary noticed Simon's worn expression. His face seemed older and more wrinkled than before. *From what Thaddeus had said it must have been a grueling and fast trip.* She assumed that as always Jesus had pushed them hard.

Salome and Mary worked together with Perpetua and the servants. Within the hour all was ready to be loaded on to the boat.

After preparing her personal items, Mary went to her usual prayer place and knelt to pray. However, this night she found it very hard to pray. As was customary, she could often observe Jesus standing on a bluff facing the ebb and flow of the lake as she prayed. This night, though, clouds covered the moon and darkness enveloped her and she could not see him. She reached out her arms toward him but could only catch an occasional glimpse.

Struggling, she stood desperately hoping to catch sight of his form, thinking, *Maybe I can move closer. But I cannot disturb him. Oh Elah! I cannot go another night or day without speaking to him. Oh! Abba, I cannot bear being separated from him any longer.* Hot tears flowed from her eyes. Losing track of time, she prayed desperately with her face against the earth. *Many days and many experiences have passed since we shared that single moment together.*

Suddenly she heard his footsteps which reminded her of the time. *The night is over, and I have hardly prayed! It is time to go in.* She caught a glimpse of him as he neared the house. *Oh! Let me run to him! But I cannot. You are my beloved. My heart aches for you. Dear Abba, forgive me for my weak and longing heart!*

Alone she trudged slowly back to her room. As she laid down on her bed, she realized her exhaustion. Her last thought was of the sound of gusting wind outside. Sleepily she whispered, *A storm is coming!* She could not know how fateful those words were. It would be the last night that she and Jesus would walk together in Galilee. Change was coming as soon as the sun rose the next day. It would be her faithfulness that would buoy her through the next phase of her life.

"Mary, it's time to rise," Salome's voice called. "Simon is calling, and we have to leave."

With everyone gathered, Simon announced, "Our schedule has changed. Instead of leaving immediately, Jesus called us together for an announcement."

While waiting, Mary noticed a change in Jesus' demeanor. Good or bad, she could not tell, for it was hard to describe. *Something is different. Is he more serious or distant?* She was not sure.

But there was no time. Jesus broke into her thoughts, announcing, "We will not return here after visiting Bethany. We will stay longer in Judea during the spring and attend the Passover celebrations in Jerusalem."

Passover! Are you going to announce our marriage? She remembered his words, *We will marry at Passover time.* Tears of joy filled her eyes, but she quickly covered her face with her scarf.

Jesus' announcement surprised Simon, causing him to become emotional. His manner sharply changed as he reminded Rabboni, "Your original plan was to return to Galilee straight away after we helped Lazarus!" With a bright red complexion, he continued, "You know the danger! We spoke about this." Uncharacteristically, Simon continued arguing and begging Jesus to reconsider, "You know that in the Sanhedrin, the Sadducees and Pharisees are planning a united course of action against you after grim reports from the Galilean religious leaders."

Simon continued, filled with concern, "They blame you! They are angered with you…for the dismal attendance in Galilean congregations and their shrinking coffers. As we speak, the Sadducees are sending out spies gathering incriminating evidence against you. Even the Roman governor is probably receiving similar troubling gossip. The rich and powerful are beginning to look at you as a danger to civil society. You are upending their hold over power. They will not allow you to continue, especially because their influence is declining!"

Simon continued on, "Rabboni, is it because of your disappointment with the rally in Bethsaida and the violence therein? And therefore, you want to barge headfirst into the whole Judean culture? Or is it because of your experience on Mt. Hermon?"

Aghast, Mary watched Simon's public disapproval. This was the first time she had heard mention about religious authorities reporting Jesus to the Sanhedrin and about their recent trip. Seldom had she seen Simon stand so publicly and openly resistant to Rabboni's plan.

Even more shocking than Simon, Rabboni retorted to Simon, "Get behind me Satan! Don't be a hindrance to me. For you are only thinking from your own point of view, not Elah's!" Accusing him, Jesus roared, "Are you thinking of the danger my plan would put you in?" Startled at Jesus's ferocity toward Simon, Mary held her breath and swallowed hard.

Then Jesus turned to everyone, "I tell you seriously! From now on you must follow my directions and trust me. Do not be ashamed of me, you adulterous and sinful generation. Whoever wants to save his life will lose it and anyone willing to give his life for my sake will find it. What good is it, if you gain the whole world, but lose your life?"

Jesus paused and took a deep breath. He seemed to rein in his raw emotion, "Do you understand, Simon?" Jesus' tone changed to benevolence. Simon's countenance fell. He was obviously shaken and humbled. He knelt and bowed with his fist over his heart apologizing. Simon's pale face was sincere as he repented. Jesus nodded acceptance of his right-hand man's humble and apologetic compliance and helped him to stand up.

Clarifying his reasoning, he continued, "I am only following Abba Elah. These times are serious, yes! But I cannot shy away from Abba's guidance to me. I, we, must follow this path from here on."

Mary knew Jesus could be stern, but a chilly feeling caused her to wonder what had happened on their trip to the north. Jesus' demeanor and attitude had surely changed. And he was no longer relaxed, but more serious than she had ever seen him.

He had another surprise announcement, "Mary and Salome go and prepare basins and pitchers of fresh water, and towels." The two women did as they were asked. When they came back with his requests, Jesus continued, "I want to perform a ceremony today with all of you. You must be raised up and understand that today I formally ordain you as my disciples. From this day forward, as you follow me believe that you will do even greater things than I do.

"Whatever you ask Abba in my name, He will do it. For Elah sent his Son into the world, not to condemn the world, but that the world might be saved through him.

This day I tell you that I am in the Father and you in me and I in you. I will never leave you nor forsake you. I give you authority over all the power of the enemy, over unclean spirits to cast them out, and over all diseases in every infirmed person.

"Firstly though, you must believe and follow my example! Have you not learned that much from me in the time we have been together?"

Surprised at his direct question, as they also felt a strange difference in their lord's spirit everyone answered solemnly, "Yes!"

"As you receive this ordination freely, you should not ask for pay from those whose lives you make better. Do not think of yourself first! Do not think of how you will live. Find those who need Abba's love and grace and give it to them and lighten their load. If you do this, your heart will be made light and your love for Abba Elah will increase. I am aware that I am sending you out as sheep among wolves, so be wise as serpents and innocent as doves.

"If you are delivered up to them, do not worry what you will say but remember the spirit of Abba Elah will fill your mind and heart with words flowing with love and truth. Remember that I am always with you even to the end of the age."

Rabboni's words of confidence in Abba Elah filled the disciples with awe and excitement. Their innocence protected them. All that Jesus gave them in this moment would come to pass and following his instructions would help them. Mary and her fellow disciples watched, not knowing the reason for this serious ceremony. But they knew that he had definitely changed and was more serious now than ever before.

After Mary and Salome arranged the water, basins, and towels, he gathered everyone. Then ceremoniously, like a father preparing his child to receive his blessing, he lined them up one by one, examining them and telling them to stand tall. Then Jesus knelt down humbly in front of them and washed their feet.

At the same time, he spoke personally to each individual. His manner was very serious as he beseeched them one by one, "If you want the people to listen to you and follow you, you must humbly serve them as I am serving you. Deny your pride, your self-centeredness, and be willing to give to others without expecting anything in return. Remember this most important request."

Finally, he asked each disciple to pledge their dedication to Elah and to him, "Are you willing to live your life giving to others? Rich or poor, Jew or Roman, man or woman? Whatever or whoever should come to you, do you swear allegiance to Abba Elah and to me?"

Every man and woman chose to answer, "Yes!" The first men were Elder Simon and Andrew his brother, and the two sons of Zebedee and Salome, also called the Sons of Thunder, James and John. These four were the first to follow Jesus when he began his ministry in Galilee.

Next, Jesus ordained Judas Iscariot and Nathaniel (also known as Bartholomew), Phillip, and Simon the Zealot. Finally, Jesus called Thomas who was a fisherman, Thaddeus (also known as Jude) and James Alphaeus, and Matthew (also known as Levi) the tax collector. These twelve men were the first to receive Jesus' anointing.

For Mary, the ceremony was exciting. She noticed the emotional James and John, and Salome their mother. Joyful and proud, they broke into tears as Jesus pronounced his special words over them.

Jesus called Elder Simon up to the front after all twelve had been ordained. Mary noticed Simon's beaming countenance despite Rabboni's strong and demanding expectations of him. He was the one man that Jesus pushed relentlessly, more than anyone else. Mary knew he did it because of Simon's strong stubborn nature. Jesus really wanted to break down his biases and prejudices. She remembered hearing Jesus teach Simon to lead from his heart and love all people.

Mary had witnessed Rabboni's tough love for Simon during the past year and a half through many rough days. It seemed to her that Jesus purposely did not explain much to Simon. She knew that Jesus believed Simon could take the pressure, though his perseverance surprised her. She watched him struggling, but no matter how Jesus treated him, he continued on. After a while Simon even prided himself on being able to withstand Jesus' harsh criticism.

Now, with Simon standing in front of him, Jesus announced with a smile, "I change your name to Peter which means Rock." For all of his faults, Jesus saw the strength of Simon Peter's leadership, commitment, and unswerving loyalty. As a result, Jesus declared officially that Peter would be their leader when he was not around. The position was coveted by others, but Jesus selected Peter.

After a pause, surprising everyone, Rabboni announced the names of seven women. They were Simon's wife Perpetua, Joanna of Chuza, Susanna of Samaria, Martha of Bethany, Salome the mother of James and John, Mary of Clopas, and lastly Mary of Magdala.

Jesus explained that even though Martha, Susanna, and Mary Clopas were not present, he included them, "I cannot forget their prayers and support. I know they are strongly devoted to my mission and are praying for us and intend to continue their support." Looking at the four in attendance that day he explained, "These seven women will be remembered for their attendance to me as well."

Just as he did with the men, Rabboni lined the women up in exactly the same manner. He washed the women's feet and then asked them to swear their complete allegiance to him. He expressed his gratitude to them, and he explained that their prayers would make it easier for all to fulfill their newly ordained missions.

Finally, Jesus addressed all his disciples, "Without your unity and your prayers, we will not be able to be successful in the next steps I will take toward Abba Elah's kingdom."

With great enthusiasm, Rabboni then asked loudly, "Can we do it?" With exuberance everyone replied, "Yes!" With that, Jesus signaled an end to the ceremony, "Let's pray."

Every head bowed with a refreshed and renewed spirit. By the end of Jesus' tearful prayer everyone wiped away their own tears.

Finally, Jesus turned to Peter and instructed him. "Prepare everything. We will leave now for Bethany and from there to Jerusalem to preach Abba Elah's word. Let me know when all is ready."

Part IV

Chapter 32

Lazarus

Very truly I tell you, whoever hears my word
and believes in God who sent me has eternal life.
He does not come into judgement but passes from death to life.
(John 5:24)

There was a joyful gathering in Lazarus' villa, celebrating his miraculous return to life. However, only a week before, when Jesus and his disciples had left Bethsaida and arrived in Bethany, Lazarus was already dead.

They had found Martha distraught with grief. Forgetting her appropriate greeting to Jesus, she instead complained to him through her tears, "Rabboni you came too late. He tried to hang on to see you one last time. You know he wanted so to tell you of his love for you. But after weeks of suffering, he gave up his spirit."

Mary saw how emotionally overwrought she was. Her swollen face was almost unrecognizable. She and Salome ran to her as she knelt crying before Jesus.

Unusually emotional, Jesus cried out to Abba Elah, "I've arrived too late, Abba! This is too painful for me! He and his family have supported me from the beginning!" Bending over to Martha, Jesus whispered compassionately to her, "Take me to his resting place."

Everyone from the household, and the disciples as well, mourned and grieved as Martha guided the way, supported by Mary and Salome.

Mary spotted Joanna and called to her, surprised, "You returned! Elah bless you!" The four women embraced and wept together. All the disciples wailed as well. Arriving at Lazarus' tomb, their small group grew to a crowd. There was so much commotion that curious townspeople had followed them.

Rabboni stood before the closed entrance and prayed amidst the weeping and wailing. He commanded the men to remove the stone. Although his request was unexpected, without hesitation Joanna turned to the men and asked them to comply with his request.

They watched as Jesus entered the crypt and remained there for some time. Peter led everyone in prayer as they beseeched Elohim, wailing in sorrow. "Abba!" Peter entreated. "Your son is overcome with grief over the death of his friend. You know that he is mourning with all his heart that he could not be here to pray for him and bring him back from death's door. You know that Your son has done all You bid him to do, even going without sleep and without nourishment! Please hear his sincere and humble requests and supplications. He knew of Lazarus' illness, but he was obediently following Your will."

Mary believed that their cries surely reached Heaven. She could not remember a time that she had ever prayed so desperately. And she noticed other residents doing the same.

It sounds like Jesus is coming out, Mary thought. She wiped away her tears and straightened her scarf, but suddenly and unexpectantly the shrouded form of a man came slowly out of the cave. Jesus followed.

Then Jesus stepped in front of the shroud and began pulling off the strips of burial cloth, one by one. When all the cloths covering the man were off, Lazarus stood wide eyed, observing the crowd of mourners. He began to cry, which in turn caused everyone to weep, but these tears were joyful.

Is this a mirage or a dream? Mary gasped just like all the witnesses and looked around observing the miracle. There was silence and it seemed that everyone forgot to breathe. Suddenly, the crowd began to cheer with joy. Everyone could hardly believe their eyes as Rabboni and Martha led Lazarus back to their home.

Days later, Mary and all the women enthusiastically prepared a magnificent celebratory banquet. News of the miracle spread by word of mouth from many of the townspeople who had witnessed it. Everyone was invited throughout the whole region. The news even reached Jerusalem and those in high places, the Sanhedrin and even to Roman authorities.

Shortly before midday, Mary received and guided guests toward Lazarus and Jesus, who stood steps away in the portico. She mused, *It is still amazing that he is really alive and greeting his well-wishers. He doesn't look sick and at least right now has no problem standing without assistance. My, how fast the news traveled of Lazarus' miraculous return to life after being dead for four days in the tomb!*

Many exclaimed their wonder and good wishes, "Adonai Elohim hayyim, it is him! He is surely well?" These phrases were repeated all morning and into the late afternoon as guests came in droves. Phillip, Thomas, and Thaddeus were assigned to move the well-wishers along, as the line grew steadily behind them.

"Is it true that you were in the crypt for four days and this preacher, Jesus, raised you from the dead?" The astonishing words were echoed everywhere all day. *The euphoric spirit is incredible! However, I see that there are some who are cynical as well.* Mary spotted them easily from their dark expressions and frowning dull eyes.

She also remembered Martha's regret for her temper, "Mary, I complained and cried in front of Rabboni in anger when he arrived. I am ashamed and I pray he forgives me! The physicians tried to save him, but they could do nothing and he passed." Mary consoled her, pointing out Jesus' compassion and love for Lazarus, his friend, and for her.

Some of Lazarus' friends reminded Jesus that they had met before. They were happy to renew their acquaintance and praised him for reviving their friend. For them there could be no better reason to celebrate than this surprising occasion.

Mary wondered, *Maybe Rabboni will announce something special today! Or speak to everyone about his mission and answer questions of the curious or tell them that he is the long-awaited Messiah. He could ask them to assist him and stand with him to announce it to the world.* The thoughts were spinning in her mind. *What then? How could anyone in power deny their words of praise about Jesus! Surely with such respected and wealthy men the Sadducees would be helpless to deny Jesus' value*. Her anticipation was mounting, and thoughts and questions were going through her mind. It was hard to stay composed.

There was a lull in greetings as the guests milled around, sharing in the festivity. Jesus had retreated and promised Lazarus and Martha to return. Mary went back into the dining hall to check with Martha and make sure everything was prepared. She caught a glimpse of Joanna and Salome talking and laughing and enjoying themselves as they worked together. Mary felt so proud of them. *Joanna came back from Sepphoris. They love Jesus so much.*

Martha was directing the women to continue arranging the palm leaves and trees and eucalyptus plants in a welcoming and beautiful manner. Foods of all kinds covered the tables. On one table there were pitted and stuffed dates, bread, cashews, and stuffed olives, almonds, and pomegranates as well as cut melons. On another table was roasted lamb stuffed with special spices. Mary knew that all of these were intentionally prepared as they were Jesus' favorite foods.

Everything was prepared with Rabboni and Lazarus in mind. Martha, overjoyed that her brother was alive, had guided the kitchen staff in preparing the sumptuous dinner at great expense. It truly was a regal banquet.

However, in the late afternoon Mary began to sense an uneasy feeling. *Something is in the back of my mind, a nagging uncomfortable feeling. Where is it coming from? Everything appears to be perfect right now and very hopeful.* Picking up an empty plate she sought to ignore the feeling and enjoy the joyful atmosphere.

Walking toward the kitchen through a hallway and about to round a corner, she overheard a man's voice murmuring and sensed a negative feeling. This caused her to halt abruptly before being seen. As she listened, the man said in a whisper, "... rumors from my contacts in Jerusalem are that some of the leaders in the Sanhedrin want Jesus arrested for blasphemy and false teachings."

Another older voice answered, "Your question is interesting because from my source there are even plans to put a price on Jesus' head. There is word that they will pay handsomely for anyone who turns him in." This man sounded a bit more sympathetic and whispered, "It sounds to me a lot like the terrible plight of the Baptist!"

Mary noticed a prickly sensation from hearing the words and surmised, *Now I understand where my unease is coming from. These men are curious, but at the same time sound dubious about Jesus.* Standing only a few meters away and hidden from them, she continued to listen.

The older man's voice continued, "I heard that the Roman governor, Pontius Pilate, is disturbed by many complaints coming out of the lawless northern regions where Jesus is from. Pilate doesn't want another situation like what happened with the Baptist. As you know, Pilate almost lost control and was chastised by Rome for that. This could be even worse. Even now there are whispers of the possibility of Rome stepping in and stopping this very celebration."

Mary took a deep breath, attempting to release her anxiety. Certainly, these two had heard of the miracle but were not convinced of Jesus' authenticity, though they were curious. Suddenly she heard footsteps coming behind her in the hallway. Quickly she continued on her path, daringly walking past the gossipers on her way to the kitchen. She decided to tell Jesus privately of what they had said as soon as she could find a moment alone with him. Suddenly she heard her name being called.

"Mary, Mary! Do you know where I can find Mary," a young boy called out as he ran into the kitchen.

She turned and responded, "I am Mary."

The lad nodded with respect and said, "Master Jesus sent me to find you. He wants you to meet him. He's in the grove." The boy pointed toward the olive trees.

Mary took off her apron and rearranged her scarf and straightened her robe. It was not uncommon for her to receive last-minute direction from Jesus. It was late afternoon when she left the kitchen and walked toward the grove of trees. She noticed the white puffy clouds gliding through the sky and the blossoms on the olive trees as she forced her anxiety and the thoughts of the nattering men out of her mind.

With high expectation she half skipped and half ran into the grove looking for Jesus. *It's been a while since we had a chance to speak privately.* Smiling the whole way, she touched her face and felt her hot cheeks. And laughed aloud. *They must be bright red*!

As she remembered his embrace, she hummed the first song that came to her mind and then sang it aloud, though not loud enough to draw attention to herself:

V'ahavta et Adonai Elohecha,
(And you shall love the Lord your Adonai)
B'chol l'vavcha,
(With all of your heart and with all your strength.)
Ur'chol nafsh'cha!
(And with all of your soul!)
Ur'chol m'odecha!
(And with all of your might!)

I feel free and a bit silly, she smiled as she strolled along. She noticed that her worries had dissipated and decided not to mention them to Jesus. Slowing down she prayed, *Oh Elah! I hope to remain calm, open, and receptive to him.*

As she neared the area where she expected him to be she took a deep breath and relaxed, pausing to look around for him. She also reminded herself to tell him the news of his mother but hesitated thinking, *I will not mention it unless he asks.*

She spotted him amongst the beautiful flowering trees. She imagined that he was praying. With feelings of adoration, she thought poetically, *The plants, trees, and even rocks seem to render him strength! He gains vigor from meditating upon even the smallest of plants or on an immense valley of wheat swaying in the wind.*

As she neared him, she scanned the surroundings confirming that they were alone. Then she ran innocently toward him, longing for his embrace.

He turned. The breeze blew his hair away from his handsome strong aquiline features. He was standing perfectly straight and she observed his strong physique. Slowing, and with more dignity, Mary approached him.

Respectfully she bowed in front of him, close enough to touch him. Enthusiastically she announced herself, "Rabboni, it is me. I received your message. How can I serve you?"

His deeply brown eyes filled her with longing for him as they stood gazing wordlessly at each other for moments. It was then that she noticed his furrowed brow. His usual relaxed and smiling expression from the first time they met alone was gone.

Surprised by his seriousness, she swallowed hard waiting for him to speak. And she again felt the weight of anxiety, *I must be feeling what he is feeling,* she thought, *but why, when there is so much joy and excitement in the atmosphere!*

Again, she swallowed hard but there was no moisture in her mouth. Tension enveloped her instead of the love she wanted to express. *Why is he sad!* she asked herself, *And why am I feeling apprehensive? Lazarus is alive. Jesus' miracle is drawing attention from many as well as the stodgy religious men!* But then she recalled what she had heard only moments before, *The gossipers in the hallway.*

"Mary!" Jesus broke her silence. It seemed that he knew she was deep in thought, "I can see that you sense my state of mind even though we have not spoken privately for a long while. I also see that you recognize something about me has changed. However, I assure you that my heart toward you has not changed. Only our situation has changed."

As he confirmed the anxiety she so much wanted to be rid of, she took a step back and held her breath in anticipation of his next words, *No! Don't say anything. There must be a way.* Uncontrollably she started to sob. Immediately she took deep breaths to compose herself. And then realized that Jesus was speaking.

"...news that will disappoint you. It disappoints me as well. Honestly you know that there has been no time for us to speak since returning from Caesarea."

Although it was a warm day, she felt chilled and gripped her robe closer. *It must be the wind,* she thought and shuddered as she wiped her tears away. It helped to concentrate her attention on Jesus. His sorrow was apparent. Angry with herself for not fostering absolute faith in him she made effort to conceal her disappointment.

He spoke with gentleness and kindness, "Mary, let me explain. This will help both of us on the way forward. During my trip to Caesarea Philippi, I was guided by Abba Elah to climb Mount Hermon. On the mountain, Moses and Elijah spoke to me giving me a sobering message from Abba. They asked me, 'What will you do if you cannot change the hearts and minds of the leaders of Hebraism? What will you do if they turn against you?'"

Jesus looked directly into Mary's eyes and though tears came to his eyes he quickly wiped them away. He waited, giving her time to consider his serious explanation and her reaction. With a nod of her head, he acknowledged that she fully understood. She also realized that he would not speak the words that they both hoped for, and then she could no longer rein in her emotions.

No! Don't speak! she thought. Uncontrollably tears flowed, but like Jesus, she fought them and wiped them away. *I understand without him needing to explain. It is too painful! Oh! Elah no!* Through maintaining control of herself for him, and knowing his total commitment to his Abba's will, she denied herself as she did not want to cause him to question Abba's guidance.

Jesus continued passionately after some very hard minutes, "I told Abba that I would work until my last breath, that I would give my life for the sake of all this misguided nation! But I beseeched Elah to forgive their ignorance. That they do not know the time of their visitation!

"Nevertheless, Abba told me that I must prepare myself for the very real possible eventuality that the Sanhedrin turns against me to silence me, and end my mission. As much as I do not want to believe it, I realized the reality and I totally submit myself and my mission to Elah. The leadership in Jerusalem is powerful and they are not ignorant of my influence, especially now after Lazarus' revival. Rome also has heard reports of me. They are also pressuring the Sadducees to control me."

Allowing his natural idealism to resurface, he insisted, "However, I pleaded with Abba. I begged Elah to give me more time!

"Truthfully Mary, what I have to say to you is tearing my heart out. I prayed and begged Abba for a different answer, but there is no other answer at this time. Unless I am successful, our life together will not transpire. Like I said, I will fight to make a foundation for you, all my disciples, and our whole nation. However, what is imperative is the total willingness and acceptance of the religious leaders and absolute unity of all my followers! And there must be no violence from our side!"

Mary refused to give up and implored Jesus, "I believe there is a way. I will not give up either." Now the reality made her sob uncontrollably, and though her heart was torn asunder she committed herself to him, "I'm sorry Rabboni that I cannot control myself. I will do anything you wish! But I am also terribly unhappy that our people who have longed for this day, encouraged by prophecies of your coming, cannot accept you!"

Jesus' face was fiery red, with moisture running down his face alongside his beard. During their passionate conversation Jesus had not realized that he was holding on to Mary's arms. Releasing her arms, he stepped back and explained, "I will not give up. I cannot waste any time. This is my plan. First, I must secure the Pharisees' acceptance and support. Nicodemus, himself a Pharisee, pledged his allegiance and loyalty to me. He continues his effort to reach the hearts and minds of the priests, the Sadducees, and all religious leaders in Jerusalem, which is what Abba wishes. Israel must become one with me."

There was a long hard pause. Stunned, Mary held her breath and tried to think and calm her emotions for Rabboni's sake.

Jesus broke the silence, "The celebration continues. We will be missed. Let's return and continue attending our guests. Abba will guide us." He turned away and walked back to the compound, breaking Mary's heart.

She wept alone. Finally, she wiped her tears away, reminding herself, *I must be strong for him now and that I will be!*

Chapter 33

The Fragrant Oil

And anyone who gives a cup of cold water to one of my followers,
Truly I say to you, he will by no means lose his reward.
(Matt. 10:42)

Upon returning to the gala, the atmosphere was joyful and celebratory; everyone was dining on the exquisite food. Mary struggled to remain hopeful, repeating the phrase, Elah will show him the pathway to victory!

She continued fulfilling her responsibilities, mingling with the guests, carrying wine, and refilling everyone's glasses. Constantly she steadied her thoughts and emotions. She analyzed everything, *Why are there conflicting emotions of assurance and doubt in my mind? This contrast is unbearable, this positivity and sullen realism.* She felt it all and was overwhelmed by the contradictory atmosphere. *Is it all a mirage? Rabboni's plans changed, then he brings Lazarus being back to life. And all the while an air of menacing concern about Rome and the Sanhedrin permeates the atmosphere.*

Standing in the shadows, she could neither move nor stop her annoying tears as she watched Jesus joining in the festivity. *Everything looks good. He is calm and cordial and compassionate as if nothing unusual has happened.*

Then out of the corner of her eye she noticed one of the religious leaders waving his arms and parleying with a group of rabbis. He was shouting suspicions about Jesus raising Lazarus from the dead, "How can this be explained? Was this a trick!"

The believers were answering, "There are credible witnesses, how can we deny it? Here before us is Lazarus walking and breathing without a doubt after lying in the crypt for days!"

Feeling regret that she could not speak up for Jesus, Mary silently begged Abba Elah, *So many are favorable to Rabboni, and many are beginning to wonder if he is the Anointed One? He is so close.*

Feeling useless, she found a quiet place and listened to the traditional music. The flutists accompanied by a harpist and tambourine player made a congenial atmosphere with their ethereal tunes. She truly missed ethnic music. It fostered an atmosphere of nationalism and their undying desire to escape the oppression by Rome. Overwhelmed, she sat alone and allowed the melodies to distract her tense mood.

Old memories flooded her consciousness, *My dream of the bridegroom so long ago. I recall the veiled bride and bridegroom clearly. It was me, wasn't it! I was the bride?* Fighting back her tears, she refused to entertain further thoughts of the dream that added to her present melancholic disposition. At that moment she committed her life to Jesus and determined that she would live or die with him.

With this renewed determination and dedication, her strength and enthusiasm returned. She pledged her undying loyalty and was inspired as she walked through the crowd directly toward Jesus and Lazarus and the surrounding guests. There she listened to their positive conversations.

With her spirit lifted, she had a most unusual idea. Inspired by her love for Jesus and the beautiful arrangements and everything around her, Mary thought of a subtle though unusual way to publicly demonstrate her love and respect for Jesus. She remembered something that had occurred in Galilee.

Without seeking approval, she went to the pantry and brought out the most expensive jasmine scented olive oil. Demurely, she bowed in front of Jesus, who was seated speaking with visitors, catching everyone's attention and causing conversations to stop. All eyes were upon her. Surprised and stunned by her actions, men whispered to each other, "What is in the urn? Who is this audacious woman?"

Fascinated, everyone stared at Jesus to see what he would do. To their astonishment, he did nothing except watch Mary with an unpretentious and affectionate expression. No one moved. The room became quiet.

Innocently but ceremonially, Mary knelt in front of him and carefully poured the expensive oil over his feet, massaging the richly perfumed oil onto his skin and then, using her hair, she wiped the excess oil away. Meanwhile the aroma of jasmine filled the atmosphere. Stunned, the guests and disciples froze in silent amazement amidst the beautiful fragrance, watching the young woman.

Standing next to Jesus, Judas brusquely intervened in an unexpectedly presumptuous and imposing voice, breaking the atmosphere of wonderment. He dismissively and disrespectfully waved his hand between Jesus and Mary and shouted, "That is enough, stop this and leave!" He chided the woman, "The oil is expensive. Woman, you have not been invited here!"

Humbly, Mary finished and bowed low before Jesus and prepared to leave the room.

As Judas' abrasive words lingered in the air, Jesus raised his hand, imploring him to stop his inappropriate rant. Strangely, it did not stop Judas from defending his actions and he continued, arguing angrily, "Our purse is limited. We cannot allow this kind of extravagance as the oil is too expensive!"

Judas turned to leave but Jesus abruptly stopped him and addressed the onlookers, "This woman did nothing wrong. Motivated by love for me she used her ingenuity in order to comfort me. Her kindness to me is beyond that which others have shown me. With humility and understanding, she displayed an appreciation of my value that has never been shown by any of my disciples. For three years most of you walked beside me and never showed me such honor. It is true, the oil is extravagant. But how long will I be with you?"

These words surprised Judas and the disciples. Nevertheless, Jesus continued, "Let this moment be remembered and Mary's name be recorded with mine forever, as she is the first person who truly understands my value and demonstrates it. This is for all of you to appreciate!"

The silence and the unforgettable moment shimmered in time. Although everyone heard his words, few truly understood Jesus' meaning. Some continued to judge her actions as vulgar and ostentatious, but they said nothing.

The pure of heart were in awe and approving of Mary's attention to her Rabboni. Simon Peter and James were sorry that they had not thought of it themselves. Nevertheless, after being hushed and disrespected by Jesus in front of everyone, Judas pompously left the hall.

Such strong and public disapproval caused Mary to wonder about Judas' real motivation. *His subtle and uncomfortable advances toward me when Jesus left him in charge, and this exaggerated anger, was this all wrought because of jealousy?* She whispered to herself, *Why did he become greatly angered and take a personal attitude toward my kindness to Rabboni?*

Then she remembered past experiences with him, *His glances at me, his attempts to get my attention. At that time, I thought it was just happenstance, but now I wonder if he was trying to entice me all the while. Does he covet my amicable relationship with Jesus? Or even worse was he trying to coax me into a relationship with him? If he is jealous of my relationship with Jesus, I wonder what kind of ideas he harbors. Oh Elah! please help me find a way to put an end to his behavior without embarrassing him in front of everyone. I will be more careful from now on. If it continues, I will bring it to Jesus.*

In order to bring order back to the hall, Peter called Martha to fill all the empty cups with more wine. Mary withdrew to the kitchen where they were already talking about her bold action. Even her closest friend, Salome, was not sure how to speak to her. But she smiled and teasing her, stammered, "I-I am amazed by you Mary of Magdala." This was Salome's endearing way of addressing her. She used it only when Mary did something surprising.

"Where did you get that idea? I did not know that you could be so brazen." The other women nodded and agreed. However, Mary continued mulling over her realizations about Judas and scarcely noticed their comments.

Mary dug into the necessary work in the kitchen as so much was needed in preparing the meals. Most of the meals took much time to prepare, and there were always dishes to wash. This was the perfect place for her. She could work and think without needing to talk.

As she worked, Mary chose optimism. Foremost was her love for Rabboni, *Abba Elah, please wait. Jesus has a plan. Abba, watch how he will change the minds of the religious establishment. You see how positive everyone is today.*

And she let herself dream, *I will be the bride of Your son. I will be Rabboni's woman.* She had never thought of Jesus in such a brazen and romantic way, *But I love him!*

Her thoughts wandered to her mother and grandmother, *Oh Elah! What will my mother think about Rabboni being her son-in-law? If only Grandmother were alive, she would be thrilled. I know she would love Jesus. Grandmother, you always wanted to meet the Messiah! Now you are going to be related to him. You are going to be the great-grandmother to his children. His children, oh my Elah, what a thought! Will I have children?* These thoughts were flooding her mind and she entertained them freely.

Unaware that her face had flushed, Martha made a comment, "Mary, are you feeling all right? You are acting rather oddly tonight. Your face is scarlet!" Her friend was trying to guess why she was so lost in thought and blushing, and said kindly, "But you should not be embarrassed about what you did. You did a wonderful thing."

Mary could hardly hold back her excitement. She really wanted to share her thoughts with Martha, but she held her mouth tightly shut. She felt like she would burst and reveal her secret as her thoughts were overwhelming her. She dropped the sponge and made a simple excuse to Martha to leave. She ran out to the orchards and the hills, escaping into the solitude of the creation.

She went outside so quickly that she almost forgot her headscarf, but quickly retrieved it. The evening air was crisp. The moon hung high in the sky and its light lit up the earth. Mary ran in the direction of the cliffs and climbed up them as quickly as a child. She was euphoric, but it was only Elah and her old friends, the stars, that she could unabashedly share with.

As she neared her familiar private spot, she heard voices. Slowing down she listened, *Who are they?* The darkness concealed her. She recognized Simon Peter's, then Rabboni's and James' voices.

Mary considered. *It is later than I thought. The dinner must have ended and as is his pattern he brought them with him to pray together.* Fondly Mary thought, *This is Jesus' favorite place to pray. He loves it so much that he even named it The Holy Rock of Judea.*

Wanting a more secluded place to pray alone, Mary turned and took a few steps when she overheard Simon Peter's voice great with concern, "... But you know that the Pharisees are trying to have you arrested at the earliest possible moment. Also, the Romans are leery of any large gathering or any sign of a popular uprising of a nationalistic hero!"

Mary froze and remained out of sight.

"It would be suicide to go into Jerusalem at this time!" James added.

There was a pause but then Jesus answered them, "Passover is but a few days away and because of the holy season the likelihood of being arrested is small. It is against custom."

"That is true. It is against the law to arrest anyone at this time," James repeated.

"Still!" Simon Peter cautioned, "Rabboni, it is very dangerous. Couldn't we continue on with gaining the support of the country people, now that there is much interest and curiosity about you? You brought Lazarus out of the grave! For Elah's sake, His power is behind you."

Jesus agreed, "But that is the very reason I consider taking my message to the Sanhedrin."

Strongly chiding Peter, like a parent would speak to a child, "Your first instinct is always trying to hold me back, but you need to trust my intuition. Before I go into Jerusalem, I will send a letter to Nicodemus and ask him to gather his broad-minded contacts for a meeting. If I can address them and answer their questions, a consensus can be formed and then it will be more likely I can obtain permission to speak to the Sanhedrin.

"For thousands of years Elah prepared this nation to receive me. He intends the leaders to listen to me and believe. This is the time. I must go. I cannot be too cautious. Abba Elah will protect me as long as I have your complete unity."

Without further discussion Jesus gave Simon Peter instructions, "Gather my disciples, including Mary and the prayer women I ordained. We will leave right after the Sabbath. As usual we will camp outside the city awaiting news from Nicodemus. Then at sunrise on the first day of the week, I will enter the city symbolizing the first day of victory for Elah.

"In the letter, give all this information to Nicodemus so that he may prepare his associates for my entry into the city. With their show of support, the Pharisees won't dare give me anything but a good reception. I want to ride a young mule into the city, as the young King David would have done in his day."

Mary remembered the prophecy of the prophet Zechariah, "O daughter of Zion, shout and see your king coming to you righteous and victorious, lowly riding on a donkey."

Jesus pointed to James, "You arrange this."

Continuing to give them encouragement, he proclaimed, "This is a great moment for Abba Elah. From this moment Elah will claim His nation." Jesus added, "The Romans, also, will see that the people are receiving me peacefully. My good news and good works will reach their ears as well. It will be hard for them to arrest me. I remind you that the Romans must also receive Elah's blessing."

Remaining hidden, Mary slipped away to a quiet place a good distance from everyone, where she could think and pray. Remembering their recent dialog that had caused her much distress, she happily realized that Jesus would not give up and this truly gave her hope.

Sitting beside an olive tree she prayed, *Abba Elah, Rabboni has a hopeful plan. Thank you, Abba for your loving inspiration!* Mary desperately prayed and she, indeed, felt hope and excitement for the future.

Quiet solitude and darkness covered the whole valley. Only the moon and stars lit the countryside. Mary sat alone pondering all the events of the day. Emotion overwhelmed her and she wept, *I am alive and live to support the Messiah…and maybe someday marry him…and help him give new life to the whole world. Oh Abba Elah! I am unworthy. Thank you for trusting me. I promise to do my best.* Realizing that it was late, she thought, *I should return to the house and be there if Rabboni needs me.*

As Mary stumbled back to the compound over the rocks, she had no way of knowing that at that same moment, not far from her peaceful place of prayer, another one of the disciples was struggling with his faith and reviewing his commitment to Jesus.

Chapter 34

Judas

This is the judgement, that the Light has come into the world.
And the men loved the darkness rather than the Light,
for their deeds were evil.
(John 3:19)

Angrily, Judas left the celebration and went out into the darkness of the night. Though it was difficult to see, he inched his way along a well-worn path toward a rivulet he had noticed earlier. It did not matter where he was going though, he just needed to get away, somewhere to think. His pride was hurt. He was disappointed that Jesus had rebuked him so publicly. As he stumbled along, he needed to think not just of his present but of his future.

Still fuming, he picked up rocks along the path and threw them toward the creek he knew was ahead. Hearing the plop of the rock hitting the water, he started looking for something to sit on. Ahead he spied an outcrop of rocks.

He sat down and continued to review his situation, *How dare he speak to me like that. There is no love or respect from him for me or my position. He needs me to speak on his behalf with the Sadducees, some of whom I know personally. He should also appreciate that I am responsible and concerned about waste.* Judas noticed that walking had not helped allay his anger as he had hoped. *How dare he scold me in front of the leaders and all the disciples! I am trying my best to control our purse. It's a responsibility I take seriously. Doesn't he understand!*

As he sat on the uncomfortable rock, he began analyzing his own life going forward, *What is my real purpose in following Jesus? Where is this leading me? What does this all mean for me?* Knowingly defensive and self-centered he continued, *Everyone gave me a hard time while Jesus was away. Initially, I thought everyone was inspired by my morning meetings and scripture reviews. But then they rebuked me and even became angry and accusatory to me. Jesus never thanked me for my leadership when he returned. During that time, I kept the schedule.*

Then his thoughts turned to Mary, *Where did Mary get that idea? How ridiculous and pompous. How dare she touch him! She will be my wife someday. She respects me and feels the same way toward me, I am sure. She watched me as I led the morning prayers. I know because I kept my eye on her.*

Unintentionally and unconsciously, mulling over his thoughts, he began to cause his heart to separate from Jesus. He even assumed that he did a better job of teaching and leading the ignorant disciples than Jesus, *At least I kept to the scriptures and reminded them of their true faith.* He had relished watching Peter's face as he gave directions during their last days in Capernaum, *At last, my knowledge and position were used.*

He pondered the past, *For a long time, Jesus confided in me and gave me the most responsibility, well except for Simon Peter. Mary and I have Jesus' special consideration because of our knowledge of scripture. He must respect me as he assigned me to lead while he was gone. Surely, because I am educated Jesus trusts me, even more than Peter.*

Feeling uncomfortable with thoughts of Jesus and Peter, he decided to move on to a more enjoyable subject, Mary. Thinking of her he smiled and imagined Mary as his wife, *She makes a man feel like a king. Her intelligence and wisdom, her beautiful voice and loving kindness, she is always on my mind. I truly want to marry her. We make a good couple because of our common knowledge and language. Though, admittedly in speaking Hebrew, her accent noticeably degrades it. But that is only a small thing.*

It is easy for her to love me…maybe she already does. Though he admitted to himself, *She is fiercely loyal to Jesus. She doesn't even acknowledge me when we are together. She only cares about pleasing Jesus. She doesn't know about my feelings, but I do want to express my love for her!*

Jesus did say that ultimately man's purpose is to marry and bear Adonai's children, but he tempered that, saying that the time had not yet come for them. Then Judas remembered a rumor, *Jesus asked Simon Peter, who was already married, to separate from his wife for the sake of the Kingdom of Heaven. And they agreed because of their love for Jesus. There is an assumed understanding that since Jesus is unmarried then they should also remain single. Funny, even the Baptist thought that way. I wonder why?*

Judas admitted that this was the first time that he had taken time to think about Mary in this way. But now, after the insulting rejection by Jesus, he allowed himself to covet her. Giving into his obsession he continued, *She is the perfect woman for me. Beautiful and faithful, graceful and generous.*

He pictured her young face as he watched from afar, smiling and laughing. *Her lips are perfectly shaped, especially her smile.* He thought sensuously of Mary's small but perfectly shaped body. *She thinks that robe conceals her body, but I know when to catch a glimpse of it. When she bends and reaches for something. There it is. Her figure, her breasts, soft and round. And when she sings, her voice is so feminine that it draws my longing for her.*

Again, he thought about her applying the perfumed oil and touching Jesus. It incensed him and made him want to shout out his secret desire to have her for himself. *Yes, I admit it! It enrages me. I must have her. I am growing weary of waiting for her!*

I wonder how much longer it will take Rome to stop Jesus' preaching. This man without pedigree or authority? There is no way the orthodoxy will accept him. I know they will not give him time or forum to speak. Am I wasting my time here? I am tired of following and not being appreciated. It is time that I announce my love for Mary.

Today, Jesus disrespected me in front of all the leaders. Am I deluding myself, or is it time for me to move on? Over the past months I have sacrificed my life for him! What is there to show for it? With Jesus, where are we headed. All this time of preaching and teaching and healing? What is this Kingdom of Heaven that John spoke of and Jesus promises?

Judas began to review his past, trying to find comfort in his memories, *Going all the way to northern Galilee at John's command. Why were the questions of such importance to John if he did not change his view of Jesus?* His thoughts became cynical as he remembered asking Jesus on John's behalf, "Are you the one…? Or shall we look for another?"

All I did for the Baptist! And for what? It all ended with his beheading! *I was as helpless then as I am now.* Driven to frustration, Judas wept like a child. Quickly looking around to make sure no one was present to see his weakness in the darkness, he wiped the salty moisture away with the sleeve of his robe.

Yes, if only I had followed my father. He wanted me to be a scribe, telling me he wanted me to do the honorable thing. I tried obediently to read and reread the Holy Scriptures. Everything was about the coming Anointed One. It was on the tip of everyone's tongue. And I became obsessed like everyone else, and like a vagabond I traveled to find him. Until that day I met John the Baptist. He convinced me I was right, and that he could help me find the Messiah. I gave up everything. Leaving everything behind, against my father's wishes.

He remembered John shouting. "Behold the Lamb of Elohim hayyim! He is the one who I am not good enough to untie the thongs of his sandals!" *But what did John mean when he added?* "Jesus must increase but I must decrease." *Why didn't he unite with Jesus? I loved the Baptist's righteousness and saw clearly that he helped many people, but why did he let Jesus walk away?*

Then Judas recalled his first meeting with Jesus after the death of John, *Jesus received me with open arms. He even gave me a position over Peter.*

He recalled the many times they had met and discussed scripture. And Jesus' broad smile of approval for his quick understanding, particularly one memorable time: "Judas Iscariot, you asked an important question and here is your answer. Elijah has already come on the cloud of purified believers, purified because of their repentance and sacrifice."

Jesus explained to me, "John the Baptist knew his mission was that of Elijah. To make ready for the Lord a people prepared. However, he failed to walk with me. He denied being Elijah after I announced that he was the prophesied Elijah. Of course, it caused people to think I was a liar! And because of his dis-unity he caused great confusion in the providence of Elohim."

Judas remembered Jesus' mystifying words, "I tell you that among those born of women there is no one greater than John. Yet the one who is least in the Kingdom of Heaven is greater than he. Can you understand this?"

Judas knew in his conscience that the words were true. And after his long search he knew when he listened to Jesus that he had found the Messiah. He recalled his jubilation and tears, *Yes! At last, I found the Anointed One.* As Judas continued reminiscing, he smiled at those joyful thoughts, *If only I could recapture the excitement of that moment. Nonetheless, regardless of all of Jesus' words and actions, I know that he is too weak so that most certainly his destiny will be the same as John's.*

He analyzed Jesus practically, from his own point of view: *He is not moving fast enough to claim Israel back from the Romans. When the Chief Priest no longer has the money to pay the invaders, they will accuse all the Jewish lawmakers and most certainly the Sanhedrin will look directly to Jesus as the culprit.*

Feeling helpless, he sat up and again let his beguilement of Mary distract him, *…using the expensive oil on Jesus' feet! She cannot touch him. She is mine.*

One self-centered thought led to another. Confused in heart and mind he was cast into a deep, dark spiritual hole. It never occurred to him to pray or ask for Elohim's help to understand. In that moment, Judas withdrew himself from the wisdom and foresight of heavenly inspiration.

***

At precisely the same hour, in Jerusalem behind the walls of the great temple, the scribes apprised the leaders, mostly the Sadducees, of pertinent news regarding the rabblerousing preacher, Jesus of Nazareth. This had started about a year before, when they noticed the coffers becoming less full.

When the scribes were originally sent off to investigate, reports came back of fantastic healings performed by a self-proclaimed preacher from Nazareth. Some of those scribes themselves were caught up in the excitement and fascination with the inspiring preacher and the thousands of enthusiastic Galileans. As were many, they themselves were inspired by his homespun lessons about Elohim. Therefore, they reported back that there was no need for concern. And so, the upper echelon dismissed it as a temporary phenomenon. The Nazarene certainly was not doing anything sordid enough to pay attention to.

However, when influential priests started making the journey from Galilee to speak with High Priest Caiaphas in the Sanhedrin, things changed. For Caiaphas was well aware of the danger of disrupters like John the Baptist, whom he had handed over to Herod for beheading almost a year before. Through experience, he had learned how to deal with perpetrators of social unrest, and the quicker the better, in order to maintain his control over society and keep his position. Cynical of religious terms like Anointed One, hearing such reports tended to raise his hackles.

That put Jesus at the top of the list of disrupters of society. His spy surprised him with the astounding report about Lazarus, an influential landowner in Bethany, being raised from the dead by this Jesus after four days in the tomb. The reporter confirmed the "miracle" being witnessed by many credible sources. Details, like Jesus removing the burial cloths from the man standing on his own outside the tomb, captured the High Priest's attention.

Caiaphas brought in his father-in-law Annas, a Zadokian priest, to participate in the discussion and together with the Sadducees and Pharisees they considered what to do with the Nazarene. Their biggest concern was not that Jesus was sent by Elohim but how long Rome would tolerate the decrease in taxes they owed.

One Pharisee, Nicodemus, stood before the council and spoke judiciously in Jesus' defense. He tried to allay their fears, though he also knew that the self-interest of the leadership would come first, before the good of society. Nevertheless, Nicodemus tried to bring clarity regarding Jesus' good character. Courageously he expressed himself, "The fact is that Jesus' true desire is to revive Judaism. He is a peaceful man, advocating compassion and care of all citizens."

Reassuringly he spoke on Jesus' behalf, "The man has not announced to anyone that he is the Anointed One. This Jesus is a humble peaceful man. He speaks of Elohim as Abba. And he is not averse to Rome." Nicodemus gave an example, "A countryman once asked him about paying Roman taxes. Jesus did not answer against Rome. In fact, he gave a fair and clear direction to the man and all that listened, 'Give to Caesar what is Caesar's and to Elohim what is Elohim's.'"

Another Sadducee questioned, "This self-proclaimed preacher, Jesus, does he have official education in a synagogue school? I hear that there are rabbis in outlying areas who are beginning to take Jesus' preaching seriously." Becoming passionate, he continued with his own bias, "Apparently, he claims audaciously that his authority comes from Elohim. My reliable source told me that Jesus makes it clear to the people that he needs to rectify misunderstandings in the scripture of our Torah!"

Then another priest, inspired by the previous speaker, became very emotional. Standing, he demanded to be given a chance to speak. With outstretched arms, he screamed out, "This Nazarene is going to attract the Romans, and then they will come after us and remove us from our positions, claiming we have no control over him. They will replace us with men whom they will have more control over, here in Jerusalem, in the Judean countryside, and all of Israel!"

Another leader fell into agreement with him as the give and take became passionately demonstrative, striking at the Sadducees' greatest fear, loss of their livelihood, "Tales of the Nazarene's healings are spreading like wildfire throughout Judea and Galilee. Those of you seated here in high positions should wonder how long you will hold your positions if Rome detects our inaction and disregard of this fanatic." It was growing late so they decided to reconvene their discussions the following day.

The whole time Caiaphas had maintained a cool façade, though mutely he determined to act before any trouble arose with the Romans. In a whisper to Annas he commented, "The only way to prevent Jesus' continued success is to have him arrested."

One of the more judicious priests heard him and argued, "Yes, but in doing that the people will rise up and rebel. His popularity has grown such that there will be mass disorder drawing the ire of Rome. This will create a messy situation. From your experience you know that because we acted early and quietly, that is why John the Baptist could be taken out without dissent or uprisings." His shrewd analysis gained a consensus and was able to curb Caiaphas' proposed solution.

When Caiaphas noted the apprehension of the men standing before him, he diplomatically relented, "Yes, I see. Therefore, we will hold back on hasty action at this time. However, if there are any further rebellious reports about the Nazarene we will act swiftly."

Chapter 35

Preparation for Passover
Spring, 30 CE

Hosanna to the Son of David!
Blessed is the one who comes in the name of the Lord!
(Matt. 21:9)

"The Galilean preacher, Jesus, is in Bethany and celebrating the new life of a friend and wealthy landowner whom he raised from the grave." This fascinating gossip spread like wildfire among the caravans of pilgrims making their way toward Jerusalem to participate in the Passover celebrations. "He is still in Bethany on Lazarus' homestead but will celebrate the holiday in Jerusalem." The rumor was spread throughout the now mobile society in Judea.

This was wonderful news to many Galilean pilgrims who remembered Jesus' captivating messages as they sat on the hills of Galilee. Their hearts were bound to him, especially after he had prayed over their families. They longed to hear more from him but did not know where he was.

Finally, after many earnest inquiries had been made throughout their travels, the news spread that they might find him in Bethany. This excited them and many decided to make the trip there in hopes of meeting him.

To their surprise they were not only able to find the owner's property, but he gave them permission to set up their campsites on his land. And as luck would have it, Jesus came to speak with them, making this a most memorable Passover. Sitting upon a knoll with families gathered all around, Jesus spoke to them as if they were all family. He also listened to their experiences and felt their joy to be with him.

An enthusiastic mother told him, "Since hearing your message, Rabboni, I have no trouble getting up earlier every morning to take care of my family. I joyfully prepare food for my husband and children to break our fast. I happily make sure they are properly dressed. My eldest daughter noticed the change in my attitude and now she doesn't argue like she used to. Now she willingly helps me around the house, watching the children and doing housework with me. Our family is much happier. Life is not easier but now I have hope. It is because of your simple messages, Rabboni."

A laborer stood and passionately begged to give his good news after meeting Jesus, "My boss is always a stickler for perfection. He always points out my mistakes. I used to get angry with him and harbored ill feelings all day. Of course, I never told him, because I wanted to keep my job."

Everyone laughed nervously. The man, not used to being laughed at, turned red and shyly hunched his shoulders in embarrassment. Taking a deep breath, he continued, "But since hearing your refreshing good news about practicing kindness and forgiveness, I decided to try it. My attitude changed and I surprised myself. Now he never shouts at me and I can tell he even wonders what happened to me."

Everyone laughed and shouted praises to him.

Jesus called Simon and Martha, "Prepare lunch for all of us." Pausing, he prayed, "Abba Elah, bless these humble sojourners. They are joyful witnesses to Your new words and concepts. Inspire them to continue applying Your new message that we all may praise You with new understanding seeing You at work in their lives."

Then Jesus continued to explain his plan and invited them to join him, "In the morning, my disciples and I are going to the temple. Would you like to come with us?"

In overwhelming unison, they shouted, "Yes, we are honored to go with you!"

One gleeful spokesman stood and said, "I think I speak for everyone here. There is no other rabbi that we would rather attend Passover celebrations and offerings with. Most of us are from Galilee and witnessed your sermons. We are overjoyed to find you again. We truly believe you are a special messenger from Elah! You comfort our dried-up hearts. Your actions and words make sense to us and fill us with great hope."

These humble men and women moved Jesus' heart. He smiled brightly, adding, "Would you like me to tell you more heavenly secrets?"

Unanimously, they shouted. "Yes!"

"With your permission I will tell you more about our Creator, Abba Elah. The brother and sister who just spoke changed their lives by changing the way they looked at their situation. Like farmers, they reap what they sow. And likewise, all of you who are members of communities should go out and perform good actions toward your neighbors, and then good relationships will develop. Am I right?" he asked.

They answered exuberantly, "Yes!"

"Now let me take your understanding a step further. For instance, one day you are walking by your neighbor and you see he is very cold and has no coat. He may even ask for your coat."

Mary noticed a woman clinging to her robe in response to Jesus' narrative.

"I suggest, don't ignore his suffering and don't walk past him and his absurd request."

Some of the people chuckled knowing that that was probably what they would do. And Jesus nodded, knowing their thinking and went on with his story.

He chided them and suggested an even more difficult response, "Rather give him your coat and if he is really cold, give him your cloak also. Then go on your way rejoicing that you could help him."

A man sitting close to the front, surprised at Jesus' suggestion, incredulously repeated Jesus' choice of word aloud, "Rejoicing?"

Jesus laughed and said, "Yes, rejoicing! Because first you had a coat and cloak to give and then rejoicing because you realize that now you have no coat and cloak for yourself. But now you know that Abba within you will shortly return to you a coat and cloak in some surprising way. Remember that you reap as you sow."

Jesus paused, looking tenderly into the faces of those in front of him, giving everyone time to think about his preposterous suggestion. "However, if you leave him, grumbling to yourself, 'why did I do that?' Thinking as you walk, 'Now I am cold instead of him. I am foolish. People will laugh at me and what will my wife say when I get home?'"

Everyone laughed at the man's farcical predicament. Jesus knew that the people were enjoying their imaginative picture of the man giving away his coat and then being angry with himself for giving his coat away.

Jesus knew that his listeners had similar situations in their own life and would feel regret just as the man in the story. Again, Jesus looked around him and waited for the idea to sink into their consciousness. Then he shouted in a loud voice, "Remember, we reap what we sow. As a farmer sows his seed into the earth, his crops will reflect his care, the quality of the seeds, and so forth. Therefore, your thoughts and actions create your future circumstances, as you know from what I have told you. Yes, of course, now you will be cold and your wife will scold you for giving away your garments. But don't be surprised when fortune comes to you in the future.

"And here is my main point. You do not want to regret or be angry with your generosity. Remember that your thoughts and actions create your future. Otherwise, with a poor attitude and action you will seal yourself and your family into poverty brought upon by your own negative attitude. Therefore, make a habit of giving generously to others with an open heart of gratitude. Then one day you will suddenly realize what a good life you have."

Mary noticed the expressions of the audience were no longer laughing and smiling, but in fact they were thinking intently. She thought, *We have never heard such words before.*

Another man stood and begged to ask a question, "Not only do I pay tithing to my rabbi, but I also am required to pay taxes to Rome. What do you think about giving Rome taxes?

Jesus said to him, "Show me your coin." He looked at the coin and asked, "Whose likeness is this on the coin?"

The man said, "It is Caesar's."

Then Jesus said, "Give to Caesar the things that are Caesar's and to Abba Elah give the things that are Elah's." There was complete silence.

Then Jesus left the front and walked closer to the people and prayed, offering the afternoon to Abba Elah. And as was his habit, he went about gathering families together and praying over them. Squatting down, he played with the children as mothers gathered near to him.

Simon Peter, Martha, and servants from Lazarus' household brought food for everyone. Peter announced, "Rabboni invites you to enjoy this early dinner. We plan to leave at sunrise. He greatly appreciates your desire to walk together with us to the temple."

In the darkness of the night, with only the half moon and stars and a small fire to light their meeting, Jesus gave instructions to his disciples, "Peter will give you my plans for tomorrow. But I want to leave you with an earnest message from my heart as time is growing short." Everyone thought that he was talking about their day ending.

"It has been a while since we met together, wouldn't you agree?

"Yes!" they answered.

"I want to give you special instructions that you will need as leaders in the future. When we are not able to be together, you will remember my words and example and be encouraged. I want to remind you of my experience with Abba the Creator. He shows me His presence with us now and always. Throughout the past months and years, I freely explained to you about Elah in words, but experience with Abba is more important to truly know Him with your heart. Always remember our relationship. You are very special men and women to me.

"Beware of the influences Hebraic doctrine has on your conscience and teachings, it is hard for you to realize how ingrained it is in you. Therefore, listen closely and try to feel my meaning, my entirely new concepts, in your heart. My messages are in most cases the opposite of what is ingrained in you, in all Jews and in all human beings. Listen to me and believe me, as you never know how long I will be able to continue speaking these radical concepts!

"Elah does not dwell in the heavens. He dwells here with us in our lives.

Abba Elah showed me…" Jesus paused, and his face became crimson as he cleared his throat.

Mary perceived him become curiously emotional, as if holding back tears and she wondered, *Why is he so emotional and why has he started talking about the future? It must be the atmosphere and all the Galileans professing their love.*

Jesus continued, "Everything Abba Elah created expresses His love! All things on this earth He created. As a loving Creator, He gave everything that moves the instinct to protect itself, feed itself, find comfort, heal itself, and continue its own kind."

He patiently emphasized, "I alone have seen Abba Elah. His love…the closest I can describe it as…" pausing and taking a deep breath, he continued, "…is that of an ideal parent. It is for us, His children, that He created the world, everything in the heavens and on earth. And like human parents for their children, He desires us to know joy, happiness, and free will. And then become caretakers of all creation. And also, like all His creation, He gave us the ability to protect ourselves, to seek comfort and heal, receive nourishment and procreate.

"Abba Elah implanted in humankind a highly developed conscience that if developed can access Elah's own consciousness and thus make a personal relationship with Him. And therefore, our Creator gave us the freedom to seek Him and conform to Him.

"However, tragically the first human pair decided to follow Abba's servant, to do the bidding of the archangel. They took on its nature, which was rebellious unbridled selfishness, thereby becoming servants of the servant. These negative traits gave rise to sadness, disease, loss and anguish, and never-ending struggle. Greed and hatred, killing, revenge and atrocities are all the result of separating from their true Parent, the Creator Elah.

"Abba Elah did not create selfishness! Humans did when they consciously rejected Elah's intent and lost their connection to Him from the very beginning of time. Thus, they created a hostile environment. As beings of intellect, they soon sought to reconcile their lost relationship with Elah by explaining and justifying Him from their own distorted view of themselves and the world around them. Do you understand?"

Jesus knew that his disciples heard his words and wanted them to understand, but he knew that it would take them a long time to resist their earlier learning. "Remember my sermon about the sheep, how the shepherd tends to and protects his flock from danger?"

In unison they answered, "Yes."

Then he turned to his assistant, using him as an example, "Simon, do you love me?

Surprised, Simon immediately looked up at him, "Yes, Rabboni! You know I love you." And he bowed down to Jesus.

Jesus told him, "Then feed my sheep."

Jesus scanned all the men and women seated in front of him. This was not the first hearing of these ideas but tonight seemed more somber than in the past. After giving them time to ruminate on his seriousness, Jesus asked, "Does anyone have a question?"

Mary became emotional as she grasped the preciousness of the moment. Not wanting to draw attention to herself, she grabbed her scarf to conceal her tears. There was silence except for the crackling wood and the chirping of the crickets. Jesus broke the silence and asked if anyone would like to comment.

Phillip asked, "Rabboni, when will you show us the Abba so we will know that which you speak about?"

Jesus answered, "What? I just explained about Abba Elah! You have heard my numerous sermons. How long have you been walking side by side with me? How many speeches, how many examples have you heard and seen?

"Don't you know by now that anyone who sees and hears my messages has seen Abba Elah in action? Again, Elah is not up in the sky but is living in the consciousness of all that you see with your own eyes and feel with your heart. It is He whom you felt when you first met me. I am in Abba, and Abba is in me. And Abba wants the same for you as for me. All that I speak is not on my own authority but comes from the authority of Abba who created me and who dwells in me.

"If it is difficult for you to understand what you cannot see with your eyes, then believe in my words and what you see me do, and pray to Abba. For this is the work that you will do as well, even after I am gone. If you believe me, then the same things I do, you will do; in fact, you will do even greater works than I do. Whatever you ask of your Abba Elah in my name, He will hear and answer you."

Mary could not stop her tears from flowing as she prayed, *How great is my Rabboni's frustration with us! How long have we been with him but still all we see is a man walking, talking, and living life and think that he is just like us. Yet we hear his words and pray that we can clearly understand him. For he is truly Elah's Anointed One. It is because of the shallowness of our awareness that we cannot see.*

Jesus broke into her thoughts, speaking to Simon Peter, "I will leave you to prepare for the morrow. Be aware that it is a very important day for us." He added one more important request, "I want James and Thaddeus to go into the village of Bethpage, not far out of our way, and find a young colt that has never been ridden. Tell the owner that you will return it after Jesus of Nazareth rides it into Jerusalem." With that said, Jesus took his leave.

Drying her tears, Mary truly felt excited for the coming morning. She envisioned everyone walking with Jesus into Jerusalem. It would also be her first time to attend the Passover worship in person.

As soon as Peter released everyone, she walked into the countryside to try to find Jesus and pray close by him. However, because of the many tents and the darkness she could not find him. Nevertheless, she found a quiet and vacant place.

Mary pondered his sermon earlier with the wayfarers, *Rabboni is the example of the man who gave his coat away. And throughout my whole life with him, I have witnessed that no matter the difficulty, he never harbored resentment toward anyone, but he deplored ignorance and unwillingness to consider his practical and simple concepts. Nevertheless, he continues on without fear or worry, regardless of Peter's unease.*

As she prayed, she remembered that Peter reported that there were at least seventy adults attending Rabboni's speech. She witnessed their excitement and enthusiasm to be able to accompany him to the temple tomorrow.

Mary also recognized some of the Galilean travelers from Jesus' speeches. Especially those who had followed Jesus to their compound in Capernaum after his sermon. They truly wanted to stay with him. But because of family responsibilities they could only serve and attend his sermons occasionally. Jesus appreciated their aspiration but also understood the hardship and burdens that they carried.

In one of her conversations with a mother of five children, Mary had listened to her complaints about her callous local religious officials. But the woman also expressed her fascination with Jesus, "Rabboni not only is sympathetic with our difficult life, but he gives us hope like we never felt before. My friends and I are enthusiastic and every opportunity I have, I relate his words to my neighbors.

"I tried to speak to my local rabbi about Jesus' sermons and how much he inspired me. Can you believe that the hypocritical rabbi rebuked me? He told me not to listen to Jesus, whom he called an impostor with no qualification as a religious teacher. Nevertheless, I paid him no attention because I know in my heart what sounds and feels right. My husband and I took Jesus' advice, to do our best for others as we would expect for ourselves. To me and my husband, Jesus' simple concepts make more sense than any Sabbath message. There is no doubt that Elah lives in him."

That evening after dinner many continued sharing testimonies with their neighbors, strangers sitting adjacent to them. Mary listened to the humming of peaceful voices throughout the countryside.

Chapter 36

Day of Victory

Rejoice greatly, O daughter of Zion! Shout aloud...
Lo, your king comes to you; triumphant and victorious...
Humble riding on a donkey, on a colt, the foal of a donkey.
(Zechariah 9:9-10)

At sunrise on a beautiful springtime morning outside of Bethany, Jesus' cadre of disciples and his devoted fellow Galileans began their parade toward the capital for the celebration of Passover. Excited to share the day together with Jesus, songs broke out all along their long procession while their children scampered playfully around their parents. Many other people coming from side roads joined with them, as there was a great feeling of excitement and joyful festivity.

Peter announced, "We will go together into the main courtyard of Jerusalem. It may be hard to stay together. From experience you know the crowd is enormous, the place filled with thousands of pilgrims. But as much as possible let us try to stay together."

As they filed in two lines along the road, their procession was full of joyful singing. Several favorite songs they sang repeatedly, ethnic Hebrew songs—many taken from King David's psalms and praising Elah:

V'ahavta et Adonai Elohecha
B'cho l'vavcha
And you shall love the Lord your Adonai,
With all of your heart.

Ur'chol nafsh'cha
And with all of your soul
Ur'chol m'odecha
And with all of your might.

Further down the road, James and Thaddeus appeared with a young donkey in tow, bringing it toward Jesus. Peter and another disciple pulled their robes off and put them upon the back of the colt. Jesus mounted it, leading the procession.

Some of the exhilarated pilgrims were so excited that they threw their robes ahead of Jesus, making a path for the donkey to walk on. The joyful atmosphere inspired many men to cut leaves from the palm trees and give them to all the people, who then waved the palm branches toward Rabboni, all the while singing Hebrew songs of praise.

The Lord is my rock, and my fortress and my deliverer,
My Elohim, my rock, in whom I take refuge,
My shield and the horn of my salvation,
My stronghold and my refuge,
My savior: thou save me from violence,
I call upon the Adonai, who is worthy to be praised,
And I am saved from my enemies.

Jesus was their champion. He alone consoled them with advice and ideas to solve their daily predicaments. Rabboni taught them that Elah was their loving and caring Abba and wanted nothing more than for all the people to come to Him. Now believing that Elah was neither vengeful nor angry toward them, they had hope that their lives could be made better by using his simple pastoral stories.

Finally, within sight of the great wall of the capital, many hundreds of pilgrims began to filter into their line. Everyone knew from experience that from the Mount of Olives it would take a few more hours to enter the gates of Jerusalem.

They continued laughing and singing while they walked, enjoying the festive atmosphere, as mothers kept close eyes on their hyperactive children. It was an unavoidable and habitual experience but accepted as the common custom before Passover. Jesus and his followers and the curious who caught an interest in their elated group all blended into the triumphant atmosphere. There were also Roman sentries interspersed among the throngs of people.

The donkey carried Jesus between lines of supporters on each side of the road. Mary walked beside John, who was holding the reins of the donkey. Both looked back often, concerned for Rabboni's safety. Jesus' tranquil expression impressed Mary. She imagined he was communing with his Abba Elah.

Mary felt the ecstatic atmosphere, echoing songs of praise and prayers to Abba Elah all around. It was contagious, the closer they got to the temple. She prayed, *Abba Elah, this is Jesus' day of victory. The inspired people are praising Your son! Surely the officials will be notified and will want to speak with him. This is a grand and special day! You must also feel hope! Please aid Jesus and help him arrange an audience with the High Priest of the Sanhedrin. Please let him bring fortune to Your people. The leaders cannot overlook the widespread support of the people. And someday let our marriage bring the old and new together. Truly the time has come.* Hopefully, Mary continued escorting the donkey carrying Rabboni Jesus of Nazareth. It was an idea she could not let go of.

Then chanting in the crowd began, at first muffled and hard to understand but becoming clearer, "Jesus, son of David. King David rode on a donkey for his coronation." Exuberantly, shouts of "Return" and "King David" and "Anointed One" were reverberating throughout. As Jesus nodded and waved to the people solemnly, he continued along the road toward the temple. Women lifted up their children hoping to catch a special blessing from the man of Elah. Mary imagined Abba Elah Himself was praising His son.

As the crowd continued singing the same verse over and over in the procession, it attracted many who wondered what all the enthusiasm was about. The travelers who had spent time with Jesus in Bethany explained to the curious. Some of the newcomers even joined them in their joyful march.

At last, Jesus dismounted. As he took his first step toward the temple the well-wishers spontaneously threw their branches onto the ground, carpeting his path into Jerusalem. And as Jesus passed by them, the crowds formed behind him, singing other psalms of David and cries of "Hosanna to Elah!" Jesus continued until he reached the entrance to the temple.

Standing under the great archway of Jerusalem's eastern gate, Jesus made a declaration to the hundreds of pilgrims standing around him, "This wall shelters the Temple Mount and the Holy of Holies. It is considered the most hallowed place worshiping Adonai, El Shaddai."

He questioned, "Though I wonder, do the leaders truly know the living Elah and are they aware of the auspicious time we live in? Let us see."

The disciples encircled him for protection and Jesus' exuberant crowd followed, pressed in by the thousands of other pilgrims. Thomas led the way, shielding Jesus with his large body. A sword hanging at his side was hidden under his robe. Simon Peter, James, and John protected him from behind, while Mary and the other women trailed behind, desperately trying not to get separated from Jesus.

Mary, unfamiliar with Passover, was whisked along by the momentum of the crowd of worshipers going toward the main courtyard and thought, *What a difference this visit to the great temple is from the last time we were here! There were not as many people.* Climbing the stairs from the street, she nearly stumbled on the narrow steps, but the many bodies acted as a barrier, and Martha walking behind her prevented her from falling backwards. Finally, as they stepped into the immense open-air public gathering arena, worshipers continued to be pressed into any vacant area.

As they went further into the populated open-air square, Mary heard the sounds of bleating sheep, and fluttering, squawking birds, and the familiar high-pitched sound of oxen. As the crowd spread out, she spied hundreds of pigeons, sheep, and oxen in cages and pens. Mary gasped with pity, knowing that all the animals were headed to their death. At the same time the stink overwhelmed her, causing her to gag.

Ahead of her, she saw lines of men waiting their turn to buy the best animal for their family's blood offering. There was much haggling about prices, some louder than others, which she realized was the reason the lines were so long.

Why do they do this year after year? Their shouting disrupts the assumed sanctity of the event. Yet, as heads of their families, they do this because they believe that by offering the best sacrifice Elah will give them the most protection from evil for their family the rest of the year. If they truly believe that, then, of course, that is why haggling is so important to them, she reasoned sympathetically.

On each table, Mary saw stacks of coins and coin filled baskets piled one upon the other. Merchants stood behind and around the tables. She was so engrossed in her surroundings that she wandered away from her sisters. Suddenly she became frantically afraid, because this was her first time in such a large crowd. *There are so many people I might not be able to find them. I could get lost!* Tears came to her eyes, and she felt her chest tighten as she looked to her right and left. Suddenly she heard Jesus' voice behind her. She turned quickly and moved closer to him, relieved not to be lost.

Jesus was speaking to the people next to him and Mary saw his closest disciples behind him. Even though there was much noise, she clearly heard him shouting out his message and pointing toward the tables of money, "Those are the money changers. They sell animals to be sacrificed by each of you observant families. But do you not realize that you are taken for fools to believe this will appease your jealous and vengeful ha Elohim? Look at the priests' hands covered in blood. They slit each animal's throat and catch the blood in a bowl and then take the bowl of blood to sprinkle on the altar."

Jesus' compassion and disgust was apparent to Mary. With heavy resentment, Jesus continued, vehemently waving his hands toward the priests, "They are fascinated with death and blood. They actually think this is pleasing to Adonai. But I tell you that Abba Adonai does not require such actions. Elah is the Creator Abba of all and, like your own abbas, He wants only your love for Him and for each other."

Mary could not take her eyes off Rabboni's expression as it was bright as lightning and wet with emotion. His words were desperately trying to get the attention of the people standing around him. She heard a loud scornful murmuring of worshipers within earshot. The temperature within the whole area became like an oven, even though above them was open to a deep blue sky. Mary's heart ached for him as she became aware of anger rising all around him.

Abruptly Jesus charged through the crowd toward the money changers. He pulled something out of his sleeve. Mary was shocked. *Is that a rope? What is he going to do?* she wondered. What happened next was an act of violence that she had never seen before from her Rabboni. Aghast, she covered her gaping mouth and froze in shock, holding her breath as she watched.

Jesus shouted, "You stand in the way of worshipers coming to pray!" One of the dealers looked up just in time to see Jesus unfurling a rope as its end whipped the top of the table, tossing baskets and coins and sheets of papyrus into the air and casting everything upon the floor. Then Jesus heaved the heavy wooden tables over, with everything on them flying helter-skelter, casting the baskets and ledgers asunder. Loud crashes echoed throughout the huge chamber. Coins spun around on the stone floor like a child's toy. Still, no one moved.

Stunned into silence, the worshipers in the area of buying and selling were caught by surprise and stopped all movement. It took a brief amount of time for everyone to process what had just happened. Then the money handlers (*shulhanim*), those who had lost everything, began to scream in retaliation, "Call the High Priest! A great injustice has disturbed this holy atmosphere! A madman has interrupted our Holy Day."

The pilgrims also began to rebound, with shouts which reverberated all around them and to all the people throughout the arena of worshipers. Hundreds of traditional customers stood around the edge of the venue, shouting and yelling. Those who were in the center surrounding Jesus just stood stunned, trying to understand what was happening. Finally, after a few minutes, people began to query the stranger next to them, "What kind of man is this who would disrupt the holiday in such a way? Who is he?"

The situation was surreal, and no one wanted to make the first move. His behavior was so bizarre that they could not rationalize what they had perceived. But it was not finished. Astoundingly, Jesus dashed to the cages and pens and threw open the gates. Doves flew into the open space with feathers filling the air. Men and women began screaming and running for the exits.

Docile sheep stared out of their enclosure and the cattle mooed and roamed. The whole courtyard was chaotic and full of animal and human noise and clatter.

Mary held her breath with her eyes moist as she also was trying to comprehend Jesus' outlandish actions. She noticed that James, who had moved closer to her, was as surprised as she was.

Finally, guided by those who had snapped out of their baffled state, the money changers and worshipers together encircled Jesus. They observed him to be a Galilean and a commoner from his clothes, but most did not know who he was.

However, one man found his voice and screamed out in anger, pointing his finger at Jesus, "I know you! You are the Nazarene. Jesus is your name. You are a disrupter everywhere you go. You are the talk of all Galilee, your healing and miracles. I am a merchant, and everywhere I go, there is talk of you and the Baptist. You strike a note of discord with many in the establishment. Is this another one of your sensational deeds you have to show us today?" the formally dressed man taunted.

Majestically Jesus shouted, "It is written that this house is the house of El Shaddai and thus should be a house of prayer, but you have made it a den of thieves."

Meanwhile, anger had now reached fevered pitch, with merchants running to call the temple guards and the head of the Sanhedrin about the attack on the Holy of Holies.

Standing close to Jesus, with swords drawn, Thomas and Thaddeus forced open a path while Peter motioned for Jesus to leave. Mary and James, who were closest to Jesus physically, protected him with their bodies, while the other disciples moved the crowd aside. Jesus threw down the heavy twine and turned to exit through the thousands of baffled worshipers, many of whom had no idea what had happened.

Mary prayed desperately, *Abba Elah help Jesus speak with the head of the Sanhedrin.* She had overheard earlier that John had been unable to reach Nicodemus to request his assistance in setting a meeting up with the chief priest. Remaining faithful, she continued to pray, *I know you will show him a way.*

Then suddenly Jesus turned and shouted righteously, "There is no difference in what you are doing now and the defiling of the temple in the days of Solomon! I will destroy this temple and raise it up again in three days." Meanwhile the temple vendors were going wild with rage.

Jesus almost went back into the hall, but Thomas, his body tensed as if expecting an immediate fight, bellowed with his sword drawn, "Peter! James! We have to get him out of here!"

"Jesus, Rabboni," James strongly entreated in Aramaic. "We have to get out of here before they attack us. We are surrounded. Let's go now!" Immediately Simon, James, and John surrounded Jesus and with Mary covered they pushed through the shocked bystanders and out of the closest temple portico.

In a few short minutes, it was as if war had been declared. Jesus' attack had caught the merchants by surprise. They amassed the guards and called on the priest designated to alert the High Priest. However, the throngs covered Jesus' escape, leaving behind the innocent and stunned worshipers. Some of the celebrants understood Jesus' distaste for the money lenders. They stayed and proudly proclaimed to the confused pilgrims around them, "Jesus of Nazareth is a great preacher!"

Jesus' name resounded throughout the atrium and even reached the ears of the priests inside the inner chamber. Many of them remembered that Jesus of Nazareth was the very man they had discussed the night before. These curious priests sprinted to the courtyard and tried to catch him in action. But they were too late, the incident was over.

Though it had only lasted moments, it left strong resentment brewing in the minds and hearts of the merchants and temple workers, and confusion in all the participants. The incident was so unusual that it even interrupted the devout prayers of the priests around the altars of blood sacrifices. The money lenders knew the message was heard loud and clear by the Chief Priest as a report was already being carried to Caiaphas.

Chapter 37

Joseph of Arimathea

You prepare a table before me in the presence of my enemies.
You anoint my head with oil.
My cup overflows.
(Psalm 23:5)

After the morning procession, the name of Jesus the Nazarene could be heard and repeated by the peasants of Galilee making him into a folk hero. Stories of his love and good will, his healings and homespun tales spread by word of mouth.

The excitement grew even more intense after reports from many witnesses escaped the inner walls of the temple. His righteous words and violent actions toward the callous money changers were deemed heroic and righteous.

An exhilarating atmosphere of great expectation surrounded that simple stratum of society. Echoes of "Anointed One" and "Return of King David" could be heard in the large groups of pilgrims filling the streets of Jerusalem. To these witnesses he was their hero. Of all their Passover experiences this was certainly their most memorable. There was great excitement and anticipation that possibly an announcement from either the Elijah or the Anointed One himself could occur.

One man was heard making a hopeful proclamation, "This is the day the Lord has made. I can feel it. Something big is coming!"

Though reports of Jesus the Nazarene's miraculous healing and defiance toward the money changers inspired the massive crowds of humble Hebrews, the leadership saw only the danger and disruption as they regarded Jesus' rebellious actions. But Jesus got everyone's attention, as was his plan.

After all, the traditional Judeans were comfortable in their positions of power and they did not feel a need for change, nor did they want it. Their view was hardly acceptance, but rather the opposite. The Nazarene was a danger to everything they held near and dear and therefore his affront to their complacent life was bound to have ramifications.

Jesus knew this disruption would happen, but he had no other recourse. His time was running out. He had to announce his purpose, Elah's purpose. Rousing the prepared leaders, awakening the honorable and sincere priests and leaders like Nicodemus, was imperative.

With no John the Baptist claiming to be the Elijah, thus fulfilling the prophecy to announce him as the Anointed One, he would have no chance to speak to the Sanhedrin. He had to find a way to speak Abba's new truth if he could remain alive.

In late afternoon, surrounded by his disciples, amidst throngs of thousands maneuvering through the narrow streets, Jesus traveled slowly to his destination. Mary could see that Jesus was aware of the confusion his action had caused most of his followers. She felt confused as well, but she prayed to understand, and she prayed for everyone to await Jesus' explanation. In Mary's mind there was not even one doubt that he would find a way. She just humbly prayed that in time everyone would understand.

Jesus' prearranged destination was the home of Joseph of Arimathea, a Pharisee and member of the Sanhedrin, and a relative. He was a successful merchant and man of influence. But time was of the essence.

Jesus called Mary to his side, "This will take much longer than expected. You and James should go ahead to the villa of my uncle, Joseph of Arimathea. James knows the way. Help my uncle prepare for our arrival. Joseph is a Pharisee and also a wealthy merchant. We have to preserve his standing as a member of the Sanhedrin. Therefore, this meeting must be kept discreet. Do you understand?"

Mary looked directly into Jesus' serious and intense gaze and nodded assurance and understanding. Just then, someone in the crowd bumped against her causing her to stumble. Jesus caught her forearm preventing her fall. Recovering quickly, Mary turned toward James, though she treasured the sensation of Jesus' hand on her covered arm. Yet without a word, she and James quickly left the group and maneuvered through the crowd much faster by themselves.

When the elderly Joseph received her, Mary recognized him as one of Lazarus' guests at the latest celebration. She particularly recollected him listening respectfully and speaking with Jesus. *The celebration must have been where Jesus arranged this meeting,* she guessed.

But after the incident today, she appreciated the importance of men like Joseph and Nicodemus and their need to be circumspect in order to help Jesus. She was especially grateful that this haven was available for her master this day.

Standing before the dignified elderly man, she first noticed his uncommonly tall stature, even with hunched shoulders, and his long thin silver white hair on his head and chin. But his bright eyes were those of an energetic youngster juxtaposed on his otherwise older physique.

Joseph of Arimathea's wizened expression was filled with a wealth of knowledge and experience. His whole physique gave an impression of a formidable character, *I can imagine a once energetic young man standing in front of me.* Recognizing the danger he was risking gave her more respect for him. *He is bold to hold a dinner for his controversial nephew. However, he seems undisturbed and fearless.*

Mary whispered a blessing, *Elah bless him and his house. I am humbled standing in front of such a respected official, hosting Jesus. How wonderful and yet dangerous.* She once again appreciated the great risk that good men like Joseph and Nicodemus and like-minded leaders were taking.

She and James bowed respectfully as the Elder proudly admitted them into his palatial home, "Welcome. I am pleased that my great-nephew, Jesus, and his disciples will visit me."

Mary respectfully announced Jesus' imminent arrival and introduced herself and James. She was surprised that he was wearing a modest homespun beige robe, not at all what she expected, though she immediately felt comfortable in front of him, especially because of his kind and respectful expression and hospitable reception. She wondered, *Certainly, a man of his esteem would have been formally dressed.*

Proudly he announced, "I have already prepared everything for him." He added genuinely, "In his message he asked that I arrange a handful of like-minded associates to meet him. Not only did I do that, but I also took it on myself to prepare a dinner for them in honor of my nephew." Joseph's eyes sparkled with unusual glee, and he seemed truly excited and without concern.

Speaking with an air of mischievousness, he told them, "You know that my brother, Jesus' grandfather, and I were young men during the time of Herod the Great. Compared to this time there is no comparison. My brother was killed during the pogroms. I escaped only because of my merchant business which took me to many countries around the Mare Nostrum, far from Herod's control."

Changing the subject back to the present he added, "I was happily surprised when my friends requested to bring more of their like-minded contacts. I accepted but I did remind them to be prudent and circumspect, though in our current political climate that is always assumed. I believe that this will be a good night for discussion, something that I look forward to and believe that my nephew will approve of. I certainly will!"

Calling a servant, he instructed, "Give Mary all she needs and help her make all my guests comfortable. James come with me. I will put you to work on the preparations."

Mary was fascinated by Elder Joseph's rebel like attitude. *His lineage must all fall into that category.* Smiling to herself she went about preparing an inner room for Jesus' privacy and a public room for dining and speaking. As she worked, she thought of Joseph's considerate words, "I will inform my servants to prepare everything with solid confidence that this will be a night to remember."

When Jesus and his disciples arrived, it was already dark. Proudly, Joseph embraced Jesus showing his familial relationship and unashamed to display his affection. Throughout the evening he constantly infused his pleasure at being Jesus' great-uncle and brother of Jesus' late grandfather.

"How can I make you comfortable? Nephew, several of my close friends are coming and want to meet you. Also, the lady Mary prepared rooms for your use. Please wash up. When you are ready, come and meet your guests for dinner and discussion." The elderly man added, "My servant will stand by to assist you."

After everyone was settled, Jesus asked Mary, James, John, Peter, and Judas to come into his inner chamber. He gave them instructions on how to accommodate the guests while he prepared in prayer, saying that he would come to them soon. Mostly out of concern for his uncle, Jesus reminded Peter to remain alert to anyone who might be a spy for the Sanhedrin and added, "Use Phillip and Thomas as sentries, stationing them around Joseph's home."

As Jesus was leading Judas into a side room, Mary waited for direction at the door and asked if she could bring him watered wine. Jesus nodded and asked for two goblets, indicating they were for Judas and himself. Mary left for the kitchen.

In the room there was a protracted period of silence as Judas stood by silently. He wondered if Jesus had forgotten he was there, so he impatiently interjected himself by clearing his throat. Jesus turned to Judas and motioned for him to come closer to him and to sit across from him. He knew Judas was struggling and was particularly concerned about him. Without a word, he nodded and gestured for Judas to speak.

Eagerly, Judas spoke his request with an improper attitude of blunt candor, "Master, I would like to go to the Sanhedrin as soon as possible on your behalf. As a scribe and accepted scholar of Hebraic law, I am familiar with their protocol. And as your disciple, I would like to give them a proper explanation of my own experiences with you. I believe that my elucidation will help them feel more inclined to want to hear from you directly. I can introduce you to them."

His contrived humility was not missed by Jesus, and neither was his assertive attitude. He had already assumed a positive answer, so he pushed aggressively for a rapid answer, "I will set up a meeting straightaway." With a brusque attitude he waited for Jesus' reply.

Jesus sat listening with his eyes closed. After prayerfully connecting with Abba, he spoke candidly, "Judas, you must not go. Listen to me. For what may seem to you a good idea, it may not be a good idea from Elohim's viewpoint. Judas, as you probably know, this is a precarious time. Abba Elohim has told me that everyone must stay together and unite to protect His providence. We will go together to the Sanhedrin in a couple of days and in this way, Abba Elah can protect us. But only if we remain united in heart. Do you understand?"

Whether or not he truly listened to Jesus' words was not clear, but Judas could hardly conceal his disappointment. He was so confident in the efficacy of his plan that he tried again to convince Jesus, but to no avail. Rejected and frustrated, he grew impatient. Combined with the unresolved scolding days before, and the incident in the temple, his unity with Jesus began to slowly dissolve. He feigned acceptance and nodded his head.

Jesus turned to Mary standing by the door, surprising Judas who had not heard her come in, and said, "You can bring the wine." As she served them, she also sensed Judas' belligerence. There was strained silence while the two men drank somberly.

Finally, trying to change the atmosphere of Judas' discontent, Jesus stood up with an air of benevolence and confidently indicated, "Come now and let us go together to receive the people of Jerusalem." With outstretched arms, as a father embracing his children, Jesus guided Judas and Mary into the main hall.

As instructed, Simon Peter had all the disciples, men and women, waiting. Jesus asked him, "Do you know if Joseph's associates have arrived?"

"Yes, they are presently visiting with Joseph."

Jesus explained to everyone in the room, "These respected men have heard enough about me that they are curious and interested to hear for themselves what I have to say. Please help me welcome them. Through their influence, I believe my chance of meeting with the clerics and even with Caiaphas in the Sanhedrin is possible."

Elder Joseph led the guests into the meeting room and presented Jesus to each one. Mary counted ten well-dressed and dignified men file in front of

Jesus, who received them with kindness and dignity. Mary was fascinated by Rabboni's loving graciousness. Finally, when the last guest was introduced, Joseph instructed the servants to seat everyone.

Elder Joseph went to the front of the room and began to speak. To Mary he was no longer a simple wizened old man but a deep hearted diplomat and man of great wisdom. With the dignity and influence of a statesman he spoke, and the weight of his words, guided by his experience, proved to be immensely helpful for Jesus.

Mary whispered to herself, *This is the first highly placed person to speak so highly of my Lord and with such pride.* The thought brought tears to her eyes.

Elder Joseph gave a short introduction, "You can see how proud I am of my nephew. It is my hope that when you leave you will have had this night a hopeful and positive experience. We come from a long line of compatriots, and Elohim needs more of them. Please allow Rabboni to give his introduction, then you may ask questions. And I invite you to have a meal together with him afterwards."

From the back of the room, Mary was glad to see the arrival of Nicodemus. She was happy to see the familiar nobleman speaking amicably to Jesus, though she noticed Nicodemus' demeanor to be unusually serious and anxious, unlike the other guests, and wondered what was causing his uneasiness. Once Nicodemus was seated, Joseph took his place in the audience as well.

After a moment of silence, Jesus stood and confidently asked, "Do you have a question to ask me?" At first there was silence. Then, Jesus began, "I assume you have heard that I preached and healed and brought together crowds of curious residents on the Galilean hillsides. In Gennesaret and Bethsaida, particularly, thousands of interested worshipers were moved as I expressed to them my personal experience with Abba Adonai Elohim and how all humankind can also have a personal experience with Him."

Jesus asked candidly, "But first, what stimulated your curiosity that you would risk your reputation to meet me?"

Again, silence from men who usually had no problem giving their opinions. After a few minutes an enthusiastic young man stood and asked, "How do you heal people?"

"Ah, a very good question." Jesus answered. "When I first experienced Abba Adonai a few years ago, like you, I thought Adonai was all about power and control of humankind through revenge and punishment. As you notice I refer to Adonai Elohim, the Creator, as Abba. For truly as my creator and your creator He is our Abba.

"I was greatly surprised when He opened my consciousness, my eyes, to His love and His consciousness. He showed me the world around me and surprised me when He showed me that everything was designed out of His love. The best example of Abba Adonai's love is that of a parent's love for their children, which is curiously common to both animals and humans. Take a human father or mother for example. He or she applauds their child's success and laments when their child is in danger or sick. They likewise forgive the mistakes of their child over and over and, if need be, willingly sacrifice their own life for their child. This is the same love as our common Abba, Adonai Elohim. Parents do not seek revenge or want to cause calamities to any of their children, no matter how great their disappointment. Likewise, neither does our Creator.

"I witnessed and experienced His love. And I learned that it is love that motivated Adonai to create the symbols of His love, for example the plants and animals. And to each kind of creation, He lovingly and individually gave a singular and unique way to live and thrive. Through Creator Adonai's invisible life essence or consciousness, if you will, He did not just create a being, but He also provided for each living kind in unique ways. He gave them awareness to seek ways to fulfill their own individual needs. For example, procreation, growth, nourishment, protection of the individual beings and their offspring, the need for comfort, and to some extent a natural ability to heal themselves from disease or injury. It is Abba Adonai the Creator who created these things for all beings including His own direct descendants, His children, humankind.

"Here is an example: Look at the mother fox or bird. She prepares a nest of soft fur or straw for her offspring's comfort. She cleans them and feeds them when they are young and teaches them how to live and how to find nourishment when they mature. And we see this same nurturing tendency even more so in human beings, whom Abba Adonai made specially in His own image.

"Here is another simple example of Adonai's protective design," Jesus pointed to his eye. "Consider your eyes, one of the most important senses that creatures, including humans, have. Why?" Jesus looked around demonstrating opening and closing his eyes. "Try this." His audience followed his example.

"Our vision enables us to experience the incredible world of Abba Adonai's creation and to experience each other. And the eyelids and eyelashes were designed with the specific purpose of protecting the eye and for maintaining its comfort. These are not accidental or coincidental. The eye is, after all, our window to the world around us. Thus, in order to last throughout a lifespan, the functions of blinking and watering protect our eyes from dust and debris and overuse.

"Or, think of beasts of burden or animals that attract flies. For their comfort Elah created a tail that constantly moves back and forth, slapping away the buzzing flies. Again, I repeat, this is not a coincidence!

"How joyfully these examples of love and caring are expressed in the smallest and most inconsequential physical attributes and yet have a profound bearing on the comfort of all living things. Clearly the basic physical designs are the product of an intelligence which intended for the life of all creatures to be comfortable and free from the stress which would have been experienced by man and beast if these necessary items were not given."

The audience began to hum with astonishment and comment among themselves at the simple but extraordinary insight, something they had never considered before.

Indicating the young man who asked the question, Jesus continued, "Now let me move on to healing, in answer to your question. It should be natural for people to be able to heal from disease or injury and even know what they can do to prevent illness, but human beings are unaware of those possibilities. And worse, they believe that these calamities come to them as punishment from ha Elohim."

"Yes!" Many in the audience affirmed.

Jesus continued to speak, at times placing emphasis on a some of his words, "When I come upon an infirmed person, my heart feels compassion toward them. I sincerely ask Elohim hayyim to heal them, and I completely **believe** that He will heal them. I simply rejoice in the power of Abba Elohim within me who is ready and waiting to heal His child the moment I ask. And most importantly, Abba showed me that **He** is not the cause of humankind's maladies!

"To explain simply, sickness is nothing but a lowering or reduction of the liveliness in the affected part. Thus, I simply recognize where the lack is and call upon Abba Elohim's vitality, His life elements. I ask Elohim, Abba inside me, to restore the health of the person."

Jesus paused and gave time for the audience to absorb his absolutely exceptional explanation. In the audience some sat thoughtfully while others talked among themselves.

A young man sitting toward the front of the audience boldly asked, "Is it lawful to heal on the Sabbath, or not?"

Jesus enthusiastically praised him for his excellent question. Instead of answering directly, he appealed to the man's own reason, asking, "What would you do if your child was sick, or if your animal was giving birth? Wouldn't you immediately call for a doctor on any day of the week and even the Sabbath? Believe me, your Abba Adonai wants you to care for anyone or anything at any time with compassion, regardless of what day it is. And He is always there when you call upon Him. Yes, even on the Sabbath.

"Abba the Creator showed Himself to me. And showed me that He lives in all of us as He is alive in all the natural world around us and wants us to be aware of His presence. You perceive the physical world but are unaware of the world of essence or spirit. However, if you reject your selfish tendencies and act compassionately to one another, you will find Abba within you and all things."

Jesus noticed an intently listening older man, and asked him if he had a question.

The man stood and humbly introduced himself, "Yes! I am Ephraim of Hebron. My elder brother has betrayed my trust many times over the years.

Because of that I broke my relationship with him. But because he is my brother, I felt I should try to resolve these difficult feelings. I asked him to forgive me for my resentment toward him. We reunited; however, he continues to disrespect me and my family. My question is, how many times should I forgive my brother?"

Jesus nodded, "Some say seven times, but I tell you to forgive seventy times seven." He noticed the surprised expressions and agreed, "Yes! My words are revolutionary, are they not? But how many times do we expect Elohim to forgive us? Of course, many times. Therefore, we should think of how we feel about this and other things and mimic Elohim.

"Many of us have an immature understanding about Adonai Elohim. Our parents taught us to believe, so we believe. But there comes a time in our life when problems cause us to desire to know more about Him, especially when we pray and do not see a good result from our prayer. Let me use the mustard seed as an example of a hidden mystery about Elohim. Have you ever seen a mustard seed?"

Everyone emphatically answered, "Yes!"

"From that tiny seed, planted in the soil and water, a trunk will begin to form that grows bark and branches and leaves. All from a tiny seed. How? Where did the wood come from and the leaves that adorn the tree? Is it not a miracle like you heard I have performed? Think about it. Is not the growth of the tree as much the work of Abba Elohim as the healings which you heard I performed?

"What is a seed, then? Can you tell me? No, you cannot, but I can." Jesus emphasized emphatically, "A seed is a tiny entity of Elohim's consciousness, knowledge of what the seed is to become. It is a fragment of Abba Adonai, which when planted in Mother Earth and receives nourishing elements, for example rainwater, will clothe itself in visible matter, the knowledge of which it possesses deep within itself. This invisible knowledge is a principle of the consciousness of Elohim. All forms of life arise from this principle. It is what separates them from the inanimate soil and rocks. The soil and rocks are consciousness in a dormant form.

"Why am I telling you this? Because your mind is like the seed. If you have in your mind the 'seed' of a plan and you truly believe what you ask for from Abba Elohim, it is possible that you will see it take shape around your original idea. The idea takes on a life of its own, growing like the tree. If you do not doubt during the process of accomplishing your idea, it will grow like the trunk of the tree. You will be able to move mountains. However, mountains can themselves become barriers of doubts, negative influence, uncomfortable conditions, or even selfishness on your way to implement your idea. These can discourage you. But if you are aware that these problems may come in one way or another, remember the tree. Knock on the door of your world, asking Abba Elohim's consciousness, and you will have entrance into the secrets of His world."

Again, he repeated, "Elohim is alive and lives within everything we see and inside all of us. He is never judgmental. He never casts us away or into hell, even if we disobey His laws or we miss Passover celebrations or fail other religious requirements."

Jesus paused and glanced around the room, "I would like to offer a prayer: Our Abba, grant us the awareness of Your presence. Grant us a willing heart to look for You and imitate Your love. Help me forgive and be compassionate toward others. Let us not hold on to old ideas that prevent us from knowing and loving You and others. Amen."

Elder Joseph stepped in and invited everyone to partake in the dinner prepared in Jesus' honor. As Mary, Martha, Salome, and Joanna served they noticed friendly conversations. Some were more vocal than others, but everyone enjoyed discussing points of Jesus' speech.

After the meeting was over and everyone had left, Jesus met privately with his uncle. He asked Mary to attend him.

"Uncle, frankly speaking, I have news that there is a possibility that I may be taken by Rome or the Sanhedrin sometime in the near future. I hope not, but I have information that the Sanhedrin and Rome are investigating me. I told Abba Adonai that if I am unable to change the minds of the High Priests, who are the only ones who can protect me from Rome, then I am prepared to give my life."

Joseph's complexion paled. As a worldly and experienced man, he was not naïve and knew of the grip of power the Sanhedrin held. He also knew that many of them used their religious position to disguise worldly aspirations and enjoyed manipulating others. He had seen this from his youth in the time of Herod. Not surprised, he nodded sadly, "What can I do to help you? I have a fleet of ships and can get you and a few of your disciples out of Jerusalem and out of Israel!"

Jesus smiled and calmly shook his head, refusing that kind of help, "No! That is not what I wanted to ask you." He paused, "Rather, if it comes to my death, I would like you to claim my body and secretly take it to Galilee. As a respected citizen of Israel and Rome from your business dealings, you will not be suspected or implicated with me. Rather, you can ask to take my body to your own family sepulcher here in the area and embalm it. Then in the darkness of night take my body to the hills of Galilee."

Jesus handed his uncle a map and pointing to a spot on it, he instructed, "These are the caves that I frequented as a boy. In secret, together with my family, lay my body in there. Do not tell anyone. This must remain a secret. Will you do this for me?" Jesus asked. "Of course, I hope this will not be necessary, and therefore that you can forget this request."

There was a long pause. Joseph of Arimathea could not help but remember how his own brother, the grandfather of Jesus, a Zadokite priest himself, was murdered during the days of Herod's pogroms. They were carried out on account of Herod's feverish search for descendants of David the King, because of prophecies that the Anointed One would come from the ruler's lineage. Joseph, with tears in his eyes, lovingly agreed, "Yes, of course, my nephew."

Jesus took his uncle's hands and offered a prayer of gratitude to Abba Elah.

***

While inside the protected Arimathea refuge good and broadminded men welcomed and listened to Elohim's son, another meeting of powerful leaders of Israel took place in the Sanhedrin, only hours before and with opposite designs.

This body of political and religious men, led by the Chief Priest Caiaphas, was composed of different parties, representing different points of view and concerns. The Sadducees predominantly represented the wealthy, while the Pharisees mainly represented the common people. This central power controlled all districts in the whole of Israel and Judea. They were directly responsible to the Roman governor, Pontius Pilate. The decisions they made were not always in the interest of Hebraism but were greatly influenced by the ruling empire of Rome and Herod, who was merely a civil figurehead.

The Sanhedrin was centrally responsible to keep the peace, especially in the religious world. Whether or not Jesus continued to preach in the nation of Israel would ultimately be their decision. The Sanhedrin was composed of the nation's most influential and prestigious scholars who urged fair and objective religious decisions for all Jewish citizens. However, they were mere proxies of the Roman empire that ultimately ruled the nation.

Whenever there was disruption in Israel, the current Chief Priest, Caiaphas, was the first to feel the wrath of the empire. His position was tenuous, as ultimately the true substantial indicator of a vigorous nation to Pontius Pilate, the Prefect of Rome, was the coffers. Taxes required by Rome were to be paid without question. This was the crux of the success or failure of the Chief Priest.

Therefore, when Caiaphas' position was put under scrutiny heads rolled, as was experienced by John the Baptist. Even though the preacher was much loved by his countrymen, he was a disrupter and Caiaphas was the first to face the consequences. No citizen of Israel would be allowed to rob the High Priest of his station. It was not a religious decision, it was simply personal, as no one was allowed to eclipse the High Priest.

When initial tales of unauthorized preaching by Jesus of Nazareth reached the attention of the assistants of the Chief Priest, they were dismissed as gossip. These clerks were the closest to the common man and had affinity for them. But when the tithing reports fell below normal, superiors checking the reports became concerned, sending messengers to the principal rabbis in all the districts of Galilee. It took time. But when the reports came back blaming Jesus of Nazareth for the decrease in funds, the next level of bureaucratic clerics sent out spies and requested specifics.

Finally, after nearly three years of collecting reports, the all-important financial news reached Caiaphas and the alarm was sounded. By the time the full report came out, already the coffers were below the required yearly amount. When the full amount of required taxes could not be sent to Rome, a red-faced Caiaphas quickly called a synod. He knew he had to get control of the situation as quickly as possible, before Rome became aware.

"Get me credible witnesses! Pay informers. Not another month can go by, or else Rome will be requiring that I step down, including all of you!" Caiaphas ordered.

Payments were sent out for credible information on the preacher and healer. But after the most recent astounding report about the Nazarene raising Lazarus from the grave came in, Jesus became a personal threat to Caiaphas putting him in danger of losing his position. Caiaphas convened the full Sanhedrin at once.

As the full assembly heard the reports, they immediately presumed that Roman spies had already reported to Caesar. The idea sent most into a frenzied fear of repercussions.

One middle aged Sadducee screamed above the chaotic hostility, "There is no time to waste. We have to act decisively, before Rome steps in!"

Their selfishness and desire for power made them insulated and narrow minded. Fear gripped them. Religious fervor was the least of their secular concerns. While a handful of dispassionate academics begged for rational consideration, they were frenetically drowned out. Thus, the irrational clerics ruled, and called for the immediate entrapment of Jesus.

Caiaphas and Annas sat back and let the ferocity continue throughout the body of officials. They agreed with those calling for the immediate arrest of Jesus, but did not want to appear to make the decision alone. Vindictively smiling at each other on the dais set apart from their cohorts, they enjoyed the lynching-like atmosphere and let it accelerate on its own. They relished it, as they were tired and bored with the dullness of life.

The Sadducees continued, greatly incensed. Many voices called out, "We agree that this Jesus of Nazareth must be stopped immediately!"

The Pharisees, Nicodemus for one, pressed for a more measured investigation. But already the fearful emotion of losing their livelihood had taken over the debate.

Annas, the previous Chief Priest and respected advisor to his son-in-law Caiaphas, cleared his throat, loudly prompting the attendees to be still. Coolly, the ornately dressed elderly man sat relaxed on his throne-like chair. He weaved his hand from side to side, like a sorcerer casting a spell. He announced his devious plan, all the while disguising his own selfish agenda, "We must find one of the rabblerouser's own and get him to lead us to the Nazarene. Give him all the silver he wants. This can be done quietly before news gets out to his followers, who would cause a messy scene. They will try to protect him and make us the villains. If we strike quickly, he can be tried and silenced before the news reaches most of his Galilean followers."

The soft magical quality of his voice seemed to stop the bantering, as if putting them under a spell. Those most frightened for self-preservation liked and agreed to the idea. And so, the plan to take Jesus at the earliest possible opportunity was instituted.

Chapter 38

The Last Supper

Everyone who drinks of this water will thirst again,
but whoever drinks the water that I shall give him will never thirst.
(John 4: 13-15)

Jesus, wrapped in a cloak, quickly disappeared from Joseph of Arimathea's compound into the darkness. After the temple incident and Nicodemus' information, Jesus and Simon Peter were under no illusion that they were safe. They assumed that the Sanhedrin leader Caiaphas had already sent spies to collect information about him.

So, moments after arranging a stealthy exit for everyone else, with only Thomas and his hidden sword for protection, Jesus took a separate direction. Simon Peter and the rest of the disciples left out of the front of Joseph's house, and broke up into two groups with plans to regroup outside of the city's walls.

Protected by a shield of darkness, the two groups took different meandering paths through the back alleyways of the great city. Finally, when each group determined that no one was following them, they left the City of David through the same gate that they had so openly and majestically entered earlier that day.

The immense city and outlying areas of Jerusalem held many possibilities for a secret rendezvous. Peter and James, who had planned the whole entrance and exit, had also prepared for Jesus' protection. They suggested the familiar Mount of Olives. It was the most secluded place, due to its rocky and dense foliage making it uncomfortable for pilgrims to camp.

Thus, after leaving Joseph's home and going in different directions, everyone met there. With a remarkably hopeful demeanor, Jesus instructed everyone to make camp. It would not be comfortable, but it was safe.

Jesus remained encouraging though, and asked Mary to sing and Martha to play her lyre. Mary remembered that once Jesus had told her how much her singing gave him peace and a feeling of closeness to his Abba. The simple music truly seemed to allay the tension and relax everyone after their great and terrible day.

Certainly, everyone believed that these tensions had begun with Jesus' outrage in the temple. Dazed, they wondered, "How could one day go from such incredible hope and praise and exaltation of Jesus as King David to death threats and great fear for Jesus and for their own lives?"

Although Simon Peter, following custom, asked for testimonies, only Simon the Zealot gave his, "I have never seen such righteousness. This action by Rabboni made me so proud to be considered his disciple. Although I have attended every Passover during my life, I never realized why going through that gauntlet of venders to offer prayers always made me uncomfortable. Jesus opened my eyes. Of course, it was the buying and selling of innocent animals just to make blood offerings. The animals are then burned, for what? Aw! It's disgusting. Not to mention all the poor people unable to feed their families, who at the very least would appreciate carcasses for food." He threw up his arms in disgust.

They were all exhausted. And almost everyone had no problem sleeping, even in the uncomfortable environment.

At sunrise, on the second day of Unleavened Bread, also known as Passover, everyone rose to a sultry but bright day. Mary noticed that Jesus' spirit was noticeably lighthearted and cheerful. It was almost like yesterday's incident had never happened. Their rest had erased the tensions of the previous emotional and long day.

The disciples were especially excited and looking forward to the evening's Passover dinner. This was the first time that they would join together with Jesus in Jerusalem and celebrate their most loved, traditional high Holy Day together.

Jesus gathered everyone together and instructed James and John with a specific task, "Go into Jerusalem and look for a man with a donkey carrying a water jug and follow him. He will lead you to a householder. Tell him that Teacher Jesus the Nazarene sent you. Ask him for a guest room where we will celebrate the Passover dinner. The man will show you a large upper room, furnished and readied for us to prepare and conduct our feast."

Then he told Simon Peter to direct the food preparations with the women Mary, Martha, Salome, and Joanna. Jesus warned them to keep their plans secret and be discreet as they moved around the city. He continued explaining his plan, "Have the women buy all the foods from the marketplace and the men prepare the dining hall. Invite only my ordained disciples, twelve men and our sisters who are with us now to the supper." He reminded them, "Our unity in heart is most important!"

He continued, "On the foundation of our recent victories, I plan to go to the Sanhedrin with you, my disciples, and with Abba Elohim. The Sanhedrin knows that I am backed by the Galilean people. I hope to win that body of religious leaders' hearts and thereby the allegiance of all the sects of our Hebrew faith. After this victory, Abba Elah will be able to bring incredible blessings to our country and the liberation of all His children from Satan's bondage."

The inn was sought out and procured by Peter, just as Jesus envisioned. The disciples began preparations under close direction by Peter and Judas. Mary, Joanna, and Salome prepared the dinner.

Nevertheless, Mary felt the tension increasing. During preparations and waiting for everyone to arrive, a lone messenger arrived to speak with Jesus. Mary, standing close enough, overheard the message in Hebrew, "The Chief Priest, Caiaphas, with the full consent of the Sanhedrin intends to have you surreptitiously arrested so as not to cause an outcry from your followers."

Shock and terror nearly burst from her mouth, but she quickly covered her mouth to remain concealed. Uncontrollably tears spilled from her eyes as she quickly turned away from her sisters, wiping them away with the edge of her sleeve so they would not become alarmed. She quickly commented, "Oh! these onions are so strong they are making my eyes water."

Praying and trying to control her trembling, all she could do was maintain composure and trust in Abba Elah's help. She knew how devastating and disheartening it would be if the others found out. Everyone except Mary believed that they were safe.

As she continued to do her part in preparing the meal, she recalled a hopeful comment that Peter reported to Jesus only a few days before, *Rabboni, the common custom during the Passover holiday protects all citizens from arrest and prosecution.*

Memory of the comment gave her hope. However, the messenger's panicked and urgent expression caused her to feel unsettled, with a gnawing sense of dread of the worst possible outcome. Nonetheless, she willed herself to remain prayerfully calm and hopeful while she silently worked diligently as a condition for Abba Elah's protection.

In the evening, the customary Passover meal was served on a traditional communal tray. The women carefully displayed the unleavened bread, charoset sauce, karpas, the bitter herb chazeret, and lamb on the platter and at each seat they placed a cup of the Passover wine. It was humble, but with much of the similarity of past Passover dinners. Mary remembered her grandmother's and mother's efforts and the joy that this her favorite holiday brought her.

Before the dinner officially began, John and Judas, with all the disciples sitting around the table, recalled the events of the original Passover. Judas recounted everything in vivid detail, "Each family was told by Moses to kill an unblemished lamb and paint its blood on their doorpost to protect the Hebrew family from the coming Angel of Death. Elohim Adonai sent his angel to punish all the Egyptians for holding them in bondage, preventing them from returning to their homeland as Moses had demanded of Pharaoh. As a result, all the pagan Egyptian's first born, both human and animal, were cursed to die."

Judas, unaware of how insensitive his words were, continued trying to make the recounting of the first Passover as vivid as he could. At the same time his master, unknown to him, was meditating and considering the possibility of his own death.

Jesus, who had been sitting and praying separately from everyone else since the stranger brought the ominous news, overheard and observed the fascination for death in everyone's expressions around the table. Suddenly he shouted out, uncharacteristically scolding John and Judas, "How can you continue to treasure such a gruesome tale, after all I have taught you about Abba Elah."

Rabboni's unusually loud and reprimanding voice caught Mary's attention.

"Our Creator has never acted with malice or punishment to His children. This story was conjured up by men who did not know their Abba Elah! They looked at everything through their own avenging and prejudiced mindsets."

Jesus' opposing comments surprised and dismayed Judas because this was a story that was required to be told at every Passover. Though Jesus' original disciples, including John, truly understood and felt remorse.

Insensitively Judas argued, "Master it is customary to recount the Passover story as we celebrate it to remind us of our proud history and our heritage."

Again, Jesus sighed disappointedly and chided him, "After all these months and years for some of you and all I have taught you about the Creator, Abba Elah."

Jesus repeated patiently his mantra, reminding them like a parent toward foolish children, "These horrid stories are ancient! Leave them in the past. Haven't I taught you about Abba's heart. His love is the same toward all His children throughout the world since the beginning. Let this Passover be a new beginning. Renew your understanding about our Creator Abba and leave the false understandings in the past."

Mary noticed how surprised and ashamed John was, that he could not even look up at Jesus for the shame he felt. Most of the others also understood, all except for Judas, as they suddenly realized how easily it was for them to revert to their old way of thinking.

Then Jesus used the solemnity of the moment to explain the forthcoming likelihood of his arrest, "Surely you are aware of the ominous atmosphere and our tenuous situation here in Jerusalem?" Everyone nodded.

Jesus paused, and Mary understood that this was the most difficult moment of his life to give them such terrible news, "Though I will continue giving my message until my last breath, I have news that the Sanhedrin will arrest me within days and bring me before the court to find a fitting punishment for me." Immediately his words caused chaos.

Since the messenger had brought the news Mary had not been able to stop her tears. But now there was a cascade of tears from everyone, even the stoic Simon Peter. Then after the moaning waned it was immediately followed with everyone's fearful expressions. They began to worry about themselves. Nathaniel and Thaddeus whispered and wondered aloud what everyone else was thinking but did not verbalize, "What will we do without Rabboni. We gave up everything. Could we be arrested also?"

Mary watched the whole scene through tears. She watched Jesus' stoic expression when their immediate thoughts of self-pity and concern came out. Nevertheless, Jesus allowed the discussions to go on for a time. Then, calmly with his exceptionally forgiving love, he continued encouraging his disciples, "Nevertheless, while I am with you, I will continue helping you understand the heart of our Abba Elah. I am determined to continue for as long as possible, though I am prepared to give my life if it is required to help progress Elah's providence. However, until then I will continue giving love. And no matter what happens, I will not leave you as orphans. With Abba Elah, there is always hope. Before long the world will not see me, but you will see me. I will ask Abba Elah to send another Counselor to be with you forever, the Spirit of Truth. Soon you will understand that I am in Abba, and you are in me and I am in you."

After a period of silence giving everyone a chance to realign themselves with his heart, Jesus motioned for the women to be seated in an empty space around the table. Then he sat quietly composed and expressionless.

He began by offering a prayer, "Abba Elah, let us enjoy this special meal together as Your sons and daughters chosen to bring Your message of love to this ancient land. Permit us to remember this special time together and know that You are always with us." Jesus, sitting upon the wooden floor, continued silently praying for their courage.

At the center of the long low table, with the disciples huddled around, the women served the traditional Seder meal. The only aspect that was not usual was the tense atmosphere in the room, as it would normally be an exalted and joyous time.

Many silently contemplated their own situation and painfully looked around at the companions. However, Jesus' countenance was still. They knew him long enough to know not to question any longer and be resolved to whatever would come about. Though most could not stop worrying about their personal situation.

After everyone was seated and the atmosphere settled down, Jesus prayed a short prayer of gratitude to Abba Elah for allowing them this blessing to be together. After which he made a dramatic change which surprised everyone.

Formally, Jesus instructed Mary to sit next to him on his left side. This broke tradition as not only did women not sit at the same table with men in public, but they especially did not sit at the head of the table. And then he asked Judas, not Simon Peter, to sit next to him on his right side, where normally Peter would have sat.

Mary obeyed his direction without question, but his request was so unusual that she could not help feeling awkward. Humbly, she took her place.

Jesus addressed all the men and women with a still and calm expression. "You are my closest and dearest companions, chosen by Abba Elah. We have shared many difficult and wonderful experiences together over the past few years. Haven't we?" he asked.

Everyone responded affirmatively but uncomfortably because this Passover's celebration was so very different from what they were accustomed to. They did not know what to expect and they were still shocked by Jesus' ominous words about their future.

Jesus nevertheless started the supper, "Let this be a new beginning in our effort to bring Abba Elah's will and truth to humankind. In this moment, push away any doubt or worry and become one with me, one with my heart. If you don't, you will be swept away by many even greater problems in the future."

Mary understood his severe sentiment and willed herself to trust him. She wanted to look at him but resisted.

Jesus continued, "Your complete unity with me is vital. Remember your ordination and commitment to me and Elah's will. Yes, this is a very serious time but your unity with me is more important than any other time we have shared together. We are close to securing Elah's Heavenly Kingdom. This is the moment which all ages in our history have hoped and prayed for. Through your oneness with me, you have power over sin and can do even greater things than I do."

In an unusually ceremonial gesture, Jesus broke off a large piece of the unleavened bread from the tray and lifted it up toward them, "This bread is symbolic of my body." Jesus explained, "As you take it into your mouth, it becomes part of your body. This is the beginning of the process of rebirth through me, the Son of Man, on our way to the Kingdom of Elah. Do this in memory of me."

He broke off a small piece and respectfully gave it first to Mary on his left side and then on his right side he gave a piece to Judas, equally respectfully. Then he gave a piece to each of his disciples, men and women alike. Together they took it and ate the bread slowly, not knowing what to expect.

He then lifted his wine goblet and handed it to Mary who sipped its sweetness and then handed the goblet to Judas to drink. And then he passed it around the table to each person to drink.

Jesus explained, "This wine is symbolic of my blood, the center of my being. The mainstay of life. Symbolically, you are drinking the core of my being. As you take my body and blood, you are reborn through me. When you eat this bread and drink my blood, it symbolizes you engrafting yourself to me. I am the Tree of Life. Remember this ceremony and take it to others as you continue spreading my words of life and love throughout the nation."

Then Jesus whispered cryptically in Hebrew, a heavenly secret meant only for Mary and Judas to understand, "You must be engrafted to me as I represent the first Adam, Elah's first son. When Eve was still with her brother Adam, death did not exist. When she departed from him, death came into being. If they had become complete and had attained Elah's original value, then death would be no more. Now as the new Adam I must find and marry the new Eve with Elah's blessing, then all humankind will be reborn."

Jesus said this with a twinkle of hope in his eyes, "You are to be reborn into the new life and lineage of Abba Elah. This is the purpose of my life to be Elah's instrument to restore all humankind to their original value. Now it can begin."

Judas began to wonder what this all had to do with him.

Jesus turned to Mary and, as if praying to a great multitude and with great ceremony, he declared in Hebrew, "Mary, this is the beginning ceremony of our marriage. You are symbolic of the first daughter of Elah whom Elah brought forth from the rib bone of Adam, His first son, the first man. Judas, you are symbolic of the archangel that took Eve from Adam and from Abba Elohim. Now this day you represent the archangel being separated from Eve. You cannot have her as your own."

Jesus proclaimed this privately and soberly to Judas, knowing very well the emotions that it would provoke. Silently he prayed that Judas would not act impulsively but would pray for understanding. However, Judas' face looked like someone had kicked the life out of him.

Mary's blushing and tears were uncontrollable. She did not truly understand Jesus' meaning, but she tried and with faith she silently promised him, *I will keep this deep in my heart and pray that Elah will help me understand and be worthy of this precious moment of our betrothal.* She nearly passed out but then took a deep breath. Jesus' unexpected formal proposal shocked her, and she felt ashamed of her unworthiness. Nevertheless, overwhelmed with happiness, she could not stop her tears of joy. *How could this be happening?* She asked herself.

At the same time, Judas' face turned ashen white as he took immediate offense. He was mortified and angry because his secret thoughts had been discovered and Jesus' intentions shocked him. Judas panicked, *Oh my Adonai! He's taking her for himself.* Then in Hebrew, he blurted out a whisper to Jesus, "This can't be! She is mine!"

Jesus nodded to him, but continued sincerely staring at his frustrated countenance. Jesus prayed that Judas would stop and think, hoping that he would eventually understand.

Meanwhile, everyone else sat in ignorance, wondering what Jesus had said to cause Mary's tears and Judas' erupting emotions.

As Jesus' demonstrative ceremony proceeded, Mary heard everything but internally Jesus' words to her were still repeating in her mind, *This is the beginning ceremony of our marriage. …marriage!* Her cheeks radiated heat as she felt she would explode with joy, all the while helplessly trying to understand, *I truly believed that our marriage would not happen! But now is it possible?*

Judas' shouting jolted her out of her thoughts. Sitting across from James, she first saw his horrified expression. She followed his stare to Judas standing beside Jesus. Judas was clearly outraged and shouting in Hebrew, "She is mine!" His eyes wildly filled with pain and disgust.

But before he stormed out of the room, Jesus predicted in Hebrew, "Judas, I know of your plans to betray me. Woe to the one who would betray the Son of Man. It would be better for him if he had not been born." With those words from Jesus, Judas left.

Though not understanding anything that had just happened, Peter was not surprised because of the man's brashness and conceit. He thought, *Judas never let go of his past. He never really understood Rabboni's love and compassion.* During the time Jesus was speaking to Mary and Judas in Hebrew, Peter presumed that Jesus had harshly scolded him for something. He thought, *Goodness knows that there are plenty of examples of his haughtiness and aloofness. He probably deserves it.* And he knew that everyone shared the same hard feelings toward him.

Jesus turned to Peter and predicted, "Peter do not judge. You also will betray me."

As if slapped by his Rabboni, Peter was shocked and hurt. Shaking his head, he assured Jesus, "No, no Rabboni, even if all fall away, I will never leave you."

Jesus assured him, "I tell you the truth, before the rooster crows you will disown me three times."

"No, no, no! Rabboni, even if I have to die, I will never disown you!" Peter moaned. And immediately all the disciples also repeated Peter's words, "We will never leave you."

However, Jesus spoke compassionately of Judas, "Judas has much to think about as do we all. Every person must examine his heart and motivation. The next few days will be challenging for us all."

Rather than feeling angry toward Judas, Mary pitied him. She understood that Jesus' words were a hard saying for him. But she also remembered her uncomfortable feeling being around Judas since months ago. She knew that he had falsely assumed an eventual relationship with her. She regretted being the cause of his struggle.

Jesus explained to everyone, "If blessing comes but we entertain self-centered thoughts and our heart is conflicted, we will miss it. I say this now because of what is coming."

Everyone began to feel uncertain anxiety. Jesus' ominous words were unsettling. Mary's joy faded because of the anxiety in the room. She prayed, *Abba, firstly, I will support Rabboni and remain outwardly composed. I don't know what the future will bring but I offer myself to you Elah.*

She also hoped for an opportunity to speak with Jesus but now was not the time. She wondered about the Hebrew words that Jesus spoke over Judas and herself. However, because of Judas' angry parting, she made a mental note to ask Jesus about them at another time.

Everyone was hungry and so the dinner and celebration continued. A pervasion of uncertainty nevertheless continued.

Jesus prayed that his disciple, Judas, would resist his blinding anger and take a moment to contemplate. He knew well the suffering he had caused Judas, however Jesus could not withhold the words, for they were Elah's words. He, like Elah, had to trust Judas in this pivotal moment. He turned to Peter and asked him, "Simon Peter, please take care of our brother Judas, for he has much to think about tonight. Please love him and try to bring him back from what I fear he might do."

Then at the end of dinner, Jesus finalized the ritual in Hebrew, ending with these words, answering Mary's question, "This is the beginning of the symbolic process of changing humankind's blood lineage. In a few days, I will hold another ceremony in which complete rebirth from Satan's lineage to Abba Elah's lineage will take place. This ceremony will complete your engrafting process to me."

Part V

Chapter 39

The Price of Disunity

Could you not stay awake with me one hour?
(Matt. 26:40)

After the Passover seder dinner of food and wine, Jesus led his disciples in a Psalm of David:

I will lift mine eyes unto the hills. From whence cometh my help.
My help cometh from the Lord, which made heaven and earth.
He will not suffer thy foot to be moved: he that keeps thee will not slumber.
Behold, he that keeps Israel that shall neither slumber nor sleep.

The song seemed to relieve the tension that was evident throughout the celebration, and especially from Judas' abrupt departure. Afterwards Rabboni invited everyone to come to the Mount of Olives with him. Most, however, requested to go visit with their families who were celebrating in the area.

Jesus asked Peter, James, John, and Mary to come with him to the serene Garden of Gethsemane in the Kidron Valley, preferred for its privacy and an ideal place to pray. Mary had noticed that Jesus' usually bright personality had changed to a heavy subdued demeanor after their dinner. Though she understood why, she hoped that the calming atmosphere of the garden would help him regain his usual positive and hopeful disposition.

Upon arriving in the garden, Peter, James, and John sought comfortable positions in the quiet lush area, sitting upon the ground and propping themselves up against a tree or rock. After the satisfying holiday dinner and measurable amounts of drink, it was obvious that their eyelids quickly began to feel heavy. Nevertheless, as Jesus' chief disciples, which they asserted proudly, they agreed to support Jesus throughout his prayer and keep watch.

James asked Rabboni, "Could Mary sing another hymn to get us started?"

"Yes, my Rabboni," Mary nodded. But because she felt Jesus' heavy spirit and a lump in her throat, her voice trembled. Nevertheless, she chose to sing a psalm of David and recited it with all her heart to uplift his:

The Lord is my shepherd I shall not want...

She paused, desperately trying not to cry out. Her voice was almost silent due to her emerging tears.

He leadeth me beside the still waters.

She truly wanted to uplift his heart and spirit but she became helpless, as she whimpered out of overwhelming love and concern for her suffering Rabboni.

"Please Rabboni," Mary whispered. "My heart is so sorrowful that I can't support you properly that my voice quivers from sadness and concern for you. I only want to relieve your worry. Yet, I fear that I am not doing that but causing you more sadness. Please forgive me!"

Jesus nodded, understanding her heart.

Finally surrendering himself to the greater design, Jesus stood, breaking the silent serenity and made a simple request. Regarding his three disciples' bobbing heads and heavy-eyed expressions, he pressed them, "Remain awake. It will not be easy, but I need your support. Stay one in heart with me and pray that Elah can continue our protection. I know the fresh balmy air and your full stomachs will tempt you to sleep, but you must stay alert and awake with me for one hour."

He confessed to the sleepy men, "My soul is overwhelmed with sorrow, and I feel like I will die just from the grief. Our unity will determine the outcome. Do you understand?"

In unison they reassured him, "Yes, Lord, we will."

Leaving them to their responsibility, he went through the foliage to pray. A stone's throw away was a small cave familiar to him, where once before he had found comfort from the cold. The small carved out crevice was a perfect place for him to bare his heart to his Abba for guidance and receive ideas on how to go forward.

As usual, Mary followed to support him in prayer at a distance. It was so quiet that she could hear his every word and every sigh.

Continuing to feel an overwhelming melancholy, she willed herself to remember the many times she spent nights with him as he prayed. For every evening she thanked the bright full moon for its light, enabling him to see where to put his feet so that he would not stumble.

Gradually the words of his prayer became louder and more desperate. The prayer reached a crescendo where she could no longer concentrate on her own prayer. To the depth of her soul, she regretted that she was so powerless to help him. Tears came uncontrollably as she tried to stifle her sobs so as to not disturb him.

He pleaded with Abba Adonai first in Hebrew and then interchanging with the endearing words from his mother tongue, Aramaic, "Abba Elah, in You there is always hope. Throughout the ages, inspired men and women prepared and made great sacrifices for this moment. Desperately, I am determined to fulfill this mission that You called me for, in one way or another! Abba, give me inspiration that I may reach the hearts and minds of the leaders and educators of Your chosen people. Forgive them. They are confused. Their minds are closed and unaware of how damaging selfish motivation is."

Pausing, and then in a softer endearing tone he begged, "My Abba, if it is possible…take this cup away from me! Give me more time!" Suddenly he cried out imploring his Abba, "Help me open their hearts. Show me a way!"

Feeling restless, Jesus returned to his men and found them asleep. The sound of his footsteps caused them to immediately arouse from their stupor and with half opened eyes they jumped up. Sincerely they apologized for falling asleep.

Jesus encouraged them to fight against their physical desire for sleep, "I understand your desire to sleep but, like I said before, you must fight the temptation to give in at this crucial moment."

Kindly as if speaking to children he said, "Your spirit is willing, but your flesh is weak. It was predicted by the prophet Zechariah that you will fall away. It was also prophesied that they will strike the shepherd and his sheep will be scattered." Then Jesus prophesied, "Peter, this night before the cock crows you will disown me three times. And the rest of you will run away."

The three men swore in disbelief, "No! Rabboni, we will never do that and even if everyone falls away, we will even die with you!"

Jesus trudged back to continue his search for a plan and to gain strength to endure what he knew was coming. He knelt down and spoke as if Abba was right beside him, "I remember my experience with You in the desert, Abba. Your love that I felt for the first time moved me into connection and harmony with Your Divine consciousness. Your love dissolved all my angst and fear. I feel that confidence now as I felt it then."

Mary was awed by his closeness to Elah.

"My fear is that I will not be able to endure the provocation of their words or the pain of possible corporal punishment and fail You. I want only to express the love that You taught me, the love that fills my heart even now. Help me not respond to them in my previous aggressive and sarcastic way. Help me to endure to the end and hold tight to Your forgiving and unselfish compassion toward all your misguided children."

But continuing to fight the eventuality he pleaded again, "Abba, there must be a way to reason with the authorities. Help me answer them with love and not lose my temper but instead to impart to them Your truth."

This time his prayer was so passionate and serious that, in the light of the full moon, Mary spotted sweat and blood pouring from his eyes and nose, dripping from his chin and forming a puddle upon the ground. Without inhibition or concern for custom, Mary rushed to wiped away the secretions from his face with the edge of her scarf. He did not seem to notice her as he continued to beseech Abba. His tearful, urgent prayer continued until he finally surrendered, "If it be possible, take this cup away. Not as I will, but let Your will be done."

He paused as if waiting for inspiration. Suddenly Jesus' countenance became exuberant. It seemed to Mary that Jesus had an idea, or even that Elah had impressed on him an idea that he had not thought of. "Yes, Abba Elah, in this tough situation I will appeal to their hearts. I will simply love them even in the face of their hatred and anger and fear."

Nearing the end of the hour, Jesus again found the disciples asleep. He woke them and returned to pray with even more intensity.

Again, continuing his fervent prayer, followed by moments of silence, and then gentle whispered prayer, finally ending in self-assurance, "Not as I will, but let Your will be done. It is now set in motion. Abba I already feel strength knowing your everlasting and enduring love for me and all of humankind. I am ready."

Staring at Mary in the light of the moon he announced portentously, "Let us prepare the others, as tonight at this very moment I am betrayed in the Sanhedrin. They will come for me soon."

Chapter 40

The Betrayer

If anyone wants to be my disciple,
They must deny themselves and take up their cross and follow me.
(Matt 16:24)

Judas, a Hebrew scholar, the most educated disciple of Jesus, stormed away from the Passover dinner in a fit of rage, recalling Jesus' insolent words to him, *How dare he call me Lucifer! Announcing to everyone that I would betray him. And revealing his bold idea to take Mary as his wife!*

Disregarding Jesus' instruction to him the day before, he thought, *He wouldn't even give my idea a thought. I only wanted to connect Jesus to the priests in the temple as a qualified cleric. I have influence with the Sanhedrin. I will show him that I can arrange for them to meet. And help them understand that Jesus poses no threat to them. I can even promise them that I will advise him how to see things their way.*

But as he navigated through the overcrowded and hot granite streets of the city, Jesus' emphatic words echoed in his consciousness, "Do not go to them."

Nevertheless, convinced by his own ego, Judas felt he knew better as he crisscrossed the meandering crowd. His self-centered mindset took over, trying to analyze his own life of intersecting paths that he had taken, *How did I get to this point? How can I make sense out of my life? I'm neither orthodox nor rebel. It all began when I got involved with the Baptist's uprising against the religious snobs.*

Judas smiled and admitted, *Oh yes, I thought it exciting to be a rebel.*

Although a humble preacher, John no doubt had an outstanding pedigree and to some degree still had authority with the orthodoxy. However, John's unexpected demise left me thunderstruck. I believe that is why I felt compelled to join with Jesus. And though uneducated, his followers believed him to be the Anointed One.

He remembered John's words. "The Anointed One…the Anointed One I am not even worthy to untie his sandals" *John preached constantly. It was all what John was about, constantly preaching and looking for the Anointed One. So even though Jesus was a self-proclaimed Galilean preacher, my interest in joining him seemed only natural. I tried to find out for myself why his followers believed in him so passionately. Initially he respected me, even gave me the power of the purse. But as time went on, I saw that he never took my opinion or advice nor did his followers. Though his charismatic folkish stories and dissent against the leadership attracted many….*

Judas wanted to stop that train of thought. It was too painful after receiving the scolding from Jesus and it was clear the disciples did not respect him.

Admitting to himself, *I caught an interest in their spirit, but now I am not sure anymore. All I feel now is that Jesus is a hopeless agitator.*

He realized, *All my life I never let down my defenses to anyone. Not even to my father or John or Jesus. It was in my best interest to preserve my own ego. Only I know what I want.* Laughing haughtily, he remembered doubting John every day. *That habit continued with Jesus of Nazareth. Somehow, I could not truly connect or submit myself to either of them. I trust only myself.*

It never occurred to him to pray for guidance. He was more comfortable with his own heart to lead him. Egocentric in his own thoughts he succumbed to anger and disrespect for everyone. In addition, the only woman he had ever loved had disparaged him. Therefore, Judas could think of nothing better than returning to his roots. Thus, in his narrow mindedness he continued on his path. Swiftly he tracked his way to the temple and toward the court of the Sanhedrin. Arriving after sunset, it was vacant and quiet, unlike the overcrowded streets.

Stopping and standing alone in the courtyard he felt so small and nearly decided to turn around and return the next day. *It's Passover! Of course, who would be here? They're celebrating with their families. Well, I've never been here when not a soul is around. Except for the firelit torches casting dark dancing shadows around the porticos everything is dark. I'll just take a look around the court,* he thought while going through an entrance toward the Holy of Holies.

There were more torches, which allowed him to see the beautifully designed white marble. *This edifice is truly awe inspiring. I've never been here alone and have never taken the time to notice its majesty.*

Soon after entering the court area, he was surprised when a wizened old priest emerged from the shadows, greeting him kindly and respectfully. Judas explained his desire to speak with the Chief Priest, Caiaphas, or someone who could take a message to him.

"I am Annas," the priest introduced himself proudly. "My son-in-law is Chief Priest."

Judas immediately remembered the name Annas, who was Chief Priest during the time he studied in the temple's religious school. He was greatly respected and quoted back then. Knowing this immediately put Judas at ease.

Annas noticed that the visitor recognized him and smiled, feigning a humble posture. Feeling a need to explain why he was there and not a lowlier priest, he explained, "It is my turn to stay late in the temple to keep the fires burning." He stood waiting for the stranger to further explain his reason to be there as it was unusual to have visitors, especially on such an auspicious evening.

Judas cleared his throat. He was so relaxed from the temple's awesomeness that he almost forgot his reason for coming. He thought to himself, *My, I have been all in my head these past couple of hours that I hardly know where to begin.* Then, getting right to it he blurted out, "I am Judas Iscariot. I am a cleric educated right here in Jerusalem's religious school, and most recently I am a disciple of the Galilean Jesus of Nazareth. You may have heard of his healings and other miracles."

Annas nearly choked, but he held back his great surprise and giddy delight. Obviously, the man in front of him had no idea of their recently decided upon plan. Like snakes, he and Caiaphas had planned to ensnare an unsuspecting believer of the Nazarene, one who would naively provide information and thus cover their devious tracks. Thus, without alerting Jesus' followers and sympathizers, the guilt of Jesus' death would then fall on the betrayer.

Presently, they were trying to come up with a plan but had put it off due the days' celebrations. The priest realized that this man, Judas, might be just the person Caiaphas was looking for to solve their dilemma. Annas nodded diplomatically, with a fake smile so as to not scare him away, "I will send for Caiaphas. He is always available for important purposes."

Trying to control himself, Annas walked a few meters away and out of earshot of the naïve disciple. He called for a servant and whispered a verbal instruction, "Go to my son-in-law Caiaphas' home. Tell him to come immediately to the court, for I have some very important news for him. Go quickly."

Annas knew that Caiaphas' resolve to silence Jesus would work better if they took care of him without convening the synod of religious leaders. Much discussion had already taken place, and they had already passed judgment. There was no need to bother them again on such a Holy Day. He and his son-in-law could act on their own authority as judge and jury.

When Caiaphas arrived, Annas filled him in as he appraised the Jew standing near to the entrance. Caiaphas coldly stared at Judas whispering, *How fortunate for us! What an unsuspecting fool, so innocent and trusting.*

Caiaphas made small talk with Judas and then moved on to the main course, "We have heard much about your Jesus of Nazareth. And just yesterday we heard how regally he entered the city leading dozens of his countrymen, Galileans, right? Many calling out his name, Jesus of Nazareth, and claiming that he is the return of King David!" Unnaturally cordial, Caiaphas asked, "Were you there also? What did you say your name was?"

"I'm Judas Iscariot and yes, I was there." Without a pause he continued speaking naively to the head of the Sanhedrin, "I would like to speak on behalf of Jesus of Nazareth as I am a follower of his. He would like to meet with you at your convenience and give you a message from Elohim."

Caiaphas and Annas looked at each other as Caiaphas raised his eyebrow with a nod. And then, carefully cajoling so as to keep Judas free of concern, he suggested a plan, "We would like to meet this Jesus. Do you think he could come tonight to meet with us?"

Judas thought to himself, *Actually, this may be a good time, since not all the other priests are here. Jesus may have a better chance to speak personally to influence the Chief Priest.* With naïve trust, and no idea that he was being set up, he agreed with a smile and a nod. It excited him to think he would be the one to get Jesus in to speak with the Chief Priest, "Yes, I believe he would be able to come. I can go and ask him to come right now."

"Oh, that would be wonderful," Annas said. "I will send a temple escort of men with you to protect you and to usher you back with Jesus." They wove their package of lies insidiously, to entrap Judas as well.

Annas and Caiaphas hoped that Jesus' supporters would be surprised and caught off guard. Before they could mount a defense, the Nazarene would be whisked away. And once they had him in their snares, they would swiftly silence him for good.

Chapter 41

Worse than Hell

Woe to that man by whom the Son of Man is betrayed.
It would be better for him if he had not been born.
(Matt 26:24)

Dawn was approaching in the Kidron Valley on the Mount of Olives. Peter, James, and John stood sheepishly facing Jesus, having failed to meet their responsibility. Peter was offering his apology to Jesus when suddenly Mary turned toward a noisy commotion approaching them. Initially she heard heavy footsteps and tinny metallic sounds. *It sounds like soldiers marching!* Mary whispered as she felt the dryness in her mouth.

As ominous dark figures approached, the light from their torches reflected off their armor and the swords hanging at their waists. Again, she whispered, *Soldiers? No! It can't be? Why?* Exhausted from the long emotional night she searched for a coherent answer. She shook herself and rubbed her eyes as she perceived a familiar face among them and thought, *Judas is leading the guards? Oh, Judas what have you done?* And then she remembered Judas' meeting with Jesus and the answer Jesus gave him, "Do not go to the Sanhedrin!" *He defied Jesus!*

Spurring Mary out of her thoughts, Judas boldly strode forward facing Jesus, surprising him and greeting him with a kiss on his cheek. Immediately the soldiers surrounded Jesus, thrusting Mary aside.

Judas gullibly announced their purpose, "Master do not confuse this armed guard with ill will but rather it is meant to protect you as a friendly escort sent by Caiaphas."

Peter snapped out of his stupor and quickly drew his sword to protect his Rabboni. Before anyone could blink an eye, Peter sliced off the ear of one of the intruders.

Immediately Jesus raised his hand and ordered Peter to put down the sword. He sternly chided his chief assistant, "No more of this! If one uses a sword, then he will die by the sword!"

Judas heartlessly ignored the violence, but quickly signaled the troops with his hand to allay any further violence. "We come in peace, Lord. I met with Caiaphas, the Chief Priest, and his father-in-law Annas. They very much want to meet you as they have heard of your miracles. I told them you were a man of Elohim." Judas continued naively and arrogantly, "Caiaphas told me that he would like to hear your message for himself. Therefore, he asked me to escort you to him."

It was obvious to Mary that Jesus would not or could not refuse, especially surrounded by armed guards. In a solemn but peaceful manner, he nodded his consent. But as soon as Jesus relented, the diplomacy was over. With overwhelming strength, the guards roughly grabbed him and tied his wrists together, rendering him helpless.

Mary followed the guards, praying desperately that someone would come to Jesus' aid. Overwrought, she tried to think of how she could help him. She looked around for her fellow brothers, but they were gone.

This is not a friendly escort as Judas says. Obviously, because they are wearing knives and swords. Judas deceived and disobeyed Jesus! From the long emotional day and night, she suddenly felt exhausted. Unable to control her emotions, she sobbed as liquid poured from her eyes and nose. But she continued praying that she could find help. Powerlessly, she looked behind her again for support, expecting to see Peter, James, and John. *Where did they go? Perhaps they went for help.*

Deserted by the disciples, she alone followed the soldiers. Nevertheless, she would not leave him, and she determined to stay with him for as long as it would take to see him freed.

She kept her distance and fell back in the darkness as the column of soldiers neared a huge villa, lit up with torches all around the property. *This must be the High Priest's home, but why are they taking him here instead of a more public place like the temple court in the center of Jerusalem?* she wondered.

The guards led Jesus into a ground level entrance. Judas did not follow them but rather went up the massive stairs and inside the palace-like edifice.

Mary stayed in the shadows of trees encircling the estate. She had no idea what time what it was. All was quiet. She wanted to move closer but there were no other shaded areas, and she knew that as a woman she would be shooed away if she was caught. Therefore, she sat and pondered what she should do.

After a desperate prayer Mary finally decided to go in search of her companions, with a plan to bring them back to this place. *With their support, we will have more influence to defend Rabboni!* Desperately she prayed for Jesus' protection until she returned. Unknown to Mary, Peter, James, and John were in a small crowd of men gathered on the lawn of the huge estate.

Elah, where can I find the disciples and supporters? We had no particular meeting place here in Jerusalem, except the inn. Then a thought came to her to run to the home of Joseph of Arimathea. She found that he was not home. Mary also thought of Nicodemus, but she didn't know how to find him.

In the crisp night atmosphere Mary regained strength. Desperate to find a disciple she ran through the greyish lit streets to the inn. She found Phillip awake but sitting in a stupor-like state. She assumed that one of the three had informed him and she hoped that they were also on the way to find others to help.

Mary called out to Phillip and had to shake him to get his attention, pleading, "We have to do something for our Rabboni! Jesus was taken to Caiaphas' home as a prisoner. The guards screamed at him and pushed him, treating him like a criminal!"

But as Mary spoke to Phillip, she noticed his dark sunken red eyes and that he was immobilized and distraught with fear. He stared at her with a blank look.

Moaning he whispered, "I should have gone with Jesus last night instead of going to my family. I could not enjoy anything with them anyway because Jesus was always on my mind." Finally, he whimpered. "What can we do?"

Immobilizing fear and shock stunned Phillip as he mumbled to himself, "Is it true that Judas led the temple guards right to Jesus. Jesus advised discretion to all of us, even Judas! This is a very dangerous time." Phillip whined, "Why?"

Mary told Phillip, "Try to get everyone together to support Jesus. I have to get back to Jesus." Finally, she strongly directed Phillip, "Go find Nicodemus and find as many believers as you can and as fast as you can. Do you understand?"

Mary ran hastily back to the mansion. She followed a line of palm trees close up to the place where she last saw Jesus and tried to keep out of sight. Kneeling down, she prepared to wait beside the trunk of a cypress tree: The guards were all around the exterior of the building so she could not get closer. She guessed that the proceedings were still going on.

However, slowing down and in the quiet became a problem for her. As she leaned on the tree trunk her eyelids began to feel heavy. Fatigue caught up with her and she began to nod off. However, with strong willpower she tried to force herself to stay alert.

Finally, after bumping her head on the bark of the tree she stood up. Suddenly she heard the door where Jesus entered earlier swing open. A guard backed out pulling a rope attached to a man's bound wrists. *Is that Jesus?* She could not be sure, because of his appearance. But then she recognized that the man was Rabboni.

His homespun robe was covered in blood. Mary grabbed her mouth to stifle a cry. His face was swollen and bruised, and his eyes were swollen shut, disguising his handsome features. He stumbled, nearly falling at times. His head seemed too heavy to hold up and his gait was unsteady. Still his hands were tied as they pushed him, causing him to stumble over and over again.

The guard pulled him toward the inclined stone steps. He still had some sensibility because she saw how he tried to brace himself at each fall by turning and using his shoulder against the sharp stone edges of the steps, unable to use his tied hands. The guard practically pulled him the whole way up to the entrance, without concern for scraping Jesus' knees and arms and legs. His clothing was ripped and ragged.

Mary sobbed, *It's hard to believe this is Rabboni. He's unrecognizable, but I know it is him. His face is bloody, and his eyes are swollen shut. His lips are engorged and bleeding.* Gasping she nearly screamed and only restrained herself by burying her face in a tuft of foliage on the ground, muffling her cries. She no longer had the strength to stay upright and collapsed on the ground crying hysterically.

Up the staircase they pushed and pulled him. Numerous times the edge of his robe tripped him. Near the top, one hefty guard grabbed the back of Jesus' robe and pulled him up to the top of the stairs like a sack of spelt as his knees and legs scraped each step.

Finally, Jesus staggered into the massive edifice. Mary on the ground managed to crawl in between two large bushes. She no longer had the strength to compose herself. She began to wail, forcing the sleeves of her robe into a knot and then into her mouth. Losing all awareness of time, she wept uncontrollably and lost consciousness.

Waking from sounds of loud shouting not far from her, she picked herself up off the ground brushing herself off and found a guard, "Sir, where are they taking the Nazarene?" The guard did not look at her but stared straight ahead answering coldly, "To Pontius Pilate, in the Roman fortress."

When Mary finally found the fortress, after asking many people along the way, the light of the sun was just beginning to break through in the eastern sky. She heard brash hollering and a greatly chaotic and tumultuous atmosphere as she neared the fortress.

Because women were not allowed any closer, she only had a limited viewpoint. From there, she watched men going throughout the crowd inciting everyone, screaming "Crucify him, crucify him" over and over. *They are stirring everyone into a frenzy,* Mary thought.

Mary scanned the crowd for a familiar face and hoped to see someone calling out on Jesus' behalf, but there was no one. *Where are Nicodemus and Joseph, Jesus' uncle, or the disciples? Or even one of the enthusiastic sojourners who walked with us into the temple chanting King David and Anointed One.* She could not see a single familiar face. Jesus stood alone and undefended.

Mary reasoned, *Everything happened so quickly in the middle of darkness and there was no time to arrange supporters. Surely someone will speak on Jesus' behalf.*

But the shouts filled with loathing continued, demanding that Jesus be punished, "Death to the blasphemer! Save our nation and crucify this villain!" They were going wild, and some seemed to enjoy shouting the loudest. When there was a lull, the inciters spurred them on with more vitriolic shouting, even telling the mob what to bellow out.

She watched wondering if it was all a nightmare, *How can all this be happening? I cannot do anything for Rabboni! Who will help him? Instead of dying down, the hatred and vengeance is multiplying. Helplessly Jesus stands still with his head bowed, being made a fool and accused of all kinds of fallacies. Where is Judas who started this?*

She screamed in support of Jesus, but her voice was scarcely heard. Only a few women heard her, and they turned around and laughed at her.

Dear Abba! Mary prayed, *How can this happen? Instead of dying down and ending with Jesus' release, the intensity of the crowd is increasing. When will they release Jesus? Please Abba Elah! Help us, please help Jesus.* Mary screamed, "Ha-Elohim" with all her heart.

Helpless among all the screaming priests and commoners, she cringed from their bloodthirsty expressions and amusement at Jesus' expense. Again, she looked around for Judas, thinking that he would be there. But there was no familiar face at all. "Where is everyone?" Again, she asked herself over and over. "Are they unaware of what's happening?"

Abruptly, there was a change in the atmosphere. The roaring stopped. Mary suddenly felt a wave of nausea overwhelm her. Ignoring the sensation, she stretched to peer over and around the heads of women in front of her.

Pilate walked out onto an elevated dais giving everyone a clear view of him. As he took his seat upon a huge throne, his voice carried and the ranting ceased. But when he announced the charges, their raucousness started up again as they continued shouting for Jesus' death without mercy.

Inching her way toward the front to stand as close as she could to Jesus, she observed Pilate's elaborately carved stone throne. Jesus was callously pushed by the temple guards toward the Roman leader.

Rabboni, what should I do? She whispered in prayer, not expecting a response. But to her surprise, Jesus turned and looked straight at her. Momentarily their eyes met and through the openings of his swollen eyelids she saw the spark of his spirit.

When he turned toward her, the women standing around her in unison gave an awful cry at his gory appearance. *He's in so much pain! Ha-Elohim please help him.* Suddenly Mary heard his calming voice in her consciousness, "Mary, remain prayerful. We are in Abba Elah's hands."

Because he had turned toward the crowd, the guard pushed him even more violently toward Pontius Pilate, causing him to fall to his knees. The rest of the morning was a blur of blood and gore. Only Mary's resolve could keep her from vomiting. The ringing in her ears was deafening at times. She was only able to hear some of Pilate's questions and Jesus' answers.

Pilate coldly asked Jesus, "Are you King of the Jews? I heard reports that many Galilean visitors called you a king."

Jesus answered, "I have no kingdom in this world. Is that your own idea or did others talk to you about me?"

Pilate answered sarcastically, "Am I a Jew? You were handed over to me by your people and chief priests. What have you done to elicit such intense hatred from these people?" Almost sympathetically, Pilate motioned toward the loathing onlookers.

Jesus answered simply, "My kingdom is not of this world. If it were, my followers would fight to prevent my arrest. But now my kingdom is in a different place."

"So, you are a king!" Pilate became interested and thought, *Here we are, this may be a reason to give him the corporal punishment that Caiaphas is requesting. He has now committed a crime against Rome and the emperor as there is no king but Caesar. However, it is obvious that he is not advocating a revolt against Rome.*

"Yes, I am a king. I was born for this reason. To bring truth to the world and testify to the truth. Those who follow me are on the side of truth, listening to me and testifying to me." Jesus spoke with strong conviction.

Pilate seemed to become curious and asked Jesus, "What is truth?"

Jesus remained silent and Pilate appeared to be disappointed when Jesus would not answer his question.

Pilate sat quietly deliberating all his options. From his experience he could tell that the man called Jesus was not a danger to society and that the anger was irrational. The Prefect analyzed the scene before him, *To be fair, preaching is not a crime punishable by death.* But as he observed the bloodied man in front of him, he thought, *Caiaphas must have reason to send him for corporal punishment. Even the priest's lackeys are screaming to crucify him! This will certainly get Tiberius' attention and I don't want to rile him, not unless the punishment fits the crime. There is a provision to release a prisoner at Passover.*

Pilate, thinking he found a way around the unusually incensed reactions, announced in a loud voice, "It is customary during Passover for the Roman Prefect to release a prisoner. I will give you a choice of two prisoners: Barabbas, a terrorist and murderer, or this peaceful man, Jesus of Nazareth."

Much to the Prefect's surprise, the crowd unanimously roared, "Give us Barabbas!"

Finally, tired of the ridiculous politics of the Jewish nation, Pilate ceremoniously washed his hands of the dissident. He had one last idea, *Through physical punishment perhaps I can get the prisoner to give up.*

Pilate stood and spoke directly to Jesus, meant only for him to hear, "I have a headache and don't really know how to rid myself of it. I was hoping that the mob would choose you, but they chose a murderer. Therefore, I am sending you to meet my soldiers. I hope they will help you come to a different decision in order to save your life. Hopefully you will reconsider your current attitude and situation. If you confess your crime and repent and desist then my soldiers will bring you back to me. I will reconsider your sentence." However, Pilate had a feeling that the man standing in front of him was committed to his cause.

Immediately Rabboni was surrounded by guards and pushed and shoved away from the crowd to an enclosed area. Jesus was gone from Mary's sight. She could no longer control herself as she ran into an alley and emptied her insides.

Chapter 42

Undefended

Whoever seeks to gain his life will lose it,
But whoever loses his life will preserve it.
(Luke 17:33)

At daybreak, a cock crowed several times performing his instinctual responsibility. But this morning when Peter heard it, he remembered his actions and Rabboni's prediction. "Yes," he admitted shamefully, "I did deny my relationship with Jesus not just once but several times. The prophecy of Zechariah, that Jesus spoke of last night, also turned out to be correct. In fact, we all scattered, fearful of losing our lives. Never did we act out of our love for Jesus, but we only thought of ourselves."

The weather-beaten fisherman bowed his head in utter ignominy and cried like a baby, crouching immobilized in the shadow of a building. Suddenly a familiar voice caught his attention, though he chose to ignore it.

Mary frantically called out, "Simon Peter!" She ran straight to him, joyfully relieved to find him. *At last, I found a familiar face!* she thought.

But as soon as she came close to him, she froze, appalled by the state of the chief disciple. Disappointed as she observed his sunken appearance, she sighed, *Peter why do you look this way. Your countenance is fallen. You are disheveled. What are you doing?* She had so much to tell him. She had to tell him that Jesus needed them. *But how can I tell him? He's despondent and irrational.*

Upon seeing Mary, Peter blubbered through his salty tears and fluid discharging from his nose. She saw that he was deranged as he did not even try to wipe the secretions away. As his frightened eyes glared at her without recognition, he screamed, "Go away. I do not know him." He cowered further into the shadows so as not to be found by the authorities.

She realized that he did not recognize her, even so she desperately tried to appeal to his better self, "Simon Peter, it's me, Mary. What can we do? We have to do something to support and defend Jesus!"

Peter relaxed upon hearing Mary's voice. Her urgent words seemed to bring him back to reality. He fell to the ground, face down in despondency and muttered, "What have I done? I should have stood in front of the guards and given my life to save Jesus. Instead, the guards just took him away without any chance to defend him."

Mary hardly understood his blubbering. Ignoring his frailty, she tried to help him focus on the reality of the moment, "Simon Peter, I was just at the Roman compound watching Pilate pass his judgement." She swallowed, hating to give Peter the horrible news. But he needed to know. "Peter, they took him and are going to try to convince him to give up his mission. That is the only choice they are giving him. It is the only possible chance for him if he wants to live."

Squatting down at his eye level, Mary implored him forcefully and energetically telling him what she had witnessed. She addressed him with respect to get his full attention. Suddenly and desperately, she began to express herself like never before. She hoped that Peter would change and want to go with her to support Jesus.

"It appeared to me that Pilate did not understand why there was such incensed hatred. In his expression the ruler seemed to be analyzing the dichotomy between the rage of the priests and clerics and the humble bloodied man in front of him. His questions to Jesus seemed to be an indication of his confusion. It seemed that he did not understand why the Chief Priest sent Jesus to him in the first place. And Pilate seemed befuddled as to the real reason the priests had it out for Jesus who appeared helpless and humbled, someone they could have taken care of on their own. Pilate seemed to be looking a way out of the situation." Mary took a deep breath.

Suddenly feeling exhausted, she fell back against the wall behind her and realized that her mouth was dry from hours without water. Her throat was sore, and she could hardly speak. But she wanted to explain more.

However, Peter broke his silence and confessed, "Mary, I denied knowing Jesus over and over today. Fear took hold of me, and I realized that I am weak and have no faith." Peter continued repenting and questioning, "Why did Judas do this? Judas said he just wanted to help so he convinced the Sanhedrin to see Jesus. Then why did he come with armed guards? Why did they manacle Jesus' hands? Mary we were tricked! All that Jesus told us came true. I swore to him I would choose death to protect him. But I am a coward."

To stop his dithering, Mary interrupted him, "We have no time for all this." With outlandish strength she grabbed Peter's robe at the neck. "Simon Peter, pull yourself together. We have got to do something. Do you know where everyone is? I saw Phillip and told him to find the believers and bring them to the Roman compound. We have to help Jesus, which we can do if we are all together."

Suddenly, a frenzied mob poured onto the street in front of Mary and Peter, with Roman guards cracking their whips and pushing Jesus down the road. Mary screamed, "My Abba Elah, what is happening? What have they done to you?"

Jesus did not see her. His face was more swollen than before. It appeared he had been beaten again. Fresh blood streamed down his face and covered every part of his body. All he wore was a girdle of cloth tied around his waist. Upon his head were twigs encircling his head. As he came closer to her, she saw thorns piercing his scalp. He carried a heavy plank of rough wood across his shoulders. Leading the procession was a Roman soldier carrying a sign written in Hebrew, "Jesus of Nazareth, King of the Jews."

Jesus stumbled along barefooted, with his hands grasping the wood trying to balance it and remain standing. The same mob she had witnessed earlier walked behind and beside him, cruelly mocking and spitting on him. They screamed in Hebrew, "Crucify him!" and taunted him sarcastically calling out, "King of the Jews."

"No!" screamed Mary as she ran alongside him heedless of her own safety, until someone pushed her aside and spat in her face. Losing her balance, she wailed, blinded by her tears. She pulled herself up on a building wall to steady herself as she was nearly trampled by the huge crowd.

Unsteadily, she followed as close as she could to Jesus. Drenched in sorrow and out of breath, she continued on relentlessly. As they climbed a gradually sloping hill, she saw a gate ahead leading out of the city. She could not think apart from the mass of people she followed, trying to keep her eyes on Jesus.

"Rabboni, you're in so much pain!" she winced, but she refused to give up hope. Instead, she prayed silently that Elah would bring forth a hero, someone who would save her teacher and love.

Meanwhile her mind was racing, *Should I speak out? No, that would certainly make them angrier and they would prevent me from going all the way with him.* Instead, Mary picked up her pace and walked beside him. Jesus must have felt her heart and spirit because he turned and looked at her. With a big smile he caught her eye, as if to say, "Do not worry. Elah is with us, you and me."

Whatever was going to happen, Mary decided she would not leave Jesus' side.

***

Unknown to Jesus, Mary, and all of Jesus' followers and believers, Caiaphas had brought the trial unlawfully. At the bidding of Annas, Caiaphas had taken the Nazarene into the dungeon of his own personal palace and not into an official court of the Sanhedrin. They did not want the moderates to have time to call other moderates or supporters of Jesus, all of whom were in the great city for Passover. Those fair-minded individuals would have called for a full and impartial trial, allowing a defense for the Nazarene.

Additionally, the coward Caiaphas did not want to take the ultimate responsibility of Jesus' death on his shoulders, so he tried to goad Herod Antipas, another bloodthirsty tyrant, to condemn the charismatic preacher. Herod however, still reeling from his decision to execute John the Baptist, refused the High Priest's bait and declined.

Legally speaking, Caiaphas knew he had a weak case but he held a secret that would destroy his career. The tax coffers were practically empty, which he blamed on his incompetent clerics. Ultimately, though, he would suffer the consequences and be held responsible for not discovering this earlier, and thus lose everything.

Consequently, he devised a plan that he thought would remove the cause, that being the simple uneducated religious dissident from far away Galilee, and thus solve his problem. This rebellious Nazarene gave the people reasons to question the religious authorities and thus stop paying their exorbitant tithes.

Therefore, spurred on by his devious father-in-law, Annas, who was also involved, he devised a plan by calling on his minions, unethical rabbis and priests. Those who had grudges toward Jesus. Those who had lost congregants and funds. Temple workers who had lost livelihoods from Jesus' scolding. And those unscrupulous priests and clerics living and working in the temple who were being paid to keep quiet about unethical deeds. They owed their livelihood to the despicable High Priest. A gaggle of corruption, they were. Thus, he called on their due diligence to convict Jesus of Nazareth without a fair trial.

According to strict Roman law, all accused had the right to an impartial judgment by their peers. Thus, to bypass all the needless trial proceedings, Caiaphas had arranged to get a full conviction by his sycophants in the wee hours of dawn; and was successful. But how could he arrange corporal punishment while standing as the highest religious leader?

Herod had refused, so the only other ruler left to do the dastardly deed was Pilate. Caiaphas knew this would take diplomacy and a carefully deceptive approach. He simply appealed to the Roman's fascination for bloodletting, knowing that would be the best way to go.

Pilate however was on guard not be taken advantage of as he had been with the Baptist. Therefore, the Roman used Jesus' claim that he was a king, even if it was of another world. In this way he manufactured a charge to put the preacher to death. To be fair, Pilate tried to persuade the unfortunate man to give up, but failed.

Caiaphas knew that Pilate would interrogate Jesus. The priest's only hope was that the accused would hang himself, thus leading to the quick execution of the rebel and solution to his money worries.

Chapter 43

The Crucifixion
of God's Son

Father forgive them for they know not what they are doing.
(Luke 23:34)

Without fear and unaware of her own situation, Mary followed Jesus, trailing his footsteps as they led him to be crucified. She could do nothing to save her teacher, healer, and liberator. He was her life and, regardless of the dire circumstances, she continued to hope and pray that someone would come forward and intervene to save him.

Until today, Mary had never heard of or seen a crucifixion. She watched helplessly as the cruel soldiers continually had to prop the large heavy wooden beam upon Jesus' shoulders. He could barely walk a few steps before nearly dropping it. His balance was off from the scourging and loss of blood. Jesus nearly crumpled under the weight.

Instinctively, Mary dashed toward Jesus wanting to help him in some way with the heavy plank each time he stumbled. But a legionnaire shoved her violently aside into the crowd, harshly cursing her in his foreign tongue.

Audaciously Mary kept reappearing at the front of the crowd. Though weak herself from the long night, she pushed herself each time to the front. Besides the gawkers were the same hate filled chanters continuing to shout hoarsely taunts of "Crucify him" and "King of the Jews" over and over.

The horrific procession slowed because of the many times Jesus fell.

Though weakened from his long torture and loss of blood, surprisingly he kept going, one unsteady step at a time as he struggled with the beam.

As the roadway curved on their uphill trek, Mary noticed that they were headed toward an enormous stone gateway. It seemed that they were taking him outside the city.

It was late morning and the hot sun beat down upon them. After each stumble the heartless soldiers whipped him, forcing him to speed up, as if trying to deprive him of an easier death from collapsing and dying along the way. Suddenly a soldier grabbed a robust man from the crowd and forced him to carry Jesus' wooden plank. Jesus continued weaving unsteadily onward. At one point the guard began to push him from behind.

All the while Jesus continued to bleed from gruesome gashes, but he never lost his composure and dignity. Jesus never shouted in anger at his torturers, even as they displayed masochistic pleasure by pushing the circle of thorny branches deeper into his skull when it fell off.

Mary remembered Jesus' last words to her, "Remain prayerful. We are in the hands of Elah."

She realized that she was numb, like she was walking in a dream. She felt nothing of her physical body, only the agony of her helpless heart. But she kept herself focused, trying to be strong and support Jesus. This was a nightmare that she wished she and her Rabboni could wake from. "Abba Elah, I have no idea what to do to help Jesus. Please help us. Please help him." Keeping her dignity, she continued to follow behind her love. No one knew the sorrow of the Creator.

The rest was a blur in Mary's consciousness. Before she knew it, she was standing in a deserted, barren quarry outside the gates of the city watching the guards lay the wooden beam upon the ground with Jesus' shoulders on top of the wood that he had carried. The thumping sound of metal hitting against wood woke her from her trancelike state. Then she screamed from the horror of blood spurting out of Jesus' wrists, "Oh Elah! Please stop this! It is too much!"

She fainted and woke to find herself sprawled on the ground. But as she opened her moisture filled eyes, there he was, her precious love hanging above her on the wooden edifice. A soldier took his two feet and hammered them onto the pole. She began to retch at the sight of his blood-filled agony. "No, no!" she screamed hoarsely between sobs and gasps.

The sight was too excruciating to watch. Yet, she found strength to stand beside the cross at Jesus' bleeding feet. At times, feeling drips of blood from above upon her robe.

The soldiers sat and stood around laughing at him, making fun of him, and harshly taunting him in their language. Mary could not hold back her sobs and moans. "No, no, no! Elah, wake me from this nightmare. I am sorry that I am so helpless. Elah, I beg You to help Your son," she pleaded.

The scene was surreal. She could not be sure if this was a dream or if she was just going mad. The robe that Jesus wore had been removed, adding to the insult as he hung naked with only a loincloth. Mary looked up into Jesus' face. Blood and sweat that mingled together had mostly dried upon his face. Blood that dripped from the sharp thorns had dried along his chin and matted his hair. Caked blood covered his eyebrows and the sides of his nose.

"Abba Elah! Mary called. Is there no one to rescue Jesus?" She turned around and saw that the crowd was gone and only her sisters remained. Muttering feebly in a soft voice, not sure if he could hear her, "Surely, someone will come soon, my Rabboni. Maybe Simon Peter or Phillip or Salome's sons… where is everyone? They must be trying to find everyone and defend you."

Jesus' eyes opened and stared into the distance. When it seemed that his head was too heavy to hold upright, he looked down and saw Mary. He smiled warmly at her without any sign of pain on his face, although she knew that he was in great pain.

Mary reached up and gently touched his bare and bloody feet, the feet that she had anointed with oil only a few nights before. She caressed them softly with care, as if trying to warm them. In between gasps and struggles to breathe Jesus began to speak, softly but clearly to her, "Mary, I can see very well up here." His familiar voice and words surprised her and caused her to sob aloud. His positive words brought on a torrent of tears.

Rubbing the tears out of her eyes, she thought, *How can he continue reassuring and comforting me in this horrible and ignominious moment—stripped of his dignity and stripped of his clothes?*

"Mary, I am sorry for your disappointment. We will have to postpone our plans," Jesus said rather sheepishly. She knew he referred to his marriage proposal. She realized, *for my sake he is trying to make light of all of this.*

"Abba, Elah's heart is truly sorrowful, beyond all imagining. He is even more disappointed than you." Jesus' words faded and he cleared his throat, "Go back to Galilee."

"Where is Judas?" Jesus asked after a few minutes, wondering where his friend was. "Where are Peter and James and the others?"

Mary could not answer from irrepressible weeping. Blood dripping from his wounds mixed with her tears and smeared her face. "I do not know, Rabboni," she whispered. "I think that they are trying to find help."

Mary wanted so much to wrap a cloth around his precious body and wipe the blood out of his eyes that dripped from the thorns pressed into his skull. She was only a helpless woman.

She glanced at the two miserable men hanging on each side of Jesus, but kept her focus on Jesus. Suddenly, the man being crucified on Jesus' left began to taunt Jesus breathlessly, "A lot of good all your noble words did. Look around. No one even cares, just a crazy woman. If you are so holy, why don't you call upon your Elohim for help? While you're at it, tell Him to let me down also." He laughed, gasping for air.

The man on Jesus' right side called to the thief on the left, "Shut your idiot mouth." Realizing that his life was nearing its end, the thief repented as he recognized that Jesus was a man of Elohim. He felt Jesus' dignity and even compassion. Surprising Mary, he humbly asked Jesus, "Could you pray for me?" Then he confessed, "I have committed many sins in my life, and I am sorry for the things I have done. I wish I had more time to make up for my sins."

Jesus grunted out words to the man compassionately, "Today... you will ... join me... in Paradise."

Suddenly in a loud voice, Jesus shouted gutturally, as if to a crowd of people. Its suddenness caused Mary to jump as she turned around expecting to see the disciples finally there. But there were only the few Roman soldiers remaining as sentinels and the two prisoners next to him.

"O Jerusalem, you had so many chances to receive Elah's holy prophets, but you always killed those sent to you. I wished to gather you together like a hen gathering her brood under her wings, but you did not want to come and listen to me. You missed yet another very special time. But I assured Abba Elah that even if I give my life, I will not give up, I will return to you and bring Elah's love and compassion to you and the world."

Jesus began to struggle for air and his face became dusky as he paused between each word, determined to use every ounce of strength and every moment he had left. Straining for each breath, and fighting against his heavy body, he forced out the words, "Mary do not stop loving regardless of all you've witnessed today. These simple people do not know what they are doing."

Jesus was looking far off. Mary turned around to see what Jesus was looking at. It was the outer wall of Jerusalem, and she perceived his longing for the people of the city. Even at this moment, he loved his people unconditionally. Again, Mary sobbed hysterically. Still with hope, she continued to encourage Jesus, "I know that we will be discovered soon, and you will be rescued. As soon as they bring everyone here, we can take you down."

Jesus spoke to comfort her heart, "Mary, you must remember everything I told you and report my message to everyone. Can you do that?" Jesus' voice cracked, and then Mary caught a quick moment of pain in his face.

"Oh Rabboni, I am so sorry." Mary realized the abject certainty of his death and screamed out, "Oh Abba! I am so helpless."

Continuing to pause after each word for air and strength, "Evil… had to stop our union… so… that humans… would remain… under its… bondage. Abba Elah… will *not* … give up… and neither will I." With deep inner strength, Jesus continued to try and extend his life, "I promise… I will… my mission is incomplete. I will come again! My Abba Elah mission… must be accomplished…someday in the future." Jesus spoke quickly, before his strength failed him, "You must… keep… faith… love. Tell all the others what I am telling you." Jesus paused.

Mary began to feel light rain upon her face. The sky was becoming darker with thick clouds obscuring the sun.

Gasping for breath, he called out, "I am thirsty. Give... a drink?" Jesus humbly asked the nearest soldier.

Mary ran over to a water tub and looked for a ladle. A soldier pushed her away and cursed at her to leave. Mary screamed desperately, "Please give him some water. Look at his mouth. His tongue is swelling."

The soldier understood but cruelly dismissed her, "Get away, you stupid Jewess. This is what you wanted, isn't it?"

But when he saw her torment, he relented. He soaked a cloth in vinegar wine instead of water and shoved it into Jesus' mouth. Jesus could not take the vinegar and began to retch. Having no strength, Jesus just closed his eyes. It was mid-afternoon, but it became as dark as night.

Mary again became aware of the rain sprinkling on her face. She ran back to be close to Jesus and tried to calm her racing heart. Still, she believed someone would come to help and kept looking back for his disciples.

Jesus' voice, weaker now, could no longer mask his pain, "Mary... Mary... take care of my mother. You alone... understand."

Mary managed to answer while sobbing uncontrollably, "Yes, dear one, I will. You are forever a part of my heart and soul!" She saw that Jesus' condition was worsening, as she confronted the reality. In deep remorse, and on her knees, she clung to the wooden cross embracing it as she dreamed that she was embracing Rabboni as her spouse.

Again, she heard Jesus trying to speak. As he tried in vain to lift his heavy head, he called out, "Father... I wanted... to bring Your love." With all his willpower he stammered, "Please, forgive... them.... They... do... not... know what... they are doing."

A soldier with instructions to hasten the deaths of the condemned men, because the Jewish Sabbath was nearing, pushed Mary aside. With ruthless callousness, he lanced Jesus' left side. Fluids poured out of his side and reflexively he uttered a weak cry of pain.

In the next second, Jesus surrendered, "Father... I... give... You... my spirit." And he sunk lifelessly upon the cross.

Mary heard his last gasp. His physical life was finished. Holding her breath, then she gulped for air and screamed out, "No, Elah, no! No! No!" She collapsed to her knees upon the wet earth and leaned against the hard wood. Distraught, her hands grabbed for something, anything. There was only dirt and mud. She felt like punching or throwing or screaming but instead she tossed the mud upon herself and smeared it upon her face and her clothing, all the while wailing in despair.

Within seconds, there were flashes of lightning followed by loud claps of thunder and sheets of rain. Hardly noticing the deluge, she turned and clung to the cross, numb and void of any sensibilities.

Traumatized and helpless and in a mental space where there was no time, she became aware of being lifted to her feet. From her trance-like state, and with big raindrops obscuring her vision, she blinked away the water and saw the blurry familiar face of Joseph of Arimathea. He spoke to her, but she could not comprehend. Helplessly surrendering herself to the elderly man, she was led away from her lifeless and dearest Rabboni.

Joseph of Arimathea, Nicodemus, and Mary of Clopas and mother of James Alpheus and Jude Thaddeus, Salome of Zebedee and mother of James and John, and Joanna attended to Mary Magdalene. Joseph explained that he had received permission from the Roman governor to take responsibility for Jesus' body.

Mary listlessly heard Joseph command the solders to take Jesus' body down from the cross, "The Sabbath is only a few hours away. I need time to take him to my tomb." That was the last Mary heard as she lost consciousness again. The reality was too severe.

"Mary!" Hearing her name, she awoke in a daze and hoped, *It was all a bad dream!* But as her vision focused on the surroundings, she realized it was not a dream. *Jesus is no longer alive. He is gone!* She accepted the reality and with all the vigor she could summon, lifted herself and pushed herself to stand.

Mary Clopas whispered gently as she held onto Mary's arm to steady her, "Joseph and Nicodemus are preparing to lay Jesus' body in the wagon. Are you able to walk with us to take him to the sepulcher?"

Together they tenderly and respectfully covered him with a fine ecru burial cloth. Taking his lifeless hand, she held it to her cheek. Gone was his loving warmth and life-giving hope. Her tears flowed.

Hardest for her was covering his face. She reached out to stop the last edge of cloth meant for his head. Trying desperately to freeze the moment in time, she stared memorizing his lifeless features. Not even with all her willpower could she muster the strength to compose herself. And though she thought that she had no more tears, suddenly she wailed unconsolably.

Then Mary nodded acceptance and they were on their way. Stumbling along and with only the wagon's support, she walked alongside, unable to take her eyes off the shroud covering him. "This is Rabboni. Oh, Elah please, no." Somehow she found the strength to keep going.

Joseph and his servants led the mule as Nicodemus, Mary Clopas, and Salome and Joanna somberly walked inconspicuously behind the wagon to Joseph's family grave. As they walked together, Mary listened quietly to the other Mary. "They will not allow us to prepare Jesus properly for burial because of the Sabbath. We cannot perform the bathing ritual or anointing with oil and herbs until the morning after Sabbath. We will return at first light to honor him properly," Mary Clopas reassured her with motherly kindness and clarity.

Though traumatized from all that she had witnessed, Mary did not give up. Rather, she eulogized Jesus with his own words and deeds. Gathering her dignity, Mary lifted her head and related Jesus' heroic last moments and message for his believers, "Along the path he never cursed his torturers or those screaming for his demise. He expressed kindness toward the criminals on both side of him. He prayed that Abba forgive those who persecuted him. And claimed that they did not know what they were doing. He also expressed his sorrow for failing to succeed. But he promised not to give up. And at the very end, with his last breath he commended his spirit to his Abba Elah."

The priest Nicodemus and the merchant Joseph of Arimathea and both women relatives, Salome and Mary Clopas, could not hold back their tears any longer and wept hysterically.

Suddenly a rattle of metal and stomping of marching boots surprised the mourners. Roman soldiers sent by Pilate had come to protect Jesus' grave, expressing as much to Nicodemus.

While dabbing his eyes and ignoring the guards, Joseph instructed the servants. Together with Nicodemus, Joseph and the servants carried Jesus' holy body respectfully into the tomb and temporarily placed him upon a stone ledge. Mary noted the strong herb perfume as they left and was glad that she and her sister were able to be the last to touch Jesus' holy body most respectfully.

Ignoring the menacing armored guards standing at attention, and knowing there was nothing left to say Mary Clopas urged tenderly, "Come, Mary."

As they solemnly walked away from the cold tomb clinging to each other, they whispered a prayer and a promise that they would return. But before leaving, they watched the servants, aided by Joseph and Nicodemus, roll a large stone sealing the entrance to the tomb.

Chapter 44

The Resurrection

April 9, 30 CE

I will not leave you as orphans…
(John 14:18)

Mary Magdalene lay upon her quilt in the darkness, having no idea how long she had slept nor the hour. Her first awareness was her aching and longing heart to see Rabboni. However, she knew the reality and she prepared herself to face it. *No longer will I see his bright and hopeful countenance. How will I go on? How will we go on?*

She mourned and found no energy to rise as she helplessly reviewed her last moments with Rabboni. First, the clapping thunder, torrential rain, and someone lifting her up from her trance-like position leaning at the base of the wooden plank that held Jesus' body. The large raindrops smearing the mud and blood on her face and hands…someone lifting her body to an erect stance and helping her walk behind Jesus' body that lay upon the burial wagon.

She remembered looking up and seeing that she was being aided by her sisters, Salome and Mary Clopas. Except for her sight, she was deaf and numb until she began hearing the voices of her sisters. "Come Mary," they coaxed her tenderly, "we are accompanying Jesus' body to his grave."

Then she sobbed as she remembered leaving the cold tomb, and Joseph's servants rolling the stone over the entrance. Shivering on her bed, she also remembered the heartless priests and brash temple guards coming to keep watch over Jesus' grave and their harsh words, "Caiaphas wants us to secure the grave to make sure there is no claim by his followers that the Nazarene somehow came back to life, because of reports that Jesus claimed death would have no power over him."

As she leaned on her sisters, her next memory was Salome's tender voice as they left the cold tomb and Jesus' body, "Come, Mary, we will return on the first day of the week when Sabbath is over, as soon as it is light enough to see our way to the tomb." She remembered the kindness of Mary Clopas, and Salome leading her to their family's temporary Passover encampment.

Still lying on her bed, she felt numb as if she was living between life and death. But she realized clearly and mumbled, "Not only is Elah's son dead and all of Abba Elah's hopes but my love and the nation's redeemer is gone." Hopelessly she thought, *What are we to do now?* This recollection gave her purpose, which jarred her out of her sleepy daze, and she sat up. As she took a deep breath the reality struck her again, causing her to sob mournfully and uncontrollably.

Mary Clopas brought her food, interrupting Mary's recollections, "You haven't eaten anything since Passover. Please eat to strengthen yourself. It is a few hours before the first sunrise of the new week. Let us ready ourselves to go together to prepare Jesus' body properly."

In the darkness, Mary slowly found her way to the edge of the camp where jugs of water and basins were kept. The water refreshed her, and she remembered when Mary Clopas initially helped her wash away the crusted blood and mud and dirt on the evening of Jesus' death.

Dismissing the strong impressions in her mind, she purposed her thinking by being grateful for the clean robe that Mary Clopas had given her. At last, with her strength returning, Mary took control of her emotions and decided to reject the immobilizing traumatic flashbacks from her consciousness.

Joined by Joanna, Mary Magdalene, Mary Clopas, and Salome collected the funeral supplies and began their trek toward Jesus' tomb, quietly and deliberately knowing that it would be their final journey to Rabboni's grave. The women set out in the darkness of morning with clouds sailing across the sky, intermittently covering the moon. As the darkness slowly receded, they purposely pulled their scarves over their mourning faces, walking ceremonially through the dim and narrow streets toward Jesus' tomb.

Along the way, Mary Clopas begged Mary Magdalene to tell of her experience. Spontaneously it brought tears and they cried together at first until they agreed to reminisce about happier moments with Jesus. However, at the slightest mention of their love for Jesus they were quickly overcome with emotion, weeping with pain in their hearts. They trudged along the path, carrying a pitcher of water, embalming oils and herbs in little jars, and a papyrus wrapped clean robe and sheet.

After a while they walked without speaking and Mary realized that sometimes she felt numb, as if living in a timeless shadow, with intervals of intense shaking emotion. All hopes for the future had been taken from her. Desperately she clung to Abba Elah, as Jesus had taught her, and managed to pray short prayers.

Walking along the quiet granite road, Mary thought, *Just two days ago I followed Jesus along this road.* Mary forcefully squeezed her eyes tight, trying not to remember the sight of his precious blood oozing from his naked body. *I was helpless, he was helpless. I was worthless! He was more precious than life itself.*

Helplessly, again she revisited the events of that day. She dared not look around because it was the last road that Jesus took in his life. She feared she would become immobilized with emotion and not make it to his grave. Rather, she kept her eyes on the ground while violent memories continued to flash in and out of her consciousness.

From about twenty meters to the tomb, as the path gently sloped upwards, together the four women ceremonially prostrated themselves in full bows upon the hard ground every ten steps until they reached their destination. All the while they sobbed intensely, with such strong emotion that they had to resist the urge to tear their clothing. Instead, they grabbed at the earth, the fine dirt alongside the road, and threw it upon themselves. They wailed from the depths of their souls. Each time they bowed their faces to the ground they set the containers ahead of them to protect them from the dirt.

No-one saw their journey except Abba Elah. Though they did not realize it, their regret was also Abba's regret.

In the darkness they knelt before the tomb until the first rays of the sun began to appear. It was then that they noticed that the rock blocking the tomb's entrance had been removed.

A sickening and faint feeling came over Mary as she ran to the entrance. Frantically she tried to figure out what had happened as her eyes adjusted to the darkness of the tomb. She bent down low and crawled into the cave. Rabboni's body was gone. She shivered and gasped, questioning aloud, "Has someone taken his body?"

But then she felt another presence in the cave. She detected an ethereal figure sitting on the ledge where Jesus' body had lain.

"Who are you?" Mary whispered respectfully, as she sensed its peaceful essence. "Where have you taken our beloved Rabboni?"

Immediately he answered, surprising her with a joyful voice, "I am a messenger of Elah. Jesus, the Son of Abba Elah, the one you are seeking, has gained victory over death. His physical body is not here. Do not worry or feel sad! What is more important is that his spirit lives to give glory to the One who sent him. Go and find the other disciples and tell them what you have found. He has conquered the world of death."

Mary quickly wiped away her tears. Hardly trusting the experience, Mary repeated his statement in disbelief, "He is alive? How can this be?"

Leaving Mary Clopas, Salome, and Joanna at the entrance to the tomb, Mary ran from the cave nearly stumbling over the embalming paraphernalia. She felt as if her heart would burst with joy.

With hope in her heart, Mary's eyes scanned the desolate rocky area but saw no one. *If he was victorious over death, does that mean that he is alive? Where are you, Rabboni?* she wondered. Frantically she whispered again, "Jesus, where are you? Am I dreaming or confused?"

Suddenly she spied a figure ahead of her among the cliffs. Composing herself, she thought, *Maybe he saw Jesus and knows which direction he went?* She wasted no time darting toward the figure. Gasping for air, she frantically called out to get the man's attention, trying to stop him. As the figure turned toward her voice, she sensed a surprising familiarity about him.

She wanted so much for it to be him. "Lord, is that you?" she whispered, trying to calm her beating heart and catch her breath. But indeed, when the

man turned and faced her, she knew, *Rabboni! I know your tender expression…
I have seen it many times.*

Stunned and powerless she fell on her knees, trying with all her might
not to cry. Rather, she wanted to show him her composure and affection.
"Rabboni, Lord, are you really here? How can this be?" But she sobbed irre-
pressibly, "You are not dead?"

Jesus spoke to Mary with his usual voice and expression of benevolence,
"I have gone beyond the death that man and Satan imposed on me, and I
am alive in spirit. You can see me, can't you? This is my spiritual body. Abba
allowed me to remain on earth for some time but then I will ascend to Abba
Elah."

The sound of his voice caused Mary to long for him, so she began to
crawl toward him. She tried to touch his foot, but though her eyes could see
him clearly her hands could not grasp a physical element of him.

"You are here, Lord, but I cannot touch you. Do my eyes deceive me?
What am I viewing? Am I dreaming?" Tears flowed. Mary looked at her hands
and wondered if she was dreaming. But she felt the hard ground and asked,
"Lord, how is this possible? Where is your physical body?" she asked in great
distress, for it took her time to comprehend.

Jesus answered her kindly, "Abba is with you and sharing this moment of
sorrow and joy with us. You must go and find the others and tell them of your
experience. You will give them hope. Right now, they are scattered like sheep
without a shepherd. Remind them that I told them to go to Galilee. There we
will meet, and I will help them accept and overcome my physical death. Tell
Peter that I love him and have always loved him.

"Mary, share with them the words I gave you during my last moments in
the physical world. Those words will give them spiritual strength and hope.
And don't worry about my physical body. You must focus your love and faith
on the fact that I am alive spiritually and still with you. Make haste and find
them! My mission continues through you and my disciples."

"Rabboni, please don't go, don't let this moment end!" Desperately, Mary
begged Jesus not to leave.

"Mary, I am with you. It gives me joy that you are able to perceive me.

Blessed are you for not wavering at the sight of me. Be of good courage and go now and do all that I have instructed you to do."

Mary's heart was renewed with hope and full of amazement. The aura of death was gone. Filled with this experience, she promised, "I will spread this experience and words from you that you have conquered death. No one can keep us apart ever again. You went beyond death! You are alive! Death cannot separate us."

The two Marys, Joanna, and Salome left the cliffs and ran into the city of Jerusalem like giddy children who had discovered a treasure. Inspired, Mary thought, *The aura of death is gone, and truly in its place is the hope of Abba Elah.* She expressed to her partners, "Today let's search for all the disciples and followers to give them this good news of hope and joy. Our Rabboni is alive!"

As the four women searched with a revived spirit, Mary remembered the first moment she met Jesus, the moment of her healing. And then she remembered the unconditional love of her grandmother and mother. She realized that it was love that had guided her throughout her early life and had led to meeting her Deliverer, the king of love, Jesus of Nazareth.

Epilogue

*"Men of Galilee," they said. "Why do you stand here
looking into the sky? This same Jesus, who has been taken from you,
will come back in the same way you have seen him go."*
(Acts 1:11)

After meeting the resurrected Jesus, Mary was filled with the Holy Spirit and her faith became even greater than during all of the two years she had traveled with him. She did exactly what Jesus had told her before and after his death. She searched for all the disciples and when she found them, she relieved their sadness and feelings of guilt by telling of her experience meeting Jesus the morning after his death and she told them his message.

She poured out so much tenderness that that the disciples felt comforted and longed to experience Jesus as she had. "There is another dimension that we have no awareness of. Rabboni has won victory over death," she said with confidence and compassion.

Mary reported that Jesus' first words to her were about them, his disciples, "Jesus told me to tell you to return to Galilee and he would meet us there. He also said that he loved you and appreciated all the times we had together."

The disciples believed that if Jesus had appeared and spoken to her, then surely he would speak to them. They were greatly excited and longed to see him again. Though their consciences were filled with remorse and guilt, they felt comforted listening to Mary relate her experience. Her heart was free, and her compassion for them and high spirit exuded from her being. They could almost feel Jesus' presence. The disciples longed for him.

***

It took practically all day to find Peter. When they did, he was unshaven and disheveled. Fear was written all over his face when he first saw Mary. He had no idea what day it was or where any of the other disciples were. He did not want to face Mary for he was so ashamed and confused.

He was moaning something about all that he had worked for in the past few years just seeming to have disappeared. He had sacrificed his family life, he had given up his fishing boat, and he was now in an unfamiliar country, so far from home. He had lost his lord whom he had loved and for whom he had sacrificed everything. He had allowed his lord to be assassinated. He had no more tears, for he had cried for an undetermined number of days and not eaten for some time.

Mary was the last person he wanted to see. She had not betrayed her lord as he had. No wonder Jesus loved her so much for he somehow knew that she would be loyal to the end. But as Mary opened the door and the light of day sliced through the darkness, Peter saw her face filled with brightness. Mary's smile was such a contrast to what he was feeling that he felt suddenly stunned and curious. He spoke gruffly to the woman, "Do you not know what has happened? Are you oblivious to the disaster that has just taken place? Or have you gone mad? Or is this a dream?"

Mary, in a totally euphoric state, exclaimed without being able to control her excitement and joy, "Simon Peter, I just met Rabboni Jesus. I met Rabboni! He was standing in the garden near his tomb. He spoke to me and called my name. He is alive!" The other women added that they had seen him as well.

Everyone in the room became aware of how strange it all sounded to their physical ears. "Jesus was dead, yet he is alive." It was truly incredulous, and they all paused to think of what they were saying. It was truly a sobering moment. The women sat down and there was not a sound in the dank room.

A few minutes went by, and then Peter broke the silence with a loud and mournful sound, his hands covering his ears and head. Peter could not bear listening to the mad women. He thought, *How fortunate it is that they have lost their minds. At least they don't have to face the reality of the next day or even the next hour.*

Then Mary ran over to Peter and knelt before him, "Simon Peter, I am not mad! We went to anoint Rabboni's dead body this morning with the holy oils and perfumes and herbs. As we drew near the grave, the tomb was open. I know there was a large rock rolled to close the tomb because Joseph of Arimathea and I watched it put in place right after Rabboni's death. I was sick with grief but that I do remember, and you can ask Joseph to verify this.

"This morning the rock was gone. As we entered the tomb, our eyes gradually became accustomed to the darkness, and we could see that our lord Jesus' body was not lying in the crypt. It was not there!" Mary exclaimed. "I swear it was not there!" Mary repeated.

Salome spoke out for the first time, supporting what Mary was saying, "Then we could see there was a figure of a young man glowing white and silvery in the tomb. He told us that Jesus was not there—that he had risen from death!"

Mary quickly added to show Simon Peter that she had not lost her mind, "We could not understand, either. We began to cry in terror, thinking that someone had stolen Jesus' body. The man in the tomb told us again that Jesus, the Son of Elah, who had died was now alive."

Mary began to plead with Simon Peter, and she told him of meeting Jesus alive near the empty tomb, "Simon Peter, Jesus even asked about you. He told me to tell you that he still loved you and never stopped loving you."

Mary began to cry because just speaking about the experience brought back the memory of seeing her Rabboni. At her words everyone began to weep. Their longing to see Jesus again was so great and Peter, who thought that he had cried his last tear, was now weeping just like the women.

After some time, Peter stood up and with the sleeve of his garment wiped his wet face. Their concerted testimony was strange, but he had been so humbled that he had no choice but to listen and wonder. He spoke, "I must go to see for myself." Not knowing where his rabbi had been laid in death, he humbly asked these women of faith to lead him. Without further words they left the dismal room.

***

Later that day James, John, and Matthew came with over a dozen men from Bethany. Lazarus, Martha, and their sister Mary, were with them as well. They were overwhelmed with sorrow to hear the report that Pilate had executed Jesus in such a short time. In disbelief, they were bewildered and ashamed of themselves for not being there to protect and defend Jesus from death. There were tears and more tears. They tore their clothes and James even ran outside to vomit. There was so much sorrow. Finally, James called everyone to gather around, and he told his story of what he did after Jesus was arrested.

He had decided to return to Bethany and gather as many believers as he could to bring to Jerusalem and support Jesus, who he thought was probably thrown in prison. James assumed that the same thing that had happened to John the Baptist might happen to Jesus. He knew that Lazarus could probably bring the largest number of supporters together so he decided to go there.

James and his brother found Matthew and they rushed to Bethany. They arrived at Lazarus' home right before sundown and the Sabbath. Upon hearing of Jesus' arrest from James, disregarding the law of the Sabbath, Lazarus went to work right away to find believers and even Zealots who could come to Jesus' aid. They were particularly interested in finding the biggest and strongest and fiercest men to take to Jerusalem. By the evening of the Sabbath, all were ready, and they began at first light on the next day to travel to Jerusalem. They asked many travelers out of Jerusalem for news of Jesus of Nazareth but there was not too much that anyone knew. They came as hastily as they could.

As James finished the story, silence gripped the atmosphere. There were no other words that could be spoken.

Finally, Mary broke the silence. She related her experience at Jesus' death and then she told them of his resurrection. Her tale took their emotions from deepest sadness to joy and wonder, like running up a steep hill, struggling to reach the top, and then the exhilaration of running down the hill. Her story took everyone through the impressions of fear, confusion, sorrow, helplessness, depression, and then she turned all these feelings into amazement, awe, joy, and, yes, finally hopeful expectation.

It was late night when she finished. Everyone was exhausted, physically and emotionally. She said that the next morning they could visit Rabboni's tomb.

***

They found the tomb empty. Out of disbelief, James asked the women if they were sure that this was the right tomb. Perhaps they had made a miscalculation in their grief. Mary Magdalene reassured James that this was where they had laid their dead lord.

During the next few days, Simon Peter and James and the whole entourage helped Mary and the other women to find all the disciples. Of course, they were as devastated as Peter and James. After hearing Mary's testimony, however, all of them began to feel hope. They followed Jesus' direction through Mary. Together they all left Jerusalem for Galilee. There, they waited to meet their Lord.

Every day Mary had dreams and visions of Jesus. She had become a spiritual receptacle. When anyone came to her, they felt a pleasant kind of invigorating jolt of power and love. They asked Mary almost incessantly to relate Jesus' last moments and his last words. She had become the matriarch of the newly forming sect that they called the 'Way of the Nazarene,' that was much sought after.

From the time of their arrival in Galilee, Jesus visited the disciples often and brought many from disbelief to belief. He was spiritually preparing these physical men to be extensions of his spiritual self. Just as he had said during his physical life, they needed rebirth. He had gained victory over death through his unwavering heart of love for Abba Elah and humankind. Thus, Abba Elah permitted him to remain spiritually in the physical world, preparing his disciples for spiritual rebirth.

He reminded them that he had ordained them as his precious children and disciples and that he needed them to help him to complete his mission in the physical world. He commissioned them to go throughout the whole world to bring his life-giving words of truth to all. He warned them not to make rules beyond what he had given them. They needed to avoid becoming like their past lawgivers lest they become constrained by them.

He reminded them, "Give of yourself completely. The goodness you preach and show in your actions will be the goodness you will receive. Teach the whole world the lessons I taught you."

Jesus promised that he would walk spiritually with each one individually and help them on their path, teaching them to love one another and to live for the sake of others. When the whole world knew of him, then he would return to give physical rebirth and create a new lineage of Elah. Jesus reminded them of the ceremony that he had shared with them on the night before his death. He told them to practice that ceremony until he returned, "Remember that I am in you, you are in me and I am in my Abba Elah. We are one."

After forty days of spiritual visitations, Jesus' spirit ascended to the spiritual world. That was a difficult time for everyone. Without Jesus' constant reassurance, many then began to feel fearful again. They said, "How shall we go to the Gentiles and preach this gospel of the Kingdom of Elah? If they did not spare him, how will they spare us?"

Mary stood up and with her brave spirit she reassured the brethren, "Do not weep and do not grieve nor be irresolute, for His grace will be entirely with you and will protect you. Rather, let us praise His greatness, for He has prepared us and made us into men and women of Abba Elah."

***

Ten days after their Rabboni's spirit ascended, a day not too different from any other day, the believers gathered in a large hall. They numbered one hundred twenty men and women. They prayed fervently in deep supplication and longing for Jesus to return to them.

Earlier, Mary, since she was recognized as being with Jesus at the end of his life, as was customary had begun the meeting with the words that Jesus had spoken before he died. Then, Peter and other close disciples gave personal testimonies of their experiences. For the disciples, repentance was always their first pronouncement, and this led everyone to repent.

The fervor of their repentance, regret, and longing struck such intense desperation and sorrow that they all cried out in a loud unison prayer to Abba. With sincerely longing hearts for their Rabboni to return to them, their loud wailing cries began, the likes of which had not been felt or heard before in any of their prayer meetings. Their sorrows reached a gut-wrenching pitch, and many fell upon the floor, overcome with overwhelming grief. Even people on the street heard the loud cries, and reported they sounded like a great whirling tornado.

Suddenly, Mary and everyone in the hall saw bright spinning balls of fire appear in front of them. Though they appeared to burn, they were not hot. Sparks flew out of the balls and lit up the heads of all those gathered in the room. Their prayers continued but the words that exited their mouths were of different sounds and intonations. They were all speaking in different tongues. It was truly a great spiritual phenomenon that was manifested into the physical world. The people on the street heard the babbling and thought that everyone in the hall was drunk.

It was at that moment that Abba Elah sent His Holy Spirit as the Comforter. Each disciple received their individual rebirth as children of Jesus and the Holy Spirit. Jesus as the father and the Holy Spirit, a feminine spirit, as the mother together as spiritual parents could now give them rebirth as Abba Elah's children. At last, because of Jesus' victory over evil, Elah provided for a substantial spiritual rebirth and thus created a master plan to overcome the evil of the world.

The fire of the Holy Spirit now burned in their blood. With this new passion for Abba Elah and Jesus they were thus commissioned by the Holy Spirit.

Mary saw the disciples off on their Elah-ordained missions. As usual she gave her testimonies of Jesus repeatedly, which they never tired of, always giving them spiritual strength and courage and renewing their life.

***

It was not always easy for Mary though. Sometimes Andrew and Simon Peter questioned her guidance. They could not understand why Jesus would speak privately with a woman and not openly with them. They said, "Are we always supposed to turn and listen to her? Why did he prefer her to us?" Then Mary wept and said to Simon Peter, "My brother, Simon Peter, what do you think? Do you think that I have thought this up myself, or that I am lying about our Savior?"

Matthew answered and said to him, "Simon Peter, you have always been hot tempered. Now I see you questioning this woman just like our adversaries. If the Savior made her worthy, who are you to reject her? Surely the Savior knows her very well. That is why he loved her more than us. Rather, let us be ashamed of our own sins and go forth with the perfect man, our Jesus, and go separately as he commanded us to preach the gospel."

Peter had matured greatly over the three years he had spent under Jesus' tutelage, but his appreciation for the value of women remained in line with the archaic customs. As a result, he never truly accepted Mary's close relationship with Jesus. He even discouraged others from seeking her testimony and account of Jesus' death. He also found it hard to accept that Jesus would first appear to her, a woman, rather than to him, his first disciple.

Even after all Mary had gone through, there were rumors of her dubious relationship with Jesus. Peter knew well that she was a virtuous woman, but he never spoke up in defense of her reputation. Thus, her testimony was often suspected as being overly emotional and less authentic.

James, always her closest supporter, was one of the first to leave with great enthusiasm to preach the Good News. Mary heard a report of how after Pentecost he traveled to a faraway kingdom in the Mare Nostrum called Hispania. She prayed fervently for all Jesus' disciples and their success in spreading Jesus' love and truth. She would find out years later that James was the first disciple to be martyred fourteen years after his Lord, Jesus of Nazareth.

Mary had spent time searching for Judas before she left for Galilee. It was strange how he had disappeared. There were rumors that he was dead and possibly by his own hand, but she could not bring herself to accept that. She imagined that he probably felt responsible for Jesus' mock trial and what seemed to be his betrayal, but Mary believed that Judas did not intend for those things to happen. She decided to pray for him that someday he would return. However, no one ever reported seeing Judas again.

Shortly after Jesus' death, on her way back to Galilee Mary visited Mother Mary, just as Jesus instructed her. She told Mother Mary of Jesus' death. It was a great shock to his whole family. There was much grieving and Mary tried her best to console them. At that time, she could only stay a short while, but she promised them that she would return to take care of them.

Taking her leave from Jesus' family, she went directly to Capernaum to care for the disciples, consoling and repeating Jesus' concerns and words that he told her on the cross. She became a central point around which Elah and Jesus could rally the grieving disciples. It was through her words of hope that the disciples remained united until the great day of what is now called Pentecost.

Mary never married for she waited for Jesus, her true love, to return, as he promised. Until the end of her life she lived the love that Jesus taught her.

Often travelers from many parts of the Mediterranean and Greek world sought out Jesus' home in Nazareth. They had a need to find something tangible to make their mystical experiences of Jesus' love a reality. They all wanted to meet Jesus' mother and when they learned that the legendary Mary of Magdala was there, she was kept busy repeating Jesus' words and her sole eyewitness account of Jesus' passion and death. Her narrative reinforced their experiences of deep love with the Holy Spirit. She never spoke of herself or her life, but through relating her experiences she was like a conduit in the physical world to Jesus in the spirit world. Through her, many received the Holy Spirit and took Jesus' message throughout the world.

The inhabitants of the small frontier village of Nazareth often saw strange people of different cultures walking down their humble streets to the home of their most infamous son, Jesus. Gone was their memory of running Rabbi Jesus out of town; they kept only good memories of the boy and his family.

Mary continued speaking with Jesus, and seeing Jesus, and dreaming of Jesus until her death. Her unchanging love and longing kept them spiritually connected. Many strangers also would have spiritual experiences with Jesus while visiting her.

Mother Mary, at first, did not know what to make of all the visitors. She was extremely humble and always remained silent in front of them all. She had nothing to say—for she, in her old age, hardly remembered any of her experiences as a young woman.

Occasionally one of Jesus' original disciples would visit. That was a special time for Mary. They would share their precious memories of their time with Jesus and each other. They shed many tears together. Often, they would ask her to sing the old songs that she had sung mostly around the campfires as they went from town-to-town witnessing. They would share letters or rumors of the disciples who traveled to distant lands. They would share tears as they spoke of the many brave and zealous men and woman willing to die to bring Jesus' love and truth to the people of the world.

Mary began to hear how Rome was becoming more forceful—killing and plundering villages that harbored the Jewish Zealots working to overthrow Roman control of their nation. False messiahs popped up everywhere. There was hardly a day that went by without hearing about death and destruction at the hands of the foreign occupiers.

One day Mary relived her memories of the last day Jesus walked in spirit with them: He promised them over and over that he would come again in his physical body to finish Abba Elah's recreation of His children. On the fortieth day after his death, he told them to go out to the whole world. He said to them, "Tell the people, everywhere, that we are all children of the same Abba Elah. It's Abba Elah's will that they be reborn through me. And tell them that I will return. Elah's will must be fulfilled."

Jesus' investment during those forty days seemed to have paid off, because the spiritual state of the disciples was much stronger than at his death. They were reborn through the many spiritual experiences and prayers they had with the Holy Spirit.

Mary watched them all change and become courageous, even saying that they would willingly give their lives to tell others about their Rabboni. She thought, *What a pity that they had not reached such a spiritual strength and understanding when Jesus was alive.*

That was such a sad day in Mary's memory, saying goodbye to Jesus. All the disciples cried and begged Jesus not to leave. Mary sobbed as Jesus left. She could not control herself. A man wearing a white flowing robe came to the grieving crowd of about 120 men and women. He announced to them, "Men of Galilee, why do you stare up into the sky? Jesus, Abba Elah's son, who has been taken from you, will come back in the same way in which you watched him go. Keep watch and do not lose faith."

Grieving tearfully, Mary faced the reality of all that she and the world had lost. Frequently she pondered, "if only we had been able to marry as Jesus had hoped and prayed. It must have been Abba Elah's desire also." There was such hope in that thought. The warmth of Abba's love flowed into her heart replacing her lonely tears.

Made in United States
North Haven, CT
07 April 2023

35159386R00257